MAKING LEVELS THE FLY WAY

A 3.5E D20 LITRPG ADVENTURE

MAKING LEVELS BOOK 1

MAKING LEVELS THE FLY WAY

A 3.5E D20 LITRPG ADVENTURE

ANTHONY T ALVES

Published by Level Up in the United Kingdom in 2023

Cover illustration by Sippakorn Upama

ISBN: 978-1-83919-555-6

www.levelup.pub

To my brother Carlos

1.1 AUTHOR'S NOTE

NOTE ON 3.5E D20 SYSTEM

No knowledge of 3.5e is necessary to read this book. If you are interested in learning more the System Reference Document (SRD) is given free in full on many great websites, as it is all covered by the Open Gaming License. Simply search 3.5e SRD, and any questions you have on the system or mechanics will be answered.

The End of the Fourth Age uses a modified d20 3.5 OGL system like Pathfinder does. I took great pains to ensure no copyrighted materials were used. The system and setting is called Black Raven. While the Black Raven system itself does not make many dramatic changes to the core OGL rules (just many additions), there are some notable exceptions. Black Raven is supposed to be a more dangerous, lower magic, and a grittier system to fit the setting it was made for. The main differences between OGL content, Black Raven, and End of the Fourth Age are described in various parts of the book.

Lastly, thank you for giving this title a shot. I enjoyed coming up with pretty uniquely flawed, but hopefully interesting and entertaining, characters. I really hope you enjoy it!

PART 1 "OBSERVE"

KIM GUM, YEAR 2043

I found out the next morning about the lights. Big green explosions in the sky all over the world. Mia said it was nanites. She was right, but she's always right about everything. The nanites even affected her somehow. I guess they are a bunch of little machines. They got inside everyone and showed us words right in our eyes. And we had a bunch more information in our cd links.

There wasn't a ton of info, but I hate reading. And since this was all everyone was talking about, I didn't really have to read anything. The nanites told us we're all being sent to a contest. Every person on earth. Everyone is freaking out big time. Especially my mom. I'm kind of excited though. It sounds pretty fun.

The contest is taking the systems and rules of a real game called end of the fourth age mmcirpg. It isn't even a super popular game. It's included with the podpass – a subscription service to, like, a million games. That's not the real name of the subscription service though, just what people call it. I forget the real name. Even without the pod-pass the game is still free2play.

Everyone says fourth age is real pay2win without the podpass. Maybe even with the podpass too. I don't know about that – they say the games my mom lets me play, like candy razzle and hearts over tunnels, are super pay2win. I think both are called gacha games. I still have a ton of fun playing them and I never spent any money ever. Not even once. I'm not nearly as far in those games as other people who pay money though. I don't care. I just like looking at my cards and getting new cards. And I can just play both of my games through my cd link instead of entering the tangle.

Mia said fourth age only has about 14 million unique logins a month, and that isn't a lot. The biggest games have almost a billion unique logins per month. Candy razzle has, like, half-a-billion unique logins a month.

Fourth age uses the Black Raven setting, based on the 3.5 edition of d20. I'm not sure what any of that means. It's marketed as a hard-core, low-magic, old-school, group-focused mmcirpg with live action combat. What people call twitch combat. Lots of people are interested in hardcore and heavy rpgs – but these people usually don't like live action combat. Lots of people are interested in twitch, live action com-bat – but these people usually aren't interested in really heavy rpg stuff. I'm guessing that's why it isn't super popular.

I wonder why they picked that game? The nanites didn't tell us much. But they did tell us a date, time, and how to be sent as a group.

1.2 PREPARATION

KIM GUM

It's supposed to happen soon. We got to wait together so we'll be sent together. Everyone is dressed in the army clothes dad got for us. The same clothes he usually wears to work. We all look pretty dumb, I think. I can tell dad wants to check the tangle or do something besides just wait here. Carlos has his cd link open, and I'd bet anything mom wants him to stop. But she won't say anything because it will start an argument. Joey is being good for once, just rocking quietly. He has no idea what is happening.

Mia says, "Two minutes until the specified time. Good luck, everyone. I hope things go well for all of you. And I hope to see you all soon."

I'm the only one who recognizes she spoke. "Goodbye, Mia!"

"Goodbye, Kim," she says.

I'm excited. I don't really know what will happen but it's better than school. Anything is better than stupid school. I'm not really into video games, but that is probably because mom won't let me enter the EIPN for anything but school. Or I used to not be able to. I could play fourth age since the nanites came. To prepare. With just my family though. We all played together. It was still a lot of fun. Would've been way more fun without them. My mom is very bossy and is taking this way, way too seriously. It's a game for crying out loud! And we only got to, like, level 15 or so. If my family wasn't slowing me down I probably could've got to level 20 or higher. And had a ton more fun.

It would be so much fun to play with some friends. Real friends, like Mia. Even though she's not a person. I don't really have a lot of friends, and the couple of people I am kind of friends with make fun of me a lot. Like, they say I'm fat. The new thing is cankles. I had to look that up. Now I have to wear pants forever.

I'm not even fat. I'm just big boned and have big shoulders. Dad says I have a big frame and I'll probably be really tall and that most super models are super tall and weren't popular or traditionally good looking when they were my age either. I looked some up; they don't look anything like me. People say I look like a frog because I have no neck or chin and my mouth is wide. And that I'm fat. But I'm not that fat. My ankles aren't even that big. And mom has big shoulders too. And everyone thinks she is beautiful. I think she is beautiful.

Just a couple more minutes. Mom is really nervous. So is dad.

Mom jumps up and says, "Let's bring it in." She goes over to Joey and pulls him to his feet and we have a family hug. Joey hates this kind of thing. He starts making noises immediately.

"I love you guys so much. Everything will be okay." After a pause she adds, "Courage is not the absence of fear, but the triumph over it." She has a million sayings like this hung up all over the dojang. Dad is squishing my shoulder and Joey's face is in my side; he is probably drooling all over me.

I know dad would have to say one of his dumb jokes, and he proves me right. "There are two types of people in this world; those who finish what they start, etcetera." I don't get it. Mom snorts and chuckles. She is trying not to cry. Dad's dumb jokes to mock her dumb sayings always make her feel better. She smiles and smacks him on the shoulder, and then they peck each other on the lips.

Mom says, "I love you guys. Don't be nervous. Remember your builds. Don't get creative. You know exactly what to do and what to pick. If this is like fourth age we should have a tutorial after character creation. Don't take risks. And when you are out…" her face turns stern, "…Do. Not. Do. Anything. Stay where you are until me or dad find you." She gives a sterner look to Carlos, "That includes you, Carlos."

"Yeah, mom. I know. Sheesh! Why do you always single me out? Why not yell at officer Kim for once?"

He breaks the family hug and moves back a few steps. He calls me officer Kim because he says I'm a pig. He is such a jerk. Sometimes he is nice to me though.

"Because…just stop. Let's stop. I'm sorry. Come back. This isn't the time."

He doesn't come back.

Dad says, "Listen to your mother. Back. Now."

On his way back my vision starts fading.

1.3 CHARACTER CREATION

KIM GUM

I open my eyes and I'm in character creation. Just like from fourth age, but a little different. So this is real? I'm kind of nervous but also kind of excited. Or really excited. This is just like the game!

Is this really real?

This is so weird. I kind of didn't believe anything was going to really happen. Usually when I get excited about something it never happens.

YES! This is so awesome! I always wanted us to enter the pods, but my parents were dead against it. They're against anything fun or exciting. And even kids get paid UBI for joining a pod. And I could do whatever I wanted after school. School is so dumb. I hate it so much.

Okay, let's do this.

My parents already decided what classes and builds we'll take. My father will be a human taunt-tank. My mother an edylin monk. Or maybe half-orc monk for the extra bite attack, I forget. My older brother Carlos will be a halfling cleric with a splash of another class that lets him get a feat to use darts and slings with his wis instead of dex. They are making me become a halfling rogue using bows. At first it was an elf but they changed it to halfling, like Carlos, for some reason. I liked being small when we played fourth age for practice so I don't mind. I can't wait to customize my looks. That is so much fun! And way better than real life where you just look like you look.

We'll wait for Joey to turn 12 to take the fifth spot in the party. I think. No one knows what this contest is or how long it will last. Or what happens to kids like Joey with special needs.

Fourth age has parties of up to six people, but for some reason this contest – or whatever this is – only allows parties of five. I'm 12. Joey will turn 12 in a little less than two years. Kids under 12 years old can't play, but they have to go. Everyone has to go. Their HPs are set to 1,728 and they get free food every day. That's what the nanites said. At least until they come of age. But the UN secretary lady said we will beat the contest quickly and they will do everything they can to get everything back to normal super-fast, so we shouldn't have to worry about Joey turning 12. But mom still didn't want to have anyone else with us. Just in-case.

My first choice is alignment. I pick true neutral, as my parents told me to – I'm not sure why. I think something about equipment. My second choice is race, and I pick rusk valley halfling – the default halfling. Third is class. I pick rogue. Fourth is background. I look through the list and start worrying. The one I am supposed to take, nine lives, is gone. I get nervous I'll get in trouble for not taking it. But I can't. It definitely isn't there. Nine lives background saves you from death. If your HPs go down below negative 10 it nullifies the damage and resets your HP to negative 5 and stabilizes you. Works once a day. Game day, not a real day. Like every four hours is a game day, I think. My parents demanded both me and Carlos get nine lives as a background.

So now I have a choice. There are a lot of good backgrounds. Full of beans would be nice, but unless Carlos gets it too it doesn't matter if my land speed is higher. I didn't like being so slow when we played fourth age together, but I probably shouldn't get that one. I could take an upbringing and open up more crafts or professions. But I'm training survival so I doubt that is a good idea. Street kid would give me

+2 to hide, move silently, sleight of hand, disguise, and bluff. Not bad. But the big draw of that background is it makes those skills class skills instead of cross-class skills, and they're all already class skills for me as a rogue. Lucky duck looks like it would help the most with my role of scouting and spotting traps, and disabling traps, and opening locks and stuff. It says a natural 1 won't be an automatic failure besides for attack rolls. And it gives +1 AC too!

I don't think mom and dad can complain about that, so I pick lucky duck. I really like the name of it. It sounds silly.

Next are ability scores. They all start at 8, besides con, which is 10. Halfling gives me -2 str, and +2 dex, but that applies after. Con can't be below 10 for anyone for some reason. I have 30 points to spend. Every ability costs 1 point to raise until it hits 14, then 15 and 16 cost 2 points, 17 and 18 cost 3 points. 18 is max unless your race bumps it up to 20. Or lowers an 18 to a 16.

I set everything as I'm supposed to. Str to 10, dex, con and int to 16, and leave wis and cha at 8. I hit accept and it shows my final scores of 8 str, 18 dex, 16 con, 16 int, 8 wis, and 8 cha.

Next is deity selection. This is different too. Fourth age allows you to select "no deity," old gods, Layla, or Pekar. But this says atheist, agnostic, and a big list of religions that are real. Well, a bunch I have heard of. That's kind of neat. A lot I haven't though. They even have favorite weapons and domains. I was supposed to pick the old gods so we could join the open fist faction. I'm not sure what to pick. My parents are atheists so I just pick that.

I am presented with feats and hope there hasn't been more changes that throw off the build I am supposed to take. Nothing jumps out. I pick point blank shot like I am supposed to.

Now skills. I have 44 points. Hopefully I remember all this right. I put 4 points, the maximum at level 1, in disable device, hide, move silently, open lock, search, and spot. I put 4 points in the cross-class skills heal and survival, which only raises them to 2.

Now for the group skills. I put 4 points into acrobatics. With an int of 16, I can pick four skills under it. I think one of them should be sleight of hand, but my parents said no to that. They probably think I'd have too much fun with it. Can't have Kim having fun now, can we? I pick balance, escape, fall, and tumble.

I put 4 points in athletics and pick climb, jump, run, and swim. I put my last 4 points into knowledge and pick arcane, dungeoneering, geography, and nature. Just as I was told to.

Next is my first specialization point. I get one point at level 1, and then again at level 5 and every 5 levels after that for a total of seven at level 30. You also get three racial specialization points. One at level 8, 16, and 24. When we were playing fourth age as a family, I got to mess around with how I used specialization points. There are a ton of fun things to specialize in. My first one went into the jump skill and it allowed me to double jump. You usually can only put one specialization point in a skill. I think tumble can take two. A ton don't take any specialization points at all, like heal. A lot are boring, but some can be a lot of fun. Like, a specialization point in stealth let me move at full speed while stealthed. Stuff like that.

My first choice was already picked for me – I specialize in point blank shot. You can usually put two specialization points in most feats. The first point in point blank shot increases the range from 30 to 40, and gives me +2 to shots within 20 feet, and +1 to shots from 21 to 40 feet. My next two points, at level 5 and 10, go to precise shot, but at level 15 I put a second point in point blank shot. That will increase the range to 60, and give +2 to shots within 30 feet, and +1 to shots from 31 to 60 feet.

Next should be languages, but it isn't there. Maybe I'm just remembering wrong? I'm on the screen for hobby, crafts, and professions. Crafts and professions have kind of been reversed. The craft listed for all characters in the SRD is now called a hobby, but only for your first class. And hobbies level with your character and not your class. You can pick any profession as a free hobby choice. Crafts are focused on making things and selling them. Professions are focused on gathering mats or doing something that helps only your character, like tinker, porter, and gambler. Classes listed as having a profession now get to pick a craft or downgrade the craft to a profession. Since I trained in the survival skill, I get a bunch of free professions from that. Such as butcher, forager, hunter, and skinner. If I was a class like ranger or bounty hunter, or I had the track feat, it would also help with tracking. Survival also gives a resting xp bonus, puts a compass on the minimap, increases my speed through certain terrains, and also a bonus to weather saves. But everyone said weather saves aren't important in fourth age. Or not super important. Or something. And I set the minimap to always face north and not rotate so the compass is useless. I think so at least.

I pick tinker as my hobby, which lets me repair some durability to my equipment by myself for free. For my craft I pick culinarian. Dad only gets the hobby since his class is fighter, and he is getting tinker too. Repairing gear is expensive. Mom is getting herbalist as a hobby and alchemy as a craft. Not herbalist, the other thing. I think herbalist is for growing herbs. Well, whatever the one is called that lets you pick them. Eh, could be herbalist. Carlos is picking either mining or gemologist as his hobby, and instead of a craft is picking up whatever one he doesn't pick as a hobby as his downgraded craft to profession choice. Ores and gems sell for a ton.

Next should be where I pick my gender and customize my character's looks, or was in fourth age at least. Instead, I have to pick an equipment kit. This is new. After going through them all I pick the hunter kit. I get leather armor, leather boots, leather gloves, belt, a short bow, a spear, and a dagger. When I try to click on a skill or profession kit I get a message that I automatically get all relevant kits for all opened skills, crafts, and professions. Nice. But what about food? And thieves' tools? I see a tab for inventory and click on it. I have a ton of skill and crafting kits and also a thieves' tool in it, plus three rations.

I don't see a way I can equip anything here, and I am excited to customize my looks, so I hit next.

What is this? It is just an overview page of my character asking me to finalize my choices. Did I mess up? Where can I customize my looks? That is what I was most looking forward to. Can I not even pick a name? Ridiculous! Does it just randomize my looks? What about languages it never let me pick?

This better not make me a stupid boy. I better look cute too!

A little angrily, I click finalize and my vision fades.

1.4 ENTER THE DUNGEON

KIM GUM

I come to standing in a grass clearing in a forest. I don't feel right. My head is all jumbled. I feel really heavy. Mom is yelling something I don't understand. My head is clearing but mom's yelling has me worried. Are we being attacked? I look around and just see my family. Joey is whimpering near mom trying to get her attention. Carlos is messing with his sling. Dad is swinging a sword and hoping around. He looks like an idiot with his big armor. I don't see something attacking us. Wait…we all look like ourselves? Why do we all look like ourselves? Shouldn't I look like a halfling?

"Put your armor on." I can finally understand what mom is saying to me. The mental commands work just like the game, so I open the inventory and click on my leather armor. "We told you to equip everything before exiting character creation," she says as the countdown for equipping armor starts. I equip my short bow, which is instant. I see an infinity sign over the quiver on my paper doll. I put my spear and dagger in slots one and two of my quickslot bar. I put my healing kit, survival kit, repair kit, cooking kit, cartography kit, survey kit, and thieves' tools into my second quickslot bar. I notice it says my carry weight is (x + (26 lbs * .75). What is x? I'm at 16.5 lbs. already?

I look through weights. My boots, gloves, belt and rations weigh nothing. My armor weighs 7.5, spear 3, bow 2, dagger .5, and I have seven kits all at .5 lbs each. That still doesn't tell me what x is.

I notice I don't have my cd link anymore. I try accessing the tangle and I can't. That really sucks. "Mia?" No response. Not having Mia really stinks. She's been my only real friend my whole life. I check my pockets. My leatherman is gone. Everything is gone. Even my real belt is gone. Why did it take my belt? This is really weird.

I start navigating to the skills page to assign the ones I need to quickslots when mom says, "Carlos, don't tell me you only have a robe please. God help me, Carlos!"

Carlos jumps and says, "That's the only kit that came with a sling, ma! What did you want me to do? Jesus, you're always on my ass about everything."

"Talk like that to your mother again and that won't be all that's on your ass," dad says as he gives Carlos what I call the 'angry-dad' look. "And watch your language."

My armor is on, it takes 30 seconds to equip. I finish hotkeying the skills, professions and the craft I have into quickslots and start working on equipping my boots, belt, and gloves. They take six seconds each. That's everything I have. And everything I can do to prepare. I think.

"Over here! This is a store," I hear mom say behind me. "I have 2 gold. How much do you guys have? Well, 20 silver and 20 copper."

"Same."

"Same too."

"Yup," we all reply.

"Good, give it to Car…me, so I can buy Carlos some armor. We can only get padded. Wait, you can use a shield and sling together, right?"

There is a pause before Carlos answers, "Yeah, technically. But I suck with the sling already. I can't use a shield with it yet."

"Have you tried? Tell you what – we'll get the light shield and you try to figure it out. Either way, it's better to have and not need, than need and not have. The padded armor is five, a light shield is three. Whoa, a buckler costs 15. I hope it's as easy to get gold here as it is in fourth age."

Mom's at some sort of floating ball thing near a tree. That's a store? I feel weird. Everything is heavy. Like I'm under water or something. Past the ball thing is a rectangle of water. I look in and see stairs leading down to a door under the water. I point it out and dad says, "We'll check it out later, sweetie."

Mom is asking Carlos about what he took instead of nine lives. I bet I'm next in line to be grilled. Is this the tutorial? It is nothing like the tutorial in fourth age if it is. Since I have some time I look through my character sheet.

Key - Base (Ability Modifier) ((Misc.)) [Total]

CLASSES: 1 Rogue

RACE: Rusk Valley Halfling - Alignment: True Neutral - Deity: Atheist

HP: 2 (3) ((5 Destined for Greatness)) [10]

AC: 10 (4) ((2 Leather Armor; 1 Small; 1 Lucky Duck)) [18]

BAB: 0

Land Speed: *

ABILITIES

Str: 8 (-1) ((0)) [8]

Dex 18 (4) ((0)) [18]

Con: 16 (3) ((0)) [16]

Int: 16 (3) ((0)) [16]

Wis: 8 (-1) ((0)) [8]

Cha: 8 (-1) ((0)) [8]

SAVES

Fortitude: 0 (3) ((1 Halfling Luck)) [4]

Reflex: 2 (4) ((1 Halfling Luck)) [7]

Will: 0 (-1) ((1 Halfling Luck)) [0]

COMBAT MODE: Free Attack/Auto Attack/Game Mode

MAIN HAND

Short Bow

AB: 0 (4) ((1 Small)) [5]

DAM: 1d6 (0) ((0)) Extra Damage=0 [1-6 Piercing], C 20, CM x3

Spear

Medium one-handed or two-handed weapons. Can be thrown. A ready action can be used to set a spear against a charge, double damage is dealt on a successful hit against a charging opponent. Must have one hand free to ready against charge.

AB: 0 (-1) ((1 Small)) [0]

DAM: 1d6 (-1) ((0)) Extra Damage=0 [0-5 Piercing], C 20, CM x3

OFF HAND

NA

OTHER ATTACKS

NA

OTHER

Spell Failure: 10%

Max Dex Bonus: 6 leather Armor [6]

Armor Check Penalty: 0

HOBBIES, CRAFTS, and PROFESSIONS

Hobby: Tinker level 1 (Maximum skill level of Hobbies is character level plus feats and racial and class features. No Ability mod for Hobbies. No experience needed to level Hobbies)

Crafts: Culinarian level 0 (Allows for the advanced completion of various dishes that do not involve baking ingredients, such as meat dishes, soups, and vegetables. Bakers focus on bread, pasta, and pastry dishes. Maximum level is class level of the class used to open the Craft. If multiclassing, a Craft can be selected twice or more and class levels can be combined to increase maximum Craft level. Unlike Hobbies, both Crafts and Profession require experience to level up)

Professions: NA

SKILLS

44 points at level 1

Italics - cross class skill

*Armor Check Penalty applies

(Falls under above group skill)

Acrobatics* (Dex) 4 (4) ((0)) [8]

(Balance)*

(Escape)*

(Fall)*

(Tumble)* (10 base points in Acrobatics with Tumble selected and opened gives a +1 bonus to AC. 20 base points gives another +1 bonus, for a total of +2 bonus to AC. This counts as a skill bonus and stacks with everything)

Athletics* (Str) 4 (-1) ((0)) [3]

(Climb)* 4 (-1) ((2 Hafling Movement)) [5]

(Jump)* 4 (-1) ((2 Hafling Movement)) [5]

(Run)* (Con) 4 (3) ((0)) [7] (10 base points in Athletics with Run selected and opened gives a +5 land speed bonus. 20 base points gives another +5 for +10 total land speed increase. This counts as a skill bonus and stacks with everything. This translates into a 7.5% speed increase at 10 and 20, 15% total. This is the only benefit in this world, as the Run skill effects Stamina in End of the Fourth Age, which was not implemented here)

(Swim)*

Disable Device (Int) 4 (3) ((0)) [7]

Heal (Wis) 2 (-1) ((0)) [1]

Hide* (Dex) 4 (4) ((4 Small)) [12]

Knowledge (Int) 4 (3) ((0)) [7]

(Arcane) 2 [5]

(Dungeoneering)

(Geography) 2 [5]

(Nature) 2 [5]

Move Silently* (Dex) 4 (4) ((2 Halfling Movement)) [10]

Open Lock (Dex) 4 (4) ((0)) [8]

Search (Int) 4 (3) ((0)) [7]

Spot (Wis) 4 (-1) ((0)) [3]

Survival (Wis) 2 (-1) ((0)) [1]

Skill Points carried over to next level: 0

FEATS

* are selected feats or options, listed last

Level 1 (Rogue 1)

Destined for Greatness (Free feat given to all players of End of the Fourth Age. You were born under an auspicious sign and have a greater destiny than most born in Benekal or even all of Tibur. You receive +5 Hit Points at level 1)

Charge (As SRD besides the following. Charges take three seconds from starting point to target regardless of distance. Distance has been standardized to 60 feet for all players since there is no land speed)

Armor Proficiency [Light]

Shield Proficiency [Buckler]

Shield Proficiency [Light]

Weapon Proficiency [Simple]

Weapon Proficiency [Rogue]

Halfling Hearing (+2 racial bonus on Listen checks)

Halfling Movement (+2 racial bonus Climb, Jump and Move Silently checks)

Halfling Luck (+1 racial bonus on all saving throws)

Halfling Courage (+2 morale bonus on saving throws against fear. This bonus stacks with the Halfling's Luck +1 bonus on saving throws in general)

Halfling Aim (+1 racial bonus on attack rolls with thrown weapons and slings)

Small (Weapons and armor automatically resize. Weight is reduced by half. Damage of weapons is reduced by 2, but cannot be reduced below 1. May effect item's HPs. Carrying capacity is 3/4ths of Medium sized characters. +1 size bonus to Armor Class, a +1 size bonus on attack rolls, and a +4 size bonus on Hide checks. Base land speed is 20. Translates to -15% speed. May change prices on gear bought through store or NPCs.)

Halfling Languages

Trapfinding

Sneak Attack (1D6)

*Background – Lucky Duck (+1 AC. No automatic failure on any roll of natural 1 other than attack rolls, when applicable)

*Point Blank Shot (+1 bonus on attack and damage rolls with ranged weapons at ranges of up to 30 feet)

*Specialization Point used – Point Blank Shot (+2 bonus on attack and damage rolls with ranged weapons at ranges of up to 20 feet. +1 bonus on attack and damage rolls with ranged weapons at ranges of between 21 and 40 feet)

ITEMS

Leather Armor

Short bow

Spear

Dagger

Healing kit (Takes 1 Round (6 seconds) to complete. No benefit if interrupted. Heals 1d2 + Heal skill + enhancement bonus hit points. Check for stabilization, poison, disease, treat wounds. Can be used once between combats. Maximum charges that can be held in the inventory are 1 + (enhancement bonus x2). Maximum enhancement bonus for all kits are +6. Cannot specialize in the Healing skill)

Survival kit

Repair kit (Takes 1 Turn (60 seconds) to complete. No benefit if interrupted. Repairs weapons and armor by a total of 1 + Tinker level durability points divided by the number of damaged pieces. Priority is set by user. Maximum durability repaired on a single item is 2 + enhancement bonus of kit. Can only be used once between combats on own gear)

Cooking kit

Cartography kit (Allowed with Knowledge: Geography. The Geography skill opens up the minimap function in outdoor terrains and improves both map and minimap with higher skill. Specializing in Geography highlights detected enemies on the minimap, adds icons for events, and gives +2 synergy bonus to both spot and search checks outdoors)

Survey kit (Allowed with Knowledge: Dungeoneering. The Dungeoneering skill allows dungeon mapping, opens the minimap function in indoor terrains, and expands the range and scope of both the map and minimap with higher skill. Specializing in Dungeoneering opens the assess enemy function, adds icons for unhidden treasure chests in range, and gives +2 synergy bonus to both spot and search checks indoors)

Thieves' tools

Rations x3

1.5 WELL, THAT DIDN'T GO AS PLANNED

KIM GUM

"You look so cute, monkey." Mom gives me what I call the 'I'm so ashamed of you' smile. I hate that smile. I hate that nickname. Monkey. And I know I don't look cute. I look like a fat idiot. The leather armor I have on is tight, and it tightened right over the baggy army clothes dad got us. I'm all…what's the word? Frumpy? My feet look giant with the game boots over my army boots. I look even more like a frog now. A retarded frog.

I'm not supposed to say that word. I'd get in so much trouble if I ever did. Mom says it is really bad but especially bad because of Joey. But Joey doesn't understand anything. And even if he could he isn't that word; he's autistic. And she can't stop me from thinking it. Especially about myself. And that is how I look. Like a fat retarded frog with cankles and no neck.

We've been here for, like, hours and hours and haven't done anything. She just had me and Carlos practice hitting trees with my bow and his sling while she and dad did whatever. We found out we can't go into the forest. There is an invisible wall that stops us. But we can shoot arrows through the invisible wall.

She promised we'd be heading out soon about an hour ago.

Jeez, this is so boring. This was supposed to be fun.

Finally, mom yells, "Everyone all set? Good. We ready to head out? Remember, we take it slow and keep it safe." After a moment she says, "Cowards never start, the weak never finish, and winners never quit."

That is one of the secret posters she keeps in the storage room of the dojang. You're not supposed to say it or the school can get in trouble.

Dad smiles and says, "Two guys walk into a bar and the third one ducks."

I don't get it. Mom snort laughs and slaps him on the shoulder. Carlos laughs. I bet he is pretending he gets it but doesn't. Carlos is an idiot. He acts like he is so much older than me but he is only 14. He isn't even a full two years older. Idiot. Pretender. Fake. I'd love to punch him in his dumb face.

Carlos and I stop taking practice shots at trees and prepare to head out. I am not good with the bow. I wish mom would allow me to melee. Mom technically knows how to use a bow since her dojang is supposed to teach all the Korean martial arts; taekwondo, hapkido, subak, tang soo do, taekkyeon, and the bow one – gungdo. Or gungo. I forget. She sucks with a bow almost as bad as I do. And I suck pretty bad. She also has MMA fighting classes, but has to pretend she only has a historic martial arts school since MMA is banned. All violent sports were banned. But not historic martial arts. Well, besides any type of Jujutsu. That was banned because people used it to get around the MMA ban. Muay thai isn't illegal, but it is real hard to get a license. Her kid classes are mainly taekwondo. Her adult classes are for people she thinks are rats and are also taekwondo. Her adult hapkido class is for people she trusts to be focused on MMA fighting and just a little hapkido. It is a big family secret since it is illegal. We're not allowed to talk about it ever. And me and Carlos can't do that class since if we mess up mom can get in really, really, super big trouble. She says when we're older we can.

I learned way more about how to shoot a bow through the training room in fourth age than mom could teach me. I'm still not good, but I will get better. As another poster in the dojang says: "just because you are struggling doesn't mean you are failing. Every great success requires some sort of struggle to get there."

As I walk up to her, mom says, "Kimmy, keep Joey close to you." Cool! Thanks, mom! You make me become a rogue so I could sneak and scout but now I'm on babysitting duty. I put my hand out for Joey. He doesn't like holding hands, but he'll usually follow if he sees your hand held out. He comes closer, sucking on his hand. Hopefully he stays quiet.

He doesn't.

Mom looks at me like it's my fault, "Stay back a little. Try and keep his noises down. I know it's hard. Please." Yeah, yeah. Whatever, mom.

Carlos is walking up front with mom and dad like he is an adult too. Stupid idiot. Is this grass actually a road? Everything seems so straight. Too straight to be a forest.

A minute later we come to a big grassy open area. Everyone but me explores the area since I'm stuck with Joey. I think I'm the only one with the geography and dungeoneering skills. And the cartography and survey kits. Good job guys. Makes a ton of sense.

We head north through the only exit of the clearing. I think roads of grass are kind of weird, but no one else is saying anything about it. We come almost immediately to a four-way intersection. North looks like a small clearing. East is a long path that seems empty. West has two monsters that look like zombie dogs on the path, down a ways where it looks like it turns south.

Dad says to mom as he nods his head where the zombie dogs are, "You see that?"

"Yeah," she says.

No one speaks for a moment. Carlos surprises me by saying, "Kim should sneak down to get a sneak attack in." Why is he being nice to me? Why the confidence all of a sudden?

Dad whispers loudly, "Knock it off, Carlos."

Maybe he wasn't being nice. I don't get it though.

A little bit later Dad says, "No nameplates. I can't figure out how to inspect."

Mom replies, "I don't think you can. Nothing is working I can think of."

There is a bunch more talking but I don't really hear it. I had to move away with Joey since he was getting louder. After a while mom calls me back.

"This is what we do. Me and your father will run at the dogs and get agro as soon as you guys attack from range. Kimmy, once you attack bring Joey back down the road a little. Stay there until we finish them off. Carlos, if there is any threat to you or anyone, stop attacking and run back to that big clearing. No, the store ball thing near the water. Bring Kimmy and Joey with you. You're in charge until we get back. You attack the dog on the right. Not now! God, Carlos! When I say so. Kimmy, you attack the one the left. Toni, you get the left and I'll take the right. Remember to communicate. And avoiding attacks is better than relying on AC – at least when we played the game-game. So dodge, block, get out the way. This should be the same. Just like we practiced. Kids! Remember, don't shoot us. Stop attacking when we get close. We don't have the hit points for friendly fire or accidents. In fact, just shoot once and stop. We'll take off running as soon as you do."

I'm pretty nervous. This feels different than the game. We get in position. I enter stealth to get sneak attack damage if I hit. I wish I didn't feel so slow and heavy still. I was hoping that would wear off. But it isn't wearing off.

I nock an arrow, draw it back, aim, and hold. I wait. And keep waiting. My arm hurts. Finally, mom whisper-screams, "As the next round ticks. Now!" and I let my arrow fly. Half way there it goes into the woods. My only consolation is Carlos' bullet hit the road even before my arrow hit the woods. He sucks even worse than I do. I told mom me and Carlos should put our attacks on game mode until we get better with aiming ourselves. If it works here, game mode would aim for us. But no one ever listens to Kim!

The monster dogs don't even know we are attacking until mom and dad start rushing them. Then the monster dogs take off like race-cars. Dad charges his and the dog jumps and crashes into his shield, bounces back, and falls to the ground. Unlike in the fourth age, normal physics seem to work here. As mom and her dog meet, she punches it but the animal doesn't react at all, and it keeps on running past her. I see the attack of opportunity animation come out of my mother. What everyone calls ghost arms. A free-hit. The ghost arm hits the dog, he doesn't react at all again, and it keeps rushing at Carlos. Or me.

I remember I was supposed to take Joey back down the road. I decide to take him around the corner at least; mom will be so pissed if I just stand here with the monster dog coming. I grab Joey's arm but he doesn't move. He is doing his finger stimming thing and making a lot of noises. I go behind him and put my hands under his armpits to pick him up. He is really heavy.

I hear mom scream, "NOOOOO!" I look to where she is running and I see Carlos on his back and the monster dog's snout around his neck, thrashing Carlos around. Blood everywhere.

Is this real? This…can't be real. Right? This can't be happening for real. My scalp tightens and I feel really weird. Like tingly all over and nauseous. I can't move. I want this to stop. This can't be real.

Mom reaches the dog and punches it a bunch. A couple seconds later it starts making horrible noises as mom is furiously pummeling it while yelling like a maniac. When the monster is really good and dead she yells, "CARLOS!" and kneels over his body, crying.

I don't even notice the other dog until it makes mom go from kneeling to almost kowtowing under its weight as it lands on her back with its mouth around her head. Its teeth are blocked from biting down on her for a second, then I see a flicker and a shine all around her. The teeth connect with her scalp. And then blood. I stand paralyzed as mom screams in pain, trying to grab the monster. The dog lets go of her head and bites her right shoulder, frantically shaking its head from side to side. She stops trying to flip it off and starts punching it in the head with her weak hand – her left hand. She is in a bad position to fight back. The punches are weak.

I want to help but I'm frozen. I'm petrified. I yell, "DAD!" And hope he comes to save her. I don't hear anything in response. I look to where he is. He is laying on his stomach in the road, blood all around him. Something inside me breaks. I don't know what. I just know it. Just like I know mom is dead too. But I don't want to be right, so I don't look at her.

I want to run away with Joey but my knees are shaking. I think of throwing him forward as a sacrifice so I can get away but I don't. I can't run right now. Holding Joey is helping. Something between me and that thing.

We'll die together, as a family. I can't run. I can't even think.

I don't want to look toward the monster but I can't help it. My knees almost give out as I see it looking at me, standing over mom's body. Staring at me. With eyes calm like a pond and blood all over its snout. It doesn't look angry. It's a trick. I slowly back up off the road and into the woods, carrying Joey with me, hiding my head behind

Joey's back. My back hits a tree and I try to shuffle around it, and realize it's the invisible wall. No going around it. I can't go anywhere.

This is it.

I'm so scared.

I put Joey down and hug him from behind. He is making a lot of noises and madly doing his stimming with his fingers.

"I'm sorry. I love you so much. I'm so sorry. Please, please forgive me. Oh, God. Oh, God."

My heart feels like it is going to burst out of my chest. I quickly take a peek and duck back down. The monster is closer. And snarling. I'm still talking to Joey but I don't know what I'm saying. My hands are shaking so bad I'm almost stimming like Joey. I start peeing my pants.

"I'm sorry. Oh, God. Please. Please. Oh, God. Joey, I'm sorry."

I hear a noise and just know the monster is attacking. This is it. Joey is pushed back into me, stimming harder and making more noise than the last time he freaked out and had to be restrained. It's hard to hold onto him, but the only thing I want now is to hold him as tight as possible. I want to die holding him. As a family. We'll all die as a family. Maybe we'll wake up at home together.

It takes a moment to register - it sounds like the monster is whimpering. I don't want to look but I have to take another peek. What I see keeps me looking. The monster has backed off and is rubbing his snout in the grass, and is definitely whimpering. He has blood from injuries on his head, probably from mom. Good. I can't see anything else wrong.

Did attacking Joey hurt it? Because he is under 12 years old?

I look more closely at the monster. It looks like a dog, but also kind of like...something else. A lion? A bird? It has a big head for its body. A really short snout for a dog. A wide snout that gets pointier at the end. Kind of like a beak, but has teeth. Its front legs are much bigger than the back legs. The whole front of the body is much bigger than the back. The ears are pretty big. They were sticking up before, but not now. The skin looks like a zombie cornflower blue color, with dark pinkish spots. Kind of like a zombie-colored purple. A sick looking type of magenta.

But, it isn't a zombie. A different type of monster. Probably.

I hate it.

It starts backing up. It won't look directly at Joey now. Or me either. I think.

The back of my pants feel heavy and warmer than my groin. I figured they were warm from my pee, but now I think I went number two in my pants. I didn't even notice when it happened.

The monster is back near mom and Carlos. It looks around, ignoring us, and starts eating mom. I look back down. I don't want to see my mom get eaten. I want to stop it. But I don't. I want to get away more. I dropped my bow. What can I do? I start crying because even if I had my bow I wouldn't do anything. I can't do anything. Besides hold on to Joey. I just want to get out of here and go home. With mom and dad. And even Carlos too. Joey is trying to wiggle out of my arms. I hold him tighter and cry, and tell him I'm sorry. I'm so sorry.

1.6 SECOND CHANCE

BRUNO VAZ

As I awake in the tutorial dungeon I bring my hand to my face. I still have a beard. The first time I was here – four or five years ago – I was clean shaven. Maybe just three years ago. I don't know. It is wicked hard to tell time here.

I don't know why I grew a beard. I look stupid with one, and it's a pain to keep groomed. But now that it's grown out I don't got to worry about any in-grown hairs, which is the only real benefit of having a beard. To me at least. In-grown hairs are always an issue shaving. Especially having just a couple days growth. I'll probably shave it off before exiting. Trimming it takes way too much time, and it's getting long enough where someone could grab it in a fight.

I pull up my sleeve to check if some newer scars are still there. Yup. I definitely kept my body as well as my memories. I'm not sure if that is a benefit or not. Getting older means everything hurts more. And hurts more all the time. Despite the healing pills. My back, knees, and especially my wrists, are pure garbage. And my ankles, hips, shoulders, and elbows are slightly less garbage-y garbage. I check to see what I'm wearing under my armor. The same clothes from my first time here.

They're not supposed to, but I still wonder if any of my coins, points, or currencies carried over. Maybe auras? I don't think we asked about auras. I try to open the bag of holding on my side but it isn't there. Of course it isn't, dummy. I always use that bag to open my inventory. I hope my gestures carried over because mental commands never worked for me and I forget how to open the UI besides with gestures and bags. Well, there's verbal commands, but you sound like a crazy idiot doing verbal commands. I do the gesture to open the inventory and it works.

No dungeon coins at all. No gear gems. No points. No gold. No nothing. Just like the machine said. No auras either. I open achievements and, thankfully, they're all still there. Phew. Achievements still being open are critical to me taking over the government. If the wish machine was wrong about that, I'd be wicked screwed.

I open email – or, I should say messaging, but if it walks like a duck – and they are all gone. Goddamn it! The bus trick didn't work. Or memory bus. Or something like that. Whatever it is didn't work. I'll have to write them all over again. On my own this time. Damn! I hate writing. Or thinking. Reading too. But especially writing. There is no way I can remember everything or write it as good on my own. Mother of Christ Almighty, I hate writing, and now I got to do a ton of it. By myself. Like a filthy plebian.

The wish machine thing has been right about everything so far. My family better be okay or I will destroy it. I know it said it wouldn't be here this time, but I can destroy the cave it was in. Destroy something.

Some of my quickslots are still good, thankfully. I fill in the couple of empty ones with my new crap gear before heading out to start saving humanity. I need to crush this dungeon to establish dominance. I can't afford any mess-ups. I really, really need all circles for the early dungeons. Or 1st SS.

I still don't understand why S is better than A, and SS is better than S. Just some dork nonsense. I could actually change it now this time. Make people call 1st SS a circle, like it is. 2nd an oval. 3rd a rectangle. And regular SS a square. Just like the dungeon shows you.

Not made up dork garbage. How does S being higher than A make any sense at all?

I hope the psuchesoma thing isn't a dumb spelling question, or 1st SS is probably out the window. And I'll look like a huge idiot. I don't remember what kind it was in the tutorial. Those spelling ones are absolutely ridiculous. Only idiots know how to spell the crap it asks. Usually French words no one has even heard of before.

Well, that is enough time wasted on thinking instead of doing. The human race isn't going to save itself.

Time to get to killing.

1.7 I GOT TO GET OUT OF THIS PLACE

KIM GUM

I don't know how long we've been standing here. Way too long. It feels like forever. Joey has given up trying to get away from me. I don't hear mom getting eaten any more. I take a peek over Joey's shoulder. I don't see the monster. I look around and see it past dad's body. It is lying on the ground back where it started, before we attacked. Its head resting on its front legs. Paws?

I get excited. This is our chance. We can get away. I think as best I can, coming up with a plan. Hopefully Joey doesn't fight me on this. I can't tell if the dog is sleeping or not. I have stealth. I mentally hit the hotkey but it doesn't work. Why? I open my UI and try hitting stealth manually, and it still doesn't work. No!

I can't blow this chance. I revise my plan. I grab Joey's wrist and he doesn't resist me bringing him along. I go and grab my bow and send it to my inventory, and I push my nausea down as I move towards my family's corpses to loot them. I see the monster dog stand and look at me. I don't freeze. I start running back towards the intersection as fast as I can, dragging Joey with me.

We take the turn and keep going. We get to the open field and I drag Joey to the southeast corner. I kneel and have Joey kneel in front of me. I don't see any sign of the monster. We wait for a long time while I cry. This place is awful. How is this real? I hope this isn't real.

I want to go home so bad. I just want to go home. This place is awful. I hate it. I hate those monsters. How long have we been here? Too long. Way too long. I got to get out of here.

I haven't seen any sign of the monster since we came to the open field. Joey is asleep. Something is floating near his body. I think it's one of his free meals. I shift and the skin on my rear hurts. I remember what's in my pants back there. It must've dried.

I don't want to deal with this now. I still feel like…I don't know. My body still feels tingly in a bad way. My stomach hurts. I'm tired. I just want to rewind time and go home. This game sucks. I want my mom. And my dad. And Carlos. I just want to get out of here.

I don't know what to do. I start crying again. I lay down near Joey with my arm on his chest. He'll move away if he realizes someone is touching him. I don't care. He's all I got now.

Joey wakes me up. He's doing the jumping thing and his sign that he is hungry. It's still daytime? My rear feels stingy. I point at the meal hovering near Joey's chest and he doesn't even look. I try to grab it but my hand goes right through it. How is this right? What if he was a baby? How could people feed babies if you can't touch their free food?

I stand and grab Joey's arms and guide his hands to the meal. It works. He drops it immediately, as soon as I let go of his arms. I bend down to look at it, to see how to open it. I don't see any seams. It looks like a small, white box. It has a green picture of something like smoke on it. I don't know how I am going to prompt Joey's hands to open it if I can't even see a way to open it.

I grab it to see if there's something on the bottom. I'm holding it before I realize I can actually touch it now. There's a raised arrow on the top I missed, pointing towards the front middle seam. I press it and the top just disappears. It has some sort of paper container, an apple, some uncooked broccoli, and something that looks like a really big meatball, but smoother. I see heat waves coming off the meat thing. The paper container is filled with liquid.

It takes me a minute to figure out the liquid container. It feels like paper but I couldn't rip the top off. You have to suck on it. It is plain water. Yuck. No one ever drinks just plain water!

I grab Joey's arm to have him sit, and then I hold the container to his mouth until he finally starts drinking. Then I put the tray on his lap.

I go to sit down but feel the pull on my rear. I want to eat before I deal with that. I get one of the three rations I have out of my inventory. It weighs almost nothing. Really, really light. It works the same as Joey's meal, it seems to get heavier when you open it. Mine has a fruit I forget the name of – some kind of, like, a weird shaped apple – a ton of carrots and a smooth ball of what looks like warmed up chicken. I try the ball out. Not bad, but I don't think it's chicken. It tastes familiar though. I wish it came with more water than the little container thingy.

Way before I finish Joey gets up and starts making his want noises. He ate a little of the meatball thing but left the rest. Now that I'm done I look for the tray he left on the ground and it's gone. What? Where is it? Did it disappear?

I stand up to look around and it's definitely gone. I walk a few steps to the woodline to throw the remains of my little tray away when I step in something mushy.

"Gross! Joey! Did you poop right here?" He definitely did. "So gross! You didn't even wipe did you?" I rub my foot on the grass trying to clean it. Great. Just great. More poop to clean. So gross.

I toss my tray into the woods and it hits the invisible wall. Why could me and Carlos shoot into the woods before? The trays can't go through the walls, but arrows can?

Oh well. It should disappear soon. Hopefully with Joey's poop too.

I hate this stupid place so much. I want to go home so bad.

I start thinking about how I'm going to clean the problem I made in my pants. For just a second I'm glad Joey is the only one here to know I pooped myself, and then I feel guilty and start crying again. And I think about missing my family and cry more.

When I finally stop crying I try to think of a way to solve my problem. I guess I could use the knife to cut my t-shirt for TP? Or the army pants or top? I start removing my armor. 30 seconds. The other equipment slots only take six seconds each.

I get an idea. One that won't require me cutting up my t-shirt. The water near the store thing!

Joey is still doing his want noises. I ignore him and start walking towards the path to the water. I think better of it and grab Joey and bring him with me. Just in case.

When I get to the water I decide to check the store ball thing first. Holy moly! A waterskin costs a gold. Soap is five silver. Even a bucket is five silver. I can't find underwear but the cheapest clothes are called peasant's outfit, at one silver. Rations are the only reasonably priced thing, with a day's rations costing one copper. Day must mean three rations, right? The recharges for the kits are pretty cheap, too, at one copper per charge for each of them.

Mom has all the rest of the money. Had. Has?

I don't want to think about that. Not again. At least not until I clean my mess up.

I start undressing and look at the water. The door! Maybe that's a way out. I get excited. We need to get out of here. This could be our way. I jump in the water, dunk my head under, and swim to the door. It doesn't budge. I try everything. Go up for air and try again. I spend what feels like an hour on the door before I give up and get out and finish undressing.

We got to get out of here somehow. But I got to clean myself off first. And clean my clothes. So gross.

1.8 A SHIELD UNTO THEM

KIM GUM

The fire I made from my survival kit is weird. It makes heat but doesn't set anything on fire. In fourth age it doesn't make heat. At least, I don't remember it making heat. That is also the same as fourth age, you can put your hand right in the fire and it doesn't burn you or hurt or anything.

It's drying my clothes pretty quickly. I can't complain about that. Joey seems to like the warmth too. Even though it isn't cold out or anything. It just feels nice.

Does it ever get dark in here? I look around for the sun but can't see it. I'm not sure if I ever saw it. Maybe when I fell asleep I slept for like 12 hours and completely missed the night?

Even though mom killed one of the monster dogs my xp bar is empty. Maybe because I didn't do anything to help kill it?

We eat again while waiting for my clothes to dry. My trays never disappear like Joey's do, and Joey is playing with both of them. He ate most of his food. Good. I actually saw his tray disappear this time. I wonder if he understands what happened to mom, dad, and Carlos? That they're never coming back. Probably not. I wish he could talk so I'd have someone to talk to about everything.

Joey's poop didn't disappear either. I decided the southeast corner of this field is now the designated bathroom area. I think Joey understands. I wish I thought a little more before cleaning off in the water near the store. The rations don't give enough water and I'm not drinking poop water. Hopefully it will clean itself somehow, so we can drink it later. I only have one more ration before I have no water. Unless I start taking Joey's.

My plan is to leave Joey here with his trays to play with while I sneak and loot mom, dad, and Carlos. And the monster mom killed.

I checked out most of the field earlier. It is a square. I figured out how to bring my mini-map up, as well as the regular map. Everything is perfect angles and sharp edges. Very weird. The whole forest has an invisible wall around it. You can see butterflies and birds in the forest, but I haven't seen one insect on the grass roads or fields. Not a fly on the poop. Not a mosquito. Nothing.

My stealth works again. I don't know why it didn't work earlier.

I stand up and walk over to the bathroom corner. The fire disappears as soon as I walk about 10 feet away from it. When I'm done I go back and check my clothes. Still damp. My army boots are soaking wet on the insides still.

Well, the game armor is pretty comfortable. Even the boots. My survival kit is out of charges so if I want to dry my socks and underwear I need money and mom has all of it. I think. I hope she has money. And I hope there was a lot left after she bought all that stuff for stupid Carlos.

I shouldn't think that. Not now. May Carlos rest in peace.

I still feel really heavy, even without the army clothes and army boots. Heavy and slow.

I know he probably doesn't understand but I tell Joey to stay put. I walk north towards the intersection and as I'm about to hit stealth I notice Joey walking towards me. Holy moly! This kid is going to drive me up a wall!

Mom used to say that all the time. I'm not sure what it means exactly beyond Joey will drive you nuts. I think. What being nuts has to do with walls, I have no idea.

I miss mom so much.

When Joey gets to me I grab him and make him sit. "Don't move! Stay Here! No move!"

Hopefully he stays, but if he doesn't and the monster dog attacks I can use him as a shield again.

I hit stealth and move around the corner to the left. The monster is still laying down with his head on its paws. My heartbeat spikes when I see it. I hope stealth works. I really, really hope stealth works.

I sneak down the road and get to Carlos and almost become sick. I check the dog and he doesn't seem to be aware of me. I touch Carlos and do the loot mental command, like in the game. I loot Carlos' robe, light wooden shield, sling, padded armor, quarterstaff, belt, kits, and rations. I get the medium load debuff. I put back his sling, padded armor, shield, and kits. The debuff goes away. I take his boots. I don't know why. They weigh nothing.

I go to mom's corpse. It is disgusting. I can't even recognize her. Poor mom. I start looting. She has eight silver (yes!) and three rations I take. I leave her kits, robe, boots, belt and hand-wraps.

I go to the monster corpse next. I get a jagged fang, three leather scraps, two silver and eight coppers. No meat? My survival kit is out of charges but I still try it on him, since butchering is part of survival. It works. I get two pieces of raw beast meat and a ruined beast hide. And the medium load debuff again. I see the monster dog's corpse disappear. Instead of putting stuff back I try moving closer to the intersection to see how much the debuff hurts. I feel way slower. I still feel heavy and slow like I'm underwater, and it is definitely worse now.

The monster dog hasn't moved yet. Dad's corpse is like…a good ways down. Way closer to the monster dog. Should I risk it? I could go back and drop everything off and come back without the debuff. But my hide and move silently skills are maxed out for level 1, and I have 18 dex, and the halfling bonuses to those skills too. All added up my hide is 12 and my move silently is 10. Both pretty high. Maybe real high. Especially for level 1. The left side of the trail has some okay shade. And listen and spot are both wis checks. A monster murder dog can't be very wise. And he hasn't noticed me yet.

Since I already have the debuff I go back to Carlos and grab the light shield and padded armor.

I start sneaking towards dad. Not even halfway there the dog looks up. I freeze. My heart almost bursts. I'm so stupid. Please, please, please, please don't notice me. Please. My legs are shaking. I can't stop the shaking. How dumb am I?

Please, please let me get back. Let me get out of this. I don't want to die. I don't want to be eaten. Without even thinking I start moving backwards. His ears perk up more. He looks right at me. I freak out and start running.

I'm not running fast. Not fast enough. The corner is a little ahead. I feel a tug on my left heel and hop forward a little, then see an arrow-head icon – which means piercing damage – float on the left side of my vision. Then I feel extreme pain on my foot. I jerk my leg and spill forward and see the monster tumble by me. I'm past the corner and see Joey still sitting on the ground playing with the trays. With adrenaline on high I jet forward on my hands and knees and barrel onto joey, wrap my arms around him, and then roll over to get him on top of me. To shield me.

My foot is on fire. It hurts so bad! Holy moly! Joey is screaming and trying to get loose. I tuck my legs in and hope the monster has nothing easy to bite on me with Joey flailing around. "Shut up Joey! My foot is killing me. You're safe. Relax. Shut up!"

He starts pushing his forehead into my face as he screams. I want to punch him. The pain in my foot isn't stopping. I hear the monster growling. I can't see him. I wish he would eat Joey.

No. Stop it. What is wrong with you, Kim? My foot hurts too much to think clearly. I don't want Joey to be hurt but if the dog focuses on him I can get away. And Joey will be fine. He has the giant shield thing, and it hurts monsters when they attack him. But I don't think I can run on this foot. Or even walk either.

Owe! It hurts so bad! "Shut up Joey! Stop moving!"

We lay there like that for a couple minutes. The pain doesn't die down. Joey doesn't calm down. I'm ready to kill him. He squirmed lower down on me. His head is on my chest now. I look up and I don't see the dog anywhere. But I don't trust it. This is a trick to make me let Joey go. I know it.

One minute later still no monster dog in sight. I don't hear it either. But the monster can be quiet. And silent. And tricky.

With my good foot I start scooting me and Joey backwards on the grass. My head presses against the invisible wall of the forest and I keep scooting. After I'm out of breath I keep scooting. I scoot until we are a good distance into the field. I still don't see the dog.

I let Joey go. He hops up angrily, stimming like mad. He walks back towards the intersection and grabs the trays and walks back past me. I can tell he is mad at me. Oh well. He would be starving to death if I didn't open his food for him. Or show him the thing floating on him was food. Moron.

Seriously, what is wrong with you Kim? He is all you've got left. He's family. And you're his older sister and he needs your help. You need to stop this. Stop being mean.

I keep scooting till I get near to where the path to the store is. Where we had the campfire set up and my army clothes are. Where my brother is.

43

The pain isn't so bad if I don't move. The problem is Joey. He went to the bathroom in our area, and he won't come near me so I can get his meal for him. I love him but I can't stand him sometimes.

He has three more trays now. He really enjoys them. He hasn't eaten since I've had those three meals. I've slept a bunch too. I guess if he gets hungry enough he'll work with me.

My foot isn't bleeding but it is all brown with dried blood. The crazy thing is it doesn't look very damaged. It's getting pretty puffy though. There are three bite marks on the inside of my heel, and four on the outside. It hurts really, really bad. I wish mom was here to help. I miss her. I miss them all. So much.

The heal kit didn't do anything to help with the pain or make it heal. When I used it a green 2 floated up the right side of my vision.

I had a plan about using the quarterstaff as a crutch. I need to get to the water to wash my foot off. Using the quarterstaff as a crutch just doesn't work. My foot hurts too much to stand on it at all. I have a new plan. I wrap my army top around my foot and start scooting to the water.

1.9 NO MORE

KIM GUM

I don't know how long I was out. It seems like forever. I was real sick for a long time. Crazy dreams. Really, really crazy dreams. Nightmares. Real bad ones. I think Joey ate one of my rations that I opened. I don't know if that was real. I hope so. I don't know where he is.

I hope he is okay.

I hope he can forgive me.

It got really bad there for a while. Real bad. I thought I was going to die. But I figured some things out. I think.

I'm not sure if what got me sick was cleaning my foot in the poop water, or me drinking the poop water. I found a clay jug for three coppers in the store menu. I was real, real thirsty so I drank a lot of water. I couldn't help myself. It looked clean. Clean enough.

And my foot was throbbing. It's really crazy how my foot didn't look that bad at all after cleaning it. Just those seven bite marks and a little puffy. It did get real pink and the bites got white stuff oozing out of them. Then my foot puffed up real big and I started feeling real sick and super sweaty. And I couldn't move and had to lay there forever, being real, real, super sick with crazy thoughts and dreams.

My foot isn't too bad now if I don't touch it.

I'm not hungry but I am really, really thirsty. I open a ration and drink the water. I haven't ate in a while and the thought of food makes my stomach turn. I got throw up in the water when I first got sick. I

45

really shouldn't drink that water no matter how thirsty I get. Especially now. Better to waste the food to get clean water. I have plenty of cash for food for a long time now.

I hope Joey figured out his own meals. I hope he isn't starving.

Where is he?

I'm shaky but I still manage to stand. I use the quarterstaff to help me hobble around. My foot is getting better. It only hurts a ton when my right foot is forward and my left leg is stretched back. And only for a second. I go to the field to find Joey.

I find him immediately. In the bathroom corner stimming with trays. He looks spotless. How is he still clean? I don't see his meal floating on him. He stands up and does his jumping and noises meaning he wants something. He is not ignoring me. Good! I guess he did forgive me.

I don't know why but thinking that makes me cry. I know he doesn't like it but I grab Joey and hug him hard. I cry harder. A big sobbing cry. Joey is less aggravated than usual while I'm hugging him. How does he not smell bad? I stink.

I buy a recharge for my survival kit and start a new fire. I still can't see the sun. I haven't seen it once. And it still hasn't gotten dark. No insects still either. Warm weather all the time. Joey seems to like the warmth of the fire though, so why not? I do too for some reason. The warmth feels good on my foot.

While I have the fire going, I use my repair kit. My bow goes from 4 to 5 durability points.

The raw beast meat in my inventory looks and smells fresh still, so I use my cooking kit to make it into something called 'basic plain grilled steak.' We eat it with our hands and just sit there for a bit, with joey doing his finger thing. I get 1 crafting xp for cooking each steak. At 10 xp I'll max out my culinarian profession until I can level my class up to 2.

"Joey, I got to talk to you about some stuff. When I was sick I…for a while…I really thought I was going to die and I…I…didn't mind. That happening didn't seem so bad. I wanted this to be over. If mom couldn't beat those dogs, how am I supposed to get through this whole place to get us out? Is there even a way out? Mom knew MMA. She was real good at it. And dad was really strong too. I know mom called dad lazy because he stopped practicing, but Carlos said dad could pin mom most of the time anyways.

"I'm not sure if I can get us out of here, but I'm not giving up. Those were just crazy thoughts, defeatist thoughts, and they're gone now. My main goal right now is to kill the monster that murdered our family. That stupid zombie dog thing. I'm going to make him suffer, and then I am going to eat him. I hate him so much. I'm going to kill them all. Or die trying. If I die I don't know what will happen to you. You'll probably die too. Eventually. I'm sorry about that.

"I love you, Joey. I'm sorry I used you as a shield. I had bad thoughts about you, too. I wasn't a good big sister. I should be your shield. Not make you mine. And I'm going to be. I'm going to take care of you real good from now on. I'm real sorry about before. I just went a little crazy. And I was a coward.

"You know…it's…it's. Hmmm. I'm just going to say it all so we can have a fresh start. I hope."

I take a deep breath and a long exhale. It is scary to say this stuff. This stuff you got to keep inside and never let no one know you think it.

"Since I can remember, mom was always so proud of you. So happy to introduce you to everyone. Her special boy. She was always ashamed of me. Or she seemed so. Sure, she was mad at Carlos a lot, but she wasn't ashamed of him. But when she introduced me, she would always make a comment about my looks, like I could be a weight lifter with my frame. Things like that. You know? It hurt. Why couldn't she just love me for who I am and what I look like?

"That's another thing. I think I have a little hate for you because you look so normal. When you sit still you look completely normal. Kind of real handsome. Girls in my school would think you are super cute. How come you get to look normal and handsome when you don't even care about it? You can't even talk. I got cankles. I look like a frog. But I'm normal on the inside."

I stop for a second because that doesn't sound right. It sounds false.

"No. No. I'm not. I'm ugly on the inside too. I have a lot of anger and hate in me, and it has gotten a lot worse since we got in here. I want to break things. I want to hurt things. I want to hurt things as much as I hurt inside. And I hurt inside real bad. All the time I do.

"You know, the things they teach me – I don't agree with them. I nod my head so I don't get in trouble and so I fit in better, but none of it makes sense. Everyone they say is nice is mean. Everything they say is right is wrong. I know it in my heart. And my heart hurts from pretending.

"We have to change if we're going to get out of here. Or I have to. Not you. I hope you don't change. You're annoying, but you're my brother and I love you. I have to change to get us out of here, but I can't pretend with this, too. Like I pretend with everyone else. I have to become more. Mom would say to her MMA class…well, it doesn't matter. What matters is I got to not…just be…not scared of pain. I got to like it. I got to train. I got to get a lot better. I got to suffer some. So I can make the monsters suffer more."

Joey picks up his trays and starts rocking and stimming harder. I doubt he understood what I said. That's okay. It's probably better if he doesn't. I don't know what the right thing to do is, but my plan sounds right. Better than some of the crazy stuff I've been thinking.

It's nice how the arrows just snap into place on the string and I can shoot with gloves on. I wish the arrows just snapped to the target when I loosed the arrow. How can this place be so game like and so real at the same time? I thought about it a lot and game mode isn't good if you're solo. It doesn't allow you to dodge or block or move or nothing. Having the game aim for you and shoot arrows for you is nice, but avoiding damage is more important. I'm leaving it on free attack so I can hopefully attack more than once a round. With auto all I'll get is one attack a round, and there really isn't a benefit for auto until you get more attacks per round. So game mode and auto-attack are out. Mom was right about free attack mode. I just got to get better with the bow. A lot better.

And I am. I am getting much better with the bow.

The spear too – I think. It is hard to know since I never learned any stances or forms. Well, a little from the training room in fourth age. But not anywhere near enough to know if I am doing anything correctly now. Kind of like if you tried to teach yourself taekwondo by watching a couple classes a couple of times. But sticking the pointy end in things seems like a no brainer.

I can use the spear and the light shield, but I am better when I use the spear two handed. I noticed in the SRD it says rogues can't use shields. But the info for both Black Raven and fourth age says rogues can use light shields and bucklers. Spears are only two-handed weapons in the SRD. I wonder why? That doesn't make any sense. And that halfling military from the fourth age story all use shields and spears as rogues. At least I'm almost positive they are rogues.

The main point I'm focusing on for training is ferocity. Explode. Be fast, be strong, be relentless, and be ferocious. Don't let up. Attack, attack, attack. Every strike is an explosion of speed and strength.

I still feel really heavy and slow, but there is nothing I can do about that. Well, almost nothing.

I think I figured out a few things. Having a medium load lowers my dex by 2. It also makes certain skills go down by 2, or 3 including the lowered dex. Hide and move silently are two of those skills. I should have checked my skills page before trying to sneak around the dog. I definitely need to improve myself, but I also have to improve my knowledge of the game and systems. I've been reading the information in the SRD for d20, as well as what is included about Black Raven and the conversion to fourth age and twitch combat. But I have to piece together how things actually work here too. It ain't the same as fourth age.

Medium load makes the heavy and slow feeling worse. It's supposed to just lower my land speed, but I don't think that is how it works here. I don't think land speed is a thing here. In the character sheet it just has an asterisk for land speed. I think being a halfling makes me just slower in general. I also think the 8 str makes me weaker. In fourth age dex doesn't make you faster, just BAB and AB do. And as a level 1 rogue I have zero BAB.

I can walk normal, like I could in real life, and my legs are just as long. It has to be a total speed debuff or something. I may be just as strong now, but maybe I just feel weaker? Maybe not. It is hard to tell. I'm definitely noticeably slower though, and get even slower with the medium load debuff.

I've been running to overcome it. Or at least get used to it. I think of it like the grav training mom used to do.

I've also been thinking about HPs. I think they work as a shield. And when the HP shield is gone, you start taking real injuries. I saw mom flash when the dog bit her. And when the dog bit my foot I didn't feel anything at first. Not until a second after the damage notification.

I shouldn't think of it as a dog. The monster. Filthy, murdering monster.

My foot is mostly fine now. The injury did help me get used to working through pain.

Every day I do a ton of push-ups, mountain climbers, crunches, sit-ups, jumping jacks, up and downs, and other exercises we used to do in class. There is a big branch I use for pull ups and chin ups. I have to use my army top as a rope to climb to the branch. I would like to do rope training but getting an actual rope would cost me a gold.

I also use Joey for squats. He doesn't like it. Once in a while I run with him on my back, over my shoulder, or cradled. He doesn't hate the piggy-backs, but he is not a fan of the rest. Oh well.

Since I started training I've had 14 long sleeps. I planned on only seven but I pushed it to 14. Another monster dog has joined the one who killed mom and dad. So now I got to kill them both. I'm giving myself 14 more long sleeps as a hard deadline. That will be about four weeks total. And then it is me or the monsters dying.

I went and looted the other stuff off mom and Carlos. I have everything in a pile near the path to the store. I can sell things to the store, too. But I haven't yet, not really. Besides Carlos' sling and the extra kits. No use for those I can see. I don't know what I really need yet, and the store only gives you a fraction of what things cost to buy. And the armor and weapons have durability, so I might need to replace something important down the road. Kits don't have durability. Just charges. All the extra loot is at our little camp area.

I can't figure out the durability. My game boots say they are at full durability, but there are bite holes in them. Weird.

I look over and see Joey playing with his trays. He has a ton of them now. He really loves them. He's really easy. The only thing he does that's been driving me nuts is not eating all his food. He's always been a twig, but the meals aren't that big. I can't really tell if he is skinnier. I think he maybe is. I wish he'd eat all the food. Sometimes he does, but not usually.

We both seem fine now with the amount of water that comes in the rations. I've kind of gotten so used to being thirsty that I stopped being thirsty.

I wish I had a mirror so I can see what I look like. They cost 10 gold in the store though.

1.10 WAR

KIM GUM

Today's the day. Or now is the time since there are no days here. Whatever. Twenty-eight long sleeps.

Vengeance for my family. No more being a scaredy-cat. Being scared is the old Kim, not me.

But I'm scared.

I'm really, really scared.

I don't want to do this. I can't keep procrastinating, though. I have everything I need. Joey is playing with his trays. I didn't get mad or yell when I saw he pooped in our camp area again. Just in case, better to do this while me and Joey are getting along. No reason to start a fight over a little poop.

I walk to the intersection, but before I turn the corner I get down on my knees. Both my parents were outspoken atheists and thought religious people were morons. I don't know a lot about religion, but I never really had to face dying before. Or doing something on purpose that will most likely get me killed.

No, stop that, Kim! No defeatism. I will kill the monsters. I will get vengeance.

I don't know if praying will help, but I don't think it can hurt. And no one is here to judge me anyways. I like the idea of someone looking out for me and a place to go if I die. And being back with my family. Maybe I'm a moron for that. I don't care.

"Hello, God. If there is a heaven I hope you let mom, dad, and Carlos in. Carlos sucks real bad but sometimes he is nice. He isn't that bad. I hope you let me in, too. If I fail. Maybe you could help Joey out if I fail? But I don't plan on failing.

"I think you are supposed to be about love and peace and that stuff, but dad says that's just what you say but you really like killing and you cause all the wars. I hope he's right because I'm going to war and I plan on doing a lot of killing. My mom killed the dog thing that killed Carlos and I think that is great. One of those dog things killed and ate my mom. It killed my dad too. If you think me killing these dogs is wrong, sorry, because I'm about to do all the wrong I can.

"In school they say justice is good and vengeance is bad. But to them…when someone is really mean to me and gets caught they just get talked to for a second, or maybe detention. I'm thinking I shouldn't have ever put up with it. I'd rather get their justice after I get my vengeance. I think vengeance is better. I want vengeance for my family.

"Maybe I'm wrong. Maybe I'm going crazy or something. But I think I'm right. And I'm going to do it. I don't want to ask for your help because then it wouldn't be my vengeance. I want to do it on my own. But I hope you watch and if I do good and get my vengeance you'll be proud of me. Maybe help my family get into heaven. And if I don't make it maybe I can be put with my family in a nice place anyways? And when Joey joins us maybe make him more…better…than he is now? So we can talk.

"I'm sorry my parents said bad things about you. I hope you don't hold it against them. If you're real."

I go to stand up but decide I have a little more to ask.

"Can I ask you something? Why did you let the green stuff take us here? What does this have to do with anything? Also, why did you make me look this way? Did I do something wrong? I don't even think I have cankles; why would they say that? Do you know if I do?

"Well, that's it. I hope you start talking back to me. That would be really cool. Sorry I have so much hate in me. Have a good day. Bye, God!"

Jeez, I say dumb things! "Have a good day." I'm such an idiot.

I take a deep breath and collect myself.

This is it. This is the time. No more procrastinating.

I enter stealth and crawl around the corner. Both monster dogs are about where they were on the first day. My plan is to take down the new dog monster with my bow, and try to get enough HPs away from the other dog monster before it closes to make it easier to kill it in melee. Keep it away with my spear when it does get close. Kill it. Bathe in my vengeance. Eat my enemies.

I go to the east side of the intersection. I could go farther down the road to have more range and more shots before they close with me, but I want an easy escape in case things go bad.

I changed my quickslots. I have charge in one, my bow in two, my spear in three, and my spear and shield in four. Just in case, I also have a dagger and shield in five. I practiced changing out a ton, so even if I get nervous I should be okay.

I do the mental command for hotkey two. I kneel, nock an arrow, draw back, breath in deeply, aim at the new dog monster, and loose. I'm nervous and my hands are shaking as I nock a new arrow. I draw and see the first arrow hit and bounce off. No damage icons. The dog thing gets up and looks around. Should I retreat and try again later?

No. This is it. Me or them.

I loose and with even more shaky hands nock a new arrow. I see the piercing icon and sneak attack icon as I'm knocked out of stealth and draw back my bow again. The dogs start barreling towards me. The old dog is in front of the new dog as they run, and the only clear shot I have is against the old dog, so I have to fire at it. I nock again and see the piercing icon.

I draw and loose again quickly.

I think about running. They are both almost on me, and neither is down or injured. I am so nervous it is hard to think straight. I do the command for quickslot four as I see my arrow actually go into the old dog's back as he yelps and tumbles. No damage icon. I must be right and HPs act as a damage prevention shield. And when it's gone you actually take real damage.

The new dog is jumping towards me and I hold up my shield as I thrust my spear to where I think he's coming. I can feel my spear connect right before he crashes into my light shield. I stumble back and fall.

I try to kip up immediately but can't and scramble to my knees instead. One of the dogs is right on me, and I hold my shield up to block its mouth as I get to my feet. Where my shield is on my arm, my hand and fingers are barely covered by the lip of the shield. And like an idiot I didn't have my hand fisted. I feel the monster's bottom teeth on my palm, but there is no pain. I thrust with my spear as hard as I can at his ribcage.

Then pain. Horrible pain in my hand. But I suck it up and it doesn't stop my thrust. My spear enters the monster's side as it starts doing its head shake thing from side to side. It is hard to keep my balance, ignore the pain, and extract my spear. But I do it. And I thrust as hard and fast as I can again and again.

Something massive hits my upper body and head, and I fly backwards. My spear almost rips out of my hand, but I hold onto it for dear life. On the way down I see the maw about to close around my face. My left hand is still in the other dog's mouth, and when my arm is extended as far as it can go as I fall, I get jerked to the left by my trapped hand. I get jerked sideways way more than enough for the bite to miss my face.

I get a flash of extreme fear and my body tingles. Then it goes away as I hit the ground, with a giant dog monster on top of me, and another giant dog monster's fangs in my hand. This is it. I'm probably dead. I hope it doesn't hurt too bad.

I'm somewhat on my left side. My spear shaft is between me and the dog on top of me, luckily positioned in a way keeping it from being able to bite me. But not for long. The dog biting my hand isn't moving. There is no chance of me getting my spear into play with the dog laying on me, my arm holding the spear pinned, and especially since the shaft is saving me right now. I rip my hand with the shield out of the unmoving dog's mouth. I scream out in the extreme pain it causes me, but immediately start bashing the dog on top of me with my shield. Anywhere I can. I wish I could hit harder, but every hit sends shocks of pain through my hand.

I'm sucking air hard and weakening fast. The dog on top of me gives up on getting my face and starts biting at the shield hitting him. Thankfully just the shield, not my hand this time. The only thing I can think to do is bite the dog since both my hands are out of play now. But I can't get my head close enough to do it. The spear's shaft between us is stopping me too.

I can't get my breath back. I try to see if I can wrap my legs around the monster but I can't shift. The shaft of my spear is digging into my ribs more and more as the dog tries to shake my left arm off as he thrashes my shield back and forth.

I get an idea. That's it! I do the mental command for quickslot five. The dog shifts as my spear disappears. I get ready to move my shield in front of my face if the dog lets it go and tries to bite me again, now that nothing's stopping him from doing so. He doesn't. He is still trying to shake my arm off. I mean it, not he.

My right arm, now holding a dagger, is still trapped under the dog. I twist my hand and try to cut the dog. I can't. I can sort of stab it a little at a weird angle. It doesn't do much. I try lifting my hips to try and get more leverage to push it deeper. It kind of works. I think.

That's all I got. I'm spent. Twisting and pushing my hips up with this huge, heavy monster on me is all the energy I got. I'm sucking air like mad, and shaky from exhaustion. The dog lets my shield go and looks down on me. It looks me right in the eyes. Those watery eyes really do look calm. Just like a peaceful pond. I was right about that. I thought I was wrong because these monsters should have crazy eyes. Angry eyes. But they don't. This one has dried blood on its face. I think this is the one that ate mom.

Why isn't it attacking? Because I'm out of the fight? I can't do nothing so there's no rush? It's like a kid at school saying mean things to me because they know I can't do anything. Like, "What are you going to do? Nothing. Just take it, fatty. Loser." But I could have done something. I could have fought. I can now too. No defeatism. It's not over until I'm dead. And if I'm going to die I can at least dig deeper and try to do more damage. Go out swinging.

I think the monster notices a change in me because it pulls back its head for a bite, and I whack it with my shield. My bitten hand flares with pain, but I suck it up and hit it again. I reach deep down and with everything left I have in me I pull my right arm while pushing on my left leg. The dog slides off of me, and I sit up and stab him. It, I mean.

The monster whimpers and pulls back a little ways and I scramble to my feet as fast as I can. I don't think the stab hurt him too bad. I hit around the shoulder and I think I hit bone because it stopped going in pretty quick and hit something hard. I try to take deep breaths but I'm so out of breath I can't really control it. My throat and lungs burn.

I meet the dog's eyes. I want to wipe the sweat off my forehead but I can't. I don't got the time.

As soon as our eyes meet it rushes at me. I yell as I rush back at it. I aim my shield at his head and try to push it downwards. He tries to get his maw around my shield but fails. I take a swipe and miss. He stops going for my shield and bites my leg right above my knee. I couldn't stop it. It was too fast. It hurts but I'm so exhausted it probably isn't registering in my mind like it should. I don't even really care that I'm getting bit. I start stabbing with the dagger.

I can't really see what I'm hitting, but for some reason it isn't going in far. I do see the arrow in his lower back. So this is definitely the old one. The one that ate mom. I start stabbing madly. I remember my training. Ferocious. Explosive hits. Strong, powerful hits with all I have. He does something to my leg that makes it stop working and I almost fall. It sends lightning pain all through my body. Did he take a bite out of me?

I hear Joey nearby freaking out. That makes me real angry for some reason. I don't want Joey to see me get killed and eaten like mom. I yell, "Joey, get back!" And I get back to stabbing. Fast and furious. I shift a little and hit a spot where it goes in deep. I stab and stab and then start stabbing and ripping down. I feel the monster bite my left elbow and the arm right above it. I keep stabbing. I start yelling as I stab. He lets go and now I'm lying on him stabbing. Stabbing and yelling.

I think it's dead. I think I won. I slide down a little and look at the monster's stupid dead face. I yell at it as loud as I can. Then I yell again. "YOU. DON'T. EAT. MY. MOM!" I spit at the face. I put my mouth right next to its dumb ear and say, "Now I'm going to eat you. How do you like that? And then I am going to eat you more." I bite its ear and try to rip it off, but it doesn't work. I whisper in his ear again, "Vengeance is mine. I win, dummy. You lose, and losers get eaten. I win."

I feel Joey's hand on my bicep. He usually only does that to new people he likes. I look at him. He isn't looking at me. He is just stimming, making his want noises, and doing his want shake-dance thing.

Still sucking air I tell Joey it's okay. I won. Everything is okay. I think I tell him that.

I'm shaking pretty badly. I might die if the wound on my leg is as bad as I think it is. I turn around and lay my back on my kill to check my leg out. Phew, he didn't bite a chunk out of me. But it is pretty bad. I inventory the dagger and shield. My elbow and arm don't look too bad at all. But my hand. Holy moly, my hand looks really bad and hurts even worse. I shouldn't have put the shield away. I think it was helping my hand not hurt as much.

My hand is throbbing really, really bad. Every heartbeat makes my hand feel like it's going to explode. I put the shield back on but the pain goes up so I inventory it again. Ow. Ow. Ow.

Kim! Stop being a baby. Pain is your friend. Pain is weakness leaving the body.

What a dumb saying. I hope it is right because a lot of weakness is leaving my body if it is. I take out my healing kit and use it on my hand. Nothing happens. I see the green healing icon but miss the number. The pain is the same, the bleeding is the same, everything is the same. I open my character screen and see my HPs are 2 out of 10. It only gave me 2 HPs? That is garbage. I should check out how that works, but I'm in too much pain right now to look at things or read.

I'm finally starting to catch my breath. The pain increases. It's impossible to ignore, but I got to ignore it for now. My original plan was to take this corpse back to my camping area, but with my leg like this, and my hand, that isn't going to happen. As close as I can to the dead monster I start a campfire with my kit. It takes me a while to get part of the monster over the fire. It weighs a ton and I can't move too good right now. I finally manage to get a little part of its back and butt over it. Just doing that was exhausting. I use the rest of its dead corpse as a pillow as I wait for it to cook. I don't want to use survival on it yet – just in case it messes up the real cooking. The vengeance cooking.

The pain is getting worse. It is really throbbing now in my hand. In my leg too. I do not like it. Not one bit. I want to wrap up my wounds but besides underwear, my army boots, and socks, I'm just wearing game stuff. And the game stuff doesn't really function like real clothes where you can wrap something in it. I guess I could use my socks, but they stink real bad. I guess that is better than nothing. I unequip my game boots and…holy moly, there is no way I can get my army boots off. Crap. Guess I just got to suck it up for now. My arm wound isn't bleeding much, and my hand and leg don't seem to be bleeding too bad. Hopefully that means I won't die from bleeding. I'm not sure how that works.

I roll on my side a little so I can reach over and feel the area of the monster over the fire. Just a little warm. I hope this works. A promise is a promise, and I 100% look forward to keeping this one.

Since I got some time to kill, and to keep my mind off the pain, I use my repair kit. I use it on my shield since it looks messed up. Durability goes from 6 to 7, but it still looks messed up.

Ow. Ow. Ow. This hurts so much.

"God? Sorry I'm not kneeling but I can't right now. I know I said I didn't want any help but my injuries really, really, really, really, really hurt. I don't think the saying about pain is weakness leaving the body is based on science or anything, because it keeps hurting worse and worse. I'm supposed to be really tough now and like pain…or at least be able to ignore it, but it hurts too much. Please make it hurt less if you can. I'll kill a bunch of monsters for you if you do. Please? I'm really trying not to be a baby but come on. Please?

"Thank you, God. Have a good day. Say hi to my family for me."
It still hurts. Ow. Ow. Ow.

"Joey. It hurts real bad. I can't ignore it. Owie. Owie. Owie."

I check the monster again. This isn't working. This fire doesn't burn anything, and I guess can only cook things the fake way. The game system way. I promised I'd eat him, and I don't think looting some meat counts. I equip my dagger and try to cut some meat off. Man, I hurt so much. Just shifting weight is horrible pain.

No blood comes out of the monster. I've seen them bleed. Where is the blood now? After a lot of pain I finally manage to cut a piece of its belly off. The piece just disappears. Holy moly, why? I put my finger inside and there is nothing. This thing is an empty shell. How weird is that?

Ow. The pain just won't let up for a second. I loot the monster, then use my survival kit. I get two pieces of beast meat. Then get my cooking kit to cook the beast meat I get from it. I get a cooked steak back. I cook the second piece of meat I looted. I call Joey over to try and give him the second piece so we can both have this crappy form of vengeance but he ignores me, as usual. Fine.

I try to inspect the steak for a description but I can't. It just says 'basic plain grilled steak.' I put it in my inventory and the popup title still says 'basic plain grilled steak.' I get a description this time, but it just says, 'basic food.' I was hoping it would say something related to this specific monster so my vengeance will feel more vengeance-y. But no. I take it out of my inventory and throw that one near Joey. If he doesn't want to come to me he can eat dirty steak then. I try and eat the one I still have, but I am too tired and in too much pain. I have to hold it with one hand and rip bites off with my mouth since I don't have a fork. I guess I could use my dagger to hold it but I'd still have to bite into it anyways, so why? I get two bites down and put it in my inventory.

My promise seems hollow so I plan on trying to take a bite out of the corpse near the hole in the stomach. I have to put weight on my injured leg, and it sends ridiculous amounts of pain through my whole body and makes my brain hurt. I push through. I try for what seems like a long time to bite a piece off, but I don't succeed. I roll back over. I'll try again in a minute.

I close my eyes and try to think about other things to take my mind off the pain. My head is throbbing now. Moving made me lose my corpse pillow. Dumb monster. I will eat you. In one minute.

I open my eyes some time later. Thinking really helps ignore the pain. I was thinking about beating up Keisha Lautour and her dumb friends. And when Maria tells me I have cankles I kick her in the head with my non-cankle ankle and say, "The better to kick you with, my dear!" And then me and Amy both laugh and become best friends forever and kick dumb, stupid Maria in her dumb face all the time. I definitely don't have cankles. My ankles are pretty thick though. Ah, who cares now anyways? I probably do have cankles. I'll kick everyone in the face with my cankles.

I try moving to use the dog corpse as a pillow again, but it isn't there. It must have despawned. Dang!

I don't know how long it will take for the dogs to come back, or respawn, or whatever they do, but I'm pretty sure I have plenty of time. The pain is always there, and always hurts real bad, but thinking about beating up jerks and bullies helps deal with it.

I must have fallen asleep because Joey startles me awake. He immediately walks away and sits and starts stimming with trays. What a jerk. Ow. The pain is worse I think. Ow. It hurts so bad.

"What do you want, Joey? You know, you have a lot of bad ideas. I know you didn't really tell me, but I am going to pretend you are the one who told me that pain is weakness leaving the body. That way I can tell you off. You were wrong, Joey. Pain is awful. All the things

63

causing me pain right now make me weaker. Healing is pain leaving the body. Pain leaving your body makes you stronger. Healing makes you stronger."

Joey is ignoring me, so I raise my voice, "Where did you come up with that crazy nonsense?"

Still being ignored.

"You can shake your trays all you want, mister, but that won't change anything. You told me nonsense. Now admit how wrong you are.

"What, you are right and I am being a baby? What? Stop it, Joey. That is crazy talk. I got vengeance for us. I'm winning. I just don't like pain. What? Winning isn't whining? Where do you get this stuff, Joey? I'm not whining. I'm in a tremendous amount of pain. I'd like to see you deal with it.

"Pain is weakness leaving the body. Give me a break, Joey."

I look over and see the steak I gave to Joey still laying in the grass exactly where I threw it.

"Holy moly, Joey! You didn't even try the steak I made for you. You think steak grows on trees or something? Can you bring it to me? Please? Right there, Joey! Grab that. Please don't make me move. Joey! Joey! Joey! Look! Where I am pointing. Bring to me. Joey, bring to me. Curse you for eternity you ingrate!"

I don't want to move. What kind of jerk tells you pain is weakness leaving the body and doesn't even bring you the steak you gave him?

"You really need to work on your manners, Joey. And your dumb sayings. It hurts so bad."

I have to move out of this area. This is going to be really hard and hurt a lot. Just my right arm and right leg work normal. I scoot around the other way. I push myself over to the other monster dog nearer the intersection and loot and then use survival on it. I look around for the steak on the ground and…forget about getting that. I would have to turn back around to get it. Scooting forward is too hard. Scooting backwards is the only way to scoot. I was going to loot dad too. That is definitely not happening now either. His corpse is way too far away.

My pain is flaring up so I day dream about beating up jerks and saying super cool things while doing it. It's crazy how that really works.

Time to start skootching to my camp area. Or scooting. Is it skootch or scoot? Who cares? This is really going to hurt. This sucks so bad.

1.11 RETAIL THERAPY

KIM GUM

The next long while was kind of a blur. Getting back to camp was horrible. And then I had to psych myself up to scoot to the store. Or skootch? Whatever one. I didn't go for a while, and when I finally got there I didn't have it in me to stand and use the store ball thing.

One time I woke up and Joey was sleeping really close to me. That was so cute. I put my arm around him and he got aggravated and moved it off him like a real jerk. I wasn't hungry and didn't eat for a while. I felt real weak. Joey actually offered me some of his food by trying to push cauliflower into my mouth. That would have been nicer if cauliflower was something he actually ate. I guess it's the thought that counts.

I had to find a new way to deal with pain. You can't control pain by day dreaming while you also get up and look through the store. The way I came up with is instead of trying to control it or block it, you embrace it. You focus on it. Explore it.

If I lifted my hand up it sent throbbing pain throughout my hand and arm. Even my head. So I lifted my arm and lifted my arm until I knew the pain like I know my own face. You look forward to it. The change. The feeling. The sensation. It lets you know you're still alive. It sucks. It really hurts. But it's better than just lying there bored out of your mind.

Man, I miss Mia. I miss always having constant access to the tangle. I used to get bored so easy when I could just pull up my cd link whenever I wanted. I used to have no idea what being bored was. Now I know. Dealing with pain is not nearly as boring as doing nothing. Absolutely nothing.

I did get some studying in. Of the SRD and Black Raven. But studying and learning are boring. One thing I've been thinking a lot about is how in fourth age, players and mobs got a ton more bloody the more damaged they got. At 75%, 50%, and 25% HPs you got like blood splatter all over. At 10% HPs, everything got all red tinted and you could hear your heartbeat. I'm pretty sure that hasn't happened to me, and I've definitely not seen that with any of the stupid dogs. It's obvious. You can't miss it.

I didn't see it on my mom neither, and I was watching her when her shield disappeared. There was no blood at all until after her HP shield was gone. Too much has changed from fourth age. I wonder how much I can trust any of the information I have. I guess I just got to find out on my own.

So, I worked on dealing with and exploring the pain for a long, long time. Now I'm ready. I think.

I get up and use the store. The pain is ridiculous, but I do it. I carefully go through all the options in the store, seeing what I have missed so far.

The first screen shows armor, weapons, accessories, equipment, special materials and items. If you click on armor it shows all normal armor, an option for masterwork, ridiculously expensive +1 to +4 enhancement armor, and an option for item builder. Item builder requires something that looks like gems or something to make armor. I have zero of those. The masterwork and enhanced armor all have minimal level requirements. You need level 2 for masterwork, level 7 for +1, 12 for +2, 17 for +3, and 22 for +4. That's the most it goes. But just for enhancement. Players can craft a +4 item with a bunch of stuff besides the +4, like permanent haste and things like that. And you can get them from drops too. I've seen some when looking into fourth age.

Some stuff goes to +6. Like skills. You can get +6 for skills. Not group skills, but individual skills.

The weapons tab shows all normal armor and stuff, and item builder again for weapons. Accessories has a lot of options to click on – aura, back, belt, boots, hand, head, neck, ring, and item builder again. This item builder lists everything in accessories besides aura. No masterwork section. The aura screen is blank. I think auras were a high-level thing you got in fourth age.

Equipment is the screen I am most familiar with from using the store. It lists adventuring gear, which is what I usually look through, as well as special substances and items, tools and skill kits, clothing, poisons, and potions and scrolls. Adventuring gear has things like ropes, waterskins, and rations. Special substances and items has really weird things that are all really expensive, besides a sunrod and a tindertwig – those aren't very expensive. One seems to be like a torch, and the other a fire-starter. It is always day so who cares about torches, and my survival kit not only starts fires, it somehow also stores logs and stones for a pre-made, ready to go fire…thing. Fire pit? Tools and skill kits has some neat things. I already have all the skill kits I need. I got them automatically. But it also has a water clock. That would be great to tell the time, but it costs 1,000 gold. That's just plain nuts. A magnifying glass costs 100 gold. How crazy is that? There are also instruments and stuff like that too. Clothing only has crap. It doesn't have underwear or socks or anything. Just pure garbage that costs way too much. The only reasonably priced thing in there is a peasant's outfit for one silver. I bought it, and it feels just like my leather armor. A little thinner, but basically the same feel. Just a waste of a silver. Poisons has poisons, the cheapest being 75 gold. Potions and scrolls are almost as bad. The cheapest scroll is 12.5 gold, and that is for the stupid light cantrip thing. All casters get that for free and can cast it all they want.

Cure minor wounds is 50g for a potion or scroll. Absolute highway robbery. Even if I had the gold I'm not sure it would actually help me heal my actual injuries and not just my HP shield.

That's another thing I noticed. In the SRD all the level 1 spells in Black Raven are just cantrips. The level 2 spells in Black Raven are the level 1 spells in the SRD. Most of them, at least. Identify is a level 1 spell still. All the way up to level 8 spells in the SRD being the level 9 spells here. With just a handful of exceptions, like identify. I looked into it more and wizards can get a level 9 spell from the SRD with spell specialization and some feats, and clerics can get one per domain. The epic spells from feats casters can get are just crazy. Enough to make me wish I was a caster. But only just a little. I heard they stink at lower levels. And their damage was nerfed big time, until they get the paragon feats for getting level 10 and 20 in the same class. The dps caster paragon feats have spell damage increases built right in. Even with both of the paragon feats I think it is still lower than the SRD unless you take some other feats, too. But they are supposed to be super high damage at level 30, especially when all geared up.

The SRD also says something about a 5-foot step to not get attacks of opportunity. I wish that was implemented here. I don't think it was in fourth age either. Not that I've ever heard of or seen. I really wish we got to play fourth age more. But here, and in fourth age, you can move and tumble in the same round. You can even charge and move. The SRD says you can't do that either.

Special materials and items is the key find. It lists a bunch of nonsense that costs ridiculous amounts of gold, but it also has two other very interesting options – misc. and coin shop. In the coin shop you can buy all sorts of cool things, like extra skill points and feats, but you need these colored coins. There are four kinds and I have zero of any of them, and never heard of them before. Misc. is the absolute motherlode. I don't know what misc. means, but I love it!

Under misc. are a ton of options. Hygiene has toothbrushes, soap, lotions – everything you could think of. And cheap. This soap only costs one copper. Everything is super cheap; usually just a copper. Medical has actual, useful medical stuff for real injuries. Entertainment doesn't have a ton that interests me, but it has playing cards, dice, dominos, spinning tops, crayons, paper, blocks, and stuff like that. Nothing really exciting, modern, or electronic. But better than nothing. Better than Joey's dumb trays.

I want to keep the raw beast meat I looted. The second dog must have only given me one piece. The other two dogs gave me two pieces each. I also have three jagged fangs, seven leather scraps, and one basic beast hide. The basic beast hide is worth 1 gold and two silver. After selling everything I have three gold, six silver, and one copper.

I should only stick to necessities, but all the stuff in misc. is so cheap I go crazy and buy a bunch of stuff. I should buy a toothbrush for me and Joey but I like not brushing my teeth or being told to brush them all the time, so I don't buy any dumb stuff like that. I buy blocks for Joey. I also buy crayons and paper. I buy five underwear and five pairs of socks. My real socks and underwear really stink and are both really, really dirty.

I look through bras. I don't really need one yet, according to my mother at least, but since no size is listed I buy a sports bra. I'm practically a woman now so I should wear one. Especially since I'm basically Joey's mother now too. Mothers should wear bras. And so should women like me who are basically mothers. And everything is one size and the game stuff just seems to always fit great, so it isn't being wasted or nothing.

Everything is just one copper each. I buy a couple more sets of rations so I don't have to come back soon. I try to find sleeping bags or bedrolls or pillows under misc., but I don't see anything. There is so much stuff I could just be missing them though. I end up spending two silver to get me and Joey a bedroll each from the regular, expensive section. I want to buy more but I don't know how long it will take me to heal, so I have to be cheap for now. A real cheapo. But just until I can start killing again. There is good money in killing. I really like money.

I check through medical and buy bandages. Mom usually breaks off a piece of aloe plant when we get a little cut or scrape. For big injuries she uses this brown bottle that has stuff that bubbles when you put it on a cut. It stings too. I forget the name. I need something for my hand and leg. My hand really hurts to move and is really warm too. My leg just hurts. I can put some pressure on my leg, but touching the area really hurts. Touching it hurts more than standing on it. I cleaned out the wounds as best I could with water, but I don't want to waste too many rations just for more clean water. Waste not want not and all.

I don't really understand the names or what things do. One thing sounds perfect though – antiseptic wound cleanser. One copper. What a bargain! I also buy a real first aid kit too. Just one silver. The first aid kit comes with three antibiotic ointment packs and antiseptic cleansing wipes. I'll save those and stick with the cleanser for now. It also comes with something called hydrocortisone. It has a ton of hand sanitizer wipes too. And aspirin. Tons of gauze and bandages. This thing is a gold mine. Scissors too! Awesome!

1.12 WHEN I STAND BEFORE THEE AT THE DAY'S END

KIM GUM

"That's a crazy idea, Joey!" But, is it really? Probably not. I like it. "Never mind that, Joey. I meant to say that was a great idea of mine. It definitely wasn't your idea. It was my idea. Got it? Good. Don't give me that look."

I think Joey is going crazy. He has a lot more bad ideas now. Dangerous ideas. He also gets mad when I use the blocks. He didn't care too much for the crayons and paper so I used those all myself. I made us hats. Joey doesn't like to wear his hat, but if I hold it on his head while pinning his arms he usually forgets it is there and will leave it on for a while. I like when we wear our hats.

I'm too old and cool to play with blocks. But sometimes after training I want to mess with them. Not play with them. Just mess with them. And Joey gets mad and comes over and tries to move them away from me. He doesn't even really play with them even. He layers them all up and then leaves it alone forever. I didn't spend my hard-earned money for the blocks to go to waste. And what kind of idiot would prefer to play with trays over blocks? Blocks are way better than stupid trays.

I did find out something that Joey loves to do. If I stand right in front of him without touching him, and jump up and down and laugh like an idiot while looking at Joey, he joins in. He thinks it's the funniest thing ever. I've never heard him laugh so much.

I see poop near our camp area. "Joey! No! I made signs and you still don't get it. This is camp. See the sign? Camp. That corner over there is the bathroom. See the picture of you pooping? That's the sign for where you poop. Not here. Bad! No poop. Bad!"

He ignores my whole rant like a jerk. How does he not get it yet? Well, he is doing much better. He never had an issue back home. He always went to the real bathroom. Sometimes in his pants, but almost always the real bathroom. I don't remember it being an issue. Maybe because there isn't a real bathroom? Maybe I should try and build a toilet or something somehow?

It's crazy how he still doesn't smell. And his clothes are perfect. The same army clothes we all wore. Still clean and don't smell at all. No rips. Perfect condition.

I stink real bad. I would buy soap but I don't want to go back into the poop water. The game stuff doesn't really get dirty or smelly. You can put it in the inventory if it gets dirty and it comes out clean. The underwear and socks have no durability, so I only needed to buy one pair of each really. The game socks don't smell, but I can smell my feet through them. And they stink. Real bad.

It burns when I pee. It has for a while now. It started before I got vengeance, but it wasn't very bad then. I'm not sure what to do about it. Or what I can do. I wish it would stop though.

My leg is healing pretty good. My hand looks a lot better but I don't think inside the hand is right. It hurts when I try to make a fist, and I can't really make a good fist at all anymore. It's definitely weaker.

I still haven't seen any insects. Our poo doesn't disappear. I think poo back on earth just disappears after a while of being outside. Disintegrates or something. Here, it just gets smaller and harder. I got a little shovel under misc. called an entrenchment tool. I started burying our poop. It was gross the way it was. Real gross. This is much better.

Mom and Carlos's robes work pretty good as tiny pillows. Outside of inventory or wearing them they are a small, folded, soft block thing that you can't really open. They aren't great pillows but better than using your arm.

I figured out I don't really need my army boots. I still wear them because they're heavy, so training with them has got to be beneficial. I sneak better without them so will leave them here when I go out killing.

Training has been okay. I can't use my left arm for much, but I can hold a shield. My leg is doing much better and I started doing squats again. I can't really do mountain climbers without my left hand, but I can do one handed up and downs and things like that. I also try and pull myself up with my right arm just by holding my army top that is on my chin up/pull up branch. I can do like three or four before resting. I try to do three sets of everything. I hope my left arm doesn't fall too far behind my right arm.

The middle finger on my left hand is all silly. It doesn't really work at all. It kind of goes along with my other finger if I make a fist or open my hand, but not really. It doesn't hurt though, so that's a plus.

I've been doing a lot of jumping jacks for pain management. It hurts when my left arm goes up and over my head. So I make myself do it a lot.

I taped a bunch of gauze from my first aid kit onto the handle of my bow. Without it I can't really close my fist around the bow and hold it tight enough. So I've also been practicing with my bow. I've had to readjust how I shoot and lost a step, but I'm doing okay with it.

Joey just had a great idea. No, it was me. I had a great idea. It was my idea. Not like Joey's dumb ideas. This was a good one. The dogs, of course, are back. I'm not ready for melee again just yet, but I can sneak out and try to down real targets with my bow. The dogs can't really go south of the intersection to get to our field, so I can just run back when they get close. I want to get good enough to be able to down one 100% of the time before they get close to melee range.

Don't worry dad. I'll loot your corpse soon.

I really need a bath. I guess I'll have to suck it up and take a bath in the poop water at some point. But not until my wounds are closed. I don't know what got me sick last time. I think it was cleaning in the water with the bleeding wounds on my foot. Could've been drinking it though. I definitely don't want to get sick like that again so I got to be real careful and never do anything that could've caused it.

I also got to stop calling those monsters dogs. They aren't dogs. Dogs are awesome. These things are stupid idiot murderers.

Good news is the experience gains seem to be the same as fourth age. Just 10 xp to get to level 2. I don't think I got credit for the monster mom killed as my experience bar was always empty. Now it looks like I have a good chunk of experience. It doesn't give a number but the bar looks about 20% filled or so. In the game they have something called CR which determines experience. It's the size of the group you're supposed to have to fight the monster, and the monster's level. It shows as like 2(3). So you'd need two level 3 characters to fight it. Or vice versa. Three level 2 characters could be it too. No, it is group size and level, because the 3+(10) is the scaling one.

Either way, the experience is the first number times the second number. The tutorial of the real game didn't have a lot of fighting, but you were level 2 after. And it only lasted a couple minutes. It gave you experience for completing dumb things like the UI, gesture, and mental command tutorial quest. If these monster dogs are 1(1)s, then they are 1 xp each. So I have 2 out of 10 xp needed for level 2. I'll get there soon. Just need a little more healing. If I can get good at killing the monsters at range before they close, I'll be rolling in xp and gold soon.

1.13 AND THE STILLNESS THE DANCING

KIM GUM

I sneak up to the turd-pigeon. Joey wanted to call the monster dogs turd-dogs. But dogs are awesome, and these things suck and are stupid idiots. I think turd-pigeon is way more insulting. No one likes pigeons. Everyone knows pigeons are real stupid and dumb and pathetic. Turd-pigeon is a perfect name for the monster dogs.

I get behind the turd-pigeon and I get an idea. "Joey, that's so dumb. Okay, I'll do it," I say in my head. That Joey really has some crazy ideas! I like this one though.

I bend over and whisper in the turd-pigeons ear, "I am the darkness."

It jumps a million feet in the air, lands, and flies at me, growling. Sure, I gave up my chance for a sneak attack, but now the turd-pigeon knows who it's messing with. I dodge out of the way and spear the turd-pigeon three times as it goes by. The third hit goes in so the HP shield is down. I leave the spear in for leverage, and fall on the turd-pigeon shield first, trapping its head under my shield while applying my full weight on top of it. I pull my spear out and stab again and again until it stops moving.

I put my face near its ear again and whisper, "I told you, you filthy turd-pigeon." I loot it and use survival on its corpse.

The west road ends and goes south for a good bit before ending in a dead end. I put my parents and Carlos down there. My dad was also killed from behind too. He must have came running when mom called out and the turd-pigeon got him from behind. That filthy turd-pigeon I ate could never kill either of my parents from the front. Just from behind. Like a true coward turd-pigeon.

"Of course I kill them from behind too, Joey! Jeez. It is different when I do it. I am the darkness. You know this, Joey."

How dare Joey compare what I do to what the turd-pigeons do. What an idiot.

He's been mad at me. Or I've been mad at him. Same thing. I forced him to take a bath, which wasn't too bad getting him to do. But putting his boots back on was a real hassle. He kicked me in the face so I pinched him to let him know you don't kick the darkness. Especially not in the face. As soon as I did I was filled with overwhelming pain for...probably not too long. It felt like forever. It hurt so much I can't even describe it. It was really crazy. His magic shield thing is nuts. It hurts so bad. How much HPs did his shield have again? Like seven thousand. I think. I can't remember. Man, that shield really hurts if you intentionally cause pain to the person who has it. I'm guessing that's what happened when I pinched him. And I barely pinched him. Ridiculous. And he kicked me in the face. How is that okay?

But since I'm basically his mother now, and a great mother too, I still got his boots back on after the pain stopped. I also bought a toothbrush and make him brush his teeth. Kick me in the face, will you? Now you got to brush your teeth. How do you like them apples, Joey?

To set a good example and be a great basically-mother I also brush my teeth now.

It doesn't hurt so much when I pee anymore either. My left hand still isn't right but it's doing a lot better.

I'm doing way better fighting. Way, way, way better. I think I could beat God. I made a bet with him I could, but if I win he has to start talking to me. He chickened out. Basically, anyways. If you don't show up to the fight, you're chickening out.

I walk down to my family's corpses and kneel and quickly ask God to please take care of them and watch over their souls. I also remind him of the duel I challenged him to. No answer back.

I hit the hotkey for my search skill, and nothing again. The first time I searched down here I found a coin. In my inventory it says ancient coin. It isn't a coin I can spend in the store. The store won't buy the coin either.

I think this whole place is made out of squares. If you look at the map everything is even, like someone made this place out of Joey's blocks. Okay, more my blocks now, but really Joey's. Like this southern passageway is five blocks down. The western passage from the intersection is six blocks. Our field we live in is five blocks tall and seven blocks wide. The area with the store and water-stairs is three wide, two tall. It works out perfect. Really weird. Fourth age dungeons aren't like this.

My experience bar is full. It filled up a long, long time ago. I've killed way more than 10 turd-pigeons. I've killed like a million. Not really a million, but way, way more than 10. I think it takes like a day for them to respawn. It usually works out to one awake time, one long sleep, plus a little bit. Once in a great while it's a lot faster, but not often.

There's no level-up button, or any way to get to level 2 I can figure out. No notifications, no buttons, nothing blinking. I don't get it. I really want to level up. I need more HPs bad.

I have way over 40 gold now. I sold my father's heavy shield and armor and longsword since I can't use any of it. I had to replace my light wooden shield. It still had five durability, but it was falling apart.

That was three gold down the drain. I've also had to replace my armor. And I bought more stuff. For training mostly. And Joey too. And a new spear. Sometimes the durability goes down permanently and after a while you just got to replace it. And other stuff just breaks apart with plenty durability left.

I make sure to use repair as often as possible. Technically, I can use it after every fight, but the kit only has one charge. Going back to the store to recharge the kit after every fight wouldn't work.

I wish I could level to 2. More HPs would be wonderful. Stupid…thing…whatever is stopping me from leveling.

Another big discrepancy I found in the game manuals is HPs. In the SRD all classes get a ton of HPs. Rogues get 6 per level. Barbarians get a whopping 12 per level. In Black Raven it is half that. Rogues get 3, barbarians 6, etc. In fourth age, everyone gets 1 less than in Black Raven. So rogues get 2 per level. Wizards only get 1 per level. Barbarians get 5 per level. But, everyone gets an extra 5 HP at level 1. So I get 2 HP from rogue, the 5 extra they give for level 1, and 3 from my con. 10 total. If they stuck to the SRD I would have a ton more HP at level 20. Bazillions more. I wonder why they changed it so much. Who knows? Adults do stupid things.

I head back and the turd-pigeon corpse hasn't despawned yet. I have to pee so I pee on the turd-pigeon. I am the darkness you stupid idiot turd-pigeon. I'll pee right on your face and there's nothing your stupid dead corpse can do about it.

Peeing doesn't burn too bad, so whatever was wrong is definitely getting better. Or I'm just getting used to it. Hopefully it's getting better. I think it is.

I head back to the intersection. Right before getting to it I hit sneak. I take the north passage. After one block there's a three block by three field. Only one turd-pigeon. I hug the east wall and sneak behind it. Nice, two in a row without being detected. I know I should go for the sneak attack but sometimes Joey has good ideas. And this one is solo, too, so I'm not really in danger. Half the time I get spotted when I'm stealthing. No big deal even if it's three turd-pigeons grouped together. This is just one. Cakewalk. So I whisper in its ear that I am the darkness and I'll pee on its face if I want to. It doesn't jump. It just tries to bite my face like a real turdy coward turd-pigeon. I kill it without much trouble. Loot. I have to go back and sell soon. I can feel I am getting close to the medium load debuff. I can carry more before getting it now though.

On the middle block of the west wall of the forest was a tree with one of those ability tests. I forget the name. Something weird. And stupid. Like suki-suki or something.

Forest is a weird word. I wonder what the person who invented it was thinking. It doesn't make much sense. It's a real dumb word if you think about it. Treest would make more sense. Forest just makes it sound like there should be four of something. Or someone mastered the number four. 'I am the four-est! Foremost expert on the number four!'

The ability test was a dexterity one. I had to run then jump on a bouncy thing and fly through a hoop without touching it. I had three tries. I got it with just pure luck on my third try. After winning, the tree disappeared and was replaced with a doorway. Through the door-way was a big room with no enemies. A chest was between two statues. The bottom part of each statue was a big tub of water. I use one to bathe and the other for extra drinking water now. In the chest were two potions of cure minor wounds weighing .1 lbs. each, and a scroll of flare also weighing .1 lbs. So, somehow, paper weighs the same as a decent sized bottle filled with liquid?

I tried one of the potions to see if it would help my hand get better since it didn't heal right, but it didn't do anything. Didn't help with the scars I have now or nothing. It probably just helps with HP shields.

I take out two clay jugs and fill them with water. Clay jugs are only three coppers so I bought another. Each weigh 4 lbs. filled. I get the medium load debuff and make my way back to camp. I bathed just like a week ago so I don't smell that bad yet. But the extra water is needed for brushing teeth and stuff. I am a great basically-mother.

I'll drop off the water, make sure Joey's okay, sell loot, and head out and clear eastward. I kind of have a routine, and the faster I go the more new stuff I can find.

1.14 VOTES

KIM GUM

I became a full-fledged grown-up woman today. For the last couple of days my stomach has felt heavy. Today I started bleeding. I found feminine pads in the store. I wish someone was here I could talk to about it. Besides Joey.

But he is all I have so I tell him, "Joey. Today I am a fully grown adult woman and I can legally vote even. You have to give me more respect now. Okay? Come on. At least look at me for a second. Joey, stop ignoring me. Joey! Joey! Joey! There. Looking at me for a second wasn't so hard, was it?"

What an ingrate he is. I grab my mirror and go near the store for some privacy. The mirror cost a ton but I need it. I take off my armor. And my sports bra. Not too shabby. There is something there. It is like the chest of a tubby boy. But I don't have much fat on me now.

It is kind of crazy. I'm definitely not fat, but my waist is still pretty thick and I still have really big shoulders and arms. I put my stuff back on and look in the mirror. I still look like a frog. Maybe more so since I now have two pretty big scars on my face, and they don't seem to be fading. My hair is getting long. I cut it all off a long time ago because even after buying a brush – for only one silver– it was too tangled to bother with trying to fix. It is getting long again. Well, not really. Just the bangs.

I get the scissors from the first aid kit and cut my bangs. Now I look even more like a frog. But now a frog woman. An adult frog woman with the right to vote.

I go back to camp. Joey and his stupid trays. He just loves them. "Joey, since I'm legally an adult now and can vote I think we should hold a couple. I vote to be queen of this forest. And I vote to rename the forest to treest. Since I am the only legal adult that can vote – both measures pass. Yay!"

I do a little dance and a couple fist pumps but Joey ignores it, so my celebration seems hollow.

"How do you like me now, Joey? Why do you always ignore me? I'm basically your mother. Pay attention to me. Okay, I'll also give you a vote too.

"If you want to pass the vote on if trays are stupid or not either raise your hand or play with trays. Two to nothing. The measure passes. Trays are now officially stupid.

"No, I can't play trays with you. I have killing to do. You know that. I know. I know. I'd like to take the day off since I officially became a woman today and my stomach hurts. But the turd-pigeons aren't going to kill themselves. I am the bleeder. I make the turd-pigeons bleed and I am so much woman that I can even make myself bleed. It's called a period. That is the power of the darkness. And the darkness doesn't take the day off because of little things like becoming an adult woman who can legally vote."

I actually don't think you can vote until you are like 16 or something. Much older than I am now. Could be as old as 18 or 21 or 25. Really old like that. But Joey doesn't know that. I am the darkness. And the darkness has some murdering to do.

I've cleared most of the forest...I mean treest, and I know where the boss is. The only other enemy in here other than turd-pigeons are turd-birds. Joey named them. I would have named them something else if I could've come up with something better, but the best name we could think of was turd-birds. They really are birds. Pretty easy to kill with a shield and if you pay attention.

The turd-birds look at you with a really big, human looking side-eye. They turn their head sideways to look at you. And they make a weird face too, like whatever they are looking at is a giant idiot. If you get into, like, four or five blocks from them, they hoot and dart right at you. If they hit you without a HP shield, it really, really, really hurts and they stick in. Then they pull their beaks out and start pecking. If they hit your shield they just fall to the ground. Not HP shield. The shield-shield. It usually just takes three stomps to kill them once they're on the ground. Sometimes four. Sometimes five if you're un-lucky, or just two if you are lucky. It usually only takes two stabs with the spear. Sometimes three. I think stomps count as unarmed damage. Halflings don't do much unarmed damage, and my 8 str gives me a -1 penalty to both hit and damage.

It is much better to be safe with the turd-birds and dodge if you don't think you can get your shield up in time. There're usually three or four of them. In one dead-end road there is just one by itself. I practice trying to spear it flying at me, since if I have any HP shield at all I'm safe even if I miss. And you can wait a little bit for the turd-bird to recover and dart at you again. Doing this training made me readjust how I fight with the shield. So I can hold the shield up and still make sure I can see the target enough to aim and jab. I used to either block or stab. Now I can do both together at the same time.

I hit a plateau with the bow. I just stopped getting better with it. I can still feel myself improving with melee, so I try to fight with spear and shield unless it's a really big pull. I used to always kill one of the two turd-pigeons west of the intersection with a bow. Then run back so the other turd-pigeon resets. And practice stealth movement to sneak attack the other one with the spear. I haven't done that in a really long time. I melee them both with no problem. More than two at a time even. No sweat.

The boss, who I named king-turd, is a giant turd-pigeon. Sometimes I call him turd-king, too. He has two turd-birds in his clearing with him. Two I can see anyways. I will fight him soon. I just want to be able to spear a turd-bird charging at me 100% of the time before I do. That means hitting them with a spear as they charge to remove the HP shield, and then again before they hit the ground. Or if it takes two to break the shield, I'll just need one stomp when they hit the ground. Once the shield is gone one good stomp is all it takes to kill them.

I'm good enough to take the king-turd. I have been for a while. I just want to get through the fight without being injured bad again. Being injured really sucks a ton. I hate it. And I want to make sure I fully cleared this place first. I found the boss before I found a big whole nother section of the forest. Treest I mean. Since then I have been using search all the time. I searched that specific block a couple times before it brought up a slot in a tree just big enough for a coin. When I put the ancient coin I found a long time ago into the slot it opened up a whole big new section with three chests way at the other end of it. I can't believe I almost missed that. RNG is dumb. I hate it. In combat, but also with everything else too. You have to search everywhere a million times to make sure. And you can't just spam it. Just one search every six seconds. So you got to be careful and really pay attention.

I wish I picked a different background instead of lucky duck. I don't think it is very useful.

I haven't gotten any good loot yet. Just potions and scrolls. So far this dungeon had four chests, and two were locked. Just one was trapped. I've only found two traps on the ground. They reset just like the monsters do. All the monsters and traps reset at the same time.

Sometimes the traps go off when I disarm them. Stupid RNG again. Nothing you can do about it.

I've been selling all the potions and scrolls I get, even the unidentified ones. I have over 150 gold now. And I had to replace my shield and spear a bunch. I always have to replace them before the durability gets close to zero, and that is annoying. How damaged an item is and its durability are not the same. That is so dumb. I'm on my sixth armor. I was going to get studded leather, but I worry about the armor check penalty. I already get caught stealthing a lot. Why make it worse? It weighs 2.5 lbs. more than my armor weighs for me, and costs 25g instead of 10g. For just 1 more AC? No thank you.

I don't know what a good number is for AC or not. Mine is 19 with my shield. That seems pretty good. But I don't think monsters get a miss when they hit me much. My HP shield rarely lasts more than one hit. It's hard to pay attention during melee, but I can probably count the times I've been hit and didn't see a damage icon float up on both my hands, and the times I got hit and my HP shield didn't break on both my feet.

That's why I need level 2 so bad. I need more HP and more AC. I'm thinking about multiclassing into a ranger next level. Whenever it lets me level. I have to have a bazillion xp by now. And since I am a halfling I won't ever get an xp penalty for multiclassing since rogue is their preferred class, no matter if I stay at just 1 level of rogue and go 19 ranger levels. Not preferred class. What is it called? Favorite class.

Rangers can use heavy shields. I'll also get a pet. Not right away, at like ranger level 4 or so. When I become a level 2 ranger I can pick the bow feats since I want to use a shield in melee, so two-weapon fighting would just be a waste. And the point-blank shot feat and specialization point I already picked won't be wasted. Rangers get a lot of skill points per level and full BAB too.

I really wish I could talk to Mia. She is really smart and great at figuring out smart stuff. She would know the best thing to do. She'd figure out why I can't level up to 2 and tell me how to do it. I'd be unstoppable with Mia.

No sense crying about it. She isn't here. Just me and Joey. I grab a couple trays and play with Joey for a bit before heading out to clear the dungeon again.

1.15 WRIT IN BURNISHED ROWS OF STEEL

KIM GUM

If I can get this turd-bird with my spear that will be five in a row. I'm on the six blocks of grass leading to the path towards the solo turd-bird, hitting search on every block. I haven't found anything new yet in this place. Not for a long, long time now. As I get to the door on the fifth block that leads to the room that has a trap, and used to have a trapped and locked chest, I feel something. I'm not sure what.

That room has another exit to the west that leads south and to two more rooms. I clear them all the time. Every day basically. Nothing should be in this room. All three rooms had chests, but never any enemies. The last room has a statue with a water tub I get a drink from. I usually take a rest and eat a meal in there.

I hit stealth and nothing happens. That usually means something noticed me or is looking at me. What is going on? Are the spawns changing?

I slowly back up. I move backwards until my back hits the invisible treest wall. I've been thinking about changing the name of treest to something else. Treest sounds like it should be the name of, like, the king of trees, not a bunch of trees. Maybe tree-herd is better? Or Tree-crowd? Treest is better than forest, but just not right. Everyone agrees forest is a dumb name for a bunch of trees though. Me and Joey will have to think about it more.

The path here goes three blocks up, three blocks west, then a bunch of blocks way down to a dead end, but before the dead end I can take a one way passage back to the main treest area from this big, secret area I used the ancient coin to get to. I hit stealth again. Nothing. What is going on?

I run north, then west, and as soon as I hit the south road I quickly turn and hit stealth. It works. I just stand there for a moment thinking. I hear a weird noise. The noise in fourth age that means something near you is stealthing and you noticed something. Either passed a spot or listen check or something. Probably spot since I put points in it, and I didn't put nothing in listen. I move a little north and peep around the corner. Nothing.

I hear the noise again, real close. My heartbeat spikes and I look around frantically.

I wait, trying to strain all my perceptions. I hear it again, from the north. For a second I see a giant snake. For the first time ever since coming here I see a nameplate. It says "3+(3) Huge Viper." Holy moly! So this is made for three or more level 3 people. I'm one level 1 person.

My heartbeat goes super crazy. They named the snake good – it is really, really huge! I hate snakes. I hate them so much. And this one is way more scary looking than any snake ever. I don't want to fight this thing. I stop myself from taking off running, and stay in stealth to move south with my knees almost buckling from nervousness.

I'm having a hard time thinking right, too nervous, and I hit the wall as I look backwards while still trying to stealth away. The snake reappears, no longer in stealth, and I notice I'm not either. My stealth icon is gone. No, no, no! I take off running, or trying to run. And as soon as I take my next step a ghost arm comes flying at me, an attack of opportunity for me moving out of melee range, as the snake starts his actual attack. I turn to start tumbling and see the piercing damage icon and the poison icon. This isn't good. This isn't good. Then as I'm tumbling away I feel a stab in my lower back and pain flares through my whole body.

I tumble max distance then start sprinting. I'm too scared to look back. I run until I see the one-way passage out. I hit it and a text box appears asking if I want to enter. I hit accept and see the snake rushing towards me from my periphery as I transition out. Out of the secret passageway, kind of out of breath, I quickly inventory my spear and check my lower back with my free hand. It's warm and a little wet. It doesn't hurt much. Only a little blood and some clear liquid a little thicker than water.

I move one block up and start sprinting west down the road leading to the field we live in. I inventory my shield, and I run as fast as I can, hoping the snake can't get through the one-way passage. I had to select the secret passage, then hit accept. Hopefully mobs can't do things like that. Especially snakes. How could it select the one-way passage? And then hit accept after? That'd be impossible, right?

Not even halfway down the road I start feeling real weird. The trees are wobbling and getting longer and shorter. Everything is all crazy. I can barely keep my balance. I fall, get up, and fall again. It's like a really slow and crazy earthquake or something. Why are the colors all weird looking?

I force myself back onto my feet, sucking air to get my breath back. Everything is spinning. But I got to keep moving. Get back to safety. Mobs never go in our field. Just got to put one foot in front of the other. You can do this, Kim. Just another foot. And then the other.

Nausea hits me and my mouth starts watering. One foot. One more step. I heave a little. I feel like I got to puke. One foot. There is the intersection. One foot. Other foot. I take the turn and fall. I almost puke but don't. I get back on my feet. I make it a little bit into the clearing and see Joey playing in the far corner before I puke everywhere. I have to lay down right now. I'm sweating bad and feel like gravity is trying to kill me. Laying in my puke doesn't bother me at all. I just wish everything would stop spinning.

I retch. I retch again. I puke until almost nothing comes out. Then I dry heave. Each heave makes my stomach cramp so bad it feels like the muscles will burst.

I think I hear the stealth sound. My heart spikes. Did the snake get into our field? No!

Even with my head still spinning, I get a clear, calming thought. My heart slows. All the fear leaves me. This is for the best. I'm sick of this. I'm sick of fighting. I'm sick of getting injured. I'm sick of pain. I miss my mom. And my dad. I want to go home. I don't want to do this no more. I just want it all to stop.

Knowing the end is coming makes me feel better. Knowing I don't got to fight no more. My cheek is wet and all I can smell is puke. I open my eyes. The grass is all crazy. It starts dancing. And then vibrating. Then starts growing.

Why hasn't it killed me yet? That stealth noise had to be the snake, right? But mobs can't get in here, our field. They never come in here. I close my eyes. The grass is too crazy. Even with my eyes closed I see a mad kaleidoscope of crazy colors swirling out of control. My head starts vibrating like the grass was.

The sound of Joey freaking out in the distance forces its way into my mind. I barely manage to lift my head up from the puke and dirt and see that awful snake attacking Joey. Joey crying and wailing. Every strike from the snake causing a white flash around Joey.

I get annoyed. Why didn't the snake kill me first? Did it pass me because I'm not a threat? I don't want to see Joey die first. I was supposed to die first. Why isn't the snake being hurt? Attacking Joey hurt the turd-pigeons. Is the snake killing itself? It doesn't look like it's in pain. Why is it attacking so slow? Game rules maybe? Once every six seconds for mobs until their BAB gives them extra attacks per round?

It's hard to think. What was Joey's HP shield? They told us before. It was a lot. 12x12x12. That is like a million I think. No, thousands? Seven thousand? Something like that. A lot. I forget. I used to remember it.

I know I shouldn't but I get mad at Joey for ruining it. Ruining me getting killed first. I got to try and get up to help him now. I try to push myself up on shaky, weak arms. I get to my hands and knees before I have to stop to dry heave. I stop moving to help the nausea go away. There is something on my hand. It starts growing fast. Is that puke?

It keeps growing and growing until it fills my vision. Then all I see is black. No, something small in the distance is flying towards me. A person. With wings and a sword. And a halo of fire. And eyes like car headlights, shining right at me. It gets bigger and bigger the closer it gets. It's a giant. He's a giant. Wearing shining white armor. Black hair, tan skin, a fighter's nose, and a real big jaw. I think he might be handsome, but I'm not sure. He kind of looks a lot like Juan from mom's dojang, but…more. A lot more. Is this God?

His face is angry and he looks real mad. I feel nauseous again. Why is he coming now? I can't duel now. It's real hard to look at him with his headlight eyes. He must hear my thoughts because they get much dimmer.

"Kimberly Gum!" His voice is like an avalanche. Real deep and makes me rumble all over. I didn't even notice I looked down, so I look back up at him.

"You are the one who dares challenge me to a duel? You run from a little snake, and you cower as you watch your helpless brother get attacked over and over?"

"I was getting up to help! To fight!"

God laughs. "You were praying for death, coward. You want to die. You just want to die first."

"I...I...can I go with my mom now? Please? I don't want to do this anymore. Please?" I start crying.

"So, your mother was right then? You are useless."

"What? She said that? Why? Because I didn't want to go to classes? She didn't even teach them. It was Juan's class and he is barely older than me. Barely older than Carlos. And she had Carlos teach too sometimes. Why would I want to go? For what? She said I'd be in big trouble if I ever stuck up for myself anyways, so why? Did she really say that?"

"Did you really use your brother as a shield to protect you from the turd-pigeons? Twice?"

"Why doesn't she like me? Why did she have me if she didn't want me?" I don't get it. What did I do wrong? I cry harder.

"Look at you! Why would anyone want you? How could anyone want you?"

I start sobbing. It's true. There is no reason anyone would want me.

"Kimberly Gum! Stop crying and look up! Look at me!"

I look up. He looks different. Like the bad guy from Star Wars with the big robes and lightning. His voice is different, too, and all crackly and weird.

"Good. Now stop being a little baby. Tell me why I should let you into my kingdom?"

It takes a bit to control my crying enough to reply. "Because...I...I don't know. I got vengeance for mom. Did she see? For dad and Carlos too. Did mom mention that? Did you see? I've killed millions of turd-pigeons too. And turd-birds. I want to go home please. I want to stop fighting. I want the pain to stop. I just want everything to stop."

"You talk about vengeance yet balk at a snake? And cry and whine like a baby. Courage is not the absence of fear, but the triumph over it."

Oh great. Now God is saying mom's stupid sayings. I look down again. This isn't going how I hoped. I wish the snake just killed me and got it all over with.

His voice changes again to something higher and more sinister as he says, "Pain is weakness leaving the body."

"NO IT ISN'T!" I yell at him. It isn't. It really isn't. "I just want to go home!"

"You are fat."

Why is God being so mean to me? This can't be God. His voice turns to something familiar so I look up. He looks like Keisha Lautour now. I hate her. She's a fake friend. She's always mean to me.

"You look like a frog with cankles."

I just want it to stop. I just want to go home. "Just leave me alone if you are going to be mean." I lay my head back down.

"Kimberly Gum, look at me right now!"

He states this with such power and authority I look up immediately. He is back to his original form with his original voice. In front of him are three snow globes floating in the air.

"It is time to choose, Kimberly Gum."

He points to the snow globe on his right. Is it a snow globe? It has a giant white mansion, maybe a castle, being snowed on. "Choose this and you can be with your family forever. If they'll have you. If not you can still know peace, and you could be happy."

If they'll have me? Can still? Could be?

Does my family really even want me? Did my mother really say I was useless? She was always so...so...pretend? Maybe? I always felt like she was super disappointed in me. I always hoped that wasn't true, and she actually loved me. Sometimes it did seem like she really loved me. Maybe even most of the time.

He points at the globe in the middle. It is empty, with just snow. Or static? "Pick this one and it will all stop. This is oblivion. You will cease to be. No memories. No family. Nothing at all. A true end."

That is what I want. To just not be anymore. Just nothing. I start getting up to select it.

"Stay!" He points to the one on his left, filled with fire and sparks. "This one. This one you don't want and you won't select. This is the path of warriors. Of gods. This is for those who embrace pain and actually want to kill monsters. Not little baby pretenders like you."

"I didn't pretend! I killed millions and you know it!"

"But this. This is the real deal. This is for my champions. They spread my message. My message of death. Those who select it are the darkness. Not pretenders. It will be too painful. It is too tough, too much for you. I need real warriors. Not whiney babies who cry all the time about pain."

"Pain hurts a lot! And I am the darkness!"

"No. No you are not. Make your selection and let's end this."

"If I select the first one can Joey come too?"

"Why do you care? There are no monsters there for him to be used as a shield against."

"Can you please tell me?"

"Yes."

"Will he still go with my family if I select the second one?"

"If you select the second, it is immaterial."

"Please answer."

"Yes."

That makes me feel good. Joey's a good kid with a good heart. Everyone in the family loves him and will welcome him. At least I don't have to worry about that.

I want the second one. But do I? Yes, but I want to prove mom wrong too. I want to prove everyone wrong. I am the darkness. I know

I am. I just don't like pain. I'm good at fighting. I just don't want to. Not anymore. Not all the time. I'm tired. I'm really tired.

I think back to when I promised to change. To not pretend. Not pretend like everyone else in the world. To really embrace pain and fighting. I promised. I did pretty good. I embraced them okay. But not great. Not really. Not fully.

If I take the middle one, it doesn't matter. I won't exist to feel guilt. Or feel bad. Or care about what mom thinks. Or worry about Joey.

Joey. I also promised to be a great big sister. I'm basically his mother. If I die, he dies too. If he isn't dead already. But I don't have to care or think about any of that if I select the middle one.

But I do care. I'm his mother and I love him. I should be better than this. And good moms don't abandon their kids. But what if he is already dead? Then vengeance. I will kill and eat the snake that killed him. Or die trying.

I can do that at least. I can be a good mother at least. My mom got vengeance for her son, Carlos. I can do the same for my son, too.

I feel the rumble all through my body as God says, "No. If you want to be my champion you have to want it. You have to do it for yourself. No half-measures. Pain must be your motivation; adversity your goal.

"Before even thinking about selecting the orb on my left answer these questions – do you love fighting and do you love pain?"

I think about it seriously. I think back to how I enjoyed getting vengeance with the first turd-pigeons. I really enjoyed killing them. But not getting hurt. I know I could have beat the boss if I tried. I was scared, but I could have done it. I was just nervous to actually do it. He is a really super giant turd-pigeon. Of course he is scary.

I reply, "I love fighting and I can learn to love pain. I will learn to love pain."

"LIES! You do not love fighting and you hate pain."

I wish what he said made me angry. I'm a lot tougher when I'm angry. But my head hurts. My mouth tastes like batteries. I feel shaky and weak. But I don't want to give up. Not on Joey. And not on me neither.

I don't want to select the third one. But I should. I wish I wanted to.

"Just select the second one, coward. I know you want to. Stop wasting my time. Run like you always run. Do nothing. Be nothing. Just end the pathetic thing that is your life."

That was another promise I made. All my life it seems people have been mean to me, almost casually. Like it's okay. No big deal. Like I don't matter. It never even really made me mad. Just sad. I just wanted them to stop. But why would they when I don't fight back?

I can fight back. I may lose. But they'll know I fight back. That I'm somebody and there is a price to pay when they say mean things. I'm sick of just taking it. And I won't. From nobody. Not no more. Not ever again. Being in pain is worth giving them more pain than I get. Pain is worth winning. Pain is worth showing them that I'm not nothing. Pain is worth keeping my promises.

Anger blossoms in my chest. It clears my head some. Makes me feel less sick. I stand up. My legs feel weak. I equip my spear and shield.

"Say one more mean thing to me again and I'll kill you," I say.

He smiles. "Come then, you fat frog. Show me you deserve the third orb."

I yell out in rage as I hit charge and fly towards him. And then I'm back in the field, the free attack I get with a charge flies out of me into the giant snake. I immediately start stabbing for all I am worth. I'm dizzy and feel really weird, but I see Joey past the snake. Alive and still freaking out. Still flashing when attacked.

I've hit the snake a bunch now and I still haven't seen a damage icon. How much AC does this snake have? I start yelling as I attack to hopefully get the snake's attention and get it to attack me instead of Joey. I wish I could see Joey's HP shield. See how much more he's got.

I finally see the piercing damage icon, and the sneak attack icon too. Nice! That got the snakes attention and got him to turn around. I just have to dodge every six seconds. That's all the attacks he gets. Just one a round. The round ticks and I stand guarded, waiting for his attack. I stand ready. He doesn't attack. Just waits. Staring. As it turns from five to six seconds he finally attacks and I dodge his giant, extremely frightening head by the skin of my teeth. As I land the next round ticks and it immediately attacks again before I'm prepared for it. I barely manage to get my shield up just in time for his head to crack into it and send me flying back through the air.

I'm looking at the sky warble in strange colors before I slam down into something. Enough pain explodes in my back that I can hardly register it. Extreme agony grips me. I can't breathe. I'd scream if I could but my lungs stopped working. I can't breathe at all. It hurts more than anything ever hurt. I can't breathe. I notice I'm kicking my legs madly as I try and breathe and deal with the pain. I've had the wind knocked out of me before, but it's never been this bad. It's never been this terrifying.

Long moments later I can finally suck some air into my lungs. The panic takes a while to go away though. Joey! A crazy amount of pain shoots through me as I get to my feet. Breathing hurts. It hurts a lot. Something must have punctured my back. I'm probably bleeding to death. I can hear something click in and out when I breathe. Maybe I can just feel it, but it seems like I can hear it.

Suck it up, Kim!

I look around. I want to check out my back but now isn't the time. It still hurts a ridiculous amount. I see a lot of crazy things but I don't see the snake. Or Joey. I turn around and see a clown. A really creepy clown with snake eyes. The clown gets close and then far away and then there are tons of them. I breathe and wince in pain. The clowns turn into statues leading to a large rabbit. What in the world?

A giant mallet swings down from the sky right at me. I dodge and wince at the pain coming from my back. The mallet comes again, and I dodge. More pain. The clown statue I'm near has a target on it. I know...I know what to do. I have to destroy all the statues leading to the rabbit.

I thrust my spear forward into the target on the clown statue, causing agony to radiate through my back and arm. Nothing I can do about that. The pain will stop when I'm dead. Either in the next couple seconds, or next year, or in a decade. Someday it will stop. But not now it won't. So I got to ignore it. I thrust again, harder, causing myself even more pain. Then another mallet flies at me.

This becomes my world. Dodging mallets and striking targets on clown statues. Every attack with my spear teaching me a lesson. A lesson I don't want, but one that I need. As I start sucking air harder and harder, every breath teaches me the same. I don't give up though. I keep going. The mallets get closer, my thrusts lose power, and the agony increases.

I can't tell if I'm getting closer to the rabbit. The world keeps wobbling. I keep my feet. I keep thrusting. I keep dodging. The clowns all laugh at me.

The world warbles and then I'm in a giant ballroom, like in beauty and the beast. I look up and the ceiling turns to a red sky. The chandelier turns into the sun. I look around, wincing with the agony each breath causes me. The battery taste in my mouth making the spit I swallow burn. Where did everyone go? I turn and a giant snake's head speeds towards me. I dodge and strike it with my spear. I see Joey past the snake. In a beautiful dress. Dancing madly.

I get real light-headed and almost fall. The snake is smiling at me with a bloody grin. Waiting. It thinks it's won.

But I'm still standing.

I wait for it to attack, and then I dodge and strike. I land and dive forward to avoid its second attack, and then I thrust again. My back radiates enough pain I almost lose my grip. It hurts so bad. My strike lands, and I manage to avoid the head, but its body crashes into me and sends me tumbling. Pain makes my body spasm and I drop my spear.

I lay on the ground and lift my head to look at the snake. It is just staring at me from its bloody face. A new round ticks. I can't get up and get to my spear before it finishes me and it knows it. Is it waiting for me to make the first move?

I don't have the strength in my right arm to lift off the ground. All the colors are weird. The snake looks bad. Wait! It really does. That is how it works in fourth age. At 75% health mobs look a little bloody. It gets worse at 50% and 25%. At 10% they look horrible. Just bloody messes. This is what the snake looks like. I almost have him. I wasn't thinking about that since it never happened to the turd-pigeons, or turd-birds, or even me. Not in here. Not once.

I just need to dig a little deeper.

The snake gives up on me moving first. It opens its mouth as it moves towards me. I can see the venom dripping from its terrible fangs. I have to force myself to wait. As soon as it rears its head back to attack I roll to the right as the head slams into the ground where I was. I suck up the extreme pain that throbs through me, grab my spear, and scurry to me feet. I know thrusting is going to cause a lot of pain and I almost hesitate. But I don't. I scream out, "I AM THE DARKNESS!" With everything I have in me, I lunge forward.

I've been seeing a lot of stuff, so I can't really tell if I see a damage icon. I attack again. And again. And then I see the snake's head coming at me. I move towards the head and stab as it attacks me. My blow lands, and I don't get hit, but I get knocked back and fall down and my spear flies from my hand again.

I breathe deep and equip my dagger. I got to get up. Sucking air and sucking up the pain breathing causes, I get back on my feet. Mostly. My legs are shaking. I'm weakening bad. Is this from blood loss? I look at the snake and I'm surprised to see it isn't moving. But it isn't dead. The name tag isn't greyed out. In fourth age there are no HP shields. Just HPs. You don't die when you go negative HPs. You can stabilize and regen HP until you get back to positive. Or you don't stabilize and keep losing HPs until you die.

I put my dagger back into my inventory and find my spear. I can't bend over to get it. I have to use my foot to flip it up and grab it. That still causes a ton of pain. I think I'm fading fast. In absolute agony I go over and stab him a bunch. Or her. Probably a him. Who can tell?

I finally see the nametag grey out. The snake is dead.

I did it. I killed him before he killed me. Stupid turd-snake. I drop my spear. I should have inventoried it. Idiot. It doesn't matter now anyways. I send my shield to inventory. I try reaching back to see how bad the wound on my back is. But I can't. It hurts too much. So much pain.

I try with my left hand. I can't fully reach it but my hand comes away dry. There should be a ton of blood. Maybe the armor is getting in the way or stopping the blood from leaking down? I inventory my armor. I get my spear back and inventory it, 30 seconds later when my armor is off I try feeling again and no blood still.

I look at what I hit. It had to have been my chair. The base chair weighs 25 lbs. and cost 5g. I got the biggest, heaviest one I could, at 50 lbs. for 10g. I use it to work out with. I invented a ton of chair exercises. Pretty good ones, too. The chair is whole and undamaged. Nothing on it could have punctured my back. But it had to have.

There should be a huge, bloody wound. But there isn't. The pain is extreme. Just breathing hurts so bad it's crazy. I can feel something clicking in and out as I breathe. It hurts bad when it clicks.

Joey! Jeez. How could you forget about Joey, you idiot! What kind of mother are you? I frantically look around and see him in the bathroom corner, facing the treest. Quiet. He is usually never quiet. He looks fine. Or unharmed I mean. Not injured. I protected my baby.

I go over to him. I'm still light headed. I don't feel good. I can't sit and get up easily so I kneel and summon my spear and put it in my left hand. I use the butt of my spear to help me balance.

"You're safe, Joey." I start crying. He looks at me and holds my bicep. I look him in the face. Is he hairy now? He kind of looks like a werewolf.

"Are you a werewolf now, Joey? That would be awesome." I feel like I have to puke again. I pull out the healing kit. It gives me 3 HPs. A message flashes across my screen saying the poison debuff has been cured and +5 con. +5 con?

I open the character screen and my con says 16 still. Oh, maybe the poison debuff lowered it by 5 and now it is back to normal?

I still feel real sick. And weird. I don't think the heal kit removed the actual poison from me. Just the poison debuff. Like with HPs. The kit doesn't actually heal me. But how can a snake from fourth age actually poison me? Well, I guess it can actually damage me, so why not?

My mouth starts watering. I should leave the bathroom corner but I can't. I'm sweating bad. I dry heave and lay down and dry heave more. I watch the kaleidoscope of colors behind my closed eyes. The battery taste is worse than the puke taste. It burns.

I focus on the pain in my back. It becomes distant. The clicking is a door opening and closing. I can go through the door. So I do. I immediately regret it. On the other side are nightmares.

1.16 IN A MAD WORLD

BRUNO VAZ

I see the exit door pop as the boss drops. This dungeon is so easy it makes me wonder how it killed over half of earth's population. I loot the boss and loot the chest. Just vendor trash. With the boss down my score for the dungeon is finalized. And since time is stopped in dungeons there's no longer any need for me to rush. I got all the time I want to do whatever I want.

Man, I love this. Fighting. Proving I'm the best. This has to be a record for the tutorial dungeon. From start to dead boss, probably an hour. I suck at telling time, but I'd bet two fat babies and a donut it was less than two hours. Had to be. The psuchesoma was a good one, for me at least – a dex one.

It's like this whole world was invented for me. I don't got to hold it in all the time; I can fight as much as I want. People calling me crazy, saying I got all these issues - none of that matters here. All that matters is I'm good at killing. None of the other BS from the real world.

I think back on when it started. Well, not started. Not really. I've always had a mouth that gets me into trouble, and people always said something was wrong with me. They weren't real serious about it until they said I got a TBI. Back in '06, or '07. When the Army started converting Pope air force base over to Army control. My first mission out of there on an Army bird.

Before that they already said I had PTSD, an anxiety disorder, depression, ADHD, yadda yadda. Why not throw a TBI on top of it, use that as an excuse too? My brain was fine before and is just as fine after. A little concussion from an explosion isn't going to hurt my brain. I'm Bruno Vaz. My fuse didn't get shorter; it was always short. I've always had memory and concentration issues. I'd like to see someone with my job who isn't a little depressed and anxious. And I've always had trouble sleeping – anyone with a soul would. You work for heartless monsters, some things are going to weigh on your conscience.

The ADHD is the best one to prove the rest are lies. Boring things and people are supposed to bore you. And if something's boring you, you shouldn't be able to pay attention. It's more like almost everyone in the world has Attention Surplus Disorder. Bunch of knucklehead idiots. They just say I'm the one with a disorder so they can feel better about being sissies.

They say having hyperfocus proves I have ADHD. Ha! Being able to focus on things that interest me is normal. Telling someone they have ADHD is like telling someone their brain works correct. I know ADHD isn't supposed to be a major issue, but it does prove how much they like to make up nonsense to make sane people feel crazy. They get you to accept the little lies so they can get away with lying big.

Hearing people prattle on about all the made-up issues they say I have…that gets old real quick. Especially from my family. There's nothing wrong with me. Period. It isn't so bad at work; they just used it as an excuse for me. Bruno ignored that order because of the TBI, or turned off coms because of the TBI. Sure. If I actually had real problems they'd take me out of Delta or medically discharge me. Force me to retire. Something. I'd be considered a danger. And the CIA would stop trying so hard to recruit me. The amount of missions I get tapped for proves I don't have any real issues. What it does prove is how competent and issue-free I am.

Man, I'm not looking forward to writing all those goddamn emails.

I can't wait to see my family. I mean my kids. Not the filthy cheating whore. She didn't cheat yet, but I know it's in her whore heart. How could Minnie do that to me? Just thinking about it fills me with a white hot rage. She was perfect. Perfect. And then she had to go and get infected with another man's penis. How do I always end up being the bad guy for getting mad about it? How could I not be furious? She cheated on me!

I take some deep breaths to calm down. I push all the anger and resentment down into the ball of hate in my stomach. She didn't cheat yet, and I need her. And if I go at her again, the same thing will happen as last time – the kids will side with her and hate me. I'll end up being the bad guy again. Even though she's the two-faced cheating whore. Unfair or not, it is what it is.

I finish pushing the hate down. I'm still angry but I feel a little better. Having all those emails I got to write hanging over my head isn't making it easier to think or control my anger.

I need my wife. My ex I mean. She doesn't know she is a cheating whore yet, and I really need her help this time. She's good at everything I suck at. Talking to people, caring about nonsense, organizing, understanding female emotions, not making people angry when she talks, stuff like that. Monkey stuff. I need someone I trust doing that crap for me. Even though I can't trust her. Well, I can trust her with these kinds of things.

I don't got to spend a ton of time with Minnie anyways. She'll be safe in the city; in her own instance of the city. A nearly penis-free instance too. I got nothing to worry about for a while. I just got to suck it up and play nice when I'm around her. My kids won't hate me this time neither. I hope. I just got to not do nothing too stupid like I usually do. It would be better if they weren't so goddamn sensitive though. I need my kids in my life. Things won't start spiraling and getting crazy if they don't push me away.

I hope they're all okay. My family. They should be. I'll be able to check soon. The wish machine thing has been right about everything else, so they'll be fine. Should be safe. If not I will destroy...something. No one messes with Bruno Vaz. Not without soon regretting it.

Well, time to get planning. First I'll walk back to the store to sell and repair. Exercise to get my head on right. I got to shave, but that should be one of the last things I do. Definitely write the emails before I sleep. Goddamn emails. Get my achievement awards squared away. Make sure my head's still on right before I exit this dungeon. And make sure I exit nice and rested. It'll be easier dealing with all the pissants and their whining when I'm bright-eyed and bushy-tailed.

I'm nervous. I always somehow get into trouble just having regular conversations with the monkeys. Now I got to take charge of all of them. I really got to try and control my anger. Try to come off reasonable. It won't look good if I got to beat up a bunch of sissies for bleating their gibberish at me. I really got to make sure I don't kill no one. Well, besides that one guy. He really needs some killing. Can't get around that. And that other guy way later.

I've been thinking about some of the things I should change since I got to write those goddamn emails all over again. Make it so less of the monkeys die from being chronically stupid. Last time almost all the best crawlers died in dungeon area 10. Obviously, we got to avoid that. And we will. But we also had way more deaths than necessary from people picking classes that are awesome at level 30, but suck wicked bad until then.

People don't realize this isn't like first age. Not yet, anyways. Things are different. No resurrections or second chances. You die you die. And most won't realize they need a class fitting their strengths, and they'll end up rerolling their class a couple times until they find one that finally clicks with them. Like with me – monk seems like a perfect class for me, but it isn't. I do much better with a shield and axe.

Way too many people pick squishy classes, and min-max wrong. They die before they realize they don't know what they're doing. Wizards and other casters absolutely suck at early levels, and die when a boss just sneezes at them. Too many people took that garbage ranged healer class with the wizard HP progression. All healers get ranged heals later. And more AoE heals when they pick the usual healer epic class.

Too many imported mobs ignore taunts, and don't got the damage visuals, and other bugs. Until people know what they're doing, and what to expect, they need to focus on improving themselves. Shore up their bodies and mind for fighting. They got to be able to take a couple hits. After doing that they can get fancy and level a squishy class. First time through is the hardest.

I won't outright lie, but I'll do my best to steer people away from squishy casters and healers for now. The casters are absolutely necessary later for raids. Same with good healers. But healers should always be able to take some hits. And give some too. Females, especially, were drawn towards the squishy classes last time. And they dropped like flies – early and often. That's a real goddamn tragedy. I'll do what I can to avoid that.

I hate this. This is the type of slimy thinking politicians use to justify being horrible. Justify lying. Say you're lying to help people. I hate politicians. I hate the fact I got to be one. And try and think like one. I'd rather not, but this doesn't even scratch the tip of the iceberg of the actual horrible things I'd do to get my kids back to earth alive. I'd burn down the whole goddamn world to keep my kids safe. And smile doing it.

1.17 SLEEPYHEAD

KIM GUM

My arm is asleep and starts tingling and wakes me up. When I move it pain flares through me. I'm still really tired and I still feel really weird. My mouth tastes like puke and batteries. I want to sleep more. A lot more. No way I can. My back hurts too much. And I really got to check on Joey.

Grunting in pain, I get up. There is no way to move so I can avoid my back hurting. Even breathing hurts. I can feel something clicking in and out when I breathe. I see Joey sleeping near the camp area, on his bedroll.

The snake is gone. That stinks. I wanted to tell its corpse that I am the darkness again. Maybe pee on it a little. Show it who the boss is. How do you like me now, you giant turd-snake? I can't do any of that now.

I go over to the first aid kit and take some aspirin. I look through the whole kit again in case there is something else I can use for pain. There isn't.

I check my back for blood again. Nothing. I check out my whole body. I'm filthy and I stink. I have some pretty good bruises and scrapes, but nothing bad. I wish I could see my back.

I put my mirror on my chair and try to look over my shoulder at my back. I can get it for a split second, but I can't see the area very good. It looks a little bruised, but nothing shows that could explain why the pain is so bad.

I reach my left hand around and inch it up until I'm over the most painful spot. I push and can feel it click out. And then click back in. Doing that causes so much pain I almost fall to my knees.

Broken ribs? Do broken ribs really hurt that bad? It's a whole huge area, but the part that pops in and out definitely hurts the worst. I feel it should look as bad as it hurts.

I've had a broken leg and arm before, and neither hurt nearly as bad as this. Or I don't remember it hurting this bad. This pain is just ridiculous. Ludacris. It just won't stop or give me a second of relief.

Well, nothing I can do besides suck it up. Maybe a hot bath would help, but I can't heat the water in the statue pools now. I don't even want to walk to see if the turd-pigeons respawned. If they haven't…I just can't trust this place now. Not with 3+(3)s spawning and coming after Joey. That was crazy. Stupid turd-snake idiot.

My right arm works and doesn't hurt that much, but I can't move it or my back and side and everywhere hurts. Extreme, shooting pain. This doesn't seem like the pain you should suck up and work through. This seems like the type of pain you let heal so it doesn't get worse.

There is only a couple things I got to do I can think of. I got to pray and see if God will appear to me again. I never officially touched the snow globe of fire. I'm not sure if I'm officially his champion or not. Regardless of what he says, I'm definitely the darkness. I have been for a long time. He can't deny me that. Why wouldn't he want me to be his champion anyways? I killed the turd-snake and saved Joey. No matter what mom thinks, or even if she really told God I was useless – I'm not. I'm definitely not.

And I'm not a coward.

I embrace fighting and I dealt with and am dealing with the pain really amazingly. It's impossible to truly embrace extreme pain. It just hurts too much. And I think God should understand that. I didn't lie.

And if he doesn't show up again that probably proves I'm the champion. That he sanctions me being the darkness. I just wish God wasn't such a jerk.

I hope I didn't just hallucinate all that. I saw some really crazy stuff. Really crazy. But I'm pretty sure God was real. He looked like God. Most likely, I'm definitely already his champion. What was I supposed to do for him? Spread his word and death or something? Or his word is death. No problem. Easy-peasy. That's what I do anyways.

I was just out of my mind with that whole wanting to die stuff. The poison messed up my mind. Who would take care of Joey? That's coward thinking, not darkness thinking.

I summon my spear and put it in my left hand and get down on my knees. "Hey God. It's your champion. I won so that counts as touching the snow globe, right? The fire one. The one on the right. My right, your left. You know what I mean. You didn't really explain it or make it very clear. I'm pretty sure beating the turd-snake counted as touching the globe. If not can you come back and let me touch it so it's official?"

Nothing. No response.

"That really happened, right God? But my mother never said that, did she? Right? I bet she didn't. She wouldn't. I'm not her favorite but she loved me. And if she's watched what I've done, seen the vengeance I gave her and dad and Carlos, she'd know I'm definitely not useless. I killed the turd-snake and saved Joey. You saw that, right mom?"

Nothing still.

"Stop playing coy, God. I think I mean coy. Is that the right word? That kind of sounds like a bad word now that I think about it. Talk to me again, God. Please?

111

"If you don't talk back or show up that means I definitely touched the snow globe of fire. And it also means my mother never said that. Right?"

Nothing. I want to ask him to help make my back feel better or hurt less, but he wants me to love pain so that would be dumb.

"Okay. How about a sign? Just let me know somehow I'm your champion, okay?"

Nothing happens. I look around and see a bag on the ground. A pouch like the mobs leave in fourth age when you wait too long to loot them. Nice! That is basically the best sign anyone could want.

"Thanks, God! Love you, buddy! I won't ask you to help with my back but it would be awesome if it hurt less somehow. And you should work on being nicer and less of a jerk. Have a good day!"

I go over and open the pouch. I get a pair of boots, a ring, and a survival kit that are all unidentified. I also get 10 each of red, green, yellow, and grey coins – the ones you need for the awesome stuff in the store. All that stuff costs way more coins than what I got, but finally getting some is nice. Means I'm on track. I also get one snake eye, four leather scraps, one poisoned giant fang, three gold, three silvers, and one copper.

The pain in my back dampens my excitement. The loot makes me encumbered. The boots only weigh one lbs., but the giant snake fang weighs five lbs. Jeez. My mind isn't in shape to do math so I drop my armor and spear and lose the medium load debuff, and I head down to the store ball thing.

Scrolls of identify cost a crazy amount. 125 gold each. That is nuts. No thank you. In the game the npcs do it for a lot cheaper. A lot cheaper. I forget how much but way less than 125 gold. Doesn't my skill in arcane knowledge help identify? I look through my skills and the info I have available. It seems spellcraft is the one to identify items. Why did those scrolls and potions I got come identified? I know synergies work weird in fourth age. Different than as stated in Black Raven or the SRD. Maybe the checks were just low enough for spellcraft to identify them?

Who knows? Dumb game. 125 gold. That is the craziest thing I ever heard in my life. Do you know how many turd-pigeons and turd-birds I would have to kill to identify one item? Millions. I get like five to nine gold or so clearing the whole dungeon and selling all the crap I get. Well, clearing the whole dungeon besides the boss. 9 x 10 is 90 in ten days. So 35 gold left over. 9 x 4 is 36. Okay. So not a million. But 14 days is a lot. And that is best case getting good loot that sells for the most. It probably really takes three weeks or a month. Especially if you consider all the gold I have to spend on replacing gear and stuff like that.

After selling all my loot from the turd-snake, turd-birds, and turd-pigeons from yesterday – or before I slept at least – I have over 210 gold. Jeez. I would definitely have way, way more if I stopped buying dumb stuff. I started buying a lot of comfort items since I had so much gold. Not the smartest thing to do, but it is fun. And I deserve it. Joey too, but nothing I get him he likes as much as his trays.

I buy an identify scroll. I hold it in my hands and activate it. I get a prompt to select an unidentified item. I open my inventory and select the boots. The word failure scrolls across my screen. NO! What the heck? Why? Why would they do this? 125 gold down the drain! Jeez! Stupid game! I hate this stupid game! Why didn't it warn me or something? What dumb skill do you need to use a level 1 scroll? Stupid, ridiculous game. 125 gold gone like nothing.

Jeez, my back hurts. I go back into the store and go to misc. I look for anything for pain. Nothing besides aspirin. Holy moly I hate this game so much! I look for something for sleep. I see two things. Melatonin and alcohol. My father takes melatonin and I know he takes it to sleep. And when we are sick mom makes us a hot toddy with some crap that tastes like black licorice called anisette that is supposed to help you sleep. I don't see any of that. I buy some rum for 10 silver. I think rum is supposed to taste like coconuts. I hope it does.

I try a sip of the rum and spit it out. It doesn't taste like coconuts at all! It tastes like burning. Yuck.

While at the store I refill my healing kit.

I go back to camp and drink some water from one of the clay jugs. I drink more and hold it in my mouth. Then put in a melatonin, then add a very small amount of the awful garbage people call rum. And then I swallow. I hate pills. The aspirin from earlier did nothing. Not so far at least.

Laying down on either my stomach or back both hurt. I also don't want to get my bedroll stinky and dirty from the puke that has dried all over me so I just grab my old pillow – I bought an expensive new one – and go to the path leading to the store, a little away from camp. I try sleeping propped up against the invisible wall, but the pillow under my back hurts more than not having it there. I try a million things but everything hurts. I go back and get my bedroll. It cost a fraction of what my old pillow cost so who cares? The best I can get is lying the pillow the long way, and having it under my chest as I lay on my stomach. It still hurts more than standing, and breathing hurts every time, but I eventually fall asleep.

Hopefully Joey doesn't wake me up like a real jerk.

Hopefully that was the only giant turd-snake.

1.18 WHAT WE WANT MOST AND USE WORST

KIM GUM

I've been sleeping a lot so it's hard to know how much time has passed. Bored out of my mind. Maybe two weeks? Could be more. It feels like more. My back still really, really hurts and it still clicks when I breathe or touch it or do anything. Just moving is real agony. It always hurts.

I'm guessing it isn't going to get better, and God won't want me sitting on my butt doing nothing when I could be out spreading the word of death or whatever it is he said. Out killing. I just really hope there aren't more giant turd-snakes.

I need to farm up enough gold to make up for the money I lost on the stupid identify scroll. Just thinking about all that wasted gold makes me furious. Idiots! Why would they do that? I don't know why I need to replace the gold, but I have to. Probably just to make myself feel better and forget I wasted so much. I also need to restart the turd-bird thing I was doing. When I can hit five in a row flying at me and make up the 125g, I'll fight the boss.

I finish up selling everything from the last leg of the dungeon clear. Almost 3g. Not too shabby. Almost 8g for the day. Not a record, but not bad at all.

I don't want to but I go to the clothing tab. I got an entertainer's outfit not too long ago. It cost 3g, but was worth every cent. I dance around and have tea parties in it. Pretend I'm a fancy noble and speak all fancy like a princess. I want a real dress though. I'm hoping the noble's outfit is a nice, fancy dress. But it costs 75g. That is absolutely nuts. Way too expensive. I can't get it. Such a waste of gold.

"Get it, dummy. You deserve it."

I look around, hoping Joey actually talked for real. I don't see him. So he only talked in my head. Dagnab it. One day he'll slip and talk in front of me.

I try to stop myself from thinking any thoughts about how it isn't Joey that's talking. Talking in my head. He talks less when I think those thoughts. I know Joey can't talk. I know it in my heart. He can't talk in real life or my head.

But he does, and I don't want it to stop.

I miss talking. Talking for real. To real people in real life. I get real sad and my chest starts hurting. My eyes start watering. I miss my parents so much. I wouldn't even mind Carlos picking on me if I could just talk to him for a couple minutes. I hate this place so much. My character sheet hasn't changed one bit since I've been in here. What am I doing wrong? Why can't I level up?

I wish I understood this contest. Even if I beat the boss, then what? I level up? Get to see or join other people? What if I can't? What if I can never talk to anybody ever again?

What is the reason for this? Why would aliens do this to us? It doesn't make any sense. If you beat the whole contest, what do you win?

Before I start crying harder I clamp down on my mind. This doesn't help me. It doesn't help Joey either. I'm the darkness. I know that for certain. I'm here. I know that too. I have to beat the boss to get me and Joey out of here. I know that.

Nothing to it. I keep fighting. Keep grinding. Keep improving, even if it doesn't show on my character sheet. I get knocked down, I get up and keep going. All I can do. Being sad doesn't help with that.

Asking the big questions doesn't help. Buying a nobles' outfit doesn't help.

Actually, buying a noble's outfit could help. If it's a dress. I wish I could figure out how to get game outfits on Joey. That would be awesome! It's a ton of money down the drain, but easy come, easy go. I hit the buy button on the noble's outfit, then confirm. I start putting all my armor in my inventory. I'm more excited than I should be. I hope this is a dress.

Finally my armor's off, and the 30 second timer starts to equip the noble's outfit.

I wait impatiently. Excitedly. It takes forever. YES! It's a dress! And it's beautiful!

"No it isn't," I hear Joey say in my head.

"Yes it is! We are going to have so much fun. Ta ta, Joey," I say in my fancy voice. "I'll see you very soon for a tea party and dancing, my good sir.

There is one part of the dungeon, where if I grab a branch and pull myself up on it, I think I can see the sun through the trees. Just a little. There is something bright. It could definitely be the sun. If it was a big fire I think there would be smoke. What else could it be? Weird. Getting up on the branch is super painful because of my clicking injury.

I've made up the money a while ago. And killed way more than five turd-birds the challenging way. Way more turd-birds than you could shake a stick at. I was thinking my back was getting better, so have been holding off on taking out the king-turd for now. But it isn't getting better. Not really. I think I'm just getting used to it. I'm really tired. It is hard to sleep good with this dumb clicking thing on my back.

Breathing still hurts, but I am getting better at moving and fighting in ways that don't aggravate it too much. I haven't seen another giant turd-snake. Just turd-pigeons and turd-birds like before.

Me and Joey haven't been able to think of a better name for the treest. But treest is not good. Better than forest? Sure. But still not good. Nothing I can do about that until one of us has a better idea.

God hasn't appeared to me again yet. I think he is happy with all the killing I've been doing. I'd like it a lot more if my back would heal. Maybe he will appear to me once I murder king-turd and pee on its face. I hope so. Who knows though?

I haven't been stealthing much. I forgot one day and just walked into the intersection and started walking towards the respawned turd-pigeons to the west. I didn't even notice till they started rushing me. Joey said in my head, "Charge, dummy!" And I did. That was a good idea for Joey. He usually only has bad ideas.

Even in the big room north of the boss room that has three turd-pigeons and three turd-birds I just charge at one of the mobs and fight them all at the same time. I used to shoot them with my bow and pick off one, run and reset them, and repeat that until there was only one or two turd-pigeons left. Maybe a turd-pigeon and a couple turd-birds at most. Now I just charge in, tell them who I am, and stomp their filthy faces into the ground.

I've lost more weight. I don't think there is any fat on my body anymore. But I still look fat. Or tubby. My face is weird. My face is still kind of fat, but I always thought I would look less like a frog if I lost a lot of weight. But I am still very froggy. I think it's my chin. Or lack of one. And I have a wide mouth. And a wide neck. It isn't a fat neck, but wide. And a little puffy under my chin. A good amount of puffy, really. Too puffy.

Oh well. I'll never win a beauty contest, but I'd like to see the women who do try to be the darkness. Ha! They would cry like little babies I bet. Little, soft, weak, pretty babies.

I decided I'll fight the boss tomorrow. Joey agrees.

1.19 BOSS MODE

KIM GUM

This boss is so dumb! I started out trying to pick off the turd-birds. But when I run away the boss resets along with any turd-birds I've killed. They just respawn like I never even killed them already.

I can't down the boss with my bow either. I've tried a bunch. I've gotten three damage icons before I've had to run to reset, and all that did was make the boss stop and enter like a berserk mode or something. And there aren't two turd-birds. There are four. One in each corner. I've only just seen the two before, but I never actually went in the room or attacked the boss before today.

I think you get locked in the room if you fight in there. Outside the room to the east is just a grass road. The fight resets if I try to run the mobs to the big room to the north I cleared. I'm going to need room to maneuver, so I have to fight in the boss room. I may get locked in. At least that is how the boss fights in fourth age work. You get locked in the room with the boss.

I have a couple ideas. One – I could take out a turd-pigeon from range, and at least take the HP shield of another turd-pigeon with my bow, then go shield and spear and work my way back into the room so I can maneuver. Two – I could use my first shot on the turd-king so he gets the sneak attack damage, then take the shields of at least one, but maybe two, turd-pigeons before going shield and spear. Three – I could sneak behind the turd-king, start with shield and spear, and take out the turd-birds with thrusts or shield blocks and stomps to their filthy turd-bird heads as I fight the boss.

I can reset on the first two plans. I'll probably be locked in on the third one without any chance to run and reset. If my spear attack misses and I blow my sneak attack it would be really hard to get away and reset even if I don't get locked in. I haven't really seen what the turd-king can do melee-wise. I'm hoping he fights like the usual turd-pigeons, but is just bigger and tougher. I'm not sure what the berserker mode does. I couldn't watch long, he just stood still while radiating red. Then I had to start running to reset.

The second option is probably the smartest way to do it. But I know in my gut what I should do, being the darkness and all. Eh, why not? You only live once. And the price for losing is no more pain. Not a bad deal.

"What about me?" Joey says in my head.

"Oh, come on. I was kidding."

"No you weren't. Remember, good mothers don't abandon their kids. You're a good mother, right?"

"You're right. You're right. I'll go for plan two. That is the best plan. Okay?"

"No. I'm for plan three all the way. Just don't die, dummy."

"What did I say about calling me that? I'm way smarter than you. You're low-functioning and non-verbal. Who are you to talk?"

"That's really mean. Why would you say that to me?"

"You're right again. I'm sorry, Joey. But you called me a dummy first."

"Stop being a dummy then, dummy!"

"Holy moly I will…just stop. No more calling me a dummy. Remember, we don't say mean things to each other. We respect each other. Got it, mister?"

"Yes."

"Yes, what?"

"Yes, mommy."

"That's better. I love you, Joey. You're a good boy."

I feel like he is still calling me dummy, but all secretive-like. Filthy ingrate. What can I do though? If I bring it up he will say I'm being crazy.

Okay, well plan three it is. I get a little nervous and scared but squash it immediately. I hit stealth, equip my melee stuff, go around the door, and pray I don't get detected before I can attack. I make it behind the turd-king. He is way bigger than he looks from blocks away.

Phew. I made it. Turd-king starts looking from side to side like he notices something so I attack immediately before I'm kicked out of stealth.

I get a piercing icon and sneak attack icon. Nice! I attack again immediately as I scream out who I am and the turd-king starts turning towards me. Then I have four turd-birds darting at me. I block the one coming at my left, and spear the one coming at my right, and then switch immediately to block the other two coming from the far corners. Tink, shift, then tink. All four turd-birds are on the ground. Before I can start a' stomping the turd-king takes a swipe at me with one of his massive front arms. Forepaws? Forearms?

This is new. It's like a lion fighting. I don't think dogs use their paws in a fight like the turd-king is doing. The regular turd-pigeons don't do that. I barely get my shield in front of it in time, and I'm not braced. The blow has some real power behind it so I go stumbling back but manage to keep me feet. With regular turd-pigeons, if you can control their head with your shield, you can stab away at them while being pretty safe. This changes things. Stupid turd-king.

I jump forward and thrust at the turd-king's dumb face. I try to land on one of the turd-birds to take it out before it recovers, but the turd-king swipes at my right while I'm in the air. I can't block so I stab his arm and get pushed back and aside. I do see the damage icon though. Ha! As I get up I stab a nearby turd-bird as it starts to recover. The turd-king is jumping towards me so I tumble away while I'm still out of engagement range. I need some space to block the other turd-birds anyway. They're all recovering and will soon start darting at me again.

I roll max distance, and my back flares in pain as I roll on the clicking injury. Suck it up, lady! No time for bellyaching. I'm on my feet and turning when I see another surprise. The turd-king can charge. A game charge, like players can. None of the turd-pigeons ever charged. Not even the snake charged. Maybe what the turd-birds do is charging too, maybe more like darting, but I never expected it from a large turd-pigeon. Well, there goes my HP shield probably. There is no blocking or dodging ghost-arm free attacks.

He gets to me and his ghost-arm flies towards my chest. Ha, ha! The ghost arm didn't beat my AC. What a loser! Stupid turd-king idiot. As I think this a turd-bird whacks into my head. I swipe it off so it can't start pecking, and I look at my health bar. It didn't do much damage. I have 7 or 8 HPs left.

I stomp on it and feel a satisfying crush. I want to tell it who I am but the other two are flying at me and the turd-king is taking another power-swipe at me too. I dodge left, putting the turd-king between me and the incoming turd-birds at the last second, and thrust. I see a piercing icon. I don't see the turd-birds so the turd-king's body can block them. I smile. Nice!

I stop smiling as I see the turd-king start growling, glowing red, and shaking. It looks like there are three turd-kings blinking in and out of existence. Or like he is shaking so fast it looks like he is three blurry turd-kings. I take a couple steps back, but not far enough to lose engagement with the turd-king so he doesn't get an attack of opportunity. I take a swipe and my spear shakes when it hits something before getting to the turd-king. Like an invisible shield. Not the HP shield. Something else.

Oh yeah – bosses and some mobs get some sort of damage immunity when they do some things. Players can get them too. I forget what they're called. Some kind of frame.

The turd-king stretches his front paws forward and howls really loud. I see a bazillion turd-birds appear out of nowhere and swoop down over-the turd-king and fly at me. Slower than usual. I dive down on the ground, and wince from the extreme pain that radiates through my back from my clicking injury. I jump to my feet and twist around to look back and see what happened to the turd-birds. They just disappear. Must have been some sort of special attack.

Something hits my back. Something small, not the turd-king. Must be a turd-bird. I go to swipe it with my spear over my shoulder, and then feel pecking right near my clicking area. The pain is horrible. Stupid turd-birds! I will kill them all repeatedly. Ew, these things are just begging to get peed on. The pain means my HP shield is gone now though; I wouldn't have felt any of its pecks if I had any HPs left at all. Mother…ew. I manage to hit it off with my spear. As I go to stomp I see the turd-king swiping. He makes a million attacks in a row, and I barely manage to block the other turd-bird attack, never mind stomp it after it fell to the ground.

For what feels like a million hours I just dodge the turd-king's wild attacks while blocking the occasional recovered turd-bird. I finally get a stomp in on one. But there is still another one. Another one I look forward to stomping. I get two hits on the turd king, but neither damage. The damage immunity thing is gone. Hopefully it stays gone. Finally, as I start sucking air hard and waning pretty fast, the turd-king goes back to normal.

I get a hit in as I evade a swipe, but still no damage icon. He is much easier to fight out of berserker mode so I should get more hits in now. The turd-king starts a swipe at me as I see the last turd bird darting in. I dodge the paw and block the bird. I stomp it. I stomp it again. I go to stomp a third time but have to dodge a swipe. I thrust towards the turd-king's face as I do. No icon. I'm on his side and get two easy thrusts in. This should be much easier without turd-birds now. I'm still sucking air but breathing a little easier. Besides the clicking that always hurts when I breathe.

I start getting a lot more hits in. I got this. No way I lose now. As soon as I have this thought I see the piercing icon from my thrust, and the turd-king starts berserker mode again. Jeez. Karma must be real. I back up a little again, he stretches forward and growls, and I dive to my belly again just to be safe. I don't look back this time, keeping my eye out for any surprise turd-bird attacks. Better to be safe than sorry. I take a couple deep breathes to prepare for the onslaught I know is coming. I give him a hard thrust from my spear but it's stopped by that stupid invisible frame shield. Just like last time.

Then the barrage of attacks starts and I start dodging while trying to control my breathing. It isn't as rough this time without the turd-birds to worry about, but I start a lot more out of breath than the first time. I keep getting hits in and finally my spear starts entering his flesh. His HPs are gone. I am now actually damaging him with every hit. The berserk mode fades with his HP shield and I'm sucking air real hard. Spent. Thankfully no HP shield means no more berserk mode. I hope. Or I'm real screwed.

I jump at him and give him a good spearing, and he starts laying down.

What the heck?

Did I win? I don't think I damaged him enough, but maybe his berserker mode makes him handle being damaged better and it finally caught up to him when it ended? I look at him for a couple seconds. And to be safe and sure I go to spear his dumb face. Quick as lightning he jumps up and bites my spear arm. My spear itself saves me from a worse injury. His teeth go deep on top of my forearm, but only one of his teeth enters my wrist. The rest go into my spear. I jerk out of it and stab like mad at him before he can recover.

I get good, deep hits in. Hits that sink in far. He whines like a little baby.

Even when I'm certain he's dead I keep stabbing. My grip starts sliding. The blood from my wound. No problem. I'm completely out of breath anyways.

I loot the boss as I suck in air. Only 8 silver and 7 bronze for coins. A basic beast hide too. Those sell for way more than the ruined ones. Some other junk only good for selling. Nothing good. No unidentified items. What the heck? Bosses should have great loot. Not just a little cash and vendor fodder. What a rip off.

I check out my arm. Not good, but not too bad either. The pain isn't horrible. I'll take a wound like this over the clicking back thing every day of the week and twice on Sundays. I think I need stitches though. Two holes on top and one on the wrist are bleeding a ton. The one on the wrist wouldn't have been bad if I didn't jerk my arm out of his mouth. I didn't really have a choice though, did I?

At the same time I start looting the four turd-birds I notice a big, open door on the west side of the room that wasn't there before. Nice! Must be the door out! As I go to pee on the turd-king's dumb face I also see a chest that wasn't there before. I finish my business with the turd-king, while pulling up my pants, I turn and tell him, "Nice try, sucker, but I'm the darkness."

I open the chest and get an unidentified healing kit, and the usual chest crap. A flare scroll and two potions of cure minor wounds. I get the medium load debuff. Stupid debuff. I use my heal kit on myself and get 2 HP back. Stupid healing kit. It give me 3 HPs once in a while, but doesn't like to. I think about drinking a healing potion but they vendor for too much to waste on me. Nothing in this dungeon is dangerous to me now, so I don't need to use it anyways. Well, unless a giant turd-snake shows up. Now that thing was dangerous. Stupid poison.

I start heading back to camp and Joey. I can't help but feel like a real badass. Even with blood dripping from my hand onto the ground. Maybe even more so since blood is dripping from my hand onto the ground. I did it! I beat the dungeon!

It would've been nice if I didn't get injured though. Or more injured. Hopefully I can level up outside that door. Or figure out how to level up. At least I get to leave this dumb treest soon.

I finally get back to camp and excitedly tell Joey we can leave! That I did it. We won. He just shakes his trays and doesn't even look at me. I go over and we do the jump-laugh thing and it gets him excited, happy, and laughing. That's the response I wanted. I'm a hero! I saved the day!

I get the first aid kit and start stitching. I've had to stitch myself up a bunch of times. Big wounds heal way faster if you stitch them up, and you don't got to be so careful with your movements or worry about them opening again and again. After cleaning the wounds, I use some tape and get going with the needle and thread. It hurts. Not bad. It's more the anticipation. In movies and vids they have tough guys getting stitched going, "Do-do-do-do-do. Just another day. I feel nothing. No big deal." But those are actors, acting. In real life it hurts. To me at least. And it's very hard to do it one handed. It helps to tape it just right. I only stitch the main three holes. The rest should be okay with just tape. I hope. I wrap bandages from my wrist to mid-forearm.

Now I can move on to better things.

I take a short rest to use my repair kit. I go and sell all the new loot besides the unidentified healing kit and refill my kit's charges. And then go back to camp to see what I need to pack, what I can sell, and what we'll have to leave. I can't take the chair, and it will probably only vendor for one gold. What a rip off. All the one copper stuff we can replace cheaply – it all vendors for zero so I'm just going to leave it all. I feel bad leaving a mess but all this trash is nothing compared to the bathroom corner anyways.

I sell everything else we can't take. I think about taking a bath but I don't want to give the mobs a chance to respawn. I just want out now. I know I stink real bad, but oh well.

When everything is as all set as I can get it, I bring Joey to the intersection and drop some items. I'll get them on the way back. No sense being overloaded for a side trip. We head west, and then south to where our family is buried. I had to bury them a long time ago, they started to stink real bad and look real weird. Mom always looked real bad, but Carlos and dad looked kind of normal – until they didn't.

I don't think Joey understands what's going on. He is just shaking trays as usual. Seems like he's in a mood.

"Mom, dad, Carlos. I did it. I won. I'm taking Joey and we're getting out of here. Sorry we can't bring you with us. I'm hoping there's people on the other side of that door, so we can't do nothing weird like that. I hope you guys are enjoying heaven. I know I told you before, but I'm the one who got you all in there, even though you're atheists. You're welcome. I saved Joey too. I won. I'm not useless. I'm the darkness.

"I'll really miss you guys. I mean…I miss you now, but I won't be able to visit after we leave. I'm taking real good care of Joey so don't you worry. I love you guys. You too Carlos. Have a good day! Bye!"

My stomach starts feeling heavy and I get a sinking feeling. This doesn't feel right.

I bring Joey back to the intersection and load up again. I have a heavy load and look through my inventory to see if there is something I can get rid of to go down to medium load. I take out both bedrolls, since they are light and easy to carry and try to get Joey to hold them. Still at heavy. He makes it clear he is bringing some trays and only some trays.

"Thanks for all the help, Joey."

He is shaking trays and making noises and not even looking at me. In my head I hear him say, "No problem, dummy."

I let it go. I know he didn't really say it so no point in arguing with him. We can revisit that comment depending on what's through the door. And it'll take a while to get there since I have the heavy load debuff carrying all this crap. I inventory the bedrolls. The feeling inside gets worse.

I grab Joey's hand and he yells and moves away, all frustrated. He gets like this sometimes. Where touching him is a real bad idea and just makes things worse. These are the times he usually gets restrained. One time he bit someone. I always thought it's better not to push when he gets like this. Just leave him alone and let it pass. But we're on the clock. Sometimes the respawns happen faster. I don't know when they last respawned. Better to be safe, especially when I got Joey with me outside the safe field. And I don't want to fight the boss again.

I don't know why but I start crying. It hurts inside. I won and no one cares. I did it. Something, someone should be excited. I did it. I know I'm not really an adult woman yet. I'm just a little kid. But I did it. This dungeon killed mom, and dad, and Carlos. But not me. It didn't get me. And I saved Joey. Something should've happened. Someone should care.

I stop crying and suck it up. No one cares and no one's going to. I hold my hand out and hope Joey follows without much issue. We head toward the exit door. To the unknown. Toward victory.

2.1 INFO FROM THE FUTURE

BRUNO VAZ

PART 2 "CONJECT"

"I thank whatever gods may be
For my unconquerable soul."
- William Earnest Henley

Bruno Vaz Character Sheet

Base (Ability Modifier) ((Misc.)) [Total]

CLASSES: 1 Rogue

RACE: Stout Dwarf - Alignment: Chaotic Good - Deity: Catholic

HP: 2 (4) ((5 Special Feat, 3 Toughness)) [14]

AC: 10 (2) ((3 Studded Leather, 1 Light Shield)) [16]

BAB: 0

Land Speed: *

ABILITIES

Str: 16 (3) ((0)) [16]

Dex 14 (2) ((0)) [14]

Con: 18 (4) ((0)) [18]

Int: 14 (2) ((0)) [14]

Wis: 8 (-1) ((0)) [8]

Cha: 6 (-2) ((0)) [6]

SAVES

Fortitude: 0 (4) ((0)) [4]

Reflex: 2 (2) ((1 Full of Beans)) [5]

Will: 0 (-1) ((0)) [-1]

COMBAT MODE: Free Attack/Auto Attack/Game Mode

MAIN HAND

Short Sword

AB: 0 (3) ((0)) [3]

DAM: 1d6 (3) ((0)) Extra Damage=0 [4-9 Slashing], C 19-20, CM x2

OFF HAND

NA

OTHER ATTACKS (Bites, etc.)

NA

OTHER

Spell Failure: 20%

Max Dex Bonus: 5 Studded Leather [5]

Armor Check Penalty: -1 Studded Leather, -1 Light Shield [-2]

HOBBIES, CRAFTS, and PROFESSIONS

Hobby: Tinker level 3 (Maximum skill level of Hobbies is character level plus feats and racial and class features. No Ability mod for Hobbies. No experience needed to level Hobbies. +2 Knowledge (Dwarven Crafting))

Crafts: NA

Professions: Porter level 0 (Increases Carry Capacity by 1 + (Porter level x 3). Maximum level is class level of the class used to open the Profession. If multiclassing, a Profession can be selected twice or more and class levels can be combined to increase maximum Profession level. Unlike Hobbies, both Crafts and Profession require experience to level up)

SKILLS

40 at level 1

Italics cross class skill

*Armor Check Penalty applies

(Falls under above group skill)

Acrobatics* (Dex) 4 (2) ((ACP -2)) [4]

131

(Escape)*

(Tumble)* (10 base points in Acrobatics with Tumble selected and opened gives a +1 bonus to AC. 20 base points gives another +1 bonus, for a total of +2 bonus to AC. This counts as a skill bonus and stacks with everything.)

(Use Rope)*

Athletics* (Str) 4 (3) ((ACP -2)) [5]

(Grapple)*

(Jump)*

(Run)* (Con) 4 (4) ((ACP -2)) [6] (10 base points in Athletics with Run selected and opened gives a +5 land speed bonus. 20 base points gives another +5 for +10 total land speed increase. This counts as a skill bonus and stacks with everything. This translates into a 7.5% speed increase at 10 and 20, 15% total.)

Disable Device (Int) 4 (2) ((0)) [6]

Heal (Wis) 2 (-1) ((0)) [1]

Knowledge (Int) 4 (2) ((0)) [6]

(Arcane) 2 [4]

(Dungeoneering)

(Geography) 2 [4]

Open Lock (Dex) 4 (2) ((0)) [6]

Search (Int) 4 (2) ((0)) [6]

Spellcraft (Int) 2 (2) ((0)) [4] 10 base points in Spellcraft gives a +1 bonus to all saves. 20 base points gives another +1, for a total of +2 bonus to all saves. Stacks with everything.)

Use Magic Device (Cha) 4 (-2) ((0)) [2]

Skill Points carried over to next level: 5 (4 refunded and extra 1 applied)

FEATS

* are selected feats or options

Level 1 (Rogue 1)

Destined for Greatness (Free feat given to all players of End of the Fourth Age that reads as follows: You were born under an auspicious sign and have a greater destiny than most born in Benekal or even all of Tibur. You receive +5 Hit Points at level 1)

Charge (Same as SRD, Charges take three seconds regardless of distance in End of the Fourth Age. In new world, distance has been normalized to 60 feet for all players since there is no land speed)

Armor Proficiency [Light]

Shield Proficiency [Buckler]

Shield Proficiency [Light]

Weapon Proficiency [Dwarven Waraxe] (Dwarves may treat dwarven waraxes as martial weapons, rather than exotic weapons)

Weapon Proficiency [Simple]

Weapon Proficiency [Rogue]

Battle Training (Giants) (+4 dodge bonus to Armor Class against monsters of the giant type. Any time a creature loses its Dexterity bonus (if any) to Armor Class, such as when it's caught flat-footed, it loses its dodge bonus, too)

Battle Training (Orcs & Goblinoids) (+1 racial bonus on attack rolls against orcs and goblinoids)

Darkvision (See in the dark up to 60 feet. Darkvision is black and white only, but it is otherwise like normal sight, and character can function just fine with no light at all)

Hardiness (Poisons) (+2 racial bonus on saving throws against poison. First Racial Specialization gives an additional +1 on saving throws against poisons (total +3), and also increases saves against disease by +3. Second Racial Specialization gives an additional +1 on saving throws against poisons (total +4), and also increases saves against disease and death effects by +3. Third Racial Specialization grants immunity to poison)

Hardiness (Spells) (+2 racial bonus on saving throws against spells and spell-like effects. First Racial Specialization gives an additional +1 on saving throws against spells and spell-like effects (total +3). Second Racial Specialization gives an additional +1 on saving throws against spells and spell-like effects (total +4). Third Racial Specialization gives Spell Resistance equal to 5 + character level)

Stonecunning (+2 to Search checks indoors. Automatic Search checks indoors every six seconds with a radius of 10 feet. First Racial Specialization changes this to all environments, and increases the radius to 15 feet. Second Racial Specialization gives an additional +2 to Search checks and increases radius to 30 feet. Third Racial Specialization gives two Search checks per six seconds, automatic success to any check with a DC of 40 or less, an alarm function if something is found, and the DC of Sense Magic checks is reduced from 60 to 55)

Knowledge (Appraise) (+2 Appraise checks)

Knowledge (Dwarven Crafting) (+2 to Architect, Blacksmith, Engineer, Gemologist, Jeweler, Miner, Smelter, Tinker, and Trapsmith)

Slow & Steady (Dwarves start at land speed 20, but armor or load do not reduce a dwarf's speed. Translates to -15% speed for race, but no penalty to speed for armor or load debuffs. First Racial Specialization gives -1 Armor Check Penalty to all armors worn. Second Racial Specialization increases Maximum Dex Bonus of all armors worn by 1. Third Racial Specialization increases Dex by 2)

Stability (+4 bonus on Ability checks made to resist being bull rushed or tripped)

Dwarven Languages

Trapfinding

Sneak Attack (1D6)

*Background – Sharp as a Tack (Instead of 2 skill points to raise cross-class skills, only 1 is needed. +1 skill point per level. Retroactively refunded or added and can't be used during character creation.)

*Toughness (3 HPs when taken, and another HP on non-prime number levels up to level 20 for a total of 15 additional HPs. One specialization point increases HPs gained through the Toughness feat by 50%. Two specialization points increases HPs gained through the Toughness feat by 50% more, 100% in total)

*Specialization Point used – Diverse Upbringing (Allows a second Background to be selected) – Full of Beans (+10 land speed. Translates to 15% speed increase. +1 Reflex saves)

ITEMS

Studded Leather Armor

Short Sword

Dagger

Light Crossbow

Light Wooden Shield

Healing kit (Takes 1 Round (6 seconds) to complete. No benefit if interrupted. Heals 1d2 + Heal skill + enhancement bonus hit points. Check for stabilization, poison, disease, treat wounds. Can be used once on self, and once on other individuals between combats. Maximum charges that can be held in the inventory are 1 + (enhancement bonus x2). Maximum enhancement bonus for all kits are +6. Cannot specialize in the Healing skill)

Repair kit (Takes 1 Turn (60 seconds) to complete. No benefit if interrupted. Repairs weapons and armor by a total of 1 + skill level points divided by the number of damaged pieces. Priority is set by user. Maximum durability repaired on a single item is 2 + enhancement bonus of kit. Can only be used once between combats on own equipped gear)

Cartography kit (Allowed with Knowledge: Geography. The Geography skill opens up the minimap function in outdoor terrains and improves both map and minimap with higher skill. Specializing in Geography highlights detected enemies on the minimap, adds icons for events, and gives +2 synergy bonus to both spot and search checks outdoors)

Survey kit (Allowed with Knowledge: Dungeoneering. The Dungeoneering skill allows dungeon mapping, opens the minimap function in indoor terrains, and expands the range and scope of both the map and minimap with higher skill. Specializing in Dungeoneering opens the assess enemy function, adds icons for unhidden treasure chests in range, and gives +2 synergy bonus to both spot and search checks indoors)

Thieves' tools

Writing all those emails gave me a wicked bad headache. I slept like absolute garbage. And I still got the headache. I never really sleep good, but I barely slept at all. Man, I shouldn't be this nervous. Taking control of the government is freaking me out. I don't want to be in charge. I hate this so much. I shouldn't have come back. Sidis should've come back. Or we should have used the resurrection wishes. We could have brought five people back to life. I don't think sending me back was a good idea.

I had a real hard time controlling my thoughts while I was trying to get to sleep. That always happens, but it's usually bad memories I try not to think about. This time it was just plain useless nonsense. Natural logs and the e function. I think natural logs is some hidden formula that repeats all the time in nature, like the pattern on a pineapple. And the e function is something that makes things bigger and smaller at the same time, like in compounding interest formulas. I have no idea how I know what either of those things are, or why I keep thinking of them. They got nothing to do with nothing. I guess my brain is inventing new ways to screw me out of sleep.

No sense trying to sleep more, it ain't going to happen. I groan as I start getting up. Old age is a bitch.

I don't feel good about the emails I wrote. I know I missed important stuff, and I don't think a lot of it makes sense. Today is going to stink. "Hello everybody! I'm from the future and I'm in charge of you!" I'm not even going to try and explain my real situation. It confuses me, never mind trying to explain it to the monkeys. I'm not good at explaining. I'm good at doing. Not thinking. Not blabbing. But the actual act of getting things done. Winning. That's what I do. And I do it fantastic. Or fantastically. Is that a word? I do it fantastically. That sounds dumb, and things that sound dumb are usually right.

I think I have some fungus growing on my balls. They itch all the time now. It's driving me wicked nuts. I'm horny too.

Stop. You're always horny. Focus, dummy. What do you got to get done?

First I got to shave. First? Maybe hold off because I should read through the emails and fix stuff and see if I remember more stuff. I tried not to write anything the monkeys will be offended by, but I should double check. Nah. Who am I kidding? I'm done with reading and writing for a while. That was just too much. Now is the time for doing. Plan. Shave. Double check everything. Well, besides the emails. Double check gear, and get in the right mindset. The right attitude.

The plan – I exit the tutorial, send the emails off to everyone, beam to the city, take control, find my family, make-nice, and talk and explain and all that stuff. Portal back, hope no one yaps at me too much, and then start phase 2. Should I think about what to tell my whore ex and the kids? Nah. I'll just wing it. I shouldn't try and bang either, but I'm horny so I'm going to. She hasn't corrupted her vagina yet so there is no reason not to. It will help me relax and deal with all the jive ass turkeys. She probably won't like it though. She only likes it when I put effort in and actually try. And I still hate her too much to do that. Plus, I got a world to save. Not a world, just the humans from it. Whatever.

Beaming. Everyone calls it porting. And portals. But a portal is something you see and walk towards. At least in my mind. The pillars in area 10, 20, the epic zone, and the city – those are portals. The achievement gives you a beam, like from Star Trek. You don't slowly phase out like on the show, it just takes some time to cast and you disappear. But it seems it should be called beaming to me, and not porting. These dorks just name everything wrong. You can actually portal from the city back to area 1, but there is no portal from area 1 back to the city. I should have put that in the email. Nah, they'll figure it out quick once it matters.

The first person in the city gets to take control of the government. Or, the first person with a class. The wish machine thing said my family and the others spawning in the city won't have classes. They can get crafter classes in the city, but you have to specifically go and get them from the class thing. I should get to the city soon after they spawn, so it shouldn't be an issue. And even if they surprise me and grab a class and take control before I get there, I don't think that will mess nothing up. Unless it's Vlad's wife – she can be wicked annoying to deal with.

I hope shaving doesn't give me too many bumps. I can have my son cut my hair. Minnie will offer, but my son is better. His hair isn't like mine, but he has to be careful about in-grown hairs too. Plus, Minnie takes a wicked, wicked long time to cut hair. Or do any sort of grooming. Nate is way faster.

Damn. Goddamn it. I can't just ignore the emails. I have to double-check them, don't I? Yeah. Well, if you got to do it, let's get it out of the way.

"EMAIL 1 INTRO AND INSTRUCTIONS

Hello everyone.

First off DO NOT SPEND ANY DUNGEON COINS YET. AT ALL. I will explain why later. I know you can't afford anything now, I just want the first thing I say to emphasize what a big deal this is.

My name is Bruno Vaz. I'm from the future. Kind of. I've done this before. This is my second time doing this. I was in my timeline for

3 to 5 years or so. It is hard to tell since years are different here, and time stops in dungeons. My team and I found a wish machine. We couldn't wish to just win or advance more, and we hit a pretty big wall on being able to advance in the raids, so it was decided to send me back to the beginning to save humanity.

Why me? Because I'm the best fighter there is. I'm not the smartest, or the best leader, or even liked much. There is a guy that may be better than me at fighting, but I doubt it. He always ranked second under me, but people think he did that on purpose and could have beaten me if he wanted to. He is wicked smart, and no one knows his real name, but we called him Sidis for some reason. Sidis could be a girl, but I doubt that. No one has seen his face, or even knows where he comes from. He would send info to smart people about things they got wrong, or help them with smart stuff. Things like that. I'm hoping he will be more helpful this time, and take a more active role in helping to point humanity in the right direction to win.

After me and Sidis, the closest people to us were distant thirds. No one came close. Sidis is the one who led my team to the wish machine thing. I don't know why he didn't use it himself. He is a weird guy. In my timeline we lost our best fighters at dungeon area 10. Other than me and Sidis that is. I'm going to make sure that doesn't happen this time, so we have way more people close to us in fighting ability to help us progress and win. This means I am taking control of the city and making some rules.

The first thing I am going to do is block the level 1 Dungeon. A lot of people that survived the tutorial dungeon got carried or got lucky. Humanity needs to train and get stronger. Especially the pod people. And the fats and the olds. The pod people just need time to build their muscles and stamina back up. I don't know why people would choose to live in the internet, but that chicken has come home to roost.

How long will the level 1 dungeon be locked? Until everyone gets SS on the tutorial dungeon. SS is the square. When everyone has SS we will move on to dungeon 1, and I'll lock the first dungeon in area 2 until all SS again. Rinse and repeat.

In these emails I have included tons of builds that work for solo through five man groups. I forgot some about magic users, but I will hit the gist of it if not the specifics. This is very important: everyone likes to talk about min-maxing. What min-maxing means now, regardless of what you say or think, is minimize death and losing, and maximize living and winning. Your low constitution builds don't work. I don't care how good you think you are. 14 Con is minimum for all builds for everyone to start. Not at 30. To start. During character generation. It took a lot of people dying in my original timeline to figure these builds out. They work. This isn't the video game. This is different. Things work different. Don't be dumb and think your low con build is so amazing you can get by with 10 Con. It will get you killed. You can't kill faster or do higher damage if you are dead.

Why not use dungeon coins now or at level 5 or level 10 or even level 20? Because you will mess up something or need to reroll for some reason. Don't spend them until you are certain this is your final build. In my timeline me and almost everyone else raiding had almost plain vanilla characters instead of being the powerhouses we could've been. Remember, our groups are short 1 person already compared to the game. I would've killed last time to have a good, proven build that was all buffed out and plused up with all the extra feats and racial stuff and specializations. We could've won. Don't repeat the biggest mistake we all made last timeline. Don't be dumb. Be smart. Make certain.

There are different groups for dungeons and getting dungeon coins. Solo, 2-man, 3-man, 4-man, and 5-man. Each grouping can get circle, oval, and rectangle. Or 1st SS, 2nd SS, and 3rd SS. There are a limited amount of each in total. 100, 200, and 300 respectively (divided by the five groups). The rest can get SS. It isn't too hard to get SS. If you are solo and want to be in a group, or in a group and want to increase the group size, there is only one way to do it, and that is to reroll your character. To change your build in the tutorial dungeon and restart your character all over again. If you want a bigger group, everyone that will be in your group enters the tutorial dungeon at the same time and rerolls. If your group size goes down due to someone leaving or a death of a group member, you can keep progressing through dungeons with your smaller group size.

I highly recommend everyone change their builds, makes some friends with people, and fix their group size. A dungeon opens three times per day. I should explain how time works here. I was told it is from some space game where you colonize a different world. Death Colony? Something like that. This contest or whatever it is took the time system from that game. Just like they took the dogs from the tutorial dungeon from some game I was told is called Sherlock Versus Watson, and they are the hounds of Baskerville. And the toucan birds are from a Mario game. And the dungeon maps are taken from a bunch of games called dungeon crawlers. Wizardry, Odyssey something, Ultimate, Tokyo Zero something or other, Magic Might, Bard's Tail, and others I can't remember. Because I'm not a huge dork and never played them. Most of the mobs (mobs are what the monsters or bad guys are called, I don't know why, just as I don't understand why SS is higher than A), come from other games or the First Age game this contest took most of the rules from. And some from movies too. Some bosses and mobs are original, but most aren't. From what I am told. Again, I'm not a dork so I don't know from firsthand experience. I just know what the dorks tell me.

If it has a nameplate it is from the First Age. If not, it was imported from something else. Besides a couple bosses that are original –

but they have nameplates. A lot of imported mobs are bugged. Damage visuals don't work. Taunts don't work. They don't have the same rules and can attack as much as they want per six second round. Stuff like that. Bugs. Expect anything. Don't ever be complacent, and always maintain situation awareness. Stay alert, stay alive. The biggest threat to survival is the search for comfort and a passive outlook.

Time works different. First off, time stops in dungeons. You enter and exit at pretty much the same time. Outside of dungeons time works different than how it did on earth. I forget exactly how savage time here works, but this will be the gist. Seconds are longer. I forget how long. A minute here is like 86 civilized seconds. An hour is like 72 of the new, savage minutes. Like 104 civilized minutes. The days are 18 savage hours. I think it is like 31 civilized hours. A year is 288 savage days. 10 months of 29 days, besides summer and winter solstice months which are 28 days long. A leap year every 7 years. Or maybe 17? I forget. Oh, it doesn't really get cold here due to time of the year, just zones. Some are cold, most aren't. It just gets a little colder or warmer depending on time of year. And that doesn't mean the dungeons are cold or hot. Those are independent.

So days have three phases here: dawn, day, dusk. Hours 0 to 5:71 is dawn. 6 to 11:71 is day, and 12 to 17:71 is dusk. Oh, this may be important: I was told it is based on a different type of number system. We are used to civilized basic 10. This time uses a savage basic 12. So 72 is actually 60. 12 is really 10. It doesn't make any sense if you have a civilized mind like I do. Don't worry, it is just how day time works. All the other numbers for everything else from First Age works civilized and correct. Game time stuff adheres to civilized minutes exactly like in the First Age. So when a spell says X time, that means earth time. Or however First Age handled it. A day is 240 civilized earth minutes, or 4 hours. A round is 6 seconds. A turn is 10 rounds (60 seconds).

Dungeons open the last half hour of each day phase. So 36 savage minutes or like 52 civilized minutes. Right now it is almost day phase. In 6 savage hours a new phase starts. Or like 10 and a half civilized hours. Then the tutorial dungeon opens again. For 52 minutes. Then again for dusk phase. Then, dungeon 1 opens tomorrow dawn phase, and again for day, and then again for dusk. Then the day after tomorrow one of the two dungeons in dungeon area 2 opens, etc. You see the 3 gems above the dungeon door? That is the opening. During the "open time" for dungeons, all previously opened dungeons open too. So In a week there will be seven open dungeons.

I don't think I am explaining any of this well. I wasn't sent back because I'm good at explaining, so please keep in mind fighting is my thing, not talking, writing, or explaining.

After you clear dungeon 1 and get to dungeon area 2 you can level to 2. Area 2 has 2 dungeons. Area 3 has 3. Area 10 has 10. Area 20 has 20. Once you clear the last level 20 dungeon you enter a giant, open area where all the raids are. And dungeons too. Lots of dungeons and raids. In my timeline we were stuck on the 24(27) mythic raid. We cleared all the 6(30) mythic dungeons, all the heroic+ and epic raids (12+, and 16). So after the mythic raids, we still have all the legendary and transcendental raids (the 36 and 48s). We never even attempted them. We lost too many on the 24(27). We lost so many we would go months before getting a big enough raid group together to give it a try.

Even though I am locking dungeon 1, it will still show as open tomorrow. Just FYI. But no one will be able to enter until I unlock it. That means practice outside the dungeons, and especially INSIDE. Grind, grind, grind. If you are rerolling hand your stuff off to someone and get it back after you exit, which is almost immediately. So

143

stagger entrances, and get to trust people outside of your group. Train. Practice. Get stronger. Learn how to fight and techniques and forms outside, practice them heavily inside.

All my achievements are still open so I have access to the arena. It opens for most people around level 4. I will clear the solo arena up to level 30 or so. Once I finish you should have access to watching the arena from your UI, and can watch me to see how to fight and get some tips. There are 4 arenas. Solo, 2-man, 4-man, and 5-man. Or normal, heroic, epic, and mythic. Some people say the heroic is actually heroic+ difficulty. They all go up to level 300. Clearing them isn't too bad since you can't die, which makes arenas the best place to practice once you open it. And the arena gives a ton of great rewards.

If you die in the dungeons or out here or in the city, you actually die. Some people claim otherwise, but they have zero proof. As far as we know this is reality and real life, so treat it accordingly."

Well, that was long. And boring. And dumb. I had a hard time reading it and understanding it and I wrote it. Nothing offensive I can see though. Good enough for government work.

I'm actually not too sure this is actually reality. I'm not too sure of anything. If I'm being honest, even back on earth I had no idea what the hell was going on most of the time. Not since like '96. I had a pretty good grasp of things up until '96. Then the world just went mad and kept getting madder. I just pretend I know what's going on. It's worked so far. Kind of.

2.2 INFO FROM THE FUTURE II

BRUNO VAZ

Now the next one.

"EMAIL 2 FAMILY, SAFE PLACE, AND WHAT TO KNOW TO PROTECT YOUR WEAK LOVED ONES

My first timeline I had my family with me. My first goal was keeping them safe. This is how you do it. Get strong. Get them strong too if you aren't strong enough to carry them without worry. This is to keep them safe through dungeon 1, which is harder than the tutorial dungeon. Once dungeon 1 is done you get to dungeon area 2 and can level up to 2. In dungeon area 2 there is a door that leads to the city. It takes a while to get there. Like about 50 days, give or take. Every day a new section opens and you can progress like 15 klicks. Not too far even for the old, weak, and the invalids. The monsters that you have to fight have tentacles that cause a wicked lot of pain but don't do any actual damage to you. Your hit point shield does nothing to stop the tentacle pain. There are a lot of them but they are wicked easy to kill if you can put up with the pain. Their bite attacks are bad though. It is easy to keep your family safe, and there will be a lot of you together. I will be fighting them in the arena so you can see how best to fight them. Big groups with a lot of people to fight the tentacle monsters and protect the weak people are best. Everyone in the same instance going to the city definitely want to enter at the same time. Small separate

145

groups will be sent to separate instances of the path and have to progress and clear separately. That isn't a good idea.

At the end of the trek you get to the city. Loren. The same from the game. There are a ton of instances of the city. But all instances have 4 of the cities in it. So each instance is 4 Lorens. And holds up to 4k people. I can kind of control the instances with permissions, so we can have specialized ones. Like one instance for medical and dental, some for kids and schools, etc. For the most part the city is safe. The only threat is other humans. Not monsters. For the most part. In the city you can reroll to one of the crafting classes. Some of them are pretty good for combat too, like Alchemist, Engineer, and Armorsmith. Weaponsmith is okay, but not that great if you plan on advancing through dungeon levels. You can also enter different zones that have crafting materials from the city. They have some mobs but are pretty safe. I think they are called node zones? I forget the exact term. They call crafting materials mats.

Oh, special people. People that are not normal or nuts or specials never lose the big shield they have. Old people and cripples with normal minds that want to fight in dungeons instead of crafting, the stats will help, and also advancing in the arena will help. In each of the 4 arenas at level 50, 100, 150, 200, 250, and 300 you get healing pills. These help with wounds, injuries, and things that make cripple people crippled. It takes about 8 to 10 points to regrow a leg. I don't think they help with mental conditions. Just physical. And not all of them. I don't think. One guy I knew still had diabetes type 1 after taking a bunch of healing pills. Maybe he had enough issues the pills never got to that? It hasn't helped me much with joint pain. Anyway, these pills help make the olds and cripples more useful. But don't waste them on people that are not motivated and will not be a valued crawler if healed.

We all have to focus on saving all of humanity, not saving some olds (that are going to die soon anyways) from some pain. Save the pills for the useful and competent people progressing, so we can win and get out of here."

Not bad. Not great, but not bad. Shorter than the first one, which is good. Nothing offensive either. I had the R word in there but took it out; the future people get furious about that word. When I said it, at least. I got called it all the time by tons of future people and no one seemed to mind when I'm the one called it. It's almost enough to make me not want to save any of these filthy barbarians. I still will, but it makes me kind of not want to.

The future people get mad about everything. Even when I say normal things. Even bland or colorless things, they still get mad. So I stopped paying attention to what they bleat or what sets them off. Because everything sets them off. Why bother trying when the end results are the same? I just avoid the things that really set them off – like saying the R word, or saying that all women are nuts. Women get super crazy when you point out how crazy they are.

"EMAIL 3 STATS AND MECHANICS. WHAT THEY DO?

You've probably noticed that this version of d20 is a lot different than in the game. I've never played the game, but will list major changes and how I know this system to work. The automatic crit for hitting weak points like eyes wasn't included here. Or limb crits, etc. Abilities provide like a bonus or a penalty to you. I'm 6'5, almost 6'6, and very strong and fast. Abilities make me weaker or stronger, or faster or slower. The hard cap on stats is still 30, with the same exact exceptions as in the game. HPs you already probably figured out act as a shield. Even if you have at least 1 HP left, it will block all damage from the next hit or spell or whatever. It won't stop the physics of the attack, but it does make physics all weird. Once the shield is gone you take actual, physical damage. And once the shield is gone, you slowly lose the benefit from the bonuses or penalties of abilities. Not super-fast, but kind of fast. Takes like 10 minutes to lose them all, depending. AC is gone immediately, as well as stuff like that (saves, energy resistance, DR, etc.). But AB is still there and applies to your hits forever, unless you are fighting something that also doesn't have a HP shield, then hitting just works like it always has throughout history. One good thing about losing your HP shield is you lose most debuffs. And non-damaging spells don't work on you. So you can't be stunned or held. But illusions work still. And you can be actually poisoned or diseased. Poison and diseases don't kill you though, they just make you feel wicked sick or weak, and sometimes you'll trip your balls off. It works out of your system pretty fast. Faster if you get back any of your HP shield at all. Even just 1 HP helps a ton. And all the abilities and system stuff come back to full immediately once you get at least 1 HP.

There is an achievements tab, check it out to see what you can do or get from it. Some of them enhance what most people call the NI. The neural implant. It definitely isn't the same neural implant you guys get to use the internet. The scientists say they proved that. That is just what people call it. Some people call it the system. The scientists say the nanites are everywhere in your bodies, and aren't localized anywhere they can find. But regardless, when your HPs hit zero, you stop benefiting from them or it for the most part. You still get ghost arms, and it makes hand-to-hand fighting work better, but AC and stuff like that are gone. Stuff like extra strength from ability bonuses and extra speed start going away but last a little while. The higher, the longer it lasts. You also can't cast spells with no HPs, or use scrolls, or clickies. You can use potions though, and kits, and some clickies work.

Ghost arms are attacks of opportunity by the way. Clickies are the magic items with activated effects. If you are a monk or want to use the grappling rules, they are pretty messed up. Bugged or whatever. My first build was a monk. The speed is great, but all the weird stuff that happens makes it a hassle. It is not recommended, especially if you are solo. But be careful even if you aren't a monk when grappling. If you try to lock a limb, clinch, or just grab a limb to block, the system might decide you are grappling, and then you are teleported to your back with the monster on top of you if you lose the check. Crazy stuff like that. Just avoid binds, especially when you or the enemy has HPs. Also, avoid trip attacks unless your build is based around them. Lots of bugs, but a lot of people say you can get around them all when you finish your build and get good at knowing what to avoid doing. And getting knockdown immunity helps fix a lot of things.

Okay, ability scores. 10 is nothing. No bonuses or anything. Speed is the most complicated so I'll save that for after. The SRD covers all the mechanics side of what abilities do, and none of that has changed, but this is also how they work here in this world. I didn't figure this out, the scientists did. If you disagree with any of this, complain to them, not me.

Strength: every point over 10 is about a 5% increase in strength. At 30 strength your actual strength is doubled. If you are strong like me, this is huge. If you are a weakling, being twice as strong isn't a huge benefit. Weak x 2 is still weak. Get stronger. Work-out. If you are going high strength try and be as strong as possible. Every point under 10 makes you about 5% weaker. If the strongest guy in the world has 8 str, and the weakest person in the world has 30, the strongest guy will still be stronger, but he will always lose against str tests and grappling test and all the game stuff. Does that make sense?

Dexterity: every point above and below 10 makes you 1% faster or slower. Max is 20%. I'll cover speed later. They think dex may actually increase your ability to handle speed, reflexes, etc. Not reflex saves, but your actual reflexes. This isn't settled, and there isn't consensus like there is with speed, but I just wanted to mention it. The speed part of dex is settled though. For reflexes, take me. Mine are great normally. So they think dex isn't a huge benefit for me. They think there is a reflex cap. But if you have crap reflexes normally, you could benefit a lot from having high dex. Again, this isn't settled.

Constitution: helps with healing speed, bone density, illness recovery, things like that. There isn't a consensus, but they think you heal 50% faster than normal at 30 con. Bone density, I forget the amount it improves, but it really doesn't matter since your bones can't break with a HP shield. Illness was a big one, I wish I could remember or explain better. If you are at a certain health, your body kills the sickness so good you don't even know you're sick. But just a little less healthy and you could get sick for 3 days. And if really unhealthy like 20 days. Something like that. Maybe there is a doctor that is smart about this stuff that I can talk to and explain this better at some point.

Intelligence, Wisdom, and Charisma: I think intelligence helps with recall. I don't remember much about these. A 30 intelligence won't make an idiot smart, and having a 6 int won't make a genius an idiot. I can't think of anything about wis. The only thing I know for certain about cha is it does not alter your physical appearance in any way. I tried a Blood Wyrm Exemplar and had 14 wis and high cha and it did not make me make better decisions or be more likable. I also had an int of 20 for a good while and I was not 50% smarter or anything like that. Or even noticeably smarter. Sorry I can't remember more about these. But, smart people swear by int and wis. I just can't state I noticed anything from them personally.

Speed: this is a hard one to explain. There is no land-speed like in the game. Your real speed is your speed. If you pick a dwarf or a small race you get a -15% speed penalty. Medium armor is a -7.5% speed penalty. Heavy armor is a -15% speed penalty. The Full of

Beans background gives you +15%. The half-orc racial gives like 7.5%. Run skill gives 7.5 at 10 points and another 7.5 at 20 points. If you think these numbers don't match up with the SRD, don't complain to me. I had nothing to do with any of this. I'm just telling you what I was told and my experience with the system.

Every AB besides BAB gives 1%. Every BAB gives 3%. Dex 30 gives 20%. Haste gives 36% speed (30% and the 6% from the 2 increased BAB).

Monk speed is the hardest to explain. This is where they found out about diminishing returns. Every speed increase for a monk gets weaker and weaker. I think the hard cap is 52% from total land-speed increases. So a level 30 half-orc monk with the Full of Beans background will have the same speed as a human level 30 non-half-orc monk with a different background. Or basically the same.

No matter what your speed and diminishing returns, haste always increases it by 36%. But that is the exception. I think if you have the max BAB (20 BAB) the BAB increase from haste is diminished. I'm not positive. But changed land-speed stuff, BAB, and AB are separate and have their own diminishing returns. AB and dex are combined together. I think. Sorry I don't remember specifics better.

And a lot of speed is just wasted if your brain can't handle it. You need good reflexes and hand-eye coordination to handle it. Some say high dex helps. I can handle more speed increase than most people, even when I have low dex. But it gets to a point even I stop benefiting from more speed.

Casting speed works the same as the game. Higher caster level and DC makes you cast faster. I only tried the one caster class and re-rolled as soon as I hit level 21 or so. I tried making it a melee focused. It didn't work too great. Casters aren't for me. Sorry I don't know more about caster mechanics.

Rerolling: you can reroll at any time you want by doing the tutorial dungeon over again and selecting "character generation" instead of "enter dungeon." You lose all equipment and money and start over at level 1. But you can hand non-binded equipment off. Non-bound? You know what I mean. You keep all achievements and dungeon coins and stuff like that. But you lose all the dungeon coins you already spent and everything you already withdrew from the arena rewards.

Stamina: the stamina points show, but never go down besides from spells causing the effects of fatigued or exhausted. You are either green, yellow, or red. How many points in each do not matter. So the Endurance feat only helps with sleeping in medium armor. That is it. Higher stamina does nothing that I've heard of.

Oh. I almost forgot. People that are pathetically out of shape think con helps with not becoming winded, not stamina points. I always go high con, and I haven't noticed anything. But I was in great shape when I got here. Just figured I mention it. Especially for you pod people. Most of you are so weak I'm surprised you made it out of the tutorial. Same goes for the people that weren't in pods. You guys are all pretty pathetic, honestly.

No feats about being negative HP do anything, like Die Hard. Ignore them all. Same with stamina point feats, like Endurance (besides the armor part for resting). They are all just wasted. Resurrect spells do nothing, unless part of the spell restores HPs, that part will work. But dead is dead here. If you die you are dead.

Sorry, I don't think I am explaining things well. I had help writing this before I came back and it was explained much better. All of it. They thought some sort of bus thing on the NI would save what we wrote together, but it didn't. So I have to do all this from my own memory, and my memory stinks. I'm certain I am forgetting important information."

That was confusing. I can't think of any way to make it not confusing or explain it better so I guess it is what it is. I didn't say anything offensive, so that's good. I'm actually about 6 '7.5 inches tall. I've always lied and said I'm shorter.

2.3 INFO FROM THE FUTURE III

BRUNO VAZ

Next up: builds. One of the most important ones.

"EMAIL 4 BUILDS"

This one is just too long to read through again. I know I hit the highlights, stressed iFrames, the ways to get iFrames, 14 con minimum, and important and key feats. Leveling builds. The only builds that are kind of light on info were the dps caster builds besides blood wyrms, and I try dissuade people from going with a squishy caster class now. And I stressed the combat focused healers, or healers that can damage and take a hit or two. Especially druids. Tons of viable druid builds. Pet and heals. Caster dps and heals. Even melee and heals. Regular clerics too, with good domains for some added dps or more tanky or more melee. No sense for a cleric not to splash 1 fighter level. I hate non-damaging healers. If you can do both, why would people expect less? Why do healers and only healers get a pass to suck? Screw them and their healing-only builds and them whining all the time about the solo arena and reduced dungeon coins. Pick a build that can damage too, dummies. I extra stressed how dumb the stupid wiz HP ranged healer is. Acolyte. That class sucks so bad. Yet is so popular. Same with the stupid halfling cleric with the slings. Crazy. Not only are future people pathetically weak, they are stupid and make poor choices. This ain't a game. You got to be able to take a hit or two. I have no idea how half the people that made it to the epic zone did it. Well, I guess I do – they were carried.

"EMAIL 5 WHAT HAPPENED ON LEVEL 10 IN MY TIMELINE, AND OTHER STUFF

In my timeline I was taking my family to the city when everyone died on 10. In area 10 there is a pillar that ports you to and from the city. No one locked any of the dungeons (because they couldn't, because there was no one in charge of the government yet then) so the best fighters were progressing as dungeons opened. No one knows what happened on level 10. The groups right behind the people leading the way entered area 10 and found nothing. No sign of anything that happened. No bodies, no loot, absolutely nothing.

We got a message that someone took control of the government when we were like a month and half into the path leading towards the city. This was the groups following behind the people that dis-appeared on level 10. They used the portal in area 10 and beat us to the city. A short time later we got to the city ourselves, along with most other groups that took the path.

People that progress through the dungeons are called crawlers (some people called us players, but that is dumb. This isn't a game and we aren't playing. Not this time). The crawler that took over the city eventually handed leadership off to some politicians from the UN.

In this timeline since I'll be locking dungeons until all get SS, the people taking the path might beat the rest of us to the city. It will depend on how long we need to lock the dungeons and how many days it actually takes to get to the city from the path. Besides me, since I can port to the city and back to exactly where I was from anywhere outside a dungeon once a day. Resets at midnight. All crawlers will be able to do this eventually. And other neat things too.

We think level 10 is like level 20. On level 20 there was a big challenge when you entered. We had 20 locked, and we massed all of the good crawlers we could. We only had less than 1k total active good crawlers ready, so we didn't have to worry about more than one instance. My advice back then was to just take in the best of the best. 30 to 50 of the cream of the crop. No one listened. We fought a huge army of undead led by a what's it called? The things that you have to destroy the jar its heart is in? You know what I mean. You have to destroy the thing to destroy the guy. It was a 16(23). We lost a lot of people, but we killed it, then found its jar and destroyed that.

Since I know where the jar is, we shouldn't lose anyone this time. The level 20 area also has a portal to the city. There is another one on the east end of the epic area. The level 21 to 30 giant zone. But by the time you find that you'll probably have the achievement to portal to and back from the city from anywhere. I rerolled too much last time to remember how things usually go.

This time, I will do all I can to ensure we lose far less people and win this stupid contest. But you have to help. Get strong. Then stronger. Get better and better at fighting."

Not too bad. I wish I could remember the name of the thing. It's on the tip of my tongue. Damn.

EMAIL 6 DUNGEON COINS

Even if you are a caster you need to be good at regular fighting for when you are at zero HPs. Your build is wicked, wicked important especially at later levels, but your fighting ability and how in shape you are is also wicked important always. Especially now. Your build is less important now. But I really, really hope you study the builds I sent, and the important feats, and make changes. Now is

156

the time to reroll. But you probably will later too. You probably don't believe me, but it's true.

This is where dungeon coins come in. The four colored ones. You get really good stuff to buff up your build. But you can only spend it once. And can only spend 5k worth of each. You don't get it back. So if you reroll after spending coins all those coins are wasted. And the stuff you get and withdrew from the arena too. Most crawlers won't get near the 5k cap for each color. So do not spend a single coin, or withdraw anything at all from the arena, until you are certain of your build. Don't commit until you are 100% certain.

Dungeons 1 through 10 are normal mobs. 11 to 20 are the heroic level monsters. Bosses can be higher or tougher than their CR indicates. But for most competent people dungeons level 1 through 20 are a cakewalk solo without ever spending any coins. The build I want isn't viable for solo crawling dungeons without spending a lot of coins and the arena rewards on it, so I am rerolling as soon as I get to the epic zone. My current build, as I explained in email 4, is great right off the bat for trying for higher SS, and is a good build in general. But I am not spending one coin or using one build reward from the arena until after I reroll. I highly suggest the same for everyone. Highly. This is wicked good advice and will save you from gimping yourself. And force you to get good at fighting too.

After you pick your epic class and enter the 21 to 30 area, none of those dungeons or raids give dungeon coins. Just a different currency for raid gear sets. But you can always grind regular level 1 to 20 dungeons for rare spawns that do drop dungeon coins. The higher the level of the dungeon, the higher a chance for a spawn. It would take forever to farm a good amount of dungeon coins this way though. But people do it since it is the only way after the rewards for level 1 to 20 dungeons and the arena.

Look at the store and familiarize yourself with the prices and functions of what you can get for dungeon coins. This is all super important so don't blow it or do something wicked stupid that you will regret. Be certain. Hold off. The flaws in your build probably won't be apparent until you hit the higher CR dungeons and raids. Just consider the builds I sent, and the wicked important feats. Or what will happen is you get to 30 and start raiding and see what other people can do and realize you suck and wish you had x, y, and z. You don't get picked up in groups, whine, cry, and reroll. Because you'll actually do better rerolling than staying a plused up gimp who wasted all their coins like a dummy.

On the first emails I wrote with the other guys we broke down all the numbers and provided really good info. But this is too much writing and thinking and checking for me. I will only say that if you get 1st solo SS on all dungeons 1 through 20 you will have more than 5k of each coin, without even counting the arena. Same with 2 man group 1st SS. 5 man group 1st SS you will have more than 5k counting the arena. Don't screw other people. You get like 1600 of each coin for completely clearing all arenas. Smart people will have access to emails to break down the numbers before it gets critical and people start earning too many coins from 1st SS. But I plan to only get enough 1st SS to hit 5k of each coin including the arena and the coins earned for regular plain SS from dungeons. I could get 1st SS on all of them. Well, almost all. Besides when the psuchesoma things are the spelling ones.

Jesus, I still have to write at least one more email. I hate this so much."

Wow, that is explained really bad. Good enough though. Or maybe it makes sense? Should I add to it? Nah. Nothing was offensive and I already said it was good enough. After rerolling the 5k is reset so you could farm coins to get plused up a good amount, but it takes forever. Really forever. Wicked, wicked long. And the arena doesn't reset. Anything withdrawn and used is gone for good. I didn't really lie, but the whole truth will make people take it less serious.

"EMAIL 7 SETUP IN DUNGEON AREAS"

I know nothing offensive is in this one, so I'm skipping reading it. This is the least important one for now. It is just where the medical tent and straddle trenches should go outside the dungeons. I invented the rest, like training areas and trade areas. Put my portable AH to use. Can't hurt, right? And I figure it is a way to get people to start getting used to taking directions from me. Start thinking of me as in charge. Give them something simple, easy, and sensible as an order to ease them into taking orders.

Just one more email left.

"EMAIL 8 POLITICS AND EXPECTATIONS

I hate politics and politicians. Either by now or soon you will see I have taken control of the city, and set the government type to dictatorship. I don't care what you do as long as you are being useful and helping to advance humanity and win this contest. Be useful. Don't be a jerk. Don't be a murderer, child molester, or rapist. Just try and be a normal, useful person until we win and get out of here. Then you are someone else's problem.

I don't want to lead or be a leader. I have to ensure certain things and avoid certain things in this timeline so I have to, even if I really don't want to. Why not a democracy? The same. To avoid certain things and ensure certain other things. I'd really like the help of Sidis. Even though I don't know him he seems to feel the same way I do about leading and politics, so that means he is probably trustworthy. Sidis, please, you are smart enough where you could really help me avoid the political garbage that happened last timeline.

Can regular people be useful outside of game mechanics? Yes, definitely. I think most people take the administrator class. Some take engineer. Engineer can actually be useful in dungeons so they can also get dungeon coins too. Administrators can't. If you are a weak dentist and don't ever want to fight again after getting to the city, you will probably take administrator so you can easily advance without combat, while hopefully opening a dental office and doing the wicked useful work of a dentist. We all still need dentists, even if it isn't a class here.

We also need some people to focus on real mining or smelting outside of game mechanics for making tools that you can't buy in the shop. Like certain dental tools and doctor tools. MDs are always useful. Real MDs that help with physical injuries. Not PhDs, you guys are useless. And usually horrible people too, unless you're a scientist and do actual, useful science stuff. Real MDs are probably more useful not being a crawler even if you could be. We need them in the city and in dungeon areas outside of dungeons. They are wicked critical and helpful. But do not give these hippies any healing pills though. They waste them on useless people. We can't have that. Sorry, we can't.

If anyone threatens, touches, or even looks funny at my family I will make you suffer as much as possible until you die. Do not try to get to me through them. It will not end well for you. Do not do anything crazy or repulsive and you will be fine.

I'm missing a ton of stuff. Sorry. My head is killing from writing. When I remember important things I will email again.

Also, please try not to talk to me. You almost certainly don't like me, I almost certainly don't like you, and I will have people you can talk to that can handle all the monkey stuff. I don't want to be bothered with your nonsense. I just want to progress and win and get as many people out alive as possible, while letting you all be as free as possible. We think differently. I can't expect you all to be normal like me, or think normal like me. And that is okay. I won't give many orders, but the orders I do give that are not outside of your control (like locking dungeon progression), I expect 100% compliance.

We need to all work towards the same goal of getting out of here with as many people alive as possible so you can all go back to being weak idiots living in the internet like monkey-sheep. You don't have to like me or agree with me, but you will listen to me (the few times I give orders, like with my family). Hell, I don't even like myself or agree with myself half the time, so I won't expect you to. But I expect you to do it anyways. Might may not make right, but it certainly makes it hard to argue.

IMPORTANT: This isn't Earth. Leave Earth politics for Earth. There is no UN. There is no terrorists or sympathizers. There are just people. Crawlers, crafters, supporters. Be useful and don't ruin everything with politics like you idiots like to ruin everything with. NO EARTH POLILTICS ARE ALLOWED HERE! PERIOD! NO EXCEPTIONS! Leave your gripes for when you get back. And we can only get back by working together.

Last thing. The AI computer lady. Miya or whatever. As far as anyone can tell she has nothing to do with any of this, cannot be reached, cannot help, and is not involved at all. Too many people spent too much time on this crazy nonsense last time and I don't see how it helps or how it could be useful.

Last thing – please set your items to descriptive mode instead of immersive mode. No one wants to hear bracers of ogre whatever. Bracers of strength +2 makes way more sense and is way more helpful to useful, normal people. Only dorks use the immersive crap. Don't be a dork. Or try to be less of one. And when the forum thing opens, remember I will have control of it. If I see any of you dorks saying dork things like bracers of ogre, etc., I will ban you. Descriptive mode. Use it."

Eh. Just eh. Not bad. But people are so politicized in the future this will fall on deaf ears. These monkeys better take the part about my family seriously.

Man, I'm glad that's done. Reading through all that garbage has given me an even worse headache. Working out and diddling will help. Get rid of some of the headache, calm my nerves, and get a little bit of the devil out so I can put my best face forward. Is it face forward or foot forward? I need them both forward, and all the luck I can get too.

2.4 KISSING HANDS AND SHAKING BABIES

BRUNO VAZ

All done. Got the devil out a little, everything squared-away and double-checked. I step through the dungeon exit. People start appearing all around me. After a second it is done. There should be a thousand exactly people here. That is how many can fit in one instance of a zone at once. All of the humans alive throughout the world are here. Not here, here. But in different instances of this zone. Dungeon area 1.

The UI with the dungeon reward and ranking pops up. My ranking is a circle. 1st SS. Of course. Rewards are five gold and a rope with grappling hook. Useless now. Dungeons don't need ropes until later. Then it just gets ridiculous how much you have to use them. I close the window and see someone else pop into existence a ways away. I think that's what I saw. That was way too late though. Someone would have had to stay in the dungeon forever to pop out that late. Why would anyone stay in the tutorial dungeon that long? No sense grinding past a couple weeks or a month on high-level dungeons, never mind the lowest level dungeon there is. The tutorial dungeon isn't worth it. Unless people were training? But how would they know to do any of that their first time in the tutorial dungeon?

I must have been seeing things. Someone moving fast and jerking away from someone and it just looked like they beamed in that much later than everyone else.

Eh, oh well. Doesn't matter. I do the gesture to open my inventory and navigate to the tab with the emails and send them off one by one. Eight emails. Send to all options. Every human alive will get them. Another achievement. A late achievement. People won't be able to do any communication through their UI at all for a while.

Lich. That's the name of the thing in area 20. I make email nine and send it off to everyone.

"EMAIL 9 LICH

Lich. That is what the thing on level 20 is called."

For some reason I feel really dumb and embarrassed. Nervous too. No one knows who I am so no one will know I sent all the emails. They just see my number on the minimap, if they even have a minimap. Good old...wait! My number ends in 13. Or it did last timeline. How did it change?

C465OV0001W87-1. I can't remember all that gibberish, but it used to end in 13-1. Well, 13-1E after I got my epic class, but 13-1 until level 21. 87? How did it become 87? Because my family isn't here? That's three people. 3 + or - 3 doesn't equal 7. But we sent 10 people total to the city. But that still doesn't add up. 3 + or - 10 doesn't equal 7 either. Maybe the little kids? Hmmm.

I look around. It takes me a couple seconds but I see people I remember from last time. And then more. And more. So that's right at least. What is going on with the number? Math is supposed to be reliable. I always knew math is stupid and you couldn't rely on it and this is scientific proof I was right.

Damn! I should have explained numbers and how the dash 1 at the end is group size you are allowed and all that stuff in the emails. Eh, oh well. I can do that later. I'll wait until I have something more important to email. And who cares about my number changing? If you can't figure it out right away, it isn't worth wasting time thinking about. It is what it is.

I watch the people for a couple more seconds. Sheep. Docile, well behaved sheep. In movies people always go nuts and full on Mad Max in situations like this. I was surprised last time by how well behaved everyone was. Other than some light stealing, the only real jerks were the UN people and some opportunists. It would actually be nice if these sheep were more rowdy. Had more fighting spirit and got in fights and did normal people stuff. It's like the whole world turned into Canada.

I open my inventory and navigate through the UI to where I can beam to the city. And do. As I reappear in the city, I get a notification asking if I want to take control of Loren. I hit yes. It asks me what type of government I want to have. I select dictatorship. And that is that. I am now the leader of all humans.

A world message goes out telling everyone I am the leader of the world. It doesn't say who, just the player number.

It makes me put a tax on sales. I set it at 2%, the lowest it lets me select, then the UI disappears.

I open my inventory again and take some time finding the right section in the UI for government controls. I was going to add my family to the government but I don't have their numbers yet. So I turn this instance of the city to private and only allow direct family of current occupants in. And then I lock dungeon 1.

What a great politician I am. Promises made, promises kept. I wonder how the nanites know if you are direct family? DNA or something? But spouses DNA wouldn't match. Eh, who cares? It also works on personal housing entrances. You can set it to allow in all direct family once you rent one. Do the nanites control this or is it whatever sent us here? Or whoever? Again, big guy, stop wondering about nonsense. I have no idea how lightbulbs and remote controls work, why am I trying to figure way more advanced stuff out?

Now to find my family. Hopefully they're with the other people. I'll explain things to the other people here at the same time as my family. Less talking and questions that way.

I have a thought and my heart nearly pops out of my chest. Goddamn! Kim's babies! I almost forgot. Idiot! Kim sent two babies here. He has two wives and eight bazillion kids. He sent the two youngest here. I got to find them. He trusted me.

Crap, crap, crap, crap, crap! What do I do? This is a big city and there are four of these cities in this instance. Crap.

I come up with the best plan my mind allows. I scream as I run towards the area of town with the store node things. The portal is where all four cities intersect. The store nodes, crafting area entrances, and stuff like that is at the north end of the instance. The main city entrance is on the south. If my yelling doesn't work I will look for something loud, like a whistle, to buy. The city is dead silent. Usually it is loud. If not from the humans then the NPCs. I hear no NPCs. I'm yelling like a maniac as I run. As I take a deep breath for another yell I hear something. I stop to listen. It sounds like yelling. Far away.

I figure out where it is coming from best as I can and move towards it at a jog to listen better. My minimap is zoomed out as far as possible, but I double check to make sure. The yelling is getting closer. And closer. I see player numbers on the minimap. Then I see my son. And from behind a different building, a couple seconds later, my daughter.

I'm not an emotional guy usually. Well, not girl emotions like crying and sad and all the girl emotions. I usually only have four emotions. Normal, funny, horny, and angry. Sometimes you can add wicked on to those. Like wicked horny. Or wicked angry. And I'm usually always the horny emotion, even when I'm the others too. It's just always there at different magnitudes. Usually high magnitudes.

But crying and feeling some sort of weird 'happy enough I could cry' emotion? Not me. When my kids were born, especially my daughter, my first born? Yes. When I'd see them in plays or stuff when they was younger? Yes. I felt that way. But not in years. But seeing both my kids now. Seeing them happy and relieved to see me. No hate or anger or any of the other nonsense I've gotten used to over the years. It almost breaks my Grinch-heart. Seeing them much younger than the last time I saw them. Knowing I have more time with them at this age. More love to give and get. Doing it right this time.

My son screams, "Dad!" and runs up and gives me a tight hug. My daughter walks over smiling. She puts her hand on my shoulder. She is gorgeous. She looks so beautiful smiling. It is so good to see her smile at me and not see the resentment that was always on her face last timeline. It gives me lots of good feelings inside of me. Hippie feelings. But the clean hippies that shower. Not the filthy hippies. This is a good memory I will savor for a while. She goes to college soon to become a filthy lawyer, so I have somehow failed to make her into a completely decent person. Maybe I can change that this time? Most of all her issues with me stem from what happened due to her mother cheating on me. Which hasn't happened yet. Last time I let it ruin everything before it happened. Knowing cheating was in my ex's heart. Cheating on me. I can't tolerate it. I can't understand why my daughter always sides with her cheating mother.

But it can be different this time. It will be different. I need my daughter to love me. And to be a decent person that isn't a subhuman lawyer. My beautiful angel will be a full-fledged human. My son and I had a big falling out in the last timeline too. Not about his whore mother. Not really. But it led to something great. Something that will ensure things between us will always be okay. Better than it ever has been. In any timeline.

I say, "I love you guys so much! But we got to find some babies! Two babies, have you…"

Both kids interrupted me to say yeah. My daughter adds, "Four actually. Or, three babies, and one toddler. One young boy. And two women. Ten people total, including us. Well, eleven with you now."

"Okay. Okay. Great. That is everyone. Ten people. All we could send. Where is everyone? Never mind right now. I got to get an email off letting the guys know their family members are safe and here. That was stupid of me to forget. Too much to remember."

As I go to open my inventory my son asks, "What is going on, dad?"

"One second. You're safe. Don't worry about nothing. Let me get this email off real quick and I'll go explain to everyone. All at once. But I'd be going nuts right now if I didn't know where my family was. I got to get this out. I can't leave the guys hanging."

My son keeps hugging me, making it hard to do the gesture. I let him. Holding on to your father like a toddler at 15 is really weird for a boy. I'm just happy he didn't call me daddy. He's a sissy, but not for long. Let him enjoy his sissy ways for now.

The group with me when we found the time machine was Bam Bam, an immigrant to the States from…I forget. Haiti? Cameroon? Maybe the Ivory Coast or Congo? He wasn't nice and polite enough to be from Niger or Rwanda, and people from Canada usually don't shut up about Canada, so I doubt he is from there either. I forget. Some French speaking country other than France. We hated each other at first. He was actually part of a group that tried to kill me. He had no immediate family. Just a bunch of older brothers. And a girl-friend he split with soon after getting here. He wanted to send a niece to the city, but this was just for immediate family. Wives and kids.

We had two people each to send back, and my ex and my kids were a given. I can't stand my ex, but if I didn't send her my kids would never forgive me. And technically we're still married and she never cheated on me so she is still my responsibility. So Bam's two people were split between me and Hang Nga. Bam was the worst fighter of us all, but he was the healer so didn't have to be as good. He had a shady past and wasn't honest about it. He wasn't honest about anything. Everyone in my initial dungeon area instance is from Fayetteville, NC, but he wasn't too far from there. He went to college in NC. Not the school near Chapel Hill. The one near Raleigh-Durham. I think. He went to the city the last timeline, instead of crawling right away. Everyone in the group I ended up in did.

Hang Nga. I think he was Vietnamese. The name he gave me to replace his number was Hang Nga. I didn't know if he was messing with me at the time and was some sort of crazy racist, but he isn't that type of guy. Nga also doesn't sound like it looks like it will sound. And we all just called him Nah. Or I do. It is the closest my mouth gets to saying it right. His wife is wicked, wicked hot. And flirty. Her body is amazing seeing as she popped out two kids. Hang Nga tried telling me the A in Hang had some sort of doohickey on it, but I wasn't going to waste time trying to figure out how to find that to add it to his name in my own UI. He probably isn't going to make the cut as an A list crawler this time, but still –friends are friends and time travel doesn't change that.

Vlad. I forget his real name. Something like Dahmer. Russian. Or he seemed Russian but was from the same place that Borat from the movie was from. Not Kurdistan. Something like that though. I called him Vlad because he was Russian and calling someone Dahmer just reminds me of people's heads in refrigerators and cannibalism. Vlad seems like a good name for a fighter, like the Impaler. And it is the only Russian name I could think of quickly. Besides Ivan. But Ivan isn't as good as Vlad. And Ivan is what we used to call targets on the range when I first joined the military, so that seemed kind of disrespectful. Sometimes I don't put a lot of effort into nicknames. He has a wife and a teenage son. You could tell his wife used to be hot, but she didn't age well and is pretty hefty now. Both were sent here. At first Vlad seemed like a wicked party-pooper. Never smiled or joked around. Always serious. But once you get to know him you see he actually loves joking and laughing. He just isn't very expressive. Dry. And reliable. Keeping everyone on track. Solid. He didn't talk a ton, but when he did he always used a lot of words to say something simple. That would always drive me nuts. Smart guy too. He didn't drink often, but one of my hobbies was getting him drunk and seeing him turn into a party animal. For like an hour, then he would spend the rest of the night puking. Good times.

Last was Kim. Really dark Asian from some country I never heard of. Two words. Timber something or other. First non-Korean Kim I ever met. At least that I can remember. Maybe Kim is a nickname I gave him? I forget. Real good guy. About my age. Has two wives. His wives are tough. One of them is wicked tough. For a woman at least. Both ain't easy on the eyes, but they have a ton of personality, laughing loud and often. And they liked me and my jokes, which is rare. Especially in the future world where everyone is always offended by everything. I got along with them great. Probably my two favorite people from the future. Kim and his wives have like eight bazillion kids. He sent his two youngest kids back. Just babies. He has more babies too. So many kids. His older kids are great fighters. Kim is awesome. Always smiling. Always laughing. Always cracking jokes. Tough as nails. Not the most skilled or genetically gifted, but I'd still want him in my party now just for the esprit de corps he brings, and the laughs. He isn't an A list fighter, but real close. And I like hanging out and drinking with his wives and older kids.

Bam Bam was our weakest member. He calmed down but was still really annoying and too political about everything. We wanted to replace him with a guy that was really good from Uruguay or Paraguay. I can never get those two straight. They should have named them

Northaguay and Southaguay so I could remember which was which. A lot of good fighters came from one of those. Whichever one was fighting the UN. But I killed one of them over some nonsense so they all hated me. Those guys stick together. Great cohesion. The rest of humanity could learn to be more like that. The great thing is they have no reason to hate me in this timeline.

The future ended up being weird. No North and South Korea. Just Korea. An alliance of whatever Burma changed their named to, Vietnam, Cambodia, and Lao – all at war with the UN. The UN in control of the US after a really short and minor civil war. The UN in control of basically everything, and you bow down or they send troops. What really surprised me is all the Muslim countries went along with it. Besides Afghanistan. But they have a long history of fighting off world super powers so why wouldn't they give it the old college try this time too?

Either Uruguay or Paraguay is at war with the UN. With Chile, Bolivia and some other countries in that area too. Maybe Ecuador? Also all of south North America. All the countries besides Panama. Belize, Guatemala, El Salvador, Honduras, Nicaragua. That area mostly stuck together. Good for them. Panama was with the rest, but the UN just massed on them until they bent the knee. They needed the canal.

Surprisingly, to me at least, both Cuba and Venezuela are supporting what the future people call the terrorist countries, the ones fighting the UN, even though they are officially part of the UN. I used to be split between which country had better arepas, Venezuela or Columbia. Now I pick Venezuela for at least helping to stick it to the man.

Africa is almost 100% UN. In name at least. Every country is part of it even if the residents aren't on board. I guess there's some major issues where there are big tribes. And small tribes. One country's people who said screw off to the UN really made me proud. Cape Verde.

What I am. My people. Or half my people at least. I always wanted to go, but we never did. I wish I did. It is supposed to be the Hawaii of Africa, but much more affordable. My grandma would make these delicious tuna pastel things. So good. Pastel com diabo dentro I think. After I went into foster care I didn't see my mom or grandma very often, and when I did I didn't really get fed. There were shops you could get tuna pastels, but I never got the spicy ones my grandma made since I was a little kid.

The issue between the UN and terrorist countries seem to be over the pods. Like all things political, it ain't very clear. Both sides claim different things that sound reasonable and make sense. With the computer lady AI running things, unemployment skyrocketed. I don't know how the UN became the world government. I heard different things. The US civil war. Climate change. Super high unemployment. Terrorist threats. The truth is probably how most things happen – for a bunch of reasons. And like most things, it would happen gradually and then suddenly.

So, due to the crazy unemployment, the UN offered something called a UBI to all people of all member nations. I think it stands for Universal Basic Income. Everyone, rich or poor, got a check from the UN every month. I guess the big talking point for living in the pods was to combat climate change. When not enough people volunteered the UN changed the UBI to only be given to people who entered the pods. That forced a lot of people into them. But they wanted more, so put quotas on member countries that didn't have enough volunteers.

The quotas started the wars. Member nations broke off. Blocs were formed. I was told they saw it as a form of slavery, and the higher quotas on industrializing nations with higher employment rates was a way to keep them poor and unequal.

I can't remember anyone who lived in a pod that ever claimed they didn't volunteer. All the ones I met said they loved it too. They all said living in the internet was a blast. The pod was also supposed to exercise your body for you, so your muscles didn't atrophy. But pod people definitely had atrophied muscles.

I don't know who's right and who's wrong. All I know is I tend to sympathize with anyone sticking it to the man, or trying to stick it to the man at least. I know it is ironic, seeing as my job was often to stick it to people trying to stick it to the man.

And I know for certain none of that matters now. All that matters is working together and getting back to earth with as many people alive as possible. Then the world can go back to being weak ass pansies living in the internet. And I can build up some credit with the Big Guy for saving the world. Hopefully.

The future people being so weak and pathetic really screwed us. No one was ready for this contest.

I was. A handful of others were too. Just not enough. Not nearly enough.

I go to messages and select 'send to all.' I have no way of knowing my old party's character numbers to email them directly so I have to send it to the whole world. I have a hard time thinking of a title.

"IMPORTANT MESSAGE IF YOU DID NOT START WITH THE PARTY OR PEOPLE YOU SHOULD HAVE

I'm really sorry I didn't message about this earlier. When we found the wish machine we had 100 points to spend. Sending me back cost 90 points. With the 10 points left we could have sent me back with dungeon coins or equipment and things like that. Or, we could keep loved ones safe that were not meant to be fighters and send them directly to the city. So we sent 10 people to the city to start. 1 point per person sent.

Three where my family. Now, I am really bad at names so please forgive me about the following but I am going to have to describe the 3 other people in our party that sent people back.

Hang Nga. I don't think this is your real name. You are from Vietnam. You have a wife and two little kids. They are here in the city with my family. Safe.

Something like Dahmer from…"

I stop typing and say to my kids, "Do you know the name of the country Borat comes from? From the movie?"

Both say Kazakhstan together, and ask why. I tell them and try to type it in. I get it wrong enough that clicking on it doesn't even give me the right word to select. I ask my kids how to spell it, and my daughter nails it in the first try. I continue typing.

"Something like Dahmer from Kazakhstan. Your wife and son are here.

Kim from Timber…"

I ask my kids if they ever heard of a country in Asia called Timber-something. Dark Asians. Look a lot like them, my kids.

My daughter says East Timor. That isn't it.

"Is there a country near it named Timor-something?"

"I don't know, dad. Not that I know of off-hand. Why don't you go ask the families? They all speak English."

Jesus, Joseph, and Mary! I am an idiot. I don't even have to ask the families. I can take a picture of all of them with my UI. I can just email the picture out. Besides for Kim's kids since all babies basically look exactly the same. But I can see if anyone knows the country. Nah's family is from Asia so they probably know. My wife…ex I mean…is from Asia too, but she moved to the US too young for me to count her the same as an Asian from Asia.

And none of the other people speak English. Probably. Everything is translated. From the UI. NI, I mean. The neural implant. The weird thing is I guess the translation is the same software that does it for games and stuff on earth. The smart people say it has the same bugs and quirks and stuff. More evidence this isn't aliens that did this to

174

us. Or at least if it is aliens they really like using our own computer stuff.

But – and this is a but that led to a lot of conspiracy stuff – with computers and only with computers you could translate with lips synced to the translation. So it looked normal. Like people actually talking the translated words. You could do it on live TV but it needed software from a computer to run at the same time. You couldn't just look at someone in real life with your own naked eyes and have it sync the lips to the translation. This led to people thinking this is a game, just with some sort of advanced technology to make everything look and feel real. Most smart people say that the technology wasn't there to make a simulation like this and the NIs are like a computer so can change what you see. Like how we can see our own UI but not other people's. I don't know the answer, but I'd rather not have people thinking this is a game and it doesn't matter if you die, or you go back to the real world if you die. It is much better for everyone to treat this as 100% real.

"Siri, you are a genius. That's why you get the big bucks. Where is everyone?"

Her full name is Usasiri. Me and my wife…I mean my ex…made a deal. She gets to name the girls and I name the boys. My son's name is Nate. Full name Nathan. Named after a good friend of mine who died. Thai people do this weird thing where they never call anyone by their real name. Just a nickname that has nothing to do with their actual name. Like my ex is Min. Really Mint, but Thai people say Min. She goes by Minnie in the US. Her real first name is ridiculously long and I can't spell it or pronounce it.

My ex calls my daughter Pet and my son Ling. That translates into spicy and monkey. I think pet is spelled different, but it sounds exactly like pet. Thai people stink at spelling Thai words in English, but they get mad if you tell them that. They can't even spell the word Thai

175

correctly. Tai. Easy. Even I can do it. Thai is pronounced thigh, not tie. But don't tell Thai people that or they will talk your ear off.

Another example is the king Thai people love more than anything – Rama 9. They pronounce it Poomipoon, but it is spelled different enough you can't even connect it to what they are saying. I can't remember how they spell it, but it is completely wrong. He was born in Boston. That is probably why he was such an awesome king and everyone loved him.

All the best people in the world come from the Boston area through the south shore and Brockton and Providence. In my time it was the last bastion of civilization in the world besides Bhutan. New York was semi-civilized, but not really. Not with that many yankee fans and tourists living there. I guess you could kind of count the north shore up to Manchester, but that area isn't civilized enough. Not like the south shore. Maybe Jersey City and Philly too. The rest of the US, and world, I considered to be the Savage Outland. Just filled with silly hillbillies doing everything wrong.

I can't call my daughter pet. I love her too much to call her something like that in the US when everyone would think I am calling her a pet. Like a dog or cat. And it would feel really weird calling my son monkey in Thai, since Thai people have this weird thing with skin color and my son is part black. I don't say half because my kids came out really light. My ex is pretty light skinned. She is from the south of Thailand and she thinks she is really dark, but she isn't. A lot of Thai women obsess about it. Skin color. According to my mother I am full Cape Verdean. But I've never seen a Cape Verdean as dark as I am. I'm way darker than my mother. And that dumb whore would have no idea who my actual father was. My actual father must have been a wicked, wicked dark guy from the deepest jungles of Africa for me to be this dark with my mother being a pretty light skinned Cape Verdean. My kids look like if someone with my mother's skin color had

176

babies with a Thai. Way lighter than Tiger Woods. So I say part instead of half. Maybe my darkness skips a generation like with baldness or something?

Now that I think about it, my kids kind of look like they are from where Kim is from. Timber-something. If Kim and his wives and kids are representative of what people from there look like at least. They could have immigrated there for all I know. Maybe they don't allow multiple wives where he is from so they all moved to Timber-whatever?

My son grabs my left hand and we start walking. It makes me feel wicked weird holding the hand of a 15-year-old boy. My daughter grabs my other hand. I feel more happiness than I have in a long, long time.

2.5 CLEAN UP

BRUNO VAZ

"I got to head back," I say to my wife. I mean my ex.

"That's it? You're leaving now? Rooney-Bear, you just got here! We just got here. Can't you stay and help us a little? Help settle the kids in? The kids are scared."

Jesus. I hate getting nagged at; especially when it pulls at my heart strings.

Surprisingly, Vlad's wife was the one who knew the name of Kim's country. Oh Jesus, I forget it already. Something like Timber-Leste. It is actually the same country my daughter said – East Timber. And they speak Portuguese. Leste is Portuguese for East. Kim never spoke Portuguese or any sort of creole that sounds like it. Not that I know of at least. We hung out for, like, a year. Even with the translation software stuff I should've been able to pick that up. Or maybe I'm as dumb as people say I am. I hope not.

I got the email off, and I added the stuff about my number changing, and explained how numbers work. I had to call it character number, because most people aren't crawlers. Character number is better than player number because I hope less people will think of this as a game. But the number doesn't change when you reroll and change your character, so that isn't really a great name for it. I also explained how to change other people's numbers in your UI to an actual name and that with achievements they will be able to email people. Or message people. Whatever it's called.

I should email again at some point with what achievements do and when they will probably get them. Jesus Christ! All this writing and thinking is going to give me a goddamn brain aneurism.

Besides the missing husbands and time travel, I explained about crafting classes and everything I could think of. I explained why there is an extra two babies here and everyone was fine with it. I think they all were just extremely happy they're here, safe in the city. And feel a little guilty they didn't have to do the tutorial dungeon or fight to get here. Besides my son. He loves rpgs and thinks he would be good as a crawler. I explained that last time he hated it. Hated it passionately. Being good at rpg stuff doesn't make you good at fighting and everything that goes along with crawling – all the horrible stuff. He agreed without much of an argument. Minnie was happy about that. Me too. And for everyone else, watching over two extra babies isn't a high price for safety, living comfortably, and not fighting for your life all the time.

Man, Nah's wife is hot. Plenty new material for the spank bank. I don't remember her being this hot last time.

Explaining to my family that the year is 2043 was hard, but they took the news like champs. I thought there'd be more drama. There wasn't none. To them, this morning was 2009. February. I guess them being from the past is easier to take than everyone on earth being sent to a dungeon world. My son just turned 15 last month. My daughter turns 17 this June. My ex cheats on me in June too. I don't know with who. I don't want to know. It will just make me more angry. Unless it is someone amazingly good looking, like Denzel or Brad Pitt. I bet it was some sissy looking pansy-boy. Brad Pitt is those things too, but come on. You can't expect a girl to say no to Brad Pitt. Even I can see why girls like him so much. And girls that go nutso for fancy nonsense like Louis Vuitton? Those girls would stab each other to death to get a chance to just make-out with Brad. And I married one of those girls. If it was Denzel or Brad Pitt it would've infuriated me, but I would've understood and got over it in time. But it wasn't. Just some Fayetteville pretty boy probably. I'm Bruno Vaz. I'm about as superior as a man can get. I can't accept or forgive cheating. Especially with a lesser person that isn't even a Hollywood heartthrob. Nope.

I thought it was February of 2009 when we all got here together last timeline. But then I started remembering more. My ex cheating on me. Splitting up. My daughter hating me. My son angry with me. My daughter going to college. Then my son going to college.

I remember Thanksgiving 2012. My son was going to college at NYU. A freshman. Living with his first boyfriend. A cop. A detective. Way older. Late 20s. Pretty good guy. Surprisingly, a manly guy. Big guy. Not as big as me, but pretty big. Tough looking too. I would've had no idea he was a homosexual by how he acted and talked. He seemed so normal. I remember being proud my sissy son had good taste in guys, got one that could protect his sissy ass, and had finally got himself a boyfriend. Finally stopped being so girly and chaste about it.

My son got pretty weird too. I stayed with him for a couple weeks and on the weekend he'd dress up like a girl and say his name was Candy Vase, but pronounced vase the fancy way where it sounds like my last name – Vaz. Since I joined Delta my kid's used my wife's maiden name and not Vaz. I use a different last name too. Depending on the situation or mission my last name was either Vasquez or Barbosa. But when my son dressed as a girl it was nice of him to recognize his real name, while also keeping it a secret. Respectful.

So, Thanksgiving, 2012. My son invited me. The first holiday I spent with one of my kids since the split with the ex. This is after years of everyone telling me I was crazy and spinning out of control and ignoring me and hating on me. Everyone turning their back on me. Betraying me. But my son invited me to Thanksgiving. Supported me. Was there for me. I love that little homo. That meant so much to me I can't even express it. Everyone thought I was teetering on the rain slicked precipice of darkness. I wasn't, but they all said I was. If I was, no one tried to pull me back. Besides my son. By just letting me spend time with him. Letting me feel okay, and wanted, and like a father.

I can't remember much past Thanksgiving 2012. But I remembered that. None of my family remembered anything at all beyond February 2009. But I did. Or do. I didn't tell anyone any of that. No need for them to know. Opening that can of worms would just confuse everyone.

And the other families didn't say much about us being from 2009, but they had to think it was weird or we're crazy. That isn't my problem though. They can think what they want.

Anyway, we are here, and to everyone in the world besides us, the current year is 2043.

I met someone else from a different time too. Like 2020-something. He didn't know or understand why either. He could have been lying. Who knows? It's not like I have proof, and neither did he.

I gave over money so all three families here could all rent houses. I like how housing works. It's pretty cheap for the basic ones, and you get to them through a door in an inn. All inns lead to all people's houses. I guess the game did the same thing. You can decorate them too. Some of the crafters make furniture and that stuff sells like hotcakes. And is expensive. Crazy. The nonsense people waste money on. But irregardless of all that nonsense, the houses are cheap and 100% safe to sleep in. Unless you give permission for someone that wants to murder you to enter. Like an idiot. Or not – a lot of spouses probably aren't safe. And in my last timeline a kid murdered his whole family. And it's not like it would be hard to get away with. That kid admitted

181

it all. If he cleaned himself up after and kept his mouth shut no one would've been able to get in the house to check. Or if he canceled the house and got a new one all evidence would have just disappeared. I think.

You can give permission for people to visit your house. And they can't take nothing. That is pretty neat. No thievery. Sleight of hand doesn't even function in player houses. Character houses I mean. But there are NPC houses you can rob blind. The real game has a thieves' guild. But this contest has no factions or guilds like that. Just player guilds. Character guilds. Jesus. Get it right and make it stick in your head, idiot. Character, not player, if you can't use crawler.

While everyone went to go get a class, my wife...ex I mean...and I rented the most basic, cheapest house for a month. Only five silvers more than a room. Twenty silver total. Great price. And there is a bug. You rent rooms and houses for a month. But time with this world doesn't jive with time in the real world, and there isn't a calendar in the UI. So if you rent a room or house for a month you get it forever. Or until you cancel it. I love bugs like that. Bugs that let you save money.

My wife and kids are soft and weak and always search for more and better comfort and luxury. So they will eventually upgrade to the best house. But I'm not paying for that useless crap. As we used to say in Bat, the greatest threats to survival is the search for comfort and a passive outlook. The best houses cost like half a mil gold. There are giant mansions in the millions too. Useless. Nonsensical. Only idiots would waste resources on dumb crap like that. Like the garbage Louis Vuitton crap my wife always whines about for me to get her. I'm not paying $700 for a scarf. Not unless that scarf transforms into a robot butler and wipes my ass on demand. Crazy. You could buy 700 normal scarfs for $700. Scarfs that look just as good and are of a similar

182

quality. But that label jacks the price up to ridiculous levels of utter craziness.

One of the things my wife and I always argue about is money. I'm cheap. I value the money I earn. She just wants to blow it all on garbage like a slightly nicer house that costs twice as much, or a car that does nothing worth noting more than a regular priced car but costs three times more. Nonsense. We watch a show together called something like Extreme Cheapskates. I hoped watching it with her would get her to see the genius and ingenuity of the people on it. She hoped watching it with me would embarrass me enough to start blowing my cash on useless garbage. We were both wrong.

A normal person would have got a job and bought their own garbage with their own money, but not Minnie. She's not normal. She demands I buy her the nonsense garbage she wants and smile and be happy about it when I do it. Nope. Cheating whore.

"Sorry, I really got to go. I'd rather stay, but I got to, you know, save the world and stuff." That came out rougher than I wanted. I think. Just thinking of her cheating makes me furious. But she doesn't show it on her face if she thought I said it too angrily.

"Why not take a bath with me? You kind of smell and you always used to shower after getting your hair cut." She smiles her sexy smile at me. I'd have rathered my son give me a haircut, but I wanted to get my ex alone. A haircut was a good reason. When I'm horny, I'm horny. I got to get it out of me or I'll go wicked nuts. So, we swung by a shop node thing and got some scissors and a razor, she gave me a haircut, and I gave her a toss in the hay. And now she wants to snuggle or something. Just yap about nothing. The price women charge us for helping get the devil out.

But I could use a bath. I haven't bathed in while. And this dumb place doesn't have civilized showers. I kind of treat crawling like the field. This was a quick swing by the rear where you have no time for anything but to hit the PX. But there's like seven civilized hours until the tutorial dungeon opens again, so why not? I don't even have to go back before then. I just want to, to make sure everything in my instance is going well. And kill that one guy. But I can kill him at any time, really.

"Good idea, pancake." I always call her non-traditional nicknames as punishment for naming my kids pet and monkey. I go over to the house control node thing and pay five silvers for a hot bath. It is a giant wooden tub that can easily fit four people. It appears out of nowhere, steaming. I'd rather relax and bathe alone, but my ex is being wicked accepting of everything I asked of her, and less annoying and yappy than usual. And when I explained how when I come back tomorrow I will start a guild and make her assistant guild leader, and that her job is going to be to run things I can't, she took it like a champ. She is good at organizing. She would've been better if she worked and had actual experience doing it in a professional manner, but beggars can't be choosers. Her father paid a fortune getting her a masters. Crazy she just wasted it. She started at UC Santa Barbara and ended at BU. That had to have cost an arm and a leg.

She needs to take what's-it-called as a class. Dammit, how did I forget already? Organizer? No. Administrator? No. Wait, I think that is right. Administrator. Sounds wrong but I think it's right. And I said "things I can't do" to make her feel better about doing it. I can do anything. I can talk to people and make stupid plans and other nonsense. I just don't want to. Everyone likes talking to Minnie. And she loves making stupid plans. Controlling a budget? She loves spending money more than anything. It works out perfectly. If I was into talking and planning and other nonsense I would be an officer. But I'm not because I am good at fighting and doing things. Actions.

We say more useless gibberish and nonsense as we get in the bath. I relax, leaning my back against the tub.

"Rooney-Bear, you should send another email out about you. Maybe explain a little about how qualified you are to be a leader. You were an officer. At least for a little while you were. And I know I'm not supposed to know or talk about it, but I know you are Special Forces or something. You're..."

I kind of dur-out after that. I feel the old fear that this whole thing is a trap to get me to betray secrets or past missions, but it goes away quick. If this is a trap the enemy deserves to win and get the info. Years long and how much money would all this cost? And manpower. It's all so real it can't be fake. And no one has ever asked me about past missions or any secrets.

And if it is fake, they either turned my wife, or were able to model her exact kind of crazy perfectly. So, the enemy is either so good they deserve to win any info they ask about but never do, or this is all real.

Maybe she has a point.

She stops her inane rambling. Maybe I should do what she says. She is smarter than me when it comes to social stuff. And math. And spelling. All the useless nonsense.

"You're right. I should do that. Good idea, brussel sprout." I probably won't. It is a good idea though. Writing is for losers and I've already written a wicked lot so far. When people see me in the solo arena that should be explanation enough.

"Maybe tell them about the brain injury and your other issues, you know, so they will be more understanding when you get mad?"

Anger flares inside of me. I don't have any goddamn issues! Unless being awesome and great at everything is an issue? Is being more competent than anyone else alive an issue? My brain is perfect. The concussion of an explosion can't hurt my superior brain. I've been in a ton of them. Why does everyone make such a big deal about just that one? I take some deep breaths to calm down. She is just trying to be helpful. I push my anger down into the big ball of hate in my belly.

She doesn't understand. She is just trying to help. I don't want to get in a fight so I don't say nothing. I take more deep breaths, gather up all the hate left in me, and just push it down into my hate-ball.

I go back to relaxing when my wife starts rubbing her foot on my leg. You dirty girl. I haven't even cleaned myself off yet. Eh, I should probably put some effort into making it good for her this time. I need her help going forward and, as Bruno Vaz, I have a reputation to uphold as a superior human.

I try not to, but I can't help but pretend she's Nah's wife. Just a little bit.

2.6 KILLER KIM

BRUNO VAZ

I take the portal back to dungeon area 1. I could have beamed back, but less people will see me this way. I think. And I will be closer to the medical and training areas I designated to see how good the monkeys are obeying orders. None of them should know I am from this instance, so it is a crapshoot if they listened to the camp set-up plan from my emails.

No one sees me appear. Everyone is looking at a scene a little ways off. A little tubby feller pointing a spear at a hot Indian looking lady. I walk closer to see what's up. The little tubby guy looks familiar. No. Girl. That's Barbosa's kid. Weird looking kid. Pretty funny too, but usually unintentionally. Mostly quiet. When we were on the path to the city she always wanted to help fight the tentacle monsters. I think her mother died on 10. Her father brought them to the city with me and my family and a ton of other people. Minnie told me about his wife later. No one knew until days after we got to the city. Not specifically who died, at least. We kind of figured it out by the arena leaders no longer advancing. Watching the arena was our only real source of entertainment on the trek to the city.

Barbosa is a pretty weak fighter, but pretty good compared to the others we had with us. He is a Cape Verdean from Providence. EP I think. So we hit it off because of that. He is in the military too. UN military. There is no US military anymore. He wore BDUs and had a

187

tab that said "special operations." I guess the sissy military in the future gives out tabs like the army gave out berets in 2001. They got rid of Rangers, Special Forces, Force Recon, Pararescue, SEALs, everything. All of them are now just special operations and everyone, even non-operator pogues that support them, wear the tabs too. All airborne divisions are now special operations. No blue cords for infantry anymore. Nothing that would make the pogues feel bad.

Bragg's name change to, like, Hiss or something, but most people call it Bragg still. There's no 82nd. Or even 18th AC. Just UN special operations all with a tab and light blue beret. The Marines are separate from the UN military. They're now the US maritime defense force, along with the prior coast guard. Their replacement for Force Recon still wear the "special operations" tab though. The navy is now just UN military. The air force is UN military. The Marines in maritime defense force still call themselves Marines. And they still seem decently competent. Not like they used to be. But better than the UN military.

From what I was told, not many soldiers do much fighting in future warfare. Computer controlled little drones do most of the fighting. Not missile drones. They're more like the little flying ones we got for recon and surveillance. You still have boots on the ground, but the combat is between drones and robots and crap. Mostly the little drones, since the little drones don't scare people as much as robots, but they do have some robots. Once an element is out of drones to do the fighting, which is never the UN, the enemy element still alive just surrenders.

I'd like to see these drone fights. I guess with computers controlling them, they just zip around like mad. No way for people to fight them. Too fast.

I bet I could fight those drones. And win too.

Barbosa is a clerk or something in a pogue unit. Stills wears the special operations tab though. The future is so ate-up. Funny enough,

Barbosa was usually my fake last name in Delta for embedded missions. Vasquez for special/clandestine missions. Me and Barbosa get along pretty good. I have plans for him in this timeline. Put his pogue skills to work.

I forget his daughter's name. I never met his wife, not that I remember at least. She is supposedly some sort of martial arts expert. Barbosa has a pretty normal skin tone for a Cape Verdean. Obviously black but obviously not full black. His oldest kid looks like he may have a little something in him, but his daughter and his special son look pure white. I think his kids have different last names than he does too, but that is common in the future. I guess women keep their maiden name when they get married, and kids get the mom's last name more often than not. The future is weird. Hopefully that explains it. If he is some sort of cuckold I would rather not know about it as I'd like him less, so I never asked about it.

As I get close I notice the girl is filthy and her special brother is close by, but not her other brother or her father. Not that I can see at least. And I don't know what her mother looks like, but no one around looks like they care enough about her to be her mother. It looks like her brother is holding food trays. What a weird kid. A little closer and I can actually smell the young girl. Awful, awful stink. Wicked bad.

The Indian looking lady isn't as hot as I thought. Pretty hot, but she has ass-eyes. Like Sylvester Stallone and John Kerry. I don't know what the name of that medical condition is, but I always called it ass-eyes. She would be gorgeous without those eyes. She is still wicked hot even with them, just not wicked, wicked hot. She is dressed like she works in an office. Most sane people dressed a little more appropriately for this. They had plenty of warning and even a countdown. Not my family. We had no warning. We all just woke up in the future. She has long, straight dark hair looking like she just brushed it. It looks like she is wearing lipstick too, which shouldn't be possible. Decent

189

amount of cleavage showing. Not as much as I'd like, but better than nothing. Dress shoes without heels. The girly type. Not like guy dress shoes. Slacks in a weird style. Probably the future style, but girls always dress ridiculous so it would probably be okay in any year. Fantastic rear-end. Just a grade A ass. Nice and juicy. As Sandler would say, "So hot, want to touch the hiney." She is a full adult to. Thirty-five maybe? She can't be younger than thirty. If she is forty she ages great.

The special brother looks clean and normal looking. You can't tell he is a special by looking at him when he is standing still, which he usually never is. He could be cast as the lead of a little kid movie with those looks. He's wearing BDUs and boots. The sister is wearing very damaged leather armor spattered with dirt and blood. Spear and shield. It looks like her brother cut her hair while having one of his hissy fits. It'd be hard to give her a dumber looking haircut even if you purposefully tried to as a prank. I forget the name of her color hair. Light-ish but dark hair. Like the color of the heavy girl from Facts of Life. The same color as her brother's. I notice she isn't nearly as tubby as I remember. She just looks it because she has a big frame. A good frame for a fighter. Heavy, broad shoulders. Especially at her age. She could be a real monster if she wants to be when she grows up. Good genetics. Like me. But I'm good looking. This kid is not. Her good genetics do not apply to her face. She looks like a frog. Her mouth is very wide and thin and she frowns a lot. Pig nose. Very weak chin and the start of a gullet already. She has stitches on her arm where the armor is rolled up. Very badly done stitches.

Killer Kim. That's her name. Or what I called her. So Kim. Always wanting to help fight the tentacle monsters. Never being allowed. I always liked her spirit. The kid has heart.

The smell is potent. A girl her age shouldn't be able to smell this bad. Kids just don't produce these smells. I also notice she is favoring her right leg and holding her shield with a weak grip. What happened to her?

Up till now I haven't been able to register whatever they have been bleating at each other. I don't remember how I missed this hot lady last time, as I notice hot women more than anything else. She smells great. She just oozes sexuality. I guess her ass-eyes aren't that bad.

I cut in to their conversation with, "Kim, where's your father?"

Both the hot girl and Kim look at me. Kim's eyes go sad as she says, "My father? He was murdered by a turd-pigeon. Who are you?"

Her father died? What? No he didn't. What is going on here? Turd-pigeons must be those side-eye toucan birds that dart at you. Barbosa wasn't a great fighter, but he wasn't bad enough to get killed by a bird, was he?

"Bruno Vaz. Where is your mother and your other brother?"

Her mouth gets even wider as she frowns, "The turd-pigeons got them too. Do I know you? I think I'd remember you. You have crazy eyes, like God."

What? And what? Her mother, I think, died in area 10. But everyone else was alive. I knew things were going to change this timeline, but everything should've been exactly the same for the tutorial dungeon. Right? That's how time travel works. Everything is the same unless you do something to change it. I understand the butterfly effect and I saw a bunch of time travel movies. I know how this stuff works. How did her parents die? How could events change before I change them myself? Which I couldn't do in any way before leaving the tutorial dungeon. She had the same exact party and it should have played out the same exact way.

And I have eyes like God? That's really weird to say. Usually people say I look angry all the time. The turd-pigeon thing is the only thing she has said at all I can easily figure out. Obviously they are the toucan type birds with the one big eye people say are from some new Mario game.

I could tell she didn't recognize my name. The hot lady did though, and I hear a few gasps from some people watching.

"I'm really sorry for your loss. Losses. Are you okay? What's going on here?"

Her face fills with rage, "This lady is trying to steal my brother. Over my dead body!"

The hot lady looks between us both and says, while smiling at me and giving a stink-eye to Kim, "Steal? I am a special needs teacher. As a teacher I am an authorized agent of the UN and it is my duty to ensure the safety and welfare of children. Joseph went to my school. I know him. I know his needs. I'm better equipped to take care of him. I'm so sorry for what happened to your family. And you did an amazing job getting through the dungeon, but I don't think it is in the best interest for anyone involved to leave Joseph in your care."

She smiles at me again and is kind of staring at me. In a hot, flirty way I think. It's hard to tell with women. Especially future women. They are prone to having hissy fits if you flirt back when you think they're flirting. Man, I'd love to get my dinky wet with her.

I say, "Why? Did something happen? Did Kim hit him or something? Not feed him?"

She gives me a bigger, sexier smile – only slightly ruined by her ass-eyes. I think one of her eyes is off too. Just a little googly. That must stink, being so hot but having ass-eyes ruin it and also having one of your ass-eyes be a little googly. "No. I don't know. It's just…I'm not sure how safe she is. Look at her. And she keeps saying she is the darkness and she will kill me and eat me. And pee on me too!"

Well, that isn't good. Weird stuff, but Kim is a weird kid. I say, "Kim, what do you mean by the darkness?"

"Me. I'm the darkness."

"But...what is it? What does it mean?"

"It means me. I'm the darkness. God wants me to kill for him. Not people. The monsters. And this lady, maybe, if she keeps trying to kidnap my brother and steal him from me. And his name is Joey, lady, not Joseph. Joey. I told you a million times and you keep saying Joseph. It is so easy. Try it. Joey. So easy to say."

Okay. Good answer. Not crazy at all. Jesus, this kid was weird last time, but not full-blown nutso.

"God wants you to kill monsters for him?"

"Ahhhh, yeeeah." She said this sarcastically like it's common knowledge and I'm an idiot for asking. She continues, "I had to pass a test and everything. And I did. And it was crazy and hard, but I did it. I definitely did it."

"How long were you in the tutorial dungeon?"

She shrugs her shoulders and says, "I don't know. A long time."

"One second," I say as I pull up the dungeon rankings. I zoom in my minimap to see her player number. Character number I mean. I enter it.

Holy Jesus and his mother Mary!

Ranking is decided by four metrics. Yellow, red, green, and grey. This is something else I should have definitely explained in my emails. The smart people had to figure all this out by asking tons of questions since none of it is explained. Grey is time it took to clear the dungeon. Time is stated in the savage way. This world's time. Yellow is a percentage representing percent cleared. Was there any dark areas left on the map? What they call fog of war. Red is another percentage representing what they call perfection – doing the dungeon true blue. All first time goes. Your HP shield never breaks, no trap is tripped, and psuchesomas are beaten on the first try. Green is just a number. What they call activity points. This number goes up doing damage, taking damage, healing damage, completing scripted events, looting items.

Stuff like that. Even if you are in a group, if you don't get a lot of activity points, you don't get the full payout of coins the rest of the group will. So people can't be carried too hard. You still got to do stuff.

Time cleared is the most important. It is like a multiplier. You have to clear dungeons wicked fast to get SS. Second most is perfection. Third is percent cleared. Last is activity. Activity shoots up when you already got SS and are doing a grinding run, where numbers for everything else are garbage. Her activity points are off the charts. With a black dot above it. That means a rare monster spawned. Maybe that was the turd-pigeon she was talking about that killed her family?

Maybe…maybe…yes. That would make sense. If coming back in time gave a new RNG roll and the Barbosa family got unlucky and got a wicked rare occurrence of a rare spawn in the tutorial dungeon. That would explain it. Why events are different now.

Rare mobs have almost no chance of spawning in lower level dungeons. I never heard of one spawning in the tutorial dungeon. Ever. Maybe because everyone dies when it happens? The smart people say dungeon 1 has a .5% chance, and 2 had a 1% chance, and 3 has a 1.5% chance, all the way up to level 20 which has a 10% chance. Same with 21 to 30 level dungeons and raids in the epic area, still a 10% chance. There's a rare drop potion that increases the base chance for a rare spawn from 1% more up to 20% more. Those were wicked valued as once you clear the last dungeon and arena, rare spawns are the only way to farm more dungeon coins. And the chance is rerolled after the dungeon resets every day you spend in a dungeon. But rare spawns are dangerous. Especially if you are running solo or in a duo. That would definitely explain how her family got killed. Just blowing through the trash mobs and then getting jumped by a rare spawn when you didn't even know rare spawns were a thing.

Seeing the rare spawn is a surprise. But the biggest surprise is her time. Almost a year. 283 days. Savage time. But savage years and earth years are about the same if I'm remembering right. Just a little longer. Crazy. She got 100% cleared. A 0% for perfection. Her total rating is a dot. Rank C. The lowest rating. She deserves a 1st SS for what she's been through.

"Kim, I'm sorry to ask this, but when did your parents die? How many days in? And was it the rare spawn that caused them to die?"

"It's okay. It was the first day. The turd-pigeons west of the intersection above the safe field. What's a rare spawn?"

"A rare spawn is a different monster than all the rest. Not the boss. It would have been something different and it should have had a label and a CR rating. Something like three-two or three-three or something like that?"

"Oh. The giant turd-snake. Huge viper. That was…a long time ago. Way after the first day though. I forget the exact CR. Maybe three-three. He was real hard to kill. His poison was crazy. That day I met God and officially became the darkness. Joey almost…," she stops and looks at the hot lady. I know what she was probably going to say. Rare spawns go after the shielded. Joey almost died. She saved him.

Jesus. This is a tough kid. Definitely not right in the head, though. But not too bad, hopefully. Just a little messed up. She may just need time around people. That is a lot of time for a kid to be all alone. Well, alone besides her special brother. But he doesn't talk. Or he never talked around me at least. He made tons of noises nonstop, but never words.

"You're a tough kid. You did great. Your parents would be wicked proud of you."

"Ahhhh, yeeeah. I know. I'm the darkness. But I ain't no kid. I've had many periods. I'm a woman now."

Ha. Goddamn, I love this kid. Spunk. I like it.

I smile at her and say, "Sorry. You're right. You're definitely a woman now." I turn to the hot lady, "Can I talk to you for a second?"

She smiles back and says yeah. I say, "Kim, were you in line for medical treatment? Why not take your brother and get back in line. I'll be over in a couple to talk to you."

She says okay and grabs her brother and moves out.

I walk back towards where I ported in. Away from the gathering crowd. They give us the space. Just one guy has moved closer. Staring at me. Giving me a tough-guy look. A decent sized guy. He is white with a shaved head. What a lot of balding guys do. Earrings and eyebrow rings. He doesn't have hair but he looks like the type of guy that would use a lot of hair product if he did. And use a lot of cologne. He is wearing a tight v-neck t-shirt with a lot of hairless chest showing, tight jeans, and sneakers that look like a more colorful version of something an astronaut would wear. His t-shirt is tucked into his jeans. How broken does your mind have to be to tuck a t-shirt into jeans? He looks like he wants to go clubbing instead of dungeon crawling. Maybe thirty-five years old. Forty maybe. Looks like the whiter, southern version of the of the Jersey goombah. Our goombahs in Boston are pretty cool. The ones in NYC are almost normal. Only the Jersey and Philly ones are wicked weird.

If you think about it, it's kind of weird that guys do the same thing with guys they want to fight and girls they want to start talking to – stare at them with an angry face like an idiot. I do the same thing, but unlike the hillbilly goombah giving me the stink-eye, I can actually fight. I could roll this sissy into a ball with little effort. I don't think it will come to that. Most future people have no fight in them. Not for physical fights. Hissy-fit fight? They can do that all day. But not an actual fight.

I turn to the hot lady and put my hand out to shake. "Bruno Vaz."

She smiles and daintily shakes my hand like a fish would. "Melissa Kaur."

Kaur. That is the Sikh female name. I forget what it means. Singh means lion. I served with a Sikh guy. The guys aren't supposed to cut their hair ever. They wrap it in turbans. The guys are all supposed to be warriors and are always supposed to have this certain kind of knife on them. Most Sikhs I met never seemed that tough or warrior like. Most of them are doctors or tech dorks – sissy stuff like that. The one I served with was. Real tough guy. He had short hair though. But he always had the knife. I never really saw him do any religious stuff, so I'm not sure if he was devote or not. And I have no idea what they believe in. What their religion is about. I think it was started to be outside the Indian caste system, but I have no idea, really. If Sikh females are supposed to be warriors too, this one stinks at being a Sikh from what I'm seeing. No warrior dresses for the office when they're going to war.

"You're right about Kim. She just went through a crazy ordeal. She was in the dungeon for a year. A whole year. Can you imagine that? Just her and her brother. And just her fighting. I never even heard of a rare spawn in the tutorial dungeon, and she fought it and won. You know how hard that is? A little girl on her own. Anyone would be a little off after that."

Her eyes flash and I can see a little crazy trickle into them, "I agree. But why point out that she is a girl? Would a boy have done any better? Are you a sexist?"

God. Grant me the strength to deal with these types of people. I'll just pretend she stopped talking after saying she agreed for this conversation and my sanity.

"I'm no expert on this stuff, but I don't think splitting them up is a good idea. You offered to take the brother. Any chance you could take them both and keep them together?"

Her eyes, and her whole demeanor, softens, "I...we can't. Our group is full. Your messages said the people with shields don't count towards party size. For his own safety I think it would be best if we take Joseph with us. I can't even work with Kimberly out here; I can't even talk with her without her threatening to stab me. And I'm not the first person she has threatened to stab. I'm like number three or four. That I know of. She isn't receptive to help. She may be beyond help at this point. I knew her mother, so I wish I could help her. We weren't friends but she was at the school a lot with Joseph. I saw her around all the time."

She stops looking me in the eyes and takes a calming breath and continues like she is making a decree, like a judge would, "In my professional opinion, and by my authority as an agent of the UN regarding child safety, the kids should be split up. For both of their sakes. For their safety. Kimberly is a danger to herself and others."

Now the sexy smile is gone and she is looking at me like I'm an unreasonable criminal for some reason. Maybe she saw some anger show on my face? I don't know. It seems like she is writing Kim off. She's just a kid. A kid that's been through hell and back. That ain't right. Maybe because I grew up mainly in foster care I don't like people writing kids off. Especially people that really think they care and are good people doing good work. Splitting siblings up seems wrong. Especially in this case, when Kim kept her brother alive for a year in a dungeon. She got them both out alive. As a little kid. A little girl. She should get praised for that. Not punished. Not separated. Her whole family was killed. Her brother is all she's got.

I don't know why a self-proclaimed expert couldn't see this. And how is a teacher an expert on this stuff anyways?

Growing up every year we took something called the Iowa Test. It was like a placement exam. I did pretty good on it, but I always ended up in the romper room. Completely my fault. I was a troublemaker.

The romper room is what everyone called the special education class-room, or sped. With special education teachers. I never got along with any of them, and did my best to drive them nuts, but that was exactly why I was put in the romper room. And not a one of them ever cared about me. I dropped out of school early, and got my GED later. But a big reason for that was the – what was it called – IEDs? No IEPs, maybe? Individual Education Plan, I think. A packet they'd give you with all your classwork for the week. They didn't even try. I got pic-tures to color at 16 years old. Why would I care about people that didn't even sort of try, or care even a little bit about me? They were paid to care about me and my education, and never did.

But they all thought they were angels for doing what they did. Give a 16-year-old that always did well on the Iowa Test pages to color. Never teach anything, but always talk about politics. Make deals with little kids that if they didn't get too crazy you'd take them out for a smoke. I bet they tell all their friends they are basically a modern day Mother Teresa for doing what they do. All the kids they help. Back then they used to put the real special kids in with kids like me. We weren't monsters. We never messed with the special kids. But being with us meant the special kids were always around violence and ag-gression. And a bunch of them were normal in the head too, just like deaf or things like that.

But none of that is as bad as the embarrassment of me getting an IEP with pages to color like a five-year-old. From people claiming to be my teacher. People paid to care but never did. Same with social workers. And most foster parents.

I may not like teachers, but the worst thing about her is she is a full name user. I can't stand when people use full names. They're usu-ally the worst people in the world and probably make up 95% of the people who cruise in the passing lane and stop people from driving normal speeds. Just plain jerks. True degenerates with broken minds.

That's the best sign for if a guy is a complete narcissist and egomaniac – he uses his full, long name. It is fine when girls use their full names because they think it sounds prettier or something – girls always do dumb stuff because they think it's pretty. Like wear high-heels and have wicked long hair. Guys demanding you waste your time and half your life calling them by their full, long first name. Ew, they infuriate me. There's no excuse or good reason for a guy to do it. Ever. Those guys should be shunned from civilized, polite society.

There is one type of person that is even worse than guys that demand people use their full, long, dumb name – and those are people that decide everyone around them is going to be called by their full first names regardless of what the people around them want. These people are as awful as politicians and lawyers. The worst of the worst. Usually full-on crazies. This lady is one of those types.

This lady is hot, but I am starting not to like her. And it takes a lot for me to not like a wicked hot lady. Two can play the name game though, Ass-eyes.

"Mel, there is no UN anymore. Not here. When I help humanity beat this contest and get back to earth, you can be an agent for them and do UN agent stuff all you want. But I'm the only government here."

I see her face turn crazy with irrational anger. "Oh, really? My name is Melissa, by the way. Ms. Kaur to you. You really think you can spread terrorist propaganda and get away with it? You think you can just replace the UN because you claim to come from the future and took control of a game city? You think I…"

I interrupt, "Calm down, lady. Jesus. Relax. We're just talking."

"RELAX! CALM DOWN! WHO DO YOU THINK YOU ARE TALKING TO!!!"

I was going to interrupt and tell her to stop being so hysterical when the club goombah comes forward and says, "This guy giving you a problem, Melissa?"

Nice! I don't hit women, but I have no issues beating up their boyfriends. And be guilt free too, if he is the one to start it. I hope he tries to get physical. But he is a future guy, so probably doesn't have the sack.

"YES! This misogynist said I have to do as he says and is spreading terrorist, anti-UN propaganda, William!"

The goombah's stink-eye increases ten-fold. He is actually flexing too, I think. Ha. He says, "You have a problem with women and the UN, guy?"

Guy? Ew, I'm going to love smashing this idiots face in. "We're just talking, Billy. Is this your girl? I didn't say anything bad about the UN, and I definitely didn't say anything to make her so hysterical. You.."

"HYSTERICAL? HIS GIRL! NO ONE OWNS ME! HYSTERICAL!"

Still looking at the goombah I say, "You need to calm her down."

Melissa is about to have another hissy fit when Billy says, "Don't worry, Melissa. I got this."

Got what? I'm not the one freaking out and having a hissy fit for no reason. He steps forward and tries to grab me. He has zero chance of doing so. But this makes me very happy. I didn't think he would actually try and get physical. The way future people usually fight is by out hissy-fitting each other.

It only takes me a fraction of a second to strip his HPs and less time to blast him in the nose. It shatters and blood goes flying everywhere. He falls and as I walk forward the crazy lady jumps on my back, yelling like a psycho. Before I can fling her off, the grappling rules kick in and I end up on top of her on the ground. I quickly get up. That couldn't have looked good to people watching. Definitely not my fault though.

Goombah is rolling back and forth on the ground, yelling and holding his nose. What was this idiot thinking? How could he have thought he stood a chance against me? He tucks his t-shirt into his jeans for Christ's sake. Maybe the dungeon overinflated his ego? The future people aren't smart.

Melissa is in a full craze now and I can tell she plans on attacking me again. I grab the goombah's arm and say, "Stop, or I'll break his arm." She keeps coming so I pop his arm out of the socket. I'm pretty good at breaking bones, but it isn't a science. Not doing it this way. Even if you are careful, even if you do it real nice and good, it could compound. What is the upper arm bone called? The humorous? Or is that the elbow? Whatever it is, breaking it like this could also risk cutting the artery there. What's-it-called? Not femoral. Something like broccoli. Brachial. That's it. Anyways, too risky breaking it.

Popping it out of the socket sounds wicked awful, and the goombah starts screaming like a little baby. I know that hurts. It hurts a lot. But come on, have some dignity. I give him a kick to the button to shut him up. Thankfully, it does. He goes out. I don't want to cause the guy permanent damage or mess his brain up so another strong blow to the head wouldn't be ideal. He is either just trying to get some snappy nappy, or Mel is his girl and it was his duty to defend her. Either way, I can sympathize. Despite tucking his t-shirt into his jeans and wearing astronaut sneakers, he could be an okay guy. I grab his other arm and just look at Mel.

She stops. Smartest thing she's done all day.

"Now relax. You can think what you want. Hate me all you want. But stop yelling. You'll never be able to hurt me, or find someone that can. If I wanted I could kill everyone in this instance. You're all alive because I allow it. Understand?"

She just glares at me instead of answering. Her arms crossed. Big angry frown. The pout makes her big lips even more sexy. Too bad this went so bad. Not much chance of us banging now.

"Okay. Listen. You can't have Joey. I'm not splitting them up. But I'll take an active role in both of them. They are my responsibility. I'll watch over them. Sound good?"

More glare, still no answer. I need some help with a situation I have to resolve, and since I already found a lady trying to recruit kids, Mel should do nice.

"I got something important for you to do. Two kids, girls, under twelve. Little teeny kids, like six or so. They need help. They need someone to care about them and look after them. They aren't specials but they've been through a lot. Orphans. They got no one. I could really use a UN teacher agent to help them. Think you could do that?"

Still just more glare, no answer. But this one needs an answer so we bang in my mind as I wait her out. I can almost see the crazy leave her as she lets out a breath and says, "What about William? You almost killed him!"

"He's fine. Physically. Not in his head though. He isn't too bright. Could just be a case of bad-taste-in-women. He'll heal up fine. You should tell him it looks wicked stupid to tuck a t-shirt into jeans when he wakes up." I call some bigger guys I see standing around over and ask them to bring Billy to the medical line. Young guys, probably military from Bragg. One shakes my hand and introduces himself with a big smile and some awe. The other won't look me in the eyes. I don't care as long as he does what I say. They carry off the dummy to the medical line, being careful of his shoulder injury.

Melissa says, "You are a monster doing that to William. And for what you said to me."

"Sure, lady. Whatever you say."

"Where are the kids? I'll see what I can do. I'm not helping you. But helping kids is my duty." She stopped looking me in the eyes a ways back. She is just sadly looking at the ground now. Her eyes don't look so sassy when she's looking down.

I guess she means helping other kids besides Kim. "This way. We got to look for them. I'm not sure where they are right now."

We pass by the medical line and I tell Kim it will be I little while more before I get back, but not to worry about being split from her brother. She doesn't really react to that news, like it was a forgone conclusion and an obvious truth. I really like this kid. She lets me know I have blood on my face and I thank her and move out.

Where we walk I hear whispers and lots of people are staring at me. Word is spreading about who I am. The camp is set-up right. Mostly right. It reminds me I got a lot to do. Ways to help.

Some people try to stop me to talk, but I tell them as nice as I can I'll have to get back to them. That I'm in the middle of something important. Melissa asks me some questions. I answer as best I can. As truthfully as I can. She doesn't like my answers. Or me. She seems kind of depressed. Oh well. Her fault for messing with me and being unbearable and crazy. She freaked out for absolutely no reason at all. I didn't do nothing for her to react like that.

I finally see the girls' father. And the girls a little ways away, just sitting. Not near no one else. The little one playing. They both look defeated. The older one has wild eyes that don't match the rest of her sad composure.

"Mel, those are the girls there. After I start talking to the father go talk to the girls. Find out what you can. Please."

"I thought you said they were orphans. What am I supposed to find out about anyways? Specifically?"

"Just talk to them and find out if something is wrong. Look them over. You'll see. I don't want to put ideas in your head. I want you to find out by yourself." After a pause I remember to say please.

She doesn't say anything so I walk towards the father. Real scumbag, this guy. He doesn't look it. He looks normal. Like a regular guy. He doesn't see me until I'm like ten feet away. He doesn't say anything when he looks up. Just watches me approach. I get real close.

"Stay seated. My lady friend is going to talk to your kids. Don't talk. Don't move."

He decides he wants to talk and move. So I take his HP shield and sit him down. He could be tough to the sissy people of the future, or the sissy people in my time, but not to me. Not even a little. So controlling him isn't much of a fuss and doesn't even rile the kids up. When he tries to talk I apply more pressure. A small crowd is watching and coming closer so I yell out, "Stay back please. Give us space." Mel is talking to the girls.

I look over for a second occasionally. Not to see what Mel and the kids are doing, but to make sure no one is bothering them or interfering. She talks to each kid separately for a while. I'm not good at judging time, but it has to be over ten minutes, but probably not more than a half-hour before Mel calls me over. I wave her over to me. She lets out an annoyed and exasperated breath before storming towards me. She won't look at the father. I notice that.

"I didn't want to talk in front of him."

"Okay."

We wait in silence before she says, "So? Can we talk somewhere else? Can you tell him to go stand over there?"

"No. Just say it here. What did you learn?"

She sighs again, I think to show me how annoyed and exasperated she is by me. "Let me say first the UN has specific protocol on how to deal with situations like this."

More silence. I guess she wants a reply from me. "Okay," I say.

"So, don't do anything crazy. We'll deal with this the right way. Okay?"

"Okay."

"You promise?"

"Yes."

"The kids have signs of physical abuse."

"Anything else?"

She pauses and says, "Yes. They say…it looks like, and I think…I'm sure they have been sexually abused. Badly. Fully."

That is what I needed to hear. I do the gesture for my quickslot 3. It is embarrassing when people are watching to do gestures. My short sword appears in my hand and I start hacking at the monster's neck. I hear people screaming as I hack. Mel tries to grab my arm but I elbow her off me. It takes me a couple seconds to get his head off. It isn't easy. Not with a short sword at least. Much harder than you'd think or from what movies lead people to believe.

The monster has a pony tail so I use that to hang his head from my belt. Melissa is still on the ground from when I elbowed her off me. I didn't do it hard, but I needed her out of my way while I did what needed doing. I put my hand out for her to grab so I can pull her up. She ignores it and looks at me like I'm the monster. What is wrong with people? She heard what he did. I'm not the bad guy here. I'm certainly not the monster.

Not in this situation at least.

She keeps ignoring my hand and staring at me like I just decided to nuke the whole world and kill everyone so I give up. "Follow me, please. We need to go talk to the kids."

"You promised you wouldn't do anything crazy! That you'd do this the right way!"

"Yeah. I didn't do anything crazy and I dealt with it the right way. You know what he did."

She stays on the ground still looking at me like I'm the crazy one.

I quickly walk to the kids and kneel down in front of them. The older one isn't crying but the younger one is. I'm not good with knowing how old kids are. The older one is probably somewhere between six and ten. The younger one is probably somewhere between four and seven. Maybe? Who knows? It doesn't matter. The younger one starts crying more when she sees me. I'm blocking the head from their view. So it isn't that. Most kids are scared of me. I'm a giant guy, and people say I have a mean face.

"Hey, girls. How you doing? My name is Bruno Vaz. You don't got to worry about your father no more. None of that stuff. You know the lady that was just talking to you? She's going to take care of you now. Would you like that? She's not right in the head but she is better than your dad, right? Easy on the eyes too, huh?"

Mel isn't with us yet. And the older girl doesn't answer. The younger is still crying. Mel comes up and before she can start talking I say, "Could you do me a huge favor? Can you just go tell the crowd why I did it? In my timeline we caught that fu…that scumbag doing it a couple weeks into the path to the city. And you verified it with the kids this time so it ain't just me saying it. Tell them that's how I operate. I don't tolerate that stuff."

"Can you say that again? Your accent. I haven't heard a New York accent that thick ever outside of really old movies."

"New York? Are you re…nuts? I'm from civilization. Brockton, Mass. Jesus. New York." I repeat what I said slower and more better so even hillbillies can understand me. New York. What an idiot. Disgusting.

She looks like she doesn't want to go, but she does. Good girl. She is learning. I probably should have gone and talked to the crowd myself, but nothing good usually comes from me talking to or trying to explain things to people. Everyone gets upset or angry at the normal, regular things I say. I wish my wife was here. She could handle this easy. Mel will probably tell the crowd I'm a jerk and a monster and all her terms for how awful I am. I don't care. Should keep the monkeys from talking to me. As long as she tells them why I did what I did. She has the right to her opinion of me.

The girls don't look like they want to talk to me so much, and when I try it doesn't get us anywhere, so I just say what I think is comforting stuff and wait. Most of the time waiting I 'm banging Mel in my mind. Looking at her butt. Let me get some of that on toast.

Mel comes back and ignores me and starts talking to the kids. She does real good. A natural at talking to kids. Besides Kim I guess. With the most important thing taken care of I head of. It takes me a minute to notice Mel is following me. This is kind of weird, I have the head of the father hanging from my belt and I would have tried to block it if I knew the girls were there. I tell her to go back and check on Billy. Unless she wants to bang, I have no further use for her. I don't say that part out loud, of course. Why was she following? What a weird lady. The hotness makes up for a lot of the crazy though.

The best thing about the head on my belt? It keeps most of the monkeys from blathering their inanities at me.

2.7 WOOD THAT NEEDS IGNITING

BRUNO VAZ

I wanted to get back to Kim, but I checked out the rest of everything by walking around. I also sent out a new email explaining the Kim thing. How things changed I didn't change. Let the smart people mull over that. I also explained dungeon rankings. That should have been in the other emails I sent and is wicked important so I wrote out an explanation quickly. It wasn't good. But good enough for government work. I also explained how from dungeon area 2 onwards, you can go back to lower dungeon areas. That's pretty important and I somehow forgot it. So you can meet people outside your area. But you'll always just advance with your own area. The different instances will all eventually merge though. You could group with people from a different instance if everyone comes back to this area and rerolls characters.

Too much information to remember or try to explain. No big deal. Plenty of time. Mining is important. Real mining, just like real blacksmithing. Making real tools and things you can't get in the store. I got to talk to Minnie about that. I never saw any real mining, but I know it happened. Maybe in the city mat grinding zones?

As I walked around I kept my eyes open for hot girls that may want to bang and some other people I had plans for. I spotted a guy I forget the name of, who also went to the city with us and was probably the best fighter besides me. He wasn't good, but he was the best of what we had. I forget his real name. I called him Lurch. Also, last time I was

209

here there was a General that took charge. A Brigadier General. His job is organizing so he should be good at it. I'm going to recruit him to replace my wife until everyone gets to the city. Not recruit him for hanky-panky, but for organizing and handling questions and nonsense I don't care about since my wife can't do it yet. And Generals make people feel safer probably. Most people, since he is UN. The sympathizers won't like it, but I got to throw the bulk of people here a bone or two. And we won't mix with the terrorist countries for a while.

No hot girls so far. Well, not single ones of the right age. A lot of hot young ones. But I don't like young ones. They're ridiculous pseudo-people. I like women around my age. Thirty-five is perfect. Thirty is as young as I will usually go. I want a women that has been beat-up by life a little (or a lot) and that has had to develop a personality. Young hot girls never have one. Not a good one at least. They don't need it. And I don't consider anyone under twenty-five to be a real person, so girls younger than that don't count as people to me. It would be like banging a dog. A really hot dog.

I'm horny still. Mel got my juices flowing. Well, before she turned out to be completely nuts and irrational. I'll see my wife again tomorrow. Well, not tomorrow for me. It will be way more time than a day for me, but officially it will be tomorrow. My wife is still wicked hot anyways. Way hotter than Mel. And my wife is sane, too. Mostly sane.

My ex I mean. The cheater. I can't forget that. Filthy whore.

I spotted the General, but didn't approach. The General looked like he was going to come up to me, but I had too much writing and serious talk lately. So I didn't move before he could.

Talking to Kim was really enjoyable. Refreshing. So I plan on talking to her again, then the arena, then the General. Deal with planning the next dungeon romp, which will be both grinding and training.

I head back to the medical area and Kim is talking to what I assume is a doctor. I hope is a doctor. I don't remember if there was an actual doctor or just nurses and EMTs or whatever. Neither me nor my family got hurt last time here so I never checked. This lady looks too young to be a doctor, but I'm not the best with age. I'd be surprised if she was thirty. She is a white, and also a tubby, squirrelly little thing. Not pretty, but not ugly. She has potential if she did herself up. Her hair is like a brown with some kind of blondish parts, in a sloppy bun thing. She is wearing what looks like hide armor. And glasses. Most people's vision is fine when their HP shield is going, so glasses are rare.

I'd throw it in her if it didn't take too much effort. Well, if she is at least thirty.

I walk up and Joey grabs my bicep and starts making noises and shaking a tray at me. This kid has good taste. He recognizes my bicep is amazing. He is probably trying to tell me my muscles are awesome. Real muscles. From hard, constant work. Not fake gym muscles that are useless to the sissy-boys that have them. Souped-up suckers.

The squirrel keeps poking at Kim's back. I watch. Then Kim inventories her armor and I look away. 1 minute passes and I check to see if it's okay to look now. Kim has some sort of large sports bra on that covers everything plus some so I didn't even have to turn my head to begin with. The lady is still probing her back, so I walk up to see what the issue is.

The lady says, "Who are you?"

I put my hand out to shake and say, "Bruno Vaz."

Her eyes get huge, "Oh. Oh. I read your messages. Amazing! I'll be with you in a moment. As soon as I'm done with young Ms. Gum here. Is this about constitution and sickness? From the messages?" She smiles at Kim as she says it. Kim's last name is Gum? Barbosa is way better. Strong. Gum is dumb and stupid. Poor kid. I knew a Gummo back when I lived in Dorchester. I wonder if Gum started as Gummo but got changed when people immigrated at Ellis Island.

"Sorry, no. Not yet. I'm all talked and thinked out. I'm just check-ing on young Ms. Gum myself. What's wrong with her back?"

"Oh. Broken and displaced ribs, it looks like. Pretty serious. This type of injury heals with difficulty and usually not well. She is lucky her lung wasn't punctured. We aren't supposed to wrap chests as it risks respiratory infection, but in this case we'll have to. Another issue is placement. She can't rest on her back for it to heal. There really is no good way for her to rest. It will take a while for it to start knitting. And there are...spurs already. It started healing and broke off multiple times. This isn't good. And we don't have the equipment to properly treat it surgically. Even if there were a surgeon here."

The lady seems flustered from talking to me. Me specifically. The time travelling leader. She isn't very observant. I have a head hanging off my belt I figure she'd have an issue with. But she hasn't even sort of seen it.

"I never got your name."

"Oh. Be...Doctor Calderon. Nice to meet you. Sorry."

Calderon? No wedding ring I see. She looks pure white too.

"Nice to meet you, doctor. You see anything else? This kid...lady, I mean, has been through hell and back."

Kim smiles at the lady comment. I can tell it hurts when the doctor pokes at her back, but she is taking it like a champ.

"Yes. Multiple serious injuries." The doctor goes on to explain that Kim's left hand is all messed up. The bone healed wrong and has torn things and messed up stuff. Both legs had major injuries that healed wrong. And her right ankle had something wrong with it, and the top of her right foot too. Minor stuff like lots of bad stitches and cuts. Lots of pretty bad scars. Kid's been through a lot.

I only planned on going to 30 in the arena, but after seeing this, and how difficult it will be for her ribs to heal naturally, I'm changing it to 50 to get a healing pill for Kim. Probably. We'll see. She deserves it though. But I just can't give mine out all willy-nilly. I got to be smart about it. I'll need some of them for myself later. But broken ribs suck. I hate broken ribs. Poor kid.

After the doctor finishes up with Kim she looks like she wants to talk to me. But she is too nervous to or something. Not my problem. I'll be around if she gets the courage. I ask Kim to grab Joey and follow me. We see Mel and her now conscious boyfriend in line with the orphan girls. Billy won't look me in the eye, but Mel smiles and nods at me. What a weirdo.

The three of us walk to an open area away from everyone, but where we can view the training going on. I sit down on a downed tree and Kim sits beside me. Joey takes the ground a ways away from us, so he can focus on shaking his trays without being bothered I guess.

Kim speaks first, "What's with the head?"

It takes me a second to figure out what she is talking about.

"Someone did stuff he shouldn't have. A monster. He looked like a man but was a monster. Now he's a decoration. Keeps the monkeys from bothering me, too."

"Awesome. If that lady took my brother I would have done the same. I'd wear her head on my belt."

I didn't say anything. This isn't the usual type of stuff you talk to kids about. How old is she, even?

I was going to ask when she says, "I never killed a real person before. Just monsters. Actual monsters. Not monsters that look like a man even."

"That's good. Killing people is ugly business. You shouldn't have to worry about it. I know you are a real woman now, but you shouldn't have to think about that at your age. How old are you?"

"Twelve."

"You spent a year in the dungeon. What is your birthday?"

"July thirtieth, twenty-thirty."

"So, thirteen now, huh?"

"I guess so, yeah."

"You know how the doctor said you shouldn't do any strenuous activity for three months?"

She looks guilty when I say this. I figured she had no plans to obey the doctor's orders.

"Yeah."

"I think I may have a way to get you healed up quicker. But it depends on some things."

"What things?" She looks at me with side-eyes, all skeptical. Like I'm trying to scam her.

"Nothing right now. I just wanted to talk for a bit."

"But what is the thing later? Is it gross or…something you could get arrested for?"

"What? No. Jesus, kid. It's just something I'd give you."

"Something gross or illegal?"

"What is wrong with you? No. Actually, that's good. You don't know me well so questioning me is a good idea. Smart. But, no. Nothing gross or illegal or inappropriate or anything."

She still looks skeptical but says, "Okay. What did you want to talk about?"

Watching the people train ineptly, I remember I still have to do the arena and send off another email too, and it makes me want to rush. Seeing me in the arena will help people train, and help them realize why I was sent back. Why I'm in charge. But this is important too, so rushing would be stupid. Being impatient would be stupid. I take a deep breath and clear my head and try to focus on the now.

"Nothing important. Just talking. I'd like to ask about your mission from God though. Anything specific you wanted to ask me about?"

"Yeah. How come you say ax instead of ask? And how come you talk so funny?"

"I definitely don't talk funny. I talk right. Everyone else talks wrong. Ever hear of Massachusetts? Boston?"

"Yeah. My grandfather used to live in Attleboro. I've been there a bunch when I was little."

"Didn't you notice people talked like me?"

"No they didn't. They talked like me. Regular. Normal."

Barbosa said that too. That no one spoke right anymore in Mass or Rhode Island. What the savage outlanders call a Boston accent instead of speaking right. He didn't have one. A little tiny bit of one. Crazy. The world has gone full savage. He said he hardly saw any fights growing up either. It seems the last bastion of civilization in the world collapsed. That is so sad.

I say, "No. You talk wrong. You sound like a filthy savage hillbilly. You and all the TV people. Monkey savages. Barbarians. I'm telling you I talk right. This is the right way to say words. Anyone who says different is a subhuman monkey. Got it?"

"Jeez, alright. I was just asking. I mean axing."

"No. You don't do it. Only special people from a special place could talk right. Could talk civilized. And I guess that place no longer exists anymore. Just speak how you usually do. And ax isn't what everyone from there says. Only certain of us. Your father could do it, but it sounds wicked strange when someone like you says it. I don't know why. It just is how it is."

"What special place?"

"The last bastion of civilization in the world. The only place to make nearly fully-civilized people. Outside of Cambridge and the rich areas, and all the tourists that move there at least. All them are monkey savages. But it's gone now, I guess. According to your father. Replaced with weak sissies. Well, I guess Bhutan is pretty civilized too. Or used to be."

"Hmmm. Sounds like a nice place. Maybe I'll take Joey there one day."

"You can't. I told you. It's gone."

"But don't they have like pictures and stuff still? Old things to look at?"

"Yeah, I guess. But what made it special and normal and civilized is gone."

"You're a weird guy, you know that? You have really big muscles though. Your hands are like the size of my whole head. My dad loved old school wrestling and he watched it all the time from the olden days. There was a guy in a show that looked like you. Zeus. His eyes were like yours. He lost to the guy with the dumb mustache. The bandana guy."

I'm weird? This kid needs to look in the mirror. "Yeah. What's-his-name. He was Deebo in Friday too. It was a movie though, not a show. I know the movie you're talking about. Hulk Hogan versus Deebo. I forget the name of the movie. What was his name? Like Listen. Something Listen. Not Sonny Listen, he was a great boxer though. Jesus, I forget. I get that a lot. Not the Hulk Hogan movie reference, but Deebo from Friday."

"Your eyes are crazy like his. Like God's."

"You saw God, huh?"

"Yeah. He was mean. He changed shape a lot too. He thinks I only pretend to like pain. But, I am. Pretending that. I don't like it. But I like fighting."

That takes me by surprise. I have to think about that for a moment before replying. My reply isn't a full lie, but not the honest truth. There is certain pain I like. That I enjoy. But best not to confuse the kid, and just side with her.

"Only a maniac would like pain. Someone with a broken brain. You want to avoid as much pain as possible. I love fighting, and fighting comes with pain. A whole lot of it. But I don't like it or want more of it. I just love fighting enough to accept it when it comes. My goal is to give out way more pain then I get. And what about working out? Getting punched in the face isn't nearly as bad as doing an hour of hill sprints, right? Working out really sucks, but you got to do it. If you love fighting at least."

"Yeah. I guess you're right. Do you think it's okay I lied to God about loving pain?"

"I don't think it was God."

"Huh? Why? It definitely was. You should see him. Then you'd know."

"Have you ever heard of Jesus?"

"Yeah."

"He said that God was real nice and loved everyone. And he said a bunch of hippy stuff that don't make much sense neither. Like if someone hits you, you should just take it and turn the other cheek towards them so they can hit that one too. You should love your enemies. Crazy stuff like that. And that you shouldn't be horny towards your neighbors. Even if they are wicked hot. Not if they're married or you are. And you should spend all day being nice and giving all your stuff away to help people. Even jerks and pansies. Wash their feet too, I think. Most of it makes no sense. But, just imagine if everyone was nice all the time and no one fought. The world would be a pretty nice place, right? Probably not for people like us, though. But for everyone else, right? And some of the stuff did make sense. Like you shouldn't lie and steal and stuff like that."

She makes a thoughtful face, "I don't know. I think a world like that would be pretty okay. I think."

"Probably. And someone would not be nice and then I could beat them up even though you ain't supposed to. But one thing's clear - Jesus and God and Mary ain't in to being mean and wanting people to kill for them. So I don't think you met God God. Maybe like a lower g god that is part of this contest. A fake god. Does that make sense?"

"Kind of. What is a lower g god?"

"God, the real God, you spell his name with a capital G. But like Thor and Icarus and King Arthur and guys like that where there is a bunch of gods, they get a lower-case g. Not a capital. Does that make sense?"

"I guess so. I didn't know that."

"Well, I just don't think your god is God God. The real God. Jesus' father. But killing monsters is a good mission. We got to do it anyways. And get real good at it so we can get all the weak people back to earth. So I don't think the mission he gave you is bad."

"Yeah. It's a good mission. I am the darkness."

"You sure are. So I told Ass-eyes I would watch out for you and your brother. You okay with that?"

"Who is Ass-eyes?"

"The hot Indian lady. The teacher."

"Oh. Ass-eyes. That's funny." She starts cracking up. For a long time. Loudly. Ass-eyes isn't that funny. What a weird kid.

She finally stops and says, "Ass-eyes. I like it. That's hilarious."

"So, you okay with me looking out for you and your brother?"

"I look out for my brother. I'm basically his mother. I guess it's fine as long as you don't do anything gross. Or illegal."

"Okay. I'll try not to do anything gross or illegal. But it's hard for me to do anything illegal when I am the law."

"How are you the law?"

"Because I'm in charge of everything. You didn't see the messages about someone taking control of Loren? It should have flashed in your eyes. You didn't read the emails I sent?"

"I saw something about...something. I didn't read the messages yet. I don't like reading and there were a lot of words."

"I hear you. Reading and writing are stupid and only idiots like to do either. I hate writing, but I had to do it. You should read the emails. They have wicked important information. Not now. When you get the chance. When you are bored or something."

"I will."

We sit quietly for a minute and she breaks the silence by saying, "You fight good. I saw you beat up the slick guy with Ass-eyes."

"We should probably stop calling her that. It isn't nice, and people are under a lot of stress today. Everyone's life has been shaken up this morning pretty bad. We should give her a chance. And be respectful. She just took on two little orphan girls. That's pretty cool for her to do. Kind, selfless, you know? And if you think that was an example of me fighting, wait until you see my arena run."

"Arena?"

"It's in the emails. You get notified when you get a new email, right?"

"Yeah. New messages. I think so. I saw some before."

"Okay. Well, check your next email you get. It will have arena in the title and instructions on how to watch."

We sit in silence for a little bit again. I break it by asking, "Anything else you want to talk about?"

"Me? Umm, I don't know. Uh, there is one thing, maybe. But it isn't good."

"No problem. What is it?"

"Um. Do you think it is okay if I have a lot of anger and hate in me?"

I take a good long moment to think about it. I know what the real answer is, but I just wanted to run through it to make sure it was okay to tell to a kid.

"Yeah. That's fine. I think most fighters do. Real fighters. Some may be peaceful inside, but I've never been. And most of the people I know that are great fighters aren't peaceful inside. I think it's good. Useful. I use it. When I get angry or feel a lot of hate I push it down into my hate-ball. And…"

She interrupts, "What's a hate-ball?"

"It's a ball of anger and hate in my belly. I push all the bad stuff down into the ball. And when I need it, when it is okay to start laying down the hate and spreading my pain to others, I draw on it. I let it out. Just a little. Because I have more hate and anger than I could ever spread. Ever share. It is endless."

"Do you think it would be okay if I did that too?"

"Sure. Of course. That is the best way to deal with it, I think. You're a good kid…I mean lady, just don't let your anger and hate blind you into doing something stupid. Like killing someone that don't need killing or shouldn't be killed. Or hurting the weak or the invalids. There would never be a good reason to hurt someone like your brother, right?"

"Of course not."

"So don't ever let your hate and anger and fear let you do something dumb you'll regret. Save it for people that need it. Or just the monsters for now. And if you are going to kill, make sure they deserve it. Make sure it makes mankind better off, right?"

"Peoplekind."

"Sure, kid. Whatever. But at your age, I wouldn't be thinking about killing people. You'll mess up and get yourself killed or kill an innocent and get in big trouble. And that stuff is hard to live with.

The mistakes. Wicked hard. If you find someone you think needs killing, just get me. Okay?"

"You got it."

"Anything else."

"Not right now."

"Well, thank you very much, Ms. Gum, for the talk. I really enjoyed it. I like talking to you."

"Me too."

"You like talking to yourself?"

She laughs, "No, dummy. I like talking to you."

2.8 LOVE AND WAR

KIM GUM

I think that guy might be in love with me. I got to be careful. Mom and dad warned me about guys like that. But is it really so bad? He is really tall and has really big muscles and stuff. Eyes like God. And my God is the real God. The capital G God. I know it.

Is that guy cute? I don't know. He looks scary and angry all the time. I'd hear girls talking about cute guys but I don't think I ever felt what they feel when they talk about it. And no boy has ever liked me before. He is really old though. Really, really, really old. An old, old man. But is he cute?

I don't think so. Not like Joey is. His face is scary. I don't think he would ever get to be the star of a movie. But I'm not pretty either. And he said he was the leader of the world. I guess that makes sense for the darkness and the leader of the world to be girlfriend and boyfriend. Like the most popular kids at school or something.

I guess I am his girlfriend now. He did ask me out kind of. I guess it is okay. As long as he doesn't do anything gross like try to kiss. Yuck. I could never kiss that ugly, old man. But I guess we could hold hands once in a while if no one is looking. Maybe. This is all so fast!

And he did stop Ass-eyes from stealing my brother. I probably would've got in big trouble if I killed her. I could have too. I know it. She seemed soft. Weak. Like a teddy bear. She doesn't belong here.

How did all these people make it out of the dungeon and my parents didn't? It makes no sense.

I miss them. My family. I don't think my parents would want that guy to be my boyfriend. I don't even know his name. I think he said it a bunch but I'm not good at remembering. I recognize his armor. Studded leather. I almost got that.

I like talking to him. He sounds really weird. "Wickit dah dah dahhhh ax dah sumpin sumpin." I wish he'd come back. Did he say he'd come back? He's been gone for a while.

It's weird having a boyfriend now. I never had one.

Should I go train? I want to but the doctor said I can't do nothing forever. Almost forever. Like three months. Basically forever. How can I do nothing for three months? God will get another darkness to replace me probably. If I don't kill nothing for three months. No. I'll still be the darkness no matter what he says. I was before I even met him. Long before. No one can take that from me. Not ever. But he could tell someone else they are. Even though they aren't. But they would believe it. Who would believe me then?

Hmm. I have to fight. The doctor lady was real nice but she is wrong about this. Too much is at risk. I made a promise. I got to fight.

Should I tell my boyfriend that I was the darkness before God told me? He seems confused by the whole thing. If I tell him it was Joey that told me, I don't think he'd understand. He'll think that I think I'm really talking to Joey, but I know it isn't Joey. Not really. Just the Joey in my head that can talk. And I'm not even certain if it was Joey's idea, or if it was my idea. I think I knew I was the darkness even before that. Like I kind of knew about it, but not really knew about it. Not until I actually said it out loud.

No. Better to just keep that to myself. My mom said secrets can be weapons to smart women. I don't know how this secret could be a weapon. But I haven't been a woman for long. I like weapons. My spear is awesome.

A notification flashes that I have a new message. I go in. At the top is one labelled "ABOUT THE ARENA." It says, "Sorry about emailing so much. But this is important for training. I did the solo arena through 50. I used all the weapons I have available. I could only use the ones I am not proficient at for the early rounds as the hit to AB is too much for even some of the level 3 fights.

Some of the best rewards you can get come from the arena, besides the dungeon coins and the healing pills I mentioned before. For clearing solo 100 you get a racial spec point, for clearing solo 200 you get a racial spec point and an extra attribute point, for clearing solo 300 you get a racial spec point and regular spec point. Duo 100 is racial ability opener, 200 is a racial ability opener and an attribute point, 300 is a racial ability opener and a spec point. 4-man 100 is a token for any feat that is non-epic and not a class feature, 200 is the same plus an attribute point, 300 is the same plus the spec point. The 5-man 100 gives a token for any epic feat. Any of them. You don't have to qualify. But you got to be careful, because you could take a spellcasting feat even if you have no spells and it won't stop you from doing it. And look into if it is a replacement or stacking feat or not. Like epic weapon focus only gives you just +2 AB. It doesn't give you the benefit of the weapon focus and improved weapon focus feats. 5-man 200 gives another one of those and an attribute point. I hate to say it, but no one cleared 5-man 300 from last timeline. We assume it gives the any epic feat and a spec point.

Now, clearing all level 100 arenas gives a free feat token. Same with 200. We assumed clearing all 300s gives it too. Maybe even an extra award, since that will mean you cleared all the arenas. Who knows? Maybe it opens a whole new arena or something else too.

The arena will open for all crawlers in not too long. It is a points achievement and not an event one so most people will open it around level 4. I should probably send an email out about achievements too. Not today. Probably not tomorrow either. I promise I will pretty soon. The first main achievement opens in 3. It isn't a game changer. Just party chat that only the party leader can communicate in. Full party chat opens at 6. Know what? I'll just cover the main ones real quick and get it done so I don't have more writing to do hanging over me. 9 opens area chat, so chat everyone in your zone can see. 12 opens emails to a single person. You can email anyone you want, just one person at a time. 15 opens one world chat message a day. 18 opens email groups. Clearing a 4(21) dungeon gives access to a forum type thing. I should say that all these open when you clear a dungeon. So when you clear a level 3 dungeon you get the party leader chat. It isn't just getting to level 3. Clearing a 6(24) dungeon opens the ability to email everyone at once. We think 24(27) will open something new, but no one has done it yet. We cleared all the 16s. There should be another one at 30. Either 36(30) or 48(30). Maybe both. Who knows? Not me. Oh, clearing the first 16(x) dungeon gets you the ability to port to the city and back to where you ported from 1 time a day. There is a 16(21) dungeon, so you could technically get this before the email all one. That would be a dumb idea, but I figure people will be smart enough by then to not do it. You don't want to tackle any of the raids until you are level 30 with your final build and some good set pieces already.

The other type of achievements are point based. So when you hit x points, it opens. You probably have some done and are working on others. Try to grind out the ones you can. I know they don't have titles or descriptions, but some are easy to figure out. Like you should all have 2 that say x/100. That is for the hounds and birds in the tutorial. Kill 100 of each and get the points for the achievements. Do all the common ones and around level 4 you will open the arena. Other achievements open the ability to take screenshots, then videos, a bunch of stuff. Some housing items. A lot of useless stuff too, like pets that do nothing and just follow you around. Cosmetic pets I think they're called? A great one is a tent that gets upgraded and can be used in dungeons. Portable bank and portable AH and portable repair station. None of those can be used in dungeons, but can be used in the dungeon areas unless it isn't cleared yet.

Okay, so how to get to and watch the arena I just did, you first..." And he goes on to explain how to get there through the UI. It is so cute my boyfriend calls messaging emails. Adorable. What a boomer. I can't wait to watch the arena. I navigate to it quickly and click the play button for the only player showing. C465OV0001W87-1.

2.9 IF YOUR DREAMS DON'T SCARE YOU

KIM GUM

I sit with my mouth open. Amazed. What I just watched was a thing of magic. My new boyfriend, whatever his name is, should…I don't even know. Wow. I've seen people sparring and training my whole life. But this? This was too wonderful for words. My family, we'd all watch old UFC and MMA fights all the time. What I just watched? This guy in the arena…it's like a movie where everything is scripted and fake and made to be ridiculously exciting to watch. But this was real. 100% real.

Indescribable. The way he moved. The efficiency of movement. The power. The skill. And he did it all while talking. While showing stances, forms, strikes, and counters for a bunch of weapons and the shield. How to dodge. How to block. When to charge. When to tumble. Turtling. Everything. I learned so much about the spear, and he said he isn't good with it. Same with swords, rapier, and pole weapons. He said he wasn't too bad with an ax or daggers, but was bad with all the rest. That real weapon masters will start having the good arena runs to watch for specific weapons training once they open the arena achievement. That's how he learned too.

Most of the weapon masters died on 10.

Not this time, though. Not with my boyfriend in charge. Everyone will live.

I've been using the spear wrong. In the game you hold it in the middle of the shaft. You can't really change how you hold it. Here, you can since this isn't the game. What my boyfriend said is the big advantage of the spear is range. A spear user should be able to kill two sword users because of the range advantage, as long as the sword users ain't using shields. I fought the turd-pigeons all wrong. I should have kept them back with ranged thrusts. And you shouldn't try to use the spear to slice. It isn't effective. Just thrusts. And the only time you hold the spear higher up on the shaft is when you need more power to puncture through a thick hide or something. Other than that you hold it as far back on the shaft as you can handle for as much range as possible. And powerful thrusts, but I already knew that. One big thing with spears is they are easier to grab than swords. But that's just important if you're fighting other humans. Real humans. Game mobs won't grab it. They can try to disarm with the disarm ability, but they won't actually grab anything.

My boyfriend likes axes for a bunch of different reasons. And not all axes. He likes the dwarven waraxe. It's pretty heavy, but easy to manipulate and aim strikes with. And like his punches, he can strike with a ton of force very quickly. The reach is decent, especially with his super long arms. It just fits him. It's more natural and fighting with one just makes more sense to him. He didn't have one now though, so he couldn't demonstrate. He said it's a lot different than fighting with a handaxe. The only axe he had on him to demonstrate with.

How the arena works is you get one level 1 monster to fight on your first fight, then two, then three, all the way up to nine at once on the ninth fight. The tenth fight is a boss fight. With all the adds that it has in the dungeon it is from. Level 1 Boss. The eleventh fight is one level 2 monster, the nineteenth fight is nine level 2 monsters. And the twentieth is a level 2 boss. So the three hundredth fight will be a level

30 boss. On fight 45 he had a mini-boss too. He said all the fights ending in five from there on out will have a mini-boss.

He gave an overview on how to fight each monster and boss. Dungeon 1 has goblins, giant fire beetles, and rat swarms, with a giant goblin sergeant as a boss. The first dungeon 2 has these blob monsters with tentacles and beaks he made a big deal about, since people bringing kids and their families to the city will face them on the path to the city. Their tentacles don't do any damage, but cause a ton of pain I guess. He let some hit him so people could see how to respond when it happens, but it didn't look like it hurt him much. He said it hurts real bad though, especially for normal people not like him. Dungeon 2 also has monkeys from a movie I liked a lot when I was a little kid called "Presents for Mwamini." It was one of the first fullimmenation movies. The monkeys are hilarious. In the movie at least. They seem very dangerous here. Especially grouped up, throwing biscuits. And little things that look like lawn gnomes called brownies I think. They are casters. You got to fight them different. And if there is a group you take the casters out first. He said those ones aren't dangerous, but higher-level casters are a pain if you don't kill them quick.

The information on free attack and auto-attack was very interesting. He is using free attack now, since auto-attack doesn't help much when you only have one attack per round. But when you get more, especially when you have three or four a round, you can do something called turtling. You hit the enemy once then go full defense for the rest of the six second round. That one hit counts as hitting the enemy however many attacks per round your BAB gets you. What's called an attack chain. But all hits after the first lose 5 AB. So if you have four hits, your fourth hit is at -15 AB. There are situations you should stay on free attack, like if you are fighting one enemy that doesn't attack often. With free attack you don't lose any AB for any attack in the

229

round, and your max hit attempts is however many times you can hit the enemy with enough force for it to count.

That is another really smart thing he said – hit attempts. That's when you hit the enemy. But it isn't a real hit, because it has to beat the enemies AC to count as an actual hit. One that removes HPs. You don't got to worry about that once you remove the HP shield. All hits are hits then. But not with game monsters. Both goblins and the giant fire beetles are from fourth age, so game rules apply. They get downed at zero HPs, but can go below that and still not be dead. So you got to hit them again when they are down. Some enemies you have to do something called a coup de grace when they are below zero HPs because they regen. You can quickslot that special attack.

The second boss was a giant puppy with an acid tongue that tries to lick you. I never heard of the game it was from, but he said it was from one. When you damage it too much it gets an iframe and shoots acid everywhere. We can get iframes too, he said. Invulnerability frame. Something that makes you immune from damage for a little bit while you do it. He stressed how important getting one was for everyone. The easiest being from tumble. From using two specialization points on tumble, the only skill that takes two. He went over the other ones, but the one he planned on getting was for charge. He said it's feat heavy to get, and isn't good for a lot of builds. The tumble one is reliable. For all classes. Great in a pinch, where charge requires a setup. He went over the rest of them, but none of it mattered. I already decided. I was going to do what he did. My build would be his. I would fight like him. I would be better even. I am the darkness. He usually uses a dwarven waraxe and a shield. I'll use a shield and spear instead. I like the spear. I can't believe he's a dwarf. He's so tall. That's really weird.

He swapped back to weapons he had proficiency in for the later level 3 fights. Usually a short sword. Sometimes a mace. Sometimes a morningstar. Sometimes a spear or shortbow. Even a rapier and quarterstaff. On the level 4 fights he mainly kept to the short sword. The level 5 boss fight was a giant crab. Half the fight he had to do with the shortbow to shoot the crab in its single eye when it opened while the boss was berserking. And he explained why the true grit feat was so great for melee classes with low will saves if you fight solo. This crab had a mental attack that could stun you for 1d2 rounds. He got stunned and almost lost his HP shield. He almost had the crab when he got stunned again. Then it almost killed him. He got real injured. Lost a whole arm and his chest was all messed up. But he pulled off the win. It was close though. I knew he could do it. But it got me thinking. If he almost died the rest of us have no chance. But that was a level 5 boss and he is a level 1. We'll have a lot more HPs by then and higher will saves and more feats and stuff.

The arena heals your HP shield between fights, and he did take some damage in other fights before the crab boss. Some spells you can't dodge. They find you no matter what you do. But that was the only time he almost lost. I got real worried. How is he going to save everyone if he is missing an arm? And the chest injury looked real bad. I started running around looking for him to help. He's my boyfriend after all. I can't just sit there and do nothing while he bleeds to death. But some lady yelled at me for running around like a maniac and asked what was wrong. When I told her she laughed at me and said I should read the messages sent because they say you don't die in the arena. It's a simulation. You can't be killed. Not really. You are fine when you exit and come back out here.

So I went back to my log to find Joey. And so my boyfriend would know where to find me. Hopefully he'll find me soon. He never told me I couldn't train. I don't remember him saying anything like that anyways. If he doesn't come back soon I'm going to start training. But hardly anyone is training now. Most everyone is just standing there, probably watching the arena vid.

The awards in the arena are both great and not good. You get a ton of gold, but the only other thing he got was a red coin for each fight. Just one, no matter how many enemies he fought or if it was a boss or mini-boss. He got one gold for every level 1 enemy. He got two gold for every level 2 enemy. All the way on up. The fight before the level 5 boss was nine level 5s, so that is what? 45 gold I think. So he made a bazillion gold total. The only other thing he got was for the level 5 boss. Some sort of healing pill. Probably crap like the healing potions.

Bored, I go in my UI to watch the arena again. I could watch it a million times. My boyfriend is amazing, and this time I won't get scared when he almost dies.

2.10 JUDGE A FISH BY ITS ABILITY TO CLIMB A TREE

KIM GUM

When I finish watching the arena vid for the second time and exit the UI I see my boyfriend playing with my brother. His arm is attached to his body and his chest is fine. They are both shaking trays at each other. I get mad for a second thinking he is making fun of my brother, but I don't think he would do that. Not my boyfriend. Right?

I walk up and he says, "Give me a minute. I bet he gives up before I do."

I ask, "What are you doing?"

"Winning."

"Winning what?"

"The food tray shaking contest your brother challenged me to."

"Oh."

I wait way more than a minute. Neither seem to be tiring. I debate calling Joey or doing something to distract him so he stops. But I don't. Boyfriend or not, I want my brother to win. Shaking trays is what he does. And he does it well. My boyfriend is just playing a game. I start thinking of a way to learn my boyfriend's name without him knowing I don't know it. I think of a million ways and settle on the one I think is best and most natural and least suspicious.

"Did you ever introduce yourself to Joey? Tell him your name and stuff?"

"Why? Did you forget my name?"

Holy moly! He saw right through my plan!

"No! I just…you never told me so I couldn't forget it."

"I did tell you. I remember clearly telling you. You asked who I was pretty much right after I met you. I also said it to the doctor right in front of you too."

"Oh. I guess I did forget. Sorry. I'm bad with names."

He laughs and says, "No problem. Me too. Bruno. Bruno Vaz."

Oh, yeah. I remember now. That name is kind of disappointing. I say, "Oh. I thought you'd have a stronger name."

"What? Stronger? Than Bruno Vaz? Bruno is a wicked strong name. What's a strong name to you?"

"I don't know. Something like Aboombabambam?"

He laughs real hard at this. When he laughs hard he sounds weird. Kind of like how a really big pig would laugh. A giant pig. No oinking, but I don't know. Giant pig laughing seems right.

"Aboombabambam, huh? You know, in my last party we had a Bam Bam. A Kim too."

"Really? What was she like? Was she the darkness? Was it me?"

"She was a he. I think Kim might be his last name. It is for Koreans. He's not Korean though. Or not from Korea. He's Asian. Or Asianish. Maybe where he is from is near Korea and they immigrated there? I don't know. I guess you don't have to live near where you immigrate to either. Eh, who knows? The name of his country is impossible to remember. For me at least. Maybe if I hear it a bunch more it will stick. There's a chance I could've given him Kim as a nickname too."

He pauses and then says, "And as far as I know he wasn't the darkness. I never heard about it or met one before you."

The way he says darkness is just plain silly. Dahhhhknis. Ridiculous. It's darkness. So easy to say right.

I say, "Are we girlfriend and boyfriend?"

He stops shaking his tray and stares at me. A real scary stare. He looks real angry. Jeez. I can't even look at him. My heart starts beating faster. Real fast. I keep my eyes down and hope this stops. I look up for a second and then back down real quick. He's still staring. Jeez. What did I say?

He asks in a voice deeper and more angry than usual if I think he's a pedophile. And he swore too. The worst swear. The one I'd get in really big trouble for saying. I don't even know what a pedophile is. Jeez, why is he so angry? I didn't even say anything. Not really.

"No. Sorry. I didn't mean to."

"You didn't mean to what?"

"Get you mad."

"Then don't..." He sighs and says, "Look, I'm sorry I got mad. But no. We aren't. And we'll never be. I'm not like that. I like women around my age. Real women, with life experience. Not kids. I know you think you're an adult now, but you're a kid. A little girl. I have a daughter three years older than you. Almost four years. I have a fifteen-year-old son. I like grown adult women. I'll never like you like that. Ever. Never. Not even a little. As a friend? Yes, definitely. But not like that. Okay?"

"Okay. I'm sorry. I just thought...is it because I have cankles?"

"What? No. Jesus, kid. Did you not hear anything I just said? It is 100% because of your age. Or lack of age. And me not being a fu...filthy pedo. And you don't have cankles. Your calves are way bigger than your ankles. You do got real big ankles though. But I think for them to officially be cankles they have to be almost the same size as your calves. Right? That's what I always heard it meant."

"And I look like a frog."

He doesn't say anything for a moment. I start thinking I made him mad again.

"I won't lie. You kind of do. But who cares? You're the darkness, right? Is the darkness a beauty contest? You're not supposed to fight monsters with your looks, are you?"

"No."

"So who cares? And you have big ankles because you have good genetics. Look at your wrists. If anything, instead of cankles, you have...uh...frists. Forearm wrists. But that's just because you probably haven't done anything to develop your forearms so they're almost the same size as your big wrists. But having big wrists is good. Great for here. You need strong wrists for weapon work. Your mom teach you any hand-to-hand stuff? MMA stuff? Your father told me she taught MMA."

I thought that was supposed to be a family secret only? Oh well, I guess it doesn't matter now anyways.

"Yeah. A little. I took taekwondo since I was real little too."

"Strong wrists are crucial for a ton in MMA fighting. Besides punching. Bars, the cinch, reverses. A million things. Why would you want little dainty, sissy wrists and ankles? Wouldn't you want big strong, fighter wrists and ankles?"

"Big strong ones."

"Goddamn right you do, kid. You want big hands and feet too. Look at the size of my hands. And my wrists. Come here real quick."

I look and move closer. He grabs my forearm and says, "Try to break free." I try for a while as hard as I can. I'm out of breath when I stop. He is strong! Real strong.

"Nothing wrong with being big and strong. You got the bone structure for it. You could be a real monster when you grow up. Not like me. Not as big as me. But good sized. A giant for a women. How tall was your mother?"

"Didn't you know her and my dad? I thought you did."

"You, both your brothers, and your dad. Your dad was taking you guys to the city. Your mom stayed to be a crawler."

"Oh. My mom was pretty tall. A lot taller than me."

"You'll probably be bigger. And taller, if you're lucky. And with this lifestyle, who cares what your face looks like? Come closer and look at my face. What do you see?"

I look. He has a lot of scars. Cauliflower ears. Bad ones. Fully cauliflowered. Real puffed out. His nostrils are real wide and his nose is in bad shape. You can tell it's been busted a lot. My parents called that fighter's nose and fighter's ears. I can notice even more scars now that I look closer. A lot. Damaged lips too. More wrinkles than you can see from far away. His haircut is almost a high and tight, like most people in the army. But not a good one, and too long on the sides. Some grey, not a ton though. Real dark skin. Oily looking. Like he's greasy. His face is shiny. He has a lot of bumps on his face too. His muscles are huge but they don't look right. His biceps don't look nearly as big as his chest and shoulders, like he doesn't work out right. His muscles that connect the shoulders to the neck go way far up the neck, and it looks silly. It looks like he is flexing them all the time, but I don't think he is.

"You have a fighter's face and you're old."

He laughs. "Yeah, I'm old. And my face is all messed up. But I can still get the ladies. Hot ones too. I got perfect genetics for a fighter. Quick-twitch everything. I had pretty big muscles naturally, before I even started trying to develop them. Bones like metal. I got to have a ton of caveman DNA in me. What do they call it? Neanderthal. Want to know a secret? I'm not six-five, almost six-six, like I said in the emails. I'm like six-seven-and-a-half. I lie to piss people off. Most people say they are taller than they are, and no one would lie about being shorter. So when someone is six-five and I tower over them, I say, 'Nah, you ain't even six-three, kid.' It infuriates them. I love it. See how big my hands and feet are? That's important for fighting but it also signals something to the ladies too, you know? Something wicked important."

He looks down and kind of blushes and says, "I shouldn't have said that. Sometimes I don't think before I run my mouth. And everyone says I don't hardly ever talk. Usually. Because all the sissies get mad at everything I say, and in general it's better for survival to keep your mouth shut and your eyes and ears open. I'm just blabbing like a little schoolgirl with you, ain't I?"

He smiles a little and says, "I don't want to sound mean but I'm surprised you like boys. You look like the cover girl for 'future butch dykes quarterly.'"

What? "I don't like boys! Are you nuts?"

"So you're a lesbian?"

I heard that term before. In class, I think. But sometimes when girls were talking about cute boys or kissing boys and stuff. I'm not sure what it is, but I don't want to admit it. I guess I stay silent too long because he asks if I know what that is.

"I think so but I'm not sure."

"It means you like girls."

"Oh. Yeah, some are okay I guess. There are some I'd like to kick in the head though."

He laughs again. The big laugh too. I don't know how what I said was funny.

"No. I mean like want to kiss girls."

What? What is up with this guy? "No! Kissing is so gross! I don't want to kiss anyone."

"Really? Hmm. Kids nowadays ain't nothing like how kids were when I was growing up. Or maybe I just hung out with kids like me. I wasn't too smart when I was your age. All I cared about was girls and fighting. Well, it doesn't matter. Maybe it does. Liking guys is pretty

238

gay and will probably hurt your fighting ability, but either way you ain't got nothing to worry about. If you're worried."

He stops. I wait for him to finish...whatever the heck he is talking about. Why so many words about absolutely nothing?

I say, "Why tell me that?"

"Oh. Lesbo broads, even the real rough looking ones, they can pull some decent looking tail. So if you're worried about that, I wouldn't be."

Why is he saying all this stuff? What is going on?

"Hell, if you like guys, I'm sure there are plenty into tough girls too. Bigger, stronger girls. You got a couple scars on your face, but if you plan on continuing down this path you'll get more. A lot more. And ears like mine. And a nose like mine. And I'm sure there's plenty of guys into that sort of thing. That's the good thing about guys. Some of us are always into what some lady has. They probably won't be Brad Pitt, but you ain't Angelina Jolie neither."

This seems like a chance to change the topic. "Who are they?"

"You never heard of them? Wicked big, super good looking movie stars. In my day. Like twenty years before you were born though. I'd figure they'd still be around. Old, but still famous and making movies."

"Maybe I heard of them. I'm not good with names."

"Me either. That pep talk make you feel better?"

"Um. I guess so. Yeah."

I agree to get him to stop talking about this stuff. I'm more confused than anything. I don't like this.

"Okay, good. Because what you can have is what I have. Real power. This is what I came to talk to you about. It looks like you have the genetics for it. I saw you with the spear with Ms. Kaur. You were pretty quick. Decent movement. Every single one of my muscles is a quick-twitch muscle. All of them. The most quick-twitch muscles anyone has ever saw. That is wicked rare. Means I'm fast. Way faster than people think someone my size will be. You probably don't have that, but you could still be decently fast. We'll see."

He kneels down in front of me before continuing, "Wicked hot girls have power. A lot of power. But the power I have, that you could have too, is better. Way better. Better than millionaires and politicians too. It's always with us and doesn't require talking or putting on make-up or nothing. Just us. We always have it with us and it doesn't need other people to play along, or get paid, or be attracted to you, or follow orders.

"Those other kinds of power? That doesn't interest me. Fame? Competition? No. Not for me. Fake fighting. With rules. For a crowd. That isn't being tough. You got to be ready for no rules, and all the tricks in the ring don't matter if you're fighting five guys that know what they're doing. Try doing a straight ankle lock on someone with a knifeman coming at your back.

"I've fought the toughest. Real tough guys. No rules guys. Real monsters. We're all a lot alike. This is who we are. This is what we do. Fame means nothing. Fake winning fake things mean nothing. Real winning is everything. Being better. Proving you're better. To the only people that matter. Other people like us.

"You got the genetics. You're young but I can help you grow into it. Be stronger. Be faster. All that. I didn't have that when I was your age. I can train you if you want. I can make you a real monster. You want that?"

I don't understand why Bruno talks to me so much but doesn't want to be my boyfriend, but I do want to be just like him. I want to be able to fight like him. I want it bad.

I say, "Yes."

"Good. I have a plan. I want you to meet some guys. You and Joey follow me and we'll get started. All right, boys night out!"

2.11 TRAINING

KIM GUM

"Alright ladies! I know your girly muscles can't take no more. Tomorrow I'm done taking it easy on you, so enjoy this vacation while you can. Ball-face! Cool them down, stretch them, and help them wipe the sand out their vaginas. I'm doing my real work out now. Quiz Kim on her build when you're done, then have her bathe."

I'm too smoked to argue. This sucks so much. Everything hurts. I didn't think being this sore was possible. This is worse than the clicking injury was.

I just walk with my head-down, looking at Lurch's feet walking in front of me. Breathing. Trying to take deep breaths and get my wind back. Everyone is silent and breathing heavy as Ball-face takes us through cooldowns and then stretches. We're all miserable. This sucks so bad. I thought it'd be fun, but it's the exact opposite of fun. We finally get dismissed and I pray Ball-face forgot about the quizzing. I just want to lay down and sleep forever. Both me and Lurch go to check on Joey. Lurch is really good with Joey. Real nice to him.

Ball-face yells out, "Kim, you ready?"

Dagnab it! He remembered. I want to say something snippy, but it ain't Ball-face's fault I'm in a bad mood. He's a good guy. Funny too. I'm not sure why Bruno calls him Ball-face. His face is normal shaped. Kind of weird looking though. Big overbite and a chin like mine – meaning not much of one. I can tell he pushes his jaw forward to try and make himself look more normal. He flexes a lot too. I think he thinks he has big muscles, but he doesn't. Not compared to Bruno. Compared to Bruno he has little baby muscles. I forget his real name. The general calls him major something. Bruno calls the general Butterball, but when I called him that I got yelled at. I have to call him general.

I sit in front of Ball-face and he says, "Sorry about this. Not my call. I got a joke for you. Knock, knock."

I smile. Unlike my father, Ball-face's jokes are always hilarious. Man, I miss my dad so much. "Who's there?"

"Cow go."

"Cow go who?"

"No, cow go moo."

That cracks me up good! No, cow go moo! That's a good one. The best part is how he says it. So serious, with his goofy looking face. Cow go moo. Ha!

He smiles, "Ready now?"

I was happy, but that sours my mood again. "I guess so, but I know this stuff. Can't we go over something better? Or just something new?"

"How about running through it quickly to check the box, then we'll move on."

"Okay. Since I'm not a halfling no more I do normal damage. Spears do 1d8 damage now. Bruno wanted me to go dwarven waraxe like him since it does 1d10 damage and he can train me better with it. But I begged him and I can use the spear because the darkness uses spears and that's just how it is. We're dwarfs because we...for a bunch of reasons. Slow and steady basically gives us the level 10 and 20 fighter paragons for free right off the bat. We want to start at 18 con, and without the plus 2 con we'd of had to use six points to go from 16 to 18, and our dex would've been 8 instead of 14. We also get automatic searches, and the only other race with automatic searches is elves, and they stink because they have minus 2 con, and that would've really messed our build up. Charisma is useless and does nothing, so the minus 2 hit to it doesn't hurt at all. We don't need wisdom because we are getting the true grit feat. And all our feat picks are just the requirements for true grit. Well, true grit, rush n' attack, and, uh, shield brace. Get them all as soon as possible, but true grit is the first big one and makes wisdom useless."

While I was talking Lurch came and sat with us. The general is still lying down and recovering. I put my hand behind my back and inch it up to where the clicking injury was. It itches still. I can't believe it's healed. Man, when we entered yesterday I was on cloud nine. Bruno made me bathe and then gave me a little pill. A healing pill. I didn't think it would work, but it did. And pretty fast too. When I took it I got itchy all over and felt weird, but my clicky injury was healed. My hand was healed a good amount too. Not all the way, but pretty good. My other injuries weren't healed that much, but I'll get my own healing pill when I can do the arena myself, and heal all the way up to perfect.

Man, I didn't realize how bad that injury hurt. Now that it's gone it's like night and day. I felt great! Ready to take on the world. I even got out of the first PT session yesterday, and I was kind of mad about it. How crazy is that? PT sucks. Physical training, ptewy! More like physical torture. Bruno is torturing us. He's a heartless monster. PT in the morning, then weapons and hand-to-hand training, then a speed clear of all the trash mobs, then more training, and more PT. So much running. I hate running. And he won't let me stop to catch my breath. He says that means I was a fall-out and a broke-(bad word for male genitals). He swears a lot. I don't like it. I keep trying to get him not to swear. Joey shouldn't hear those words. And I don't like it.

Ball-face looks disappointed and says, "That it?"

243

Jeez, man. Relax. "No. Tinker as a hobby because it saves gold, and also saves time if you're trying to beat the clock and get 1st SS. And if your gear breaks you could die. We picked porter because you can never have too much carry weight allowance, and if you're going for 1st SS you won't have to drop loot or waste time hitting a shop node thing. More loot is more money. It levels up easy too, and we can keep it maxed just by training with the medium and heavy load debuffs. And we get bags of holding to increase carry weight even more. I can't wait to get those!

"Uh…oh, background and skills. Sharp as a tack. We picked our background because we're real short on skill points and need all the skill points we can get. Same reason why it's smart to pick rogue at level 1 – it gives you a ton of skill points and open a bunch of class skills. And the what's-it-called feat? Uh, trapfinding. Absolutely needed for 1st SS solo clears. Skills are all the ones we'll need to solo clear dungeons. The only skill we have that isn't 100% needed is knowledge (arcane), but since we have three open group skills, that one is just the most useful of what was left. It's not that helpful, but can be kind of helpful sometimes. The run skill and spellcraft are just nice to buff our speed and saving throws. And tumble increases our AC. At some point, when tumble gets high enough, people get immune to attacks of opportunity. But we didn't get it for that, just the AC increase. Rush n' attack will give our charge an iframe so we won't have to worry about ghost arms so much, as long as there are mobs we can ping pong off of."

The general is sitting up now, listening in. Ball-face is leaning back, pushing his jaw forward, trying to look cool or handsome or something. Lurch is throwing pebbles. I hope that was enough explaining. I want to move on. Bruno had me study the builds before we even entered the tutorial dungeon again. We could talk about a million things. Like, how weird it is time stops in dungeons. We handed all our gold and gear off to other army guys before we entered since we rerolled and would lose it all if we didn't. Supposedly, they'll see us disappear and reappear in, like, a second. Then they'll hand us our stuff back, give us their stuff to hold, and disappear for a second. That's crazy. We're going to spend like a month in here. How's that only a second? I'll believe it when I see it.

Ball-face puts a piece of grass in his mouth and says, "What's good and bad about your build?"

"Um, it's a solo clearing build. At level 20 we'll be 12 fighter and 8 rogue. Uh, I forget the epic class we pick. Grandmaster or something, but that's way, way far away anyways. We'll reroll when we have the dungeon coins to make our final build work. Our final build is high damage and good for raiding, and has a ton of survivability too. Bruno hasn't told me what it is yet, just what it will be good at. We'll reroll before we start raiding. This build is a leveling build. We can spot traps and disarm traps and pick locks, but we can't stealth or scout ahead. We can take a hit, and tank even 5-man dungeons all through the epic zone, but we'll have a hard time even off-tanking the early raids. We can do decent damage. Good damage now, but that will go down compared to other classes as we get higher levels. Damage focused casters will smoke us at 30, even though casters suck and are stupid."

Ball-face laughs. "Don't let general Edwards hear you say that."

The general laughed too, so I doubt he's mad. He stands and walks closer to us. "When I was a boy I loved Harry Potter." He waves his hands all weird and says dramatically, "Magic! Magic! Why wouldn't I pick a class that lets me do what no one ever could do, but everyone always wanted to? There's a saying, everything looks like a nail to a hammer. As a wizard, I can turn the hammer and nail into anything I want, or shoot a fireball and melt them. I say only fools wouldn't take the opportunity to master magic. Yes, we have it much harder at early

245

levels. Yes, it's easy to make the case we stink and don't contribute much now. I'd rather have it hard now and melt faces with ease later. What don't we contribute later? Even with the best fighter build imaginable, I'm still pretty old. As a wizard, my age doesn't matter so much. And remember, I'm not trying to clear dungeons by myself. I will always be in a five-man group. Magic. I'm Harry Potter."

Everyone but me laughs. The general was trying to be silly, but what he says hits home. Everything I've said about my build is solo focused because I'm going back to being alone. This is the first and only time I'll be grouped up for a dungeon. I try my hardest not to, but I start crying. Lurch hugs me and asks what's wrong. "I don't want to clear dungeons by myself. I don't want to be alone again."

I feel a pat on my head and the general says, "I'm sorry. I'm sorry. I didn't mean to upset you."

Lurch says, "It's okay, girl. You don't have to be alone. You can come to the city with my family. We'd love to have you along."

I get nervous. I don't know what to say. I don't want to hurt Lurch's feelings, but I don't want to go with his family and go to the city. I want to fight. I want to stay grouped with Bruno. Not just grouped with any people. One person specifically – Bruno. Lurch is a kind man. Really good with Joey. But, no. How do I tell him without hurting his feelings? Well, at least I'm not crying anymore.

Bruno, covered in sweat, pops up behind the general, "I still got it! This big and can still sneak like a mofo. Are you ladies crying?"

He hunches over and starts backing away. "Okay. I still got another hour of PT to do. You ladies have fun talking about your feelings and astrology or whatever. I'm sure the world will save itself. Magic! We'll just cast a spell and get back to earth. Easy-peasy."

We're all silent for a minute. The general says, "He has absolutely no people skills at all. I mean, read the room."

246

We all laugh, probably harder than we should. I feel embarrassed for crying like a baby.

"Kim, Bruno explained dungeon coins to you, right? He isn't ditching you. He has faith you can hit cap solo, and said grouping would be a waste. It's a rather large compliment, really. And he's still training and spending time with you in the outside zone too," says Ball-Face.

Talking about something new will clear the tension and lessen my embarrassment, so I say, "A little, but not really."

"Okay. You get 25 of each color dungeon coin if you get 1st SS as a solo clear. 22 with a 1st SS duo clear. And it goes down from there. Only 20, 18, or 16, for a 3, 4, or 5 person 1st SS clear. 2nd SS is just 20, 18, 16, 14, and 12. 3rd SS is 15, 13, 12, 10, and 9. Regular SS is 9, 8, 8, and 8. S is 7 for solo and the rest just 6. A is 5 and 3. B is 3 and 2. And C is 2 and 1. 1st, 2nd, and 3rd SS are only given out in limited amounts. Only 100 people can get 1st SS, only 200 can get 2nd, and only 300 can get 3rd.

"The first time a new dungeon opens is when all the big payouts are given out. We all need 5,000 of each color dungeon coin, and 1,600 of those come from the arena, and there are...what was it? 211 dungeons if I'm remembering right. Even if a five-man group gets all SSs in every single dungeon, that is only...a little less than 1,700 coins. Way under the 5k needed to cap out when added to the 1,660 for the arena. We need as many good people capped out as possible if we're getting back to earth. Anyone who can solo should to maximize coin gain. He's saying you can, so you should."

I wonder if he really thinks I understood any of that. He could've just made chickens noises and it would've made as much sense. I know his heart is in the right place, and he explained all that to make me feel better, trying to make it seem Bruno not grouping with me is a compliment, but come on? It's gibberish.

The general says, "Bruno has no tact, but he has the exact right focus. Dungeon area 10 killed humanity's chances of returning to earth during his timeline. We have a chance to correct that. And correct everything else he's described. To do better. We're all part of something far bigger than any one of us. We owe it to everyone to make as many sacrifices as needed to get them home."

2.12 DOING DARKNESS THINGS

KIM GUM

"Okay, Kim. Last pull is the biggest pull. Balls to the wall. Just don't do anything stupid, fundamentals and by the numbers," Bruno tells me.

Balls to the wall means go all out. Don't hold back. I'm pretty sure that's what it means. First time I heard that I was like, "gross!" But it doesn't mean what it sounds like. I've never seen Bruno do anything gross to the walls at least. He never tells anyone else the thing about fundamentals and by the numbers. Just me. Because sometimes I like to have fun. This dungeon is easy, especially now that I don't got the clicking injury no more. There's no reason not to have a little fun.

This is the room above the boss's room. Three turd-pigeons and three turd-birds. No problem. I say, "Hua." Bruno likes when I say hua. It seems to mean yes.

I hit charge and fly towards the furthest turd-pigeon. The one right next to the other one. I'm supposed to push it back and get some range with my spear, but instead I tell all these idiots who I am. "I am the darkness!" By the time it's out of my mouth all six mobs are coming at me. I can't really attack, and I'm barely able to block the two turd-birds furthest from me. I have to whip my shield around hard to block turd-birds as I dodge turd-pigeons, and I know it counts as an attack. For the rest of this round hitting will be much harder since I'm now taking a dual-wield penalty.

I can only go full defense, and I'm forced to jump back a little too far and get two ghost arms for it. I'm too busy to recognize if there are damage icons, and I just focus on staying alive. Balls to the wall. I lose myself in the fight, and without realizing it, the fight is over and I'm standing over the corpses of my enemies. Sure, I got myself into a little bit of a pickle, but it worked out fine.

Bruno yells, "Kim, you goddamn idiot! What did I say about doing stupid sh…crap?"

He looks mad. We've been in here for a month, so I can tell when he's actually mad or just being Bruno. "Oh yeah? And you don't? How many times do you tell your UI you will destroy it? Or other objects that can't talk back? No one tells traps or doors, 'I will destroy you!' And, 'Eeewwwwww!' Always going, 'Ew!' Angry at objects. And everything else too, all the time. "Ew!' And how about all the dumb things you say all the time? 'That's a spicy meatball!' Or, 'I Love gold!,' while putting your pinky in your mouth. Or 'Stop looking at me swan!' Or, 'Just you 50 cops against kung-fu Joe!' Or, 'It's your butt, Mr. Postman!' How is that not dumb? And weird? I'm the darkness. What's the point if I don't do darkness things?"

"Well, Kim, you make some good points," he says with a smile and a little laugh. "Except you ever see me mess around in a fight? I do my nonsense when it's safe. You're just begging to be smoked, ain't you? We got four more days in here. The last day you're doing a full clear including the boss and I'm taping it all. Don't mess around. Everyone will see it so take it serious. Strictly business. Man that was a great album by EPMD."

He always uses words I don't understand. Butterball, I mean the general, always gets suspicious of that. Bruno doesn't know things everyone knows, but knows a bunch about old timey things. Well, the general doesn't get suspicious lately. They have some sort of secret they won't tell me and it's driving me nuts. All their stupid whispering and stopping talking when I come over.

I say, "What the heck is taping?"

"Jesus Christ, Kim. It's like you're trying to give me a brain aneurism. Everyone knows what taping is. I tape you. Uh, tape record you clearing the dungeon, and then I'll email it out."

"Oh, you mean vid. You'll make a vid and message it out. You talk so weird."

"Sure, I'm the weird one. Vid is a made up, nonsense word. It's taping. Or tape recording. Always has been, always will be. Let's head back. Jesus, Joseph, and Mary, loot first, Kim! Good, there you go. Use your head once in a while. Now we can head back. I've been meaning to talk to you about something. What do you think about the other guys?"

"Um, I like them. I guess. Why?"

"Just tell me what you think of each one. What's your opinion on them?"

I haven't really thought about it. I take a minute to collect my thoughts. Ball-face is supposed to be the best fighter of all the military guys. He's going to be in charge of all the training of everyone once we get out of here. The general is going to be some sort of leader. Ball-face is super smart and figured out a ton of UI stuff. The general wrote a bunch of messages to send off when we get out of here. Well, he didn't type them out – Ball-face typed them out after he figured how to make Bruno's keyboard visible to everyone. Bruno hates that. Just sitting there. No way Bruno was going to type them himself though. Lurch is here because he's the best fighter going to the city with the families and he'll be in charge of that.

"Ah, Ball-face is nice. He's a really good fighter too, and funny. And real smart. His jokes are hilarious. A little weird though. But not as weird as you.

251

"The general is nice, I guess. But he seems kind of slick. Like he is just pretending to be nice but is real good at pretending. If that makes sense. He isn't so good at fighting. I love when we do hand-to-hand training together because I can beat him sometimes.

"Lurch is really, really nice. Great guy. He moves real slow though. He's faster when he fights, so I don't know why he's so slow when he isn't. He loves talking. He gets annoyed when I don't pay attention, but he just talks, talks, talks. How am I supposed to pay attention when he's always talking about nothing? He's awesome with Joey. Does some weird stuff though. I bet when we get back he's brushing Joey's hair. Why? The system takes care of it. Makes it all clean and nice every day. It's weird. I don't think he's very smart, either."

Bruno stops for second, and I look back and he looks mad. The real mad. The scary kind of mad. But it doesn't last long. We start walking again and Bruno starts saying, "Last timeline, on the path to the city, everyone got complacent and felt safe because I was with them. Remember what I said about the biggest threat to survival being a passive outlook and the search for comfort? Well, everyone got comfortable. Too comfortable too often. I've seen Lurch jump in to danger to save stupid people with no regard for his own safety. He did it every time. If he's stupid then the world needs more people the type of stupid he is. I don't want to hear you insult him again, we clear?"

I put my head down. That isn't fair. I didn't insult him. And I didn't even call him stupid. If I make any excuses Bruno will just ask if I want cheese with my wine or something dumb like that, even though whatever that means makes no sense. So I just say, "Hua."

Bruno doesn't care about my hurt feelings and keeps going, "Butterball was supposed to bring in the toughest solider to be the trainer, but he brought in his own aide-de-camp. Just a crony. The toughest guy is always enlisted. Officers always become poque-ass sissies after captain. It becomes more about kissing ass instead of kicking ass, you know? Ball-face isn't bad, but he isn't the toughest. And Butterball is slick. You don't make general without being slick and getting good at playing games. Yes men. But we can use it. He's not infantry. Has a pogue branch. He's the lowest general. Brigadier general, got it early but's been stuck for a while. He's 48. Assistant division commander of mobility. Good with words. Good at all the things I'm bad at. I hope I can trust him. You remember what I said our big goal is?"

"Um, get everyone back to earth with no one dying?"

Bruno laughs, "I wish. That's our long term goal, but people will die. Can't avoid that. So, that goal is right, but it's as few people dying as possible – not no one dying. What's our next immediate big goal?"

I start thinking. I think it might be everyone getting SSs before Bruno opens dungeon 1. They were all talking about that. Motivating people to grind and train to get SS on this training dungeon. The training dungeon opens one more time before dungeon 1 opens, but Bruno is going to keep it locked. All the families have to get through dungeon 1 before they can start going to the city, and dungeon 1 is harder than the tutorial dungeon.

"Is it to get everyone to SS before you unlock dungeon 1?"

"Well, Jesus, Kim. I guess we got a lot of goals. You're right. That's an important goal. And a big one. So good job. But I mean dungeon area 10. No point in any of this if all our good people die in dungeon area 10 again. No way we get back to earth. Me coming back would just be a waste. Butterball knows the UN. He knows how they think. I'm not against the UN. You know that. I wasn't in the civil war. I'm not a terrorist. I know you love the UN, and you're proud of your dad and hate terrorists and sympathizers…"

Dagnab right I do! Everyone does. Always starting wars and killing innocent people because they hate freedom and the environment and don't even believe in global warming or science.

Bruno continues, "…but it isn't as black and white as that. I can't let them have power yet. Probably after dungeon area 10. If it goes bad it won't matter, and if it goes good, hopefully the UN won't be able to muck it up and will focus on getting everyone back to earth instead of politics and power games. Just remember, no matter what you hear people say, you know my goals. You know why I'm doing this. I don't want to be in charge. I have to. I hate it. They're going to come at me. Come at me hard. Come at me sideways too. Butterball agrees, the closer me and you are, the more at risk you are. The last thing I want is for you to be hurt or killed because we're friends. Or for you to be used against me. I got enough black marks on my soul as it is, I don't need no more.

"I just want you to know that. Know I would love grouping with you, but we can't. It isn't because I don't like you. I love hanging with you. You're just a kid, but you got spunk. You're crazy, but in a fun way. If I had my druthers, we'd group for this whole thing. But life don't care and don't ask what you want. It is what it is. Me taping you won't be just to motivate people to train and get SS. It's to try and keep you safe. Make you popular enough you won't be a target, even though you're connected to me. Trying to keep you secret will put a much bigger target on you. It's how they think. Devious. Sideways. They think everyone's like them and only think like they do."

He stops for a second and I start talking before he can again. He feels bad so he's rambling. "Please. Please. I don't care. Please stay grouped with me. I don't want to do this alone. Believe me, the UN wouldn't hurt someone like me. They only go after criminals and terrorists. Everyone knows that. They're the good guys. But if you're worried, just train me to be good enough where you don't have to worry. Please? Pleeeaaasee?"

I smile and try to do puppy dog eyes, but I think that only works if you're cute or good looking. Bruno doesn't like whining, and I can tell he's annoyed, so I stop talking and try to look tough. He likes tough. He respects tough.

We walk the rest of the way back to the open field in silence.

When we arrive Bruno yells, "Okay, ladies. Weapons training. Let's go! Lurch, move with a sense of urgency. How many times do I got to tell you, always move out with a sense of purpose. No lollygagging. Moving like a turtle isn't going to get you out of weapons training."

Lurch throws up his hands, "Who is Lurch? I don't get it. Why do you always call me this?"

"He's the person you're named after."

"My name is Hector Mu..."

"Your name is what I tell you it is. And I'm telling you your name is Lurch. Shhhhh. No more talking. This is training time."

"But..."

"Shhhhhh. I'm making you stronger, Lurch. Focus on not sucking so bad, not your name."

2.13 BEGINS WITH FOLLY, AND ENDS WITH REPENTANCE

KIM GUM

We got out of the dungeon, did the equipment swap, and Bruno sent out all the general's messages. He also sent out a message with a vid embedded titled, "If you can't fight as good as this little girl, you are doing it wrong. Man-up, suckers. Stop being pansies." All of us, especially the general, told Bruno it's real bad to call everyone weak, or sissies, or invalids, or fats, or olds. So he agreed not to. And he started with new offensive words to call all of humanity. Like suckers, and Maries, and pansies, and pissants. As the leader of all humans, calling all the humans bad names. Even I can see why that's a real bad idea. He says it motivates them. But they don't like it. No one likes it. But that wasn't what made me mad.

I used to think the name-calling was real bad, but also kind of funny. And I still do I guess. But what got me real mad was I don't like when he calls me a little girl. I'm not little. He knows I've had many, many periods. I'm basically an adult women, and I'm also basically a mother too. And what does me being a girl have anything to do with anything? My mom was a girl and she was super tough. At school they say thinking girls are weaker than boys is terrorist propaganda. I know Bruno isn't a terrorist. He was friends with my dad and my dad fought terrorists. And the general and Ball-face fought terrorists too. But sometimes Bruno makes me think. He is a great man. A good man. But I think he really believes girls are weaker than boys. That makes me real angry.

But that's okay. I'm the darkness and I will prove him wrong. That's what friends do. They help each other. Like Bruno is helping me. He helps me a ton. And I know for a fact he likes me more than everyone else, too. Way more than the general, and Ball-face, and Lurch. And he tells me I have a ton of potential and I'll be one of the best in the world when I'm all grown up and he finishes training me.

That message with my video did hurt my feelings, but I do like how good I did in it. I did really good. I downed the boss quick and I did everything right. Like Bruno says, "By the numbers. Hua?" Hua, indeed. I was very hua. But I'm not little, and being a girl doesn't matter.

I was super sad since we were all breaking up, and I'd have to solo dungeons alone forever now. Well, with Joey too, but he doesn't talk out loud. He barely even talks in my head now.

Bruno said he had business to take care of and left me. He just left me. Like I was nobody. That made me sadder.

Lurch took me and Joey to his family, but he said I had to call him Hector or Mr. Murillo. He didn't want me to disrespect him in front of his family. I would never do that. Not on purpose at least. But Lurch isn't a disrespectful name. I don't think so. His family was real nice but real boring so I was happy when someone said the doctor lady was looking for me. The doctor was real surprised at how good I healed and had a bunch of questions about the healing pill I didn't remember or know the answers to. She's a real nice lady. I like her. She asked a lot of questions about Bruno too, and wanted to know where he was and stuff.

Since Lurch was boring I went to find Ball-face and see if I could help with training or anything. I'm real good with the spear now. Real good. I think so.

I could tell Ball-face was just being nice when I showed up and asked if he needed help. He let me help train. He said I should only call him major something-or-other when Bruno isn't around. So I did. I forget his real name now. I think it fit him. I just call him major. Ball-face is a way better name though. I think he was surprised I was pretty good at training other people, but I've seen people training and getting trained my whole life. For a while, when I was younger, I was trying to be an assistant instructor too, but my mom never let me.

Ball-face was training with his shirt off. He would flex as he walked around, but tried not to be obvious about it. It's always obvious. What a weirdo.

We couldn't train for too long because it got too dark. So I started to look for Bruno. I saw a bunch of kids hanging out and I knew two of them from my school. I also recognized a real little kid from my mom's taekwondo school. The class Mac mostly instructs; the little kid class. I loved that class when I was in it. I miss Mac. He was fun. I miss Mia too. I miss my family.

Well, I thought one of the kids I knew from school called me fat and said something about my cankles, but he swore he didn't. He said he just said hi. He got real nervous after I put my spear against his stupid neck. Then the other one from my school, the girl, said I was crazy. She definitely said that. 100% my mind didn't change anything on that one. She definitely said it. While I was threatening them an adult ran over saying I was in real big trouble, so I took off.

Bruno has a tent. A real big tent. He used it in the dungeon. I bet a bunch of people can sleep in it, but he won't let no one. Just him. In his big, comfy tent alone. Like a real jerk. He got it from achievements and it has a bunch of upgrades and bonuses for the owner. It always has a fire pit with a fire going in front of it. That fire was the only reason I was able to find Bruno.

I went up to the tent and called out. I was surprised to see the doctor come out of the tent first. She seemed embarrassed and left real quick. Bruno said they were talking about healing pills and the con ability. He also told me he wanted to talk to me.

As we sit down at the fire, Bruno says, "Don't forget you still owe me gold for the guild fund. I'm going to the city after dawn phase and will start the guild. Did you ID the gear you got handed back?"

There's a much cheaper way to ID stuff than scrolls. At least for lower level items. I learned the misc. section of the store stands for miscellaneous, which means something like "everything else." I missed it under there but you can ID items for a cost of 10g plus 5g times the itemization points of the item. Way cheaper than scrolls. I forgot exactly what I got now, but besides the healing kit +1, I didn't get anything useful. There was a survival kit +1, but I don't got the survival skill no more. The itemization points for +1 enhanced skill is 5, so it only cost 35g to ID the +1 kits. And IDing this was always works. No chance of failure. High level items cost way more to ID in misc. Bruno says when everyone gets to the city, people can make a lot of gold IDing items, but they spam chat way too much.

The boots and ring I got from the giant turd-snake piece of garbage in the tutorial dungeon were useless to me when I ID'ed them. The boots were move silently +1, and the ring was spot +1. I don't got either of those skills now. I guess the rare spawns usually drop loot tailored for the people that kill it, so I can't wait to fight more of them. But Bruno says we won't see many. Not until later.

We got a potion that increases the chance for a rare spawn by 1%. Bruno took it and is saving it for later. Rare spawns drop stuff that has no minimum character level, so even besides the dungeon coins you get for killing them, they are pretty awesome. The only other way to get items with no minimum character level is from the reward for completing a dungeon for the first time. One reward gives a piece that has permanent death ward. I forget which dungeon Bruno said. We won't get to it for a while anyways, but I can't wait for that.

I tell Bruno, "I got the gold now if you want it. And I did ID everything. Only thing useful was a +1 healing kit."

"Nice. That's awesome. That'll help a ton. Give me the other stuff and I'll put it in my portable bank. After I get back from the city, and our guild's open, I'm going to start putting my portable auction house out. That'll help with taxes and gold and mats and renown all that stuff."

Uh oh. Bruno won't like this next part. I say, "Sorry, I already vendored everything. I thought it didn't matter until you started the guild."

I brace for his anger but there isn't any. "Well, you only screwed yourself. Everything magic is going to sell like hotcakes for a long while. You could've made a ton of gold with that crap. You got to start listening, Kim"

No one says anything for a bit. We just sit in silence. I want to bring up us staying grouped, but I'm scared to do it, and I can't think about anything else to talk about.

Finally, Bruno breaks the silence. "I got some news you should like. Me and Butterball talked about it, and we're staying grouped up for at least one more run through the training dungeon. Dungeon 1 is staying locked for at least a couple more runs, so there's no rush. He's got a lot to deal with here, management bullsh...crap. So going into the tutorial dungeon again will give us more time to plan and whatever. He'll have Ball-face go too. He needs his typist. I'll ask Lurch, but it's up to him. He didn't like being away from his family for so long. Understandable. You don't have to go with us, but I wanted to give you the offer. What do you say?"

The knot in my stomach loosens a little. I start smiling ear to ear. Even if it's just pushing it back a little, I won't have to be alone again for a little bit longer. "YES! Of course I'm in."

"I thought you'd say that. It won't be for a month. Maybe a week. Maybe two. We'll see. I've also been thinking about something else. I don't like having other people dictate what I do or how I do it, and that's what I'm doing. I do what I want. I'd like to stay grouped with you, and if you want to stay grouped with me, that's all that should matter. Just realize, you're not seeing the full picture and this will definitely put you in more danger. Up to you, but you got to say you realize it and understand it."

As soon as he makes the offer I start crying. The knot in my stomach goes away completely. I don't say anything, because I can't. I'm crying too hard. I just go over to Bruno and hug him and cry. And he hugs me back.

2.14 CAN'T SMOKE A ROCK

KIM GUM

I keep seeing the flashing reminding me there are new messages in guild chat, and I want to check it so bad. And I'm super excited we're about to be level 2! Focus, Kim! I haven't done anything to get smoked yet, and we're at the boss. I'll be able to check soon. Patience. You can do it!

Bruno says, "You ready, champ?"

"Hua." I say it before thinking. I look back and double check Joey is there. He is. He's been following us in this dungeon for some reason. Maybe because it's new?

This should be easy. I've already seen this boss during Bruno's arena run. Just a tank and spank with some adds. This whole dungeon has been easy. But Bruno's done almost everything himself. He wouldn't even let me do traps and locks, even though our skill is exactly the same. We're exactly the same. Don't make no sense. But seeing Bruno in action is…is…amazing is the only word I can think of. I could barely keep up.

This dungeon has game mobs – goblins, giant fire beetles, and rat swarms. The rat swarms are a hassle, but not too bad. If our fort saves were lower we could've got diseased from just being near the rat swarms, but nothing happened to us. I guess going high con is less stupid than I thought. The fire beetles could be an issue for dumb people, but the fire and explosions are easy to avoid if you don't suck too bad. The goblins are a joke. At least compared to the turd-pigeons. They barely fight back. Barely even try to parry. The ones with shields at least always try to block. Sure, their HPs are a little higher, but since they only attack every six seconds and suck at fighting, this dungeon seems way easier.

Maybe it isn't. Bruno did most of the work. I'll see next time we run it. I'll be doing it all myself next time, while Bruno watches. I'll bet a million dollars he finds some dumb reason to smoke me too. Even if I do great. I hate being smoked. Stupid exercises. I hate mountain climbers so much. They should be illegal. Bruno says getting smoked so much is making me stronger, and should be making me smarter, but isn't. And if I don't get smarter I may end up being the strongest person in the world.

"Kim, goddamn it! Pay attention. Lollygag on your own time. If we don't get 1st SS I'm going to smoke you for a week. I said I'll pick up one add and the boss. Get the other two before hopping on the boss. Hua?"

Jeez, relax. "Hua."

Bruno charges in the boss' room at a trash mob, and leads it up towards the boss rushing at him. I wait a second as the other two trashes are about to get close together on their way towards Bruno. I charge when they do, and get agro on both. I down them quick. Nothing to it. I also remember to keep stabbing while they are down until their nametags go grey. Don't want any surprises.

I get behind the boss. The goblin sergeant. I'll call him turd-sergeant. Bruno's trash mob is already down. I get one hit in that doesn't even land before the turd-sergeant gets an iframe, pulls out a horn, blows on it, and grows taller as three more adds charge at us.

I get one down and turn for another, and see Bruno's already back on the boss. I jump behind the giant goblin and start thrusting. My hits are landing, and as it transitions to an iframe I get a crit on top of my sneak attack damage. The boss goes down, but the horn noise goes off like he didn't, and we get three more adds running at us. Bruno downs two in the time it takes me to down one again, but I got the crit that downed the boss, so I count our score as even.

"Just so you know, that weird thing where he went down and then the horn goes off – that was me. I got a big crit off on top of the sneak attack damage. You're welcome."

Bruno laughs as he loots the mobs and the boss. "Got a kit. Hopefully a healing kit. I want mine upgraded so bad. Where's Joey?" We both look towards the door and see Joey enter the boss room like he knew it was safe now.

Bruno says, "We definitely got 1st SS. We blew through this. Good job, Kim. I'm worried about the spelling psuchesomas since we both stink at spelling. Oh well. We'll cross that bridge when we come to it, but 1st SS will probably be out the window when we get those. You ready for the AAR?"

Holy moly, we're about to get level 2 through that door and Bruno wants to do an AAR? It wouldn't be so annoying if he said it normal, but he says aye-aye-aaahhhh. It means after action review. And no I'm not ready. I want to get level 2 so bad, and check guild chat, and do a million things besides a stupid AAR. I don't say any of that. I just say, "Hua."

"Okay, what'd we do right and what'd we do wrong? And what could we do better?"

"Any chance I can check the guild messages, big guy? It was going off like mad before we entered, and I stayed focused just like you told me to. I didn't check even when you were doing the psuchesoma. 100% focused. Could be important or an emergency."

"Yeah, go ahead. We got time. Plenty of time. Let me know if it's something I need to know about. Or if Ms. Kaur is acting up again."

Ass-eyes. That hussy is such a nut. She's always fake pretend nice in front of Bruno, but I see right through it. Bruno invited her to the guild because she is supposed to be in charge of children stuff in dungeon areas, but she went nuts and just spammed chat with how horrible Bruno is and that he's a terrorist and stuff like that. Bruno made a new chat channel called 'child emergency' and Ass-eyes can only post in that one, and he told her if it isn't relevant or child related she's going to get kicked from the guild. Bruno puts up with too much from her, just because she's watching those two weird little girls doesn't mean we should have to put up with all her craziness.

Bruno said everyone else talked too much in guild chat about nonsense, so he made a chat channel just for important information for him called 'important no bleating allowed.'

I go to the main chat channel and it's just everyone in the city wishing us luck on the new dungeon. Emina and Hanh also reminding us for the millionth time to look for their husbands. Bruno already told them there's no way they'll be in our instance dungeon area 2. Our dungeon area 2 will get a lot of new people, but it will still be people from around fayetteville and NC. No way we join with people from russia and vietnam for a long while. We'll start joining with people from farther and farther away after dungeon area 2 since most people will take the path to the city instead of staying and crawling dungeons.

I read over the messages to make sure I didn't miss nothing. It's kind of crazy this is only our third official day on this world. In this contest. So much has happened. And it isn't even the third day yet, not technically. We'll still have almost an hour of the second day when we exit this dungeon. This is the second day dusk phase opening. But we'll finally be level 2.

We ran the tutorial dungeon five times. The last two times hardly anyone was moving up in rank. Bruno and the general wanted to have people do the tutorial one more time, so we'd be exactly one day behind dungeon openings. Everyone hated that idea, so they relented. Now we'll be two opening behind.

I ask Bruno, "Are you going to the city when day phase starts again like last time?"

"No, no. We got to organize all the monkeys going to the city. That'll take a while. I want a whole phase to spend with my family, and day phase is best. I don't want to waste my beam to watch my family sleeping. They'll be busy grinding mats during day phase so it's not ideal, but last time I went I had to wake everyone up, and they weren't too happy about that. And I had to beam back early to give out guild invites and square stuff away. No phase is ideal, but day phase works out best. Remember, they ain't doing dungeons, so this is actually just the second day for them, and tomorrow will be the third, and they still got to adjust for the longer days here."

It's so adorable my BFF calls teleporting beaming. I tried explaining that port stands for teleport, and not portal, but his brain doesn't work right. Once something is fixed in his head it doesn't change. So, to him, port is short for portal – proof being the actual portals in area 10 and 20 and the epic zones. I love this big lug, but he has issues. Seeing Bruno teleport was neat. It has a long cast time, but then he just disappears. Poof. Gone. I want to watch it again.

When Bruno got back from the city last time he came to me first and I was the first person added to the guild. Well, besides the city people. That made me feel good. Important. I went with Bruno as he added the general, Ball-face, and Lurch to the guild. As he was adding people I checked out the guild. There were 6 people in it besides me and Bruno. Bruno's wife, who is the assistant guild leader, his two kids, two of his last party's wives, and one of their kids who is old enough to take a class. I couldn't tell who was who then, because it just showed numbers instead of names, but we sorted that out later in guild chat. They all went crafters.

Bruno's wife, Minnie, has a class that doesn't sound like a crafter though. Administrator? What a dumb sounding class. It counts as a crafter. I guess that class can scribe, which I think just means writing stuff down, but they get xp for a ton of dumb things. Talking in guild chat. Talking out loud to people. Even changing settings gives them xp. If they are in a guild leader position they get xp for any money changing hands for anyone in the guild, including people vendoring items. Crazy. I guess administrator is a catch all class. Even people that play fourth age just to roleplay and spend all their time as innkeepers, bartenders, or servers become administrators. They don't get a ton of xp for anything, but they get xp for a ton of things.

Bruno's son, Nate, became an armorsmith, and the boy around my age, Sergey, became a weaponsmith. His daughter, Siri, became a jewelsmith. The other ladies, named Hanh and Emina, became a clothier and a woodsmith. Bruno said the big money is with the weaponsmith and armorsmith classes, but they can't make a lot of things without a jewelsmith refining certain things, and woodsmiths and clothiers making certain things. Between their craft and hobby selections, they had all the gathering, smelting, and everything else covered to make most items. And all the crafters make a lot of money, but weaponsmith and armorsmith make the most.

They need a leathersmith real bad to make certain weapons and armors. For a lot of stuff they can substitute cloth. And the people in the city don't have a good, steady income of leather yet. They can farm the stuff they need in the crafting zones for the most part. There are mobs in the crafting zones, but not enough to supply the amount of mats needed to level up leatherworking. If someone went leathersmith, they would have to buy most of their mats, and they'd be way behind everyone else in the city. Rare mats mostly came from mobs in dungeons, just like most leather comes from dungeons too, so they can't get everything from farming crafting zones.

Bruno has another achievement award – a portable AH. You can't use it in a dungeon. It's filled with all the crafting stuff people in the city could make before he had to port back. So far it's just basic weapons, shields, and some of the bad pieces of medium and heavy armor. The ones with the worst AC and worst maximum dex bonus. A lot of scale mail, one chainmail, a couple splint mails, and two banded mails. Everything is priced way cheaper than the store sells those items for. A heavy wooden shield is 7g in the store, but is 4g 5s in the AH for a buyout. That doesn't seem like a big amount of savings, but heavy wooden shields aren't very expensive. You could save over 50g off the store price for chainmail. That's a lot of savings.

Nothing was set up for bidding, just in case if barely anyone bid and all the expensive stuff ended up selling for nothing. Crafting is expensive. Even with Bruno giving the city people money, they need to sell their stuff for more than it would vendor for to keep crafting. The other professions in the city just vendor what they make since belts and bracers and rings and other stuff they can make isn't magical.

My current spear and shield are in good shape and have almost full durability so I didn't buy nothing from the portable AH. Bruno left it in front of the dungeon. The cheaper stuff sold, but not all the expensive stuff. Not right away at least. I didn't check recently.

Bruno put the word out people should sell all the hides and leather they get to anyone who took tanner and leatherer as crafts or hobbies. Then those people could refine some hides and make specific mats out of leather that would sell real good to the people in the city through the portable AH. He also had a portable bank he let me put stuff in so we could carry more loot. Like the grappling hook rope thing we got for finishing the tutorial dungeon, and some stuff we couldn't equip until level 2, and other things we don't need to carry around yet.

Bruno told me that hopefully when we turned level 2 and mul-ticlassed into fighter, we could buy our full plate armor and heavy shields from our guild instead of through the store. It would be way cheaper than the store. We have to save up, but the people in the city should have our stuff ready for us now. It looks like we'll have to wait until after we clear dungeon 1 again to get it, since Bruno just said he isn't going to the city until day phase.

Bruno also added the doctor lady to the guild. She acts really weird around Bruno. I don't know why. He also added two more guys from the military. I didn't change their numbers to names because I don't know them. I still don't understand why Ass-eyes is in the guild, that crazy hussy.

Bruno is right though, she is real pretty.

I wonder why Bruno left so many guild slots open? We can have 30 people in the guild.

"Bruno, how come we have so many open guild slots?"

"You were right there when I explained to Butterball why, and why I picked a trading guild."

"I...I didn't listen. Sorry." I was probably talking in chat when Bruno explained it. I love chat.

"No problem, but it means I got to make you stronger."

Dagnab it! So close! Oh well, getting smoked so much really is making me stronger.

Bruno sighs and says, "Okay. Pay attention this time. There are three types of guilds. Adventurer, bounty hunter, and trading. People also call trading guilds crafting guilds. All of them can level up to guild level 3. You need renown to level up. Each type gets renown different. A main source and a minor source. Bounty hunting guilds get renown from collecting bounties and battlegrounds, neither of which are a thing here. So bounty hunter guilds are out because you can't level them at all. Adventuring guilds get renown from quests and killing bosses, and bosses is the minor renown source. Since there's no quests here, adventurer guilds take forever to level up.

"Now, trading guilds main renown source is from trading, minor is crafting and harvesting mats. Even we contribute to renown gain by looting mats from mobs and repairing with tinker. I'm not sure if porter adds anything. Maybe. But my AH is adding a ton of renown. We add renown from vendoring items too. So, trading guilds is the only way to get to guild level 3 fast.

"Guild level 3 is important for a couple things. Our member cap now is 30. At guild level 2 it will be 45, and 60 at 3. All the guilds have different bonuses. Bounty hunter guilds give extra bounty slots and bonus gold and renown for battlegrounds. Adventure guilds give temp HPs on rest and bonus xp on quest completion and boss kills. Trade guilds give discount fees on the auction house and a percent chance not to use up mats during crafting. The temp HPs are nice, but it's only 3 points at level 1 and 9 points at level 3. And you can only rest every four hours. And you would only get 3 temp HPs forever because you won't getting to guild level 2 for a long, long time. The trade guild give a 16%, 32%, and then a 50% discount on all the fees of the AH for all members, crafters or not. And the fees are wicked high. Just to post an item the fee costs 10% of what a vendor would pay for the item. If it doesn't sell you get 5% back. If an item sells you lose all that fee, plus an additional 5% of the total amount the item sold for on a buy-out, or 10% if a high-bid. I forget how the mats bonus works. I know crafters love it though.

"The big bonus of guild level 3 is everyone in the guild gets plus 1 to both AB and AC. That's huge. Doesn't sound big, but that's two feats right there. You also get bonus xp for guild levels. I think 2, 4, and 6 percent. But that doesn't matter either. Saving on gold is great for now, but when you hit the epic zone and start rolling in gold it doesn't matter. The bonus xp doesn't matter either. I told you what happens when we hit the epic zone, right?"

I reply, "Yeah, I'm super excited for it too. You pick an epic class!"

Bruno waves his hand, "Yeah, but not that. No more dungeon locks or level locks. All your banked experience from all the dungeon grinding up to then goes right into your epic class. My first time there I shot right up to level 25, and I missed out on all the grinding before 10 since I went to the city. A ton of people went straight from level 20 to 26. And you still have to hit every 5-man up to 30 so you hit level 30 wicked early. I told you my plan, right? On how I'll reroll and everything?"

I say, "Um, yeah, kind of. Actually, not really. I don't know the new class or anything."

"Not the class. The plan. I clear all epic zone 5-mans in this build, then I reroll and blow through everything all over again as a power-house. The dungeons in the epic zones don't give dungeon coins, they give gear gems. Same with raids. When I hit the epic zone in my new class, I'll probably only be level 22 or 23. I'll still hit 30 just doing all the five mans, and when I do, I'll have enough gear gems to get two raid set pieces immediately. So even though I waited so long to reroll I'll be ahead of the curve or only slightly behind it. Right around where the first people to start raiding are, except I'll be way better and blow past all those sissy-ass fruitcakes."

I give him my disappointed look. Not just for the name calling. What is it with him saying 'I' instead of 'we?' I thought we were past all this. We're in this together, forever. I say, "Bruno, you promised the general you'd stop calling everyone sissies and monkeys. Come on, man!"

His face gets serious for a second and then lets up. My heart goes back to normal, I thought he was mad and I got scared. Phew. He says, "I do what I want. And I only promised not to call them names to their faces. Like in emails or in person. I can still do it just in front of you. You got to stop nagging me. I stopped swearing for you, so give me a break, huh?"

I laugh. "No you didn't. You swear all the time."

"No I don't. Not the big ones. Sometimes I slip, but I barely ever do. But now since little Ms. High-and-mighty is getting too big for her britches, you can start knocking them out while I finish explaining why so many guild spots are still open."

Knocking them out means doing pushing-ups. I get into the front leaning rest position and start knocking them out. Bruno continues, "So, we have 15 people in the guild now. We could fill it with useless nobodies who'd only spam chat with more monkey bleatings, or we could fill it with people that add something. Butterball wants to add…hey! All the way down. All the way up. You're not bobbing for apples. Butterball wants to add important UN people. He thinks it will ingratiate them to me and they'll cause me less of a hassle. I doubt it. We'll see. I want to add some arena leaders and some people I can trust. Probably some enlisted. Depends on who we mix with going forward, and if it's safe to go back zones.

"Uh, we'll see. When the cities open we'll kick people out and add more crafters until we get guild level 3. Then we'll kick the crafters all out and this guild will be for all the best crawlers. We could get a bunch of guilds going now, but since we have all the crafters it really doesn't matter since they would hardly get any renown. And Butterball thinks it'is of more strategic value for me to be in control of the only guild for now. Hell, I'm easy, so we'll see how it goes. I don't want to be pigeonholed. Muscle failure already? That's sad, Kim. Supine bicycle. Go!"

Phew! My arms were about to give out. Bruno always knows when I'm actually at muscle failure and when I have more in me to give. I roll over on my back and start doing the supine bicycle. These aren't so bad. Push-ups are much harder. Mountain climbers are the worst.

I wonder if Bruno made a vid of this run. Probably not. People wanted a vid of him in the tutorial dungeon. It was real hard to see what happened or get anything of value from that vid. It doesn't make sense for melee fighters to vid themselves fighting. It just looks like confusing chaos and makes you feel sick. Maybe he'll vid me again on the next run. I'll do that one myself without Bruno's help.

I can't wait until I can make my own vids. I wonder how long we'll stay in this dungeon. Level 2 is right through that door. I wish you could use guild chat in dungeons. I wish I didn't get smoked so much.

I don't get smoked for much longer. The AAR goes good. Not much we could've done better. Bruno said I did perfect. I like that. I did perfect. We're only staying in here for about a week. Man, level 2 is right through that door. Patience is so overrated.

2.15 LEVEL 2 AND EVIL DEVIL HAGS

KIM GUM

Dungeon area 2 – finally! I get the dungeon completion popup and we got 1st SS. Nice! Oh, a bag of holding! I claim it immediately without even checking the amount of gold I got too. There was also a potion, but who cares? Healing potions stink. We can only drink one between resting and you can't drink them in combat. Well, you can, but it's super hard if you're melee.

I go into inventory and slot the bag of holding. It's just a tiny one and only increases carry weight by 10 lbs. It's a cosmetic item so everyone can see it when you slot it. This is the worst one, but they get super awesome. They go tiny, small, average, medium, big, large, huge, enormous, massive, and gigantic. The gigantic one increases carrying capacity by 2,500 lbs. That's just nuts! I could carry so much with that. You can have one of each type. Or have one of each type slotted in your inventory.

Well, that was exciting. I know the grappling hook is supposed to be necessary later but that wasn't exciting to get. A bag of holding is way better. But I'm way more excited to finally level up to 2. I open my UI and can finally, finally level up. Following Bruno's build I multiclass into fighter. My HPs go up to 23. My BAB goes up to 1. My fort saves go up by 2. I put a point in acrobatics, athletics, disable device, knowledge, open locks, search, and UMD. I get a bunch of free feats too. Nice! Medium and heavy armor, heavy and tower shields, and martial weapons. For my fighter bonus feat I take weapon focus, and it increases my AB by 1. I take focus with the spear, Bruno will take dwarven waraxe. Bruno already has a dwarven waraxe in his portable bank ready to go. We both already have heavy shields in there too, so our AC will go up by 1. But the heavy shields give us a -2 armor check penalty. When we get our full plate, it will add -6 to that, and raise our AC by 8, but lower it by 1 too because of the max dex penalty.

I feel on top of the world! Level 2! Finally!

This is so dumb! Our area had a bunch of new people. Everyone knew me because I'm famous and the attention was weird so I kept around Bruno. And I guess I was annoying him while he was trying to prepare all the people going to the city and handle stuff, so he made me learn something called a pace count. And klicks. Klick with a k.

For a pace count, Bruno put a stake in the ground and walked a good ways off and put another stake in the ground. He said it was 100 meters. He had me walk from stake to stake counting every time my left foot hit the ground. It takes me 69 steps to hit 100 meters. Bruno said when I finish growing it will be less steps. I'm already real tall though. At least compared to other kids my age. I tower over them.

Honestly, I don't even know what a meter is. Even still. Or a yard. I know a foot is 12 inches though. And about how long an inch is.

Bruno made me pace out the distance from dungeon 1 to 2-2. Then 2-2 to 2-1, then 2-1 back to dungeon 1 again. One klick is a thousand meters. I got a little over two klicks from dungeon 1 to 2-2. Like 2 klicks, and almost 200 meters more. I forget the distance I got from 2-2 to 2-1, or 2-1 to 1. It was more than a klick. A good amount more.

I didn't know why Bruno had me do this, but when I got back he was mad I didn't do it right and he said, "It is exactly two klicks across.

You don't think that's weird? That this place uses the most popular measurement system on earth for distance? All of the dungeon areas are like this. Exact klicks. Pretty weird, huh? Gets you thinking."

Thinking about what, I don't know. I guess I kept bothering him while he was busy because he told me to practice my pace count until I got exactly two klicks from dungeon 1 to 2-2, and closer to what I'm supposed to get for 2-2 to 2-1. He also made me memorize that it's...oh jeez, I forgot. It's something like five klicks is three miles. Close to that. That's the gist of it. I don't know how that's helpful or what I'm supposed to do with this information.

I'm just pretending I'm doing it. I didn't even walk all the way to 2-2. Who cares about any of this? Not me. And I want to get back and say goodbye to Lurch and his family. People were already heading towards the door to the city when I was sent off. It's in the top middle of the instance. I couldn't see anything on my way back since I have to look like I'm coming from dungeon 1-1 on the south part of the instance. Make it look like I really did more pace counting stupid nonsense.

I finally get back and the dungeon area seems dead. There're people, but hardly any compared to earlier. I go to the training area and Ball-face isn't here. I go to the med area and it's pretty empty too. I see the doc though, and that makes me less nervous.

I say, "Hey, doc. Where's Bruno? And everyone else?"

"Hello, Ms. Gum," she says to me with a big smile. "Bruno went with the people to the city. Just to show them how to form up and deal with the tentacle monster attacks. He'll be back soon. Everyone here is all that's left. Most people are going to the city."

I get sad. I didn't get to say goodbye to Lurch. "Have you seen Joey?"

"Yeah, a while ago. He was with Melissa. Um, Ms. Kaur. She isn't going to the city, so she's around somewhere."

"Thanks, doc."

I head out, just wandering and looking for Ass-eyes and Joey. Some people waving and saying hi. I wave and say hi back. I stop and look through chat. I leave a goodbye message for Lurch. He talks a ton in chat, so he isn't gone forever. My whole life everyone has always told me I stink at writing. They should see Lurch write. He stinks way worse than I do. Sometimes you can hardly tell what he wrote. I guess the translator is responsible for some of it. It isn't perfect. But still, Lurch writes real bad.

I talk a little bit to Nate and Siri. Nate is real nice. I can't wait to meet him. Siri is okay. She seems a little snooty. Maybe she'll be different in person. She is a lot older than me though, and older kids don't usually waste time on younger kids.

Sergey seems okay. I like him, but I guess he is always staring at Siri's boobs and butt and it creeps her out. Siri is real pretty and all the boys always like her a lot. That's what Nate said.

I finally see Joey, hanging out with some old lady.

Filthy devil hag! Hussy! Devil witch! Spawn of Satan! I hate her so much. I hate her so much it hurts. She will die by my hand. Not today, but one day. Ewwwww!

I can't believe Bruno sided with her. Stupid devil hag. Ewww, I hate her so much.

When I found Joey he was with this old hag lady who is the devil. She was real strong for being so old. And mean. And evil. I hate her so much. She caused me to send a lot of stuff down into my hate-ball. She held me and made me answer questions even though I didn't want to and Bruno says I never have to answer anything to anyone. Besides him. As long as I don't do dumb stuff like when I threatened those kids from my school and held a spear to one of their dumb necks.

So this devil was holding me and forcing me to answer questions. I wanted to stab her but figured Bruno would get mad. So I answered

277

her dumb questions. Real dumb questions. Like if Bruno ever touches me. Of course he touches me. How do you train without touching? Does it make me uncomfortable? Yes, of course. And more. Much more. It hurts. It hurts bad sometimes. Ever been in an arm lock, lady? PT is worse though, and he doesn't touch me in PT. Besides buddy carries. I can't carry Bruno yet, but when I can that will really suck. I guess we touch a little when we do the thing where I lay on the ground and hold Bruno's ankles while he stands behind me, and I have to try and kick him in the chest and he catches my feet and throws my legs down. Throws them all over. I hate those. Not as much as duck walking or mountain climbers, but I hate them a lot. Yeah, PT hurts way worse than hand-to-hand or weapons training.

She asked me a million questions about a million things. About my parents. Being the darkness. My siblings. Dumb feelings. How did this make you feel, and how did that make you feel? Everything was feelings to this devil lady. That old dragon monster, filthy devil. I hate her so much.

Bruno finally got back and the devil let me go and he and the devil got to talking. She said I had all this stuff wrong with me. Tons of stuff. I was real angry and wasn't listening good like I probably should've been. I was angry Bruno was being so nice to the devil hag, talking so nice to her. But then she started to yell at him, and after a while he started to yell back. She was yelling real loud and I could tell Bruno was getting angry. I took that as a sign to go balls to the wall so I stabbed the devil, but she was a decent fighter for being a super old filthy devil hag and dodged my next thrust. I never even broke her dumb HP shield.

Bruno grabbed my spear and was real mad at me and made me go stand away until I calmed down. When he came to talk to me later, after I calmed down, he said I had to talk to the devil for an hour between dungeon openings, and she's some sort of professional with feelings and talking. Like doc, but for brains – and is evil and worships the Satan. Probably.

Bruno says all this was my fault because I proved the devil right by stabbing her and I'm lucky she had a HP shield and didn't get hurt. Filthy devil hag. I'll spit on her filthy devil grave one day. And pee on it too, probably. She will die by my hand. I'll stick my spear right up her butt and it will come out her mouth and I will roast her over a fire and eat her. Well, I probably won't go that far. That seems really dramatic and gross. But she would deserve it if I did. A girl can dream, can't she?

Bruno smoked me real bad for stabbing the devil. Now he has me running laps. He said you always have to treat old women with respect, no matter what. And they have to do something real crazy for you to get physical with them, but it's better to just leave instead of getting physical. And if one is annoying me just avoid them. But I have to always be nice and respectful to old women. And old men too. But especially old women. And another one of his dumb rules is I shouldn't hit women, even though I am a woman. Unless they are good at fighting like me and want to fight me too. And can fight back. But that's a dumb rule and makes no sense. He also thinks I shouldn't fight guys like he does. He says I'm not smart enough yet to tell when it's okay to fight. But I will be able to when I'm full grown. Full grown in my body and mind.

He also said I couldn't avoid the devil because she was allowed to talk to me for an hour between every dungeon opening. And I couldn't be mean neither. But I could be mean if someone grabbed me and was mean to me first. Even though that's exactly what the devil hag did to me.

I see the dungeon's gem flash a half hour warning. Nice. I'm not that tired, but I don't want to be too spent if I'm clearing dungeon 1 by myself while Bruno vids it. Show these pogue sissies how to do it right. I am the darkness.

2.16 THE CLEARER WE SHOULD SEE THROUGH IT

KIM GUM

Next run on dungeon 1 I cleared the dungeon and fought the boss by myself. And I did awesome, and Bruno sent out a video of it. And the message just said, "Let the darkness show you how it's done." That made me real happy. What wasn't on the video was after I killed the boss I peed on his stupid dumb face like I should, and that got Bruno real mad at me because I didn't tell him I was going to do it and he said he saw stuff he shouldn't see and I should use my brain more and have some decency. He wasn't mad I peed on the corpse. He said I could pee on whatever I want as long as he isn't looking and peeing on your enemy's corpses can be good for the soul. I got smoked again. Being smoked so much makes me stronger. That's how Bruno says I should look at it.

So since then I have to meet with the devil hag between openings. We usually meet right after a dungeon closes. We were going to do it at the midpoint, three of this world's hours after a close, but this way is easier since I kept forgetting and missing the meetings when it was at the midpoint and the devil would come searching for me and bugging Bruno, and Bruno doesn't like to be bugged. I bet he wouldn't mind so much if the devil was pretty. But she isn't. She is an ugly old devil hag. With her dumb robes. Casters are stupid idiots.

And the worst part is if I don't talk or answer her dumb questions about feelings she rats on me to Bruno, and then Bruno smokes me. And he looks at me all disappointed. I hate that. Disappointed for what? Not wanting to waste my time talking to the devil? I don't see him talking to her about feelings all the time, but I don't give him disappointed looks, now do I? Talking about feelings is stupid.

And she is tricky. Sometimes she talks about interesting, normal things that get me talking about interesting, normal things, and then she pulls the old switcheroo. She will talk about her group and how they cleared this or that, or why casters aren't stupid but are actually good in her opinion. And we start talking all normal, like normal people talking about interesting stuff. And then she starts with the non-interesting, non-normal questions and ruins everything. Tricky old devil.

One time I peed in a cup and gave it to her but she figured it out real quick. Before even taking a sip and making it worth it. She wouldn't stop yapping her stupid devil mouth about that. Bruno got real mad as he considered that being super disrespectful to old women. And I'm not. I am super nice to them. All of them besides the devil hag. I hate her so much it hurts me inside. She has caused my hate-ball to grow fifty million billion sizes. So much hate forced down into my ball.

People were getting used to things. The gems flash on the hour. And pulsed a little 30 minutes before opening, and again at 15. Then a lot five minutes and one minute prior. The time between dungeons were getting real civilized. People were nice and helped others. A lot of joking and messing around. Mostly training. Getting better. Improving.

Things just progressed. More dungeons, level three. I got more stronger and more awesome. Then level 4. I'm level 5 now. Well, basically level 5.

Joey was finally sticking to the designated bathroom area the whole time – in dungeons, and out. I kept on a regular bathing schedule so Bruno would stop making me bathe like a child when I'm a fully grown woman. He always says I smell when I don't. And one time he made the devil talk to me about female stuff and taking care of female parts. That was so embarrassing. Talking to your arch-nemesis about private stuff. And why does Bruno think he needs to get that old devil to talk to me about being a woman? I've been one for a long time and I know how to do it. I mean, I do what she said to do and it helps, but come on.

Most of the messages he sends out now are usually through the general and typed up by Ball-face. The people in our instance said the general's messages were way better than Bruno's. When more people joined us in the dungeon area 3 there were some more NC people, but also a lot of people from out of NC. Like from virginia, tennessee, and SC. I think some from georgia too, but that could have been in area 4. I made friends with this one boy from SC, but I think he died because I couldn't find him later. I mostly just trained or helped with training in the dungeon areas. That and tried not to get in trouble. Too much trouble, I mean.

Bruno helped train a good amount, but when we were alone he said it was a waste of time because all the people there were garbage. Even the ones that always got a ranked SS. It would make him mad. Ass-eyes group would sometimes get 3rd SS, and once even got 2nd. Bruno didn't understand how since he said their group was complete trash. Two of the guys in the group, William and Duncan, were trainers. Good guys. Good fighters too. Both were soldiers at hiss. William was an MP. He always tries to get me to put in a good word with Bruno because of the incident they had way back when, but Bruno always just laughs when I tell him anything about William.

Bruno let me take a nap in his tent once. It was awesome. My nose got broke training with some guy and I felt sick after so Bruno took his tent out and told me to rest inside. It was super comfy. I got the basic tent myself now through achievement points. It sucks compared to Bruno's. Bruno's is like super magic or something. The bed is so, so, so comfy. It's amazing. I love that bed. I need it. You can't see in his tent at all from outside, or hear anything from inside of the tent if you are outside it, but when you go in you can see outside the tent. And you can, like, punch the walls from inside and it doesn't move. And you can turn off sound from outside so you don't hear anything. And it has an alarm if someone comes too close or touches it or a bunch of settings like that. It has a bunch of HPs too. His tent. My tent has 3 HPs. And my tent sucks real bad. It doesn't do anything besides be a little, teeny-tiny stupid regular tent.

After the city people left almost all the crawlers always got SS on dungeons. When they tried. You still had to grind for gold and drops so those runs were never SS. But on the first attempt of a new dungeon almost all the crawlers got SS. There were still a lot of plain S and a few A rankers, but SS was the vast majority. After three runs of a dungeon Bruno opened the next. He said after area 10 he would only lock dungeon 19-19 leading to area 20, and people could rip through dungeons and stay with the new openings if they wanted. He said we probably would too.

Two people opened the arena in area 3. Late in area 3. One was a Japanese guy everyone knew called Tora Hige. He was some famous kenjutsu expert in real life who won a ton of competitions. He was actually paid to play fourth age and they made a class especially for him called eighteen armed snake. I guess that is common. Games paying famous people to play them. Fourth age also paid an old, famous MMA fighter to play after they came out with the unarmed expansion. But the classes and subclasses added by that, and the rules and improvements to unarmed combat, aren't in this...contest or whatever this place is – the version of fourth age this contest uses. It uses patch 2. The second big patch after release. There was another big content patch after patch 2 before the unarmed expansion even came out. So this contest is way behind. They were almost ready to release a new psionic expansion soon before all this started.

Fourth age also paid another guy to play that was real good at fighting with swords like knights did. He did something called half-swording. He was super old so he wasn't what Bruno consider a top tier crawler. It didn't matter if you were old in fourth age, but it matters here. In fourth age you didn't use your real body, and in here we do. In Bruno's last timeline the knight guy ran a school in one of the city instances and was real famous.

Tore Hige's class uses an exotic weapon called a darg. The darg is clearly a katana. The class can use two types of swords only – a darg, or a cravi. The cravi is a like a chinese jain. Cravis look like a longsword but are exotic weapons with an 18-20 crit range. Someone told me why they don't just call them katana and jain. I forget the details but it had something to do with the world this game was based on. They didn't have eastern stuff in Black Raven, and without buying more licenses the makers of fourth age had to invent new stuff for this game themselves and give it all crazy names to avoid copyright issues. And they wanted eastern stuff and more appeal to the eastern market. The biggest markets are in the east now, after the west kind of stopped doing so good.

So, Tora Hige is amazing. I bet Bruno would destroy him in a fight, but he is still amazing. It took him a bunch of tries but he almost caught up to Bruno in the solo arena. I think Bruno cleared level 8 when he was level 3. I forget exactly, but Tora Hige almost caught up to him. Tora Hige's wife, Ryu Jin, is also famous from martial arts competitions, and also was paid to play the game. They had the best guild in the game. She didn't open the arena until area 4, but she was one of the first to open it in area 4. She uses 2 handaxes. She fights so beautiful. She flows. Her class is a bearserker. I thought she was a weapon sage at first because of how smooth she fought, then a barbarian when I saw her use rage, but Bruno said she was a bearserker. Bearserkers can't transform while raging until later though. She is so amazing and super beautiful too. Just watching how beautiful she fought was almost enough to make me want to switch classes.

I heard about both of them, Tore Hige and Ryu Jin, when mom started allowing us to play fourth age, but I never looked into either. I forget their real names. People call them what their character's names in the game were. I can't wait to meet them.

The other person to open the arena in area 3 was a stupid caster. No one knew who he was. His class was druid, and people assumed it was the guy, Sidis, that Bruno talked about in his messages. Druid is the class you need before going blood wyrm exemplar prestige class. But Bruno said it wasn't him. He was real good at fighting. He usually died trying to heal himself during combat. He was almost as dark as Bruno, but not nearly as tall or muscly.

Bruno told me the first people to open the arena in area 4 would be 2 rapier guys, a greatsword guy, 2 monks, and Ryu Jin. But there was only one rapier guy for the initial people. Way, way later a second rapier guy showed in the arena. It wasn't the one Bruno expected and that bothered him. He doesn't like when things change. He complains about things changing a lot.

Bruno said all these people, the best fighters of humanity (besides him), died in area 10. The half-sword guy lived too. He didn't go to the city, but he wasn't with the lead crawlers in area 10. All these people opening the arena now were 1st SS people. I was one of them. I was the first person to open the arena on level 4. Well, me along with the rapier guy, the greatsword guy, 2 monks, and Ryu Jin. We all opened it after exiting 3-3 into area 4. The others did it after the next opening. Like 50 more people. Then like a bazillion people opened it after the next dungeon opening.

The arena is crazy. Crazy fun and crazy awful. I spent a ton of time doing it. It's great training. I didn't do nearly as well solo as the other people that opened it. I died on the level 5 boss a bunch. I finally beat him, but it was more luck than skill. Bruno said he wouldn't be able to down the level 9 boss, but he did. He said it was just pure luck, and he wasn't expecting to down that boss for a bit since his will saves were so bad. Tora Hige's class has high will saves. All his saves are high – like monks. And it doesn't even matter since he is in a 5-man group and his class was made specifically for him and his strengths. But even with high will saves Tora Hige was stuck on the level 8 boss. Ryu Jin and the druid and everyone else in the arena was stuck on the level 7 boss. Everyone but me. I was still on the level 6 boss.

We also did the duo-arena. We didn't spend much time in it, and I wasn't a ton of help, but we stayed ahead of Tora Hige and Ryu Jin. Bruno said his back hurt from carrying me. In the duo the level 8 boss was a huge pain. She's caster and kept us rooted while whacking us with spells. We barely got her. When I was finally able to get some hits on her was the fight we downed her. It wasn't many hits, but I helped us win.

No one else in our area were one of the first people to open the arena. Later more did. A bunch. Ball-face, some other hiss guys, some marines from somewhere, and some guys from a big army base in georgia that joined us in area 4. Probably some others. Bruno said the military turned into a bunch of garbage sissies but he trusted military guys more, so we did the 4-man and 5-man arena with a rotation of them. Trying different comps. He did it without me a lot. I did the duo, 4-man, and 5-man with different people too. Bruno thought that was the best training. The training area got less and less action as people opened the arena.

Tora Hige's team did better than us in the 4 and 5-man arenas. He had a really old man that made the general and devil hag look young compared to him. People say that is Tora Hige's master. A caster that carried a katana. A darg I mean. That looked weird. He was real good with it, even being such an oldie. Tora Hige also had a girl a little older than me as a healer, and a guy that was another eighteen armed snake. People said the girl was his niece or sister-in-law but I don't think they know for sure. I'm hoping it is really Ryu Jin's daughter. Tora Hige's daughter too, of course. But more Ryu Jin's daughter. If that makes sense. They think the other guy is another student of the master, as he is an amazing katana fighter too. Really, really good. They almost never did the 4-man with anyone else besides four of their people. The 5-man was almost always the same five people. They got to level 7 in the 4-man, and level 3 in the 5-man. Not the level 3 boss. Only, like, early 3s.

Bruno expects we'd blow past them at level 6 when we get true grit. We'll see. The only real strong fighter in our area so far is Bruno. I wish I could say I was second. But I was like way down the list. Way, way down. I did make friends with a really tough guy. His name is Gunny. He is pretty old but not old like Bruno. Bruno gets along with Gunny real good. Gunny is mean to a bunch of marines and yells at them a lot. He doesn't yell at me though. He told me I say hua wrong, but Bruno said to ignore him.

4-2 was a huge dungeon. Six floors and a lot of fun stuff. People call it the dwarven pit. The reward for that one was pretty nice – an endless water flask.

The boss of 4-4 is a huge pain. I almost got injured bad when fighting him. I could've got killed too. I attacked from the back and Bruno warned me when I see him rushing away from the boss to do the same. But when Bruno rushed away I was confused because my hits were still landing so it couldn't be a telegraph attack. Bosses up until then got an iframe for when they start executing their telegraph attack. And the floor turns red where it will hit. Neither happened. Bruno yelled for me to tumble, and I did, but I still got hit by, like, big jagged rocks shooting out of the ground. My HP shield saved me, but I went flying into a tree's branch and got hurt. Not super hurt like before with the huge-turd-viper. Just scratched and banged up pretty good. And that got me freaked out because I already took the healing pill from beating the level 5 boss of the solo arena to heal up all the rest of my injuries I still had. I still have the 4 point healing pill from level 5 of the duo, but Bruno says healing pills are rarer than lawyers with consciences so we can't waste them. And I know he'd be real mad if I got hurt bad after just completely healing myself. My hand and everything worked perfect again. No pain. No issues at all.

Bruno yelled for me to stay back and just watch. This boss was like a rhino with snake scales for skin. He had a giant club with a huge boulder tied to the end of it. He could swing it real fast. Bruno told me his tell for the telegraph was standing still and blinking, but he never said nothing about there not being no iframe or red outline area on the ground. He did say some of the imported monsters from other games had bugs though. So maybe those two things are bugs? Either way Bruno would be mad I didn't listen and didn't move with a purpose when I saw him didi mau'ing out of the area. He hates when I don't listen or almost get killed. Doing both was going to be a real bad smoking.

I didn't see what happened after the rock spike thing. Not the first time it happened. For a bit it was a normal tank and spank, with Bruno doing both the tanking and spanking. Bruno had the rhino almost sideways, so I could see the blinking I think. And I did. Bruno ran away, the rhino holds his weapon way back over his head and slams it into the ground with a crazy amount of impact, and then rock spikes came up in a huge area, and instead of charging back like I thought Bruno would, he waited. The boss charged him, and Bruno tumbled away. You have to time that perfect, because charges aren't supposed to be able to be avoided. But you can do it with a tumble if you tumble far enough and start the tumble at the exact right time. You have to be real good to do that. And you can't charge and tumble in the same round. You can only do one in a round. You can time it so you tumble into a new round then charge immediately, so they are real close together, though.

Then the fight was tank and spank again. Then the boss blinks, rinse, repeat.

When the boss was down Bruno said he forget the boss charged after the spike things, and about the no red area. He said the iframe didn't matter since you have to didi mau and can't stick around to hit him anyways. Not if you are melee. He said he turned him canted so I could see the blinking but wouldn't be in the LOS for a charge, in case he charged whoever he saw instead of who was closest. And who knows what the charge range is for a boss who doesn't have a telegraph outline? His charge could be bugged too. And Bruno forgetting about the charge hurt him too. I didn't see it but the boss' ghost arm got Bruno good. Took 2/3rds of his HP shield.

The worst part? Next opening I am doing all this dungeon solo. Including the boss. Bruno will be there to step in if I'm in real danger. I just got finished being smoked and we're exiting now. That smoking was a doozy. Real bad. He smoked me real nice and good. I only have ten earth hours to recuperate before we enter again. But I'm still all smiles as I grab Joey and our stuff and head for the exit. I'm about to level up to 5!

3.1 REELING IN THE CRAZY

BRUNO VAZ

PART 3 "PREDICT"

"For it's Tommy this, an' Tommy that, an' "Chuck him out, the brute!"
But it's "Saviour of 'is country" when the guns begin to shoot;"
- Rudyard Kipling

I already decided we were going to exit and not stay in the dungeon and train, but now I'm having second thoughts. We haven't been training enough, and it shows in Kim's solo arena. She needs to get better. She has potential. A lot of potential. What she needs is time to fully grow and develop into her adult body, a ton more conditioning, and better weapons training with a spear than I can give her. And Kim needs a positive influence like me telling her how to think right. She's a little crazy, and I need to reel in the crazy. Make her mind as strong as I'm making her body.

And I don't want to exit. I'm nervous. I promised myself on this next trip to the city I would talk to Nate about the thing. Except I'm nervous because everything has been going so good with my kids. I don't want to ruin it. I don't think this will ruin anything, but that sissy gets upset about everything, so who knows. And this is mainly for him. To make him happier. To make his life better.

Level 5 isn't a huge jump in power. The second specialization point is going in geography and not something that helps us directly in fights. Putting the point in geography does a couple things that help get higher dungeon rankings easier, especially at the higher level dungeons when the layouts get all nuts. It puts a red dot on the map for mobs you notice – which is kind of helpful in most dungeons, but really helpful in the 3d dungeons.

I should say dungeons based on 3d maps of dungeon crawler games. The dorks say most of the dungeon crawlers were 2d, so there aren't a ton of 3d maps in this world. Maps where you go up and down on the same map, have spiraling staircases, hills, etcetera. Those are a pain because the map and minimap become far less useful since it's just a big, confusing mess smooshed all into 2d. Anything making it easier to know if you cleared an area, or where things are, is wicked helpful. If there's some red dots in an area you cleared, you know there's something above or below you, and then you just got to figure out how to get there. Or if you see some red dots off to the side where there is nothing, you know there's something. Got to find a hidden door to get there or some crap like that.

A specialization point in geography is supposed to give a +2 synergy something-or-other to search and spot just in outdoor environments. You're supposed to need a specialization point in dungeoneering to get the same benefit for indoor environments, but a bug causes a specialization point in either to give you +2 in both environments. A spec point in dungeoneering gives the ability to assess enemies and shows unhidden treasure chests and some other nice icons on the minimap. Icons like the psuchesoma and one-way passages and things like that. That's another bug. A spec point in either geography or dungeoneering gives you not just the +2 to search and spot for both, but also the event icon from geography and all the icons from dungeoneering. It works right in first age, or whatever the dork game this place is based on is called, but is bugged on this world. The good type of bug. The kind that helps us.

So, the choice is really between red dots on the map or the ability to assess enemies. Red dots always helps. I have the important enemies memorized. Most of them. My memory sucks so I forget some stuff, like I forgot the rhino-snake boss' charge after his non-telegraphed 'telegraph' ability. And a lot of imported mobs can't be assessed. But it's usually pretty simple stuff, like bash damage isn't good against zombies but great against skeletons, fire attacks can heal some fire creatures. Crap like that. And when you start raiding someone always knows the boss' mechanics. And you can use a scroll or a clicky for assess anyways. I guess you could get the red dots with the sense life scroll too. But always having red dots just seems way more useful more often. I don't really use scrolls often. I don't even like changing weapons for different mobs. Just the ones you have to. Like the golems that destroy weapon durability, or those slime things that destroy metal weapons. I hate those things.

I would never waste a spec point on whatever skill it is to get the free item ID. The dorks can cay it's necessary all they want, but it isn't. At some point all the good crawlers have more gold than they can spend, and ID'ing anything doesn't put a dent in funds. You never have more spec points than you could use in useful things. So we're only specializing one of those skills, and that one is geography.

The dorks would also say it's a waste for both me and Kim to put a spec point in geography. And they would be right, but it's better for her to be prepared. Just like why we both have the same exact build, and points in all the same skills. We aren't going to be grouped up forever. She has potential, but unless we start spending way more time in dungeons she'll still be just a kid and not strong enough to help, and she'll just hold me back. If things go as planned we'll all be back on earth well before she is fully grown and reaches her potential. When she could be a top tier crawler.

Sure, she'll be mad at me when we have to split up. Furious probably. But that's okay. She can be as mad at me as she wants. My job is to get my family, and her, and as many people as possible, back to earth alive and whole. Not be their buddy. I'm helping and taking care of her and her brother. Helping her become a real person with actual power. Putting her on the right path. Hopefully going back to earth won't kill that spark in her. Won't sissify her.

That kid has really grown on me. She's like the son I never had. Well, I have a son, so I should say the type of son I always wanted. Even though she is a girl. She's awesome. I love that knucklehead. Is she crazy? Sure. But all females are, and Kim is my kind of crazy. Not the annoying kind of crazy most females are, where they just yap and yap and yap about feelings and other silly, made-up nonsense.

Girls make up so much nonsense and believe in it fiercely. Not just invented, make believe emotions. But tons of things – like ghosts, palm reading, tarot cards, fortune telling, and colors. Colors. What a load of nonsense. The colors girls pretend exist are ridiculous. Like, the only kind-of, sort-of argument I got in with my son when I stayed with him and his boyfriend around Thanksgiving 2012. They both left and forgot something and parking in his area was nuts so they called and asked me to bring down a cayenne blazer. I heard of cayenne peppers. I have no idea what one looks like. Probably red. There was a commercial from when I was younger. I think for Pringles. Some Cajun hillbilly saying, "Cayenne pepper. Onion garlic." And what is a blazer? At first I thought it was some homosexual sex thing. Something to spice up the homo sex. I don't know what a flamer is either, but I know it has something to do with homos. So after like ten minutes they call again and ask where I was and I was freaking out tearing up their room looking for some spicy red sex toy.

Well, anyways, a blazer is what homosexuals call suit jackets. And they both thought cayenne was a color. It is a made up, invented girl nonsense color called cyan. But Nate pronounced it wrong. They both swear they didn't, but they 100% did. It's pronounced like scion, not kai-yan. So it should be spelled scian, really. I can see why he pronounced it wrong once I looked it up. But the actual color name is gay-blue. If they said, "bring down the gay-blue suit jacket," there would've been no confusion at all.

There're really only like eight actual colors. Blue, red, green, yellow, orange, brown, black, and white. All the invented ones are just mixes of those. Pink is gay red. Purple is gay blue-red. Cyan is gay blue, or gay blue-green. Etcetera. So easy and simple. But girls have to complicate everything. The homos too. Just invent emotions and colors, and even planes of existence and magic powers to explain ghosts and talking to the dead. Why? To make themselves feel better? Or just confuse guys? Well, normal guys, at least, with normal brains that work right. Crazy broads.

But, girls are pretty and smell good and have vaginas so they're definitely worth all the yapping and the headaches and made-up nonsense.

So a spec point in geography, and weapon specialization in dwarven waraxes for level 5. And level 6 I get the true grit feat. I can't wait for that. Will saves are stupid and dumb, and the magic that tests will saves is the stupidest, dumbest of all magics. And everyone knows it and that is why they made the true grit feat. The best feat ever. A real feat for real men, like me. And girls like Kim, too, I guess.

Kim, leading Joey, is almost at the door. I got to decide now. I'm not that horny. Not too horny. We haven't spent a ton of time in dungeons since my last trip to see my family, and I banged the doc

295

before entering this dungeon. That tubby broad is wild. Very needy, but not clingy. And most important, she is discreet. I can wait a couple weeks getting by on "me-time." And Kim needs the training. She is my responsibility. And she isn't doing so hot in the arenas. My libido comes second. Kim comes first. She fought like crap on that last boss, and almost got more injuries.

I say, "Kay, stop." I don't know why I say Kay instead of Kim. It just came out wrong.

"Kay?" Kim askes as she stops in front of the dungeon exit.

I hate admitting when I make a mistake, so I just go with it. "Yeah, Kay. Kim was too long. You're Kay now."

"I think Kim and Kay are the same amount of syllables. Kuh-aye. Kuh-im."

"That's not how syllables work. Kay is one syllable, Kim is two. Kay. Kih-im. See?"

"I really don't think that's right. How syllables w…"

"Keep it up and your name will be Kuh. Now come here, Kay."

She walks over and posts in parade rest, "Hua?"

"Can Joey exit on his own? Go grab him real quick just in case." She does and posts in front of me again.

"We're staying in here and training. We're not leaving until you can hit me three times. With your spear. And your arm and leg bar defense is better. Are better. Defenses are better. You know what I mean. And alignment control. Yours and mine. Not mine, how you control my alignment. Also, you reached muscle failure way too easily during that smoking. You need to get a lot stronger. And if you do good enough and put the effort in I'll go back to calling you Kim. Okay, Kay?" I add in the last part because I know I'll start forgetting to call her Kay soon anyways, so maybe that will motivate her when I do and start calling her Kim. She'll assume she is doing good.

"Hua, but don't you want level 5? Can't we do that after I clear this dungeon on my own next opening?"

"Level 5 isn't going to help with your martial skills or strength. Have you been using the grip-ball?"

"Hua!"

"Let's see. Come squeeze my wrist." She does. It's pathetic.

"Kim! I mean Kay! Come on! I can barely feel it. Have you actually been working on your grip strength?"

"Yes! Hua! Hua times a hundred. Ask Ball-face! I swear!"

"You've been trying to rip the extra leather armor too?"

"Yes! I mean hua! Definitely. All the time I do it."

I give her a suspicious and disappointed look. I know she hates the disappointed look. Her grip should be much stronger with hands and wrists like that. It's pathetic. I get in a horse stance and make my back dramatically straight and put my arms out to the sides.

"Come on. Assume the stance and freeze. Back straighter! Straighter! If you move before I do I'll show you what real pain is. Kay."

My left knee hurts a lot more than usual doing this. My right knee and both ankles seem to hurt more too. My shoulders hurt bad. Maybe I should take a healing pill and see if that helps my joints a little? Nah. Got to save them. Life is pain. Stop being a sissy.

We really got to start road marching too. I really haven't made her hump yet. I could use it too. I'm getting soft. Nothing purges the sissy out of you like getting way overloaded and doing a nice 50k hump. She isn't ready for that. And I'm not wasting a ton of gold to get over-loaded enough to really feel the pain. Too bad there isn't any super heavy things in the copper store. We can just buy a ton of cheap stuff I guess. Humping is great for hip flexors. Too bad we can't get rucks like the old Army ones, or LBEs with mag pouches that really make your hip flexors work.

Land nav too. There're no azimuth compasses. I bet I could just notch a regular compass. Maybe. Those suckers cost 100g. Should I spend it? Yes. Land nav is important for any soldier. Kim can't be a real person unless I teach her all the infantry skills. This dungeon isn't great for land nav or even humping, but it's good enough. And it's time I stopped babying Kim. The training starts for real today. She's 13. Still a kid, sure. But a tough kid that needs to be much tougher. And I can tell doing so sucky in the solo arena bothers her a lot. She wants to be better.

Pain builds character. Not knowing how long a hump is builds character. In Delta selection I had a billion pound ruck with the 60, tripod, AG bag, and 3k rounds and they just gave me an azimuth and told me to start humping. If I was off even a little I would have missed the guy waiting at the next point. Who knows how long it was. At least 30 klicks. At least. And he just gave me another azimuth and told me to start humping again. Same at the next guy, and the next, and the next. Humping for days. If I wasn't as fast as I am it would have taken way, way longer. They played it off like they weren't impressed by my time, but I know they were. I guarantee I'm the best humper in the universe. No way anyone could ever come close to being as good at humping as I am. I'm Bruno Vaz. As my Super Fly poster in my room used to say, "Never a dude like this one. He's got a plan to stick it to the man."

Curtis Mayfield. Now that was a musician. How was he not more popular?

"Move again, Kim, and we'll be here all day. I mean Kay."

3.2 MEECES TO PIECES

KIM GUM

Area 5. Level 5! Reward for 4-4 is any weapon you want with ghost-touch. Nice! Stupid concealment or whatever it is called ghosts have.

I can't wait to level up. Fighter level 4, and weapon specialization feat. Plus my second specialization point. It goes in garbage. In geography. But Bruno says it's important. So I got to waste my second point in garbage. Oh well. The last one was wasted on garbage too. I don't know why we don't use our specialization points on awesome stuff. We could. Nothing is stopping us from doing so.

We wasted a lot of money going from regular full plate and weapons to masterwork. It makes sense for the weapon, but the armor just reduces the armor check penalty by 1. Seems like tons of gold down the drain for nothing.

I get out of the level-up screen and check out my character screen to see how awesome I am.

Base (Ability Modifier) ((Misc.)) [Total]

CLASSES: 1 Rogue/4 Fighter

RACE: Stout Dwarf - Alignment: Chaotic Good - Deity: Catholic

HP: 4(18) (4(20)) ((5 Special Feat, 5 Toughness)) [48]

AC: 10 (2 -1 Max Dex Bonus) ((8 Full Plate, 2 Heavy Shield)) [21]

BAB: 4

ABILITIES

Str: 16 (3) ((0)) [16]

Dex 14 (2) ((0)) [14]

Con: 19 (4) ((0)) [19]

Int: 14 (2) ((0)) [14]

Wis: 8 (-1) ((0)) [8]

Cha: 6 (-2) ((0)) [6]

SAVES

Fortitude: 4 (4) ((0)) [8]

Reflex: 3 (2) ((1 Full of Beans)) [6]

Will: 1 (-1) ((0)) [0]

COMBAT MODE: Free Attack/Auto Attack/Game Mode

MAIN HAND

Dwarven Waraxe

AB: 4 (3) ((1 Weapon Focus)) [8]

DAM: 1d8 (3) ((2 Weapon Specialization)) Extra Damage=0 [6-13 Slashing], C 20, CM x3

OFF HAND

NA

OTHER ATTACKS (Bites, etc.)

NA

OTHER

Spell Failure: 50%

Max Dex Bonus: 1 Full Plate [1]

Armor Check Penalty: -6 Full Plate, -2 Heavy Shield [-8]

HOBBIES, CRAFTS, and PROFESSIONS

Hobby: Tinker level 5 (Maximum level is character level. No experience needed to level Hobbies. Hobbies level with character)

Crafts: NA

Professions: Porter level 1 (Increases Carry Capacity by 1 + (Porter level x 3). Maximum level is class level of the class used to open the Profession. If multiclassing, a Profession can be selected twice or more and class levels can be combined to increase maximum Profession level. Unlike Hobbies, both Crafts and Profession require experience to level up)

SKILLS

5 At level 5, 0 carried over = 5

Italics cross class skill

*Armor Check Penalty applies

(Falls under above group skill)

Acrobatics* (Dex) 8 (2) ((ACP -8)) [2]

(Escape)*

(Tumble)* (10 base points in Acrobatics with Tumble selected and opened gives a +1 bonus to AC. 20 base points gives another +1 bonus, for a total of +2 bonus to AC. This counts as a skill bonus and stacks with everything.)

(Use Rope)*

Athletics* (Str) 6 (3) ((ACP -8)) [1]

(Grapple)*

(Jump)*

(Run)* (Con) 6 (4) ((ACP -8)) [2] (10 base points in Athletics with Run selected and opened gives a +5 land speed bonus. 20 base points gives another +5 for +10 total land speed increase. This counts as a skill bonus and stacks with everything. This translates into a 7.5% speed increase at 10 and 20, 15% total.)

Disable Device (Int) 8 (2) ((1 Kit)) [10]

Heal (Wis) 4 (-1) ((1 kit)) [4]

Knowledge (Int) 7 (2) ((0)) [9]

(Arcane) 3 [5]

(Dungeoneering) ((1 Kit)) [10]

(Geography) 3 ((1 kit)) [6]

Open Lock (Dex) 8 (2) ((1 Kit)) [11]

Search (Int) 8 (2) ((1 item)) [11]

Spellcraft (Int) 3 (2) ((0)) [5] 10 base points in Spellcraft gives a +1 bonus to all saves. 20 base points gives another +1, for a total of +2 bonus to all saves. This counts as a skill bonus and stacks with everything.)

Use Magic Device (Cha) 5 (-2) ((0)) [3]

Skill Points carried over to next level: 0

FEATS

* are selected feats or options

Level 1 (Rogue 1)

Destined for Greatness (Free feat given to all players of End of the Fourth Age that reads as follows: You were born under an auspicious sign and have a greater destiny than most born in Benekal or even all of Tibur. You receive +5 Hit Points at level 1)

Charge (Same as SRD, charges take three seconds regardless of distance in End of the Fourth Age. In new world, distance has been normalized to 60 feet for all players since there is no land speed)

Armor Proficiency (Light)

Shield Proficiency (Buckler)

Shield Proficiency (Light)

Weapon Proficiency (Dwarven Waraxe) (Dwarves may treat dwarven waraxes as martial weapons, rather than exotic weapons)

Weapon Proficiency (Rogue)

Weapon Proficiency (Simple)

Battle Training (Giants) (+4 dodge bonus to Armor Class against monsters of the giant type. Any time a creature loses its Dexterity bonus (if any) to Armor Class, such as when it's caught flat-footed, it loses its dodge bonus, too)

Battle Training (Orcs & Goblinoids) (+1 racial bonus on attack rolls against orcs and goblinoids)

Darkvision (See in the dark up to 60 feet. Darkvision is black and white only, but it is otherwise like normal sight, and character can function just fine with no light at all)

Hardiness (Poisons) (+2 racial bonus on saving throws against poison. First Racial Specialization gives an additional +1 on saving throws against poisons (total +3), and also increases saves against disease by +3. Second Racial Specialization gives an additional +1 on saving throws against poisons (total +4), and also increases saves against disease and death effects by +3. Third Racial Specialization grants immunity to poison)

Hardiness (Spells) (+2 racial bonus on saving throws against spells and spell-like effects. First Racial Specialization gives an additional +1 on saving throws against spells and spell-like effects (total +3). Second Racial Specialization gives an additional +1 on saving throws against spells and spell-like effects (total +4). Third Racial Specialization gives Spell Resistance equal to 5 + character level)

Stonecunning (+2 to Search checks indoors. Automatic Search checks indoors every six seconds with a radius of 10 feet. First Racial Specialization changes this to all environments, and increases the radius to 15 feet. Second Racial Specialization gives an additional +2 to Search checks and increases radius to 30 feet. Third Racial Specialization gives two Search checks per six seconds, automatic success to any check with a DC of 40 or less, an alarm function if something is found, and the DC of Sense Magic checks is reduced from 60 to 55)

Knowledge (Appraise) (+2 Appraise checks)

Knowledge (Dwarven Crafting) (+2 to Architect, Blacksmith, Engineer, Gemologist, Jeweler, Miner, Smelter, Tinker, and Trapsmith)

Slow & Steady (Dwarves start at land speed 20, but armor or load do not reduce a dwarf's speed. Translates to -15% speed for race, but no penalty to speed for armor or load debuffs. First Racial Specialization gives -1 Armor Check Penalty to all armors worn. Second Racial Specialization increases Maximum Dex Bonus of all armors worn by 1. Third Racial Specialization increases Dex by 2)

Stability (+4 bonus on Ability checks made to resist being bull rushed or tripped)

Dwarven Languages

Trapfinding

Sneak Attack (1D6)

*Background – Sharp as a Tack (Instead of 2 skill points to raise cross-class skills, only 1 is needed. +1 skill point per level. Retroactively refunded or added and can't be used during character creation.)

*Toughness (3 HPs when taken, and another HP on non-prime number levels up to level 20 for a total of 15 additional HPs. One Specialization point increases HPs gained through the Toughness feat by 50%. Two Specialization points increases HPs gained through the Toughness feat by 50% more, 100% in total)

*Specialization Point used – Diverse Upbringing (Allows a second Background to be selected) – Full of Beans (+10 land speed. Translates to 15% speed increase. +1 Reflex saves)

LEVEL 2 (Fighter 1)

Armor Proficiency (Medium)

Armor Proficiency (Heavy)

Weapon Proficiency (Martial)

Shield Proficiency (Heavy)

Shield Proficiency (Tower)

*Weapon Focus: Dwarven Waraxe (+1 AB with dwarven waraxes)

LEVEL 3 (Fighter 2)

*Juke (Prereq: 1 BAB, 13 Dex; Charge no longer requires a clear path to target. May make up to 2 45 degree turns during charge. Charge only requires 9 feet. One Specialization point decreases the distance needed to Charge by 1 additional foot and increases 45 degree turns allowed by 1. Two Specialization points decreases the distance needed to Charge by an 1 additional foot (2 total, to 7 feet) and increases 45 degree turns allowed by 1 (2 total, 4 turns during a charge).

*Blitz (Prereq: Juke; Charge distance is not changed, by Charges are completed in 1.5 seconds instead of 3 seconds. If opponent moves during Charge, can follow up to full Charge distance. No loss to AC during the turn a Charge action was taken. One Specialization point decreases Charge time by a .35 seconds (1.15 second Charges). Two Specialization points decreases Charge time by a further .15 seconds (1 second Charges) and allows an additional attack from the MH weapon if multiple attacks are in the attack chain (2 in total))

LEVEL 4 (Fighter 3)

LEVEL 5 (Fighter 4)

*Weapon Specialization: Dwarven Waraxe (+2 damage with dwarven waraxes)

*Specialization point used – Geography (Highlights detected enemies on the minimap, adds icons for events, and gives +2 synergy bonus to both spot and search checks outdoors. Due to a bug, this also gives +2 synergy bonus to spot and check indoors, and adds icons for unhidden treasure chests in range on the minimap)

Important Items

Masterwork Spear (Equipped), Ghost Touched Spear, Spear

Masterwork Heavy Shield (+2 AC)

Masterwork Full Plate (+8 AC, -4 ACP, 1 MDB)

Bracers of Use Rope +1

Cloak of Tumble +1

Boots of Jump +1

Ring of Search +1

Ring of Escape +1

Cartography Kit +1, Heal Kit +1, Survey Kit +1, Thieves Tools +1

Pretty awesome. I wish we had better gear. But we're only level 5. You could get to level 5 in fourth age in no time at all. We got to level 10 in two days playing as a family with my parents just talking non-stop while we waited. Talk, talk, talk, talk, talk. Man, that was annoying. Man, I miss them. I even miss Carlos. We can get upgrades to every single item at level 7. Or even before if we get a stupid rare spawn again.

Jeez, that training sucked. Way more brutal than usual. Way, way more. We were in there forever. It felt like years. Humping is awful. Whoever invented it is a very evil person. Bruno said we started really slow and easy. Only going 15 klicks. Only. After what felt like weeks of pain, when my feet hurt so bad I wanted to cry, and my legs were no longer fully under my control, Bruno smiled at me and just said, "Five klicks down, just ten more to go." Smiling. Like a real jerk.

I fell out. Bruno does not like that. He does not like falling out one bit. But he walks so fast it's crazy. And why? Even in area 4 the zone was only three klicks wide. The area 20 zone will probably only be like 12 klicks wide. And you don't walk the whole thing at once. And definitely not with the heavy load debuff. And we had the super duper extra mega heavy load debuff. Why would anyone do this? Humping is so stupid and useless. It is just pain for nothing.

Your feet are so messed up after a hump. Your legs hurt so bad. At the end I was doing 25 klick humps without falling out. But why? It's nonsense. Crazy nonsense. It sucks so bad. I hate it so much. It's way worse than running. Way, way worse.

He also wanted to do some other stupid nonsense with a compass. I don't know what. He was doing something with a compass, and kept threating to destroy it, and then freaked out and started smashing it to pieces. And then yelled at me like a crazy person. Not words. Just loud screams. Then he went and attacked a tree for like 15 minutes. What a nut.

I'm just happy whatever he planned on doing with the compass didn't work out. Probably some form of torture I can't even imagine.

The thing that really bothers me is I think he let me get three hits on him. I hope not. But I think he did. He'll be sorry once I'm able to trounce him regularly. I'll say, "You ain't leaving until you can get five hits on me, sucker!" And then I'll dodge all his hits and hold him in the triangle like he's nothing and bite his nose off. Well, I won't do that. That's a little much. But I'll break it real nice and good. And then pee on it. And laugh the whole time.

But I'm still growing. I'm not a real person yet. Bruno says I won't be one until I'm 25 years old when my brain is final, but I can be an important person before then. One that matters. One with real power. My body will stop growing before my brain. Long before. And I'll be big. Bigger, I mean. I'm already big. As tall as most adults. And strong too. But I have to get much stronger. I can't break any holds with my grip yet, or my strength, but I can slip out of them if I catch them early enough. And I can with kids my own age. I trounce those suckers all the time. And women too. Adult women. And some men. I wish there were more kids my age. Maybe in this zone there will be.

That reminds me. I should re…

"KIM! Where the hell is Joey?" Bruno screams, interrupting my thoughts. I hate to admit it but I pee my pants a little. I hate when that happens. But I have to pee real bad and Bruno startled the heck out of me. Jeez! Relax boomer. Where is Joey? He was right with us when we got out.

"He was just right here. He has to be close. I only just leveled-up. It only took two-seconds. Jeez." I wanted to tell him to relax but he would probably smoke me, so I don't.

"Go find him, and come back and wait for Dr. Pauluk."

I give him a hua but try to add in some of my exasperation so he knows his ideas are bad and stupid. Dr. Pauluk is what other people call the old devil hag instead of calling her the old devil hag. She is pure evil and I hate her and she will die by my hand. She kidnapped me, assaulted me, tricks me all the time and makes me talk and I'm just supposed to be okay with that? No siree Bob.

I go to pee then go to find Joey. I see the military people are having a formation. They usually don't do that right away when we get in a new zone. Weird.

I find Joey shaking a tray at a really beautiful woman. She keeps trying to give him a flower. I haven't seen her before. I don't see many pretty women around. Most of them went to the city. Besides Ass-eyes. She's still around for some reason. This lady is wearing leather armor. Probably a bow user. I can't picture her risking her pretty face in melee. Maybe she is some kind of caster that can wear leather. Ass-

308

eyes and most casters wear robes. Magic casters. Clerics wear real armor. Or can, at least.

I go grab Joey. As I do the pretty lady says, "Oh my God! Kim! Is Bruno in this zone? Instance of the zone I mean? Is he here?"

"Yeah." I start pulling Joey away.

"One sec. Who is this? Is this your brother or something?"

Most people outside of our zones haven't seen or know about Joey. He becomes popular real fast though. Everyone loves Joey.

"Yeah. His name is Joey. I'm basically his mother now though." I try to get away again.

"Wait. One second. I just opened screenshots. Mind if I get one of all of us?"

Wow. Maybe I opened it too. More important, maybe I get a tent upgrade! That would be awesome. I'm sick of looking at Bruno's dumb, awesome tent. I want it so bad.

"Yeah. Sure." She comes in between me and Joey. I smile. And hold it. And hold it.

"I can't...I don't know how to make it point at us. Do you know how? It only points away from me."

I go into achievements. It takes a minute for me to find out where the screenshots achievement is and to claim it. Pretty lady says something I ignore as I try to figure out how to flip the camera back to point at us. I finally say, "I can't figure it out either."

"It's okay. Let me just take one of you and your brother." She does. She then says, "Want to take one of me and Joey?"

I say sure and do. I don't know why, but why not I guess? She gives me the flower she was trying to give to Joey.

"That's for you, Kim. Or your brother. He doesn't seem to want it though. Oh, where is Bruno, by the way?"

I tell her and we say our goodbyes and I head back. She doesn't follow for some reason. When I am a good distance away I get down on my knees to pray.

"Dear capital g God. The one and only capital g God. I am the darkness to your light. I swear to you one day the devil hag will die by my hands. Please don't let her stupid session go for too long. Please. Amen"

I do the hand thing for the father, son, and holy spirit like Bruno taught me. He doesn't like when I pray to the real God – the God I met, which is the same as his even if he is too dumb to realize it. But he makes me pray some dumb prayers before we go to bed. One is "our father," and the other is "hail Mary." They are dumb and make no sense, and are about things like doing art in heaven. My way of prayer is much better. I do like the father, son, and holy spirit hand thing though.

Bruno is where he was before. Usually the general and Ball-face and those other two guys meet him here. And they talk and do their dumb stuff while I talk to the devil hag. Where is the devil hag? Maybe she figured out she can do other things besides harassing poor, innocent young girls like me?

Bruno says, "Where the hell is everyone? I'm supposed to go see my family after the dungeon closes. I will destroy them!"

"I don't know. I saw the military guys were forming up below the training area. Maybe they're with them?"

Bruno gives me an angry look. I don't think he is angry with me. Just angry. Anger is one of the actual emotions, and not one of the invented emotions, so it is okay to be angry. Good to be angry. Sometimes. Not all the time. According to Bruno. But he also tells me to calm down and control my emotions a lot. It's confusing.

Bruno starts pacing around, mumbling to himself, so I play with Joey. A game my mom used to tell me not to do, but Joey likes it. I hold something in my hand. It could anything. And when he tries to take it I move it away, just out of his reach. He gets angry if you move it too far away and starts making angry whines, but if you keep it close, he just keeps trying to get it. And it makes him happy. He makes a "duga, duga, duga" noise the whole time. That's a good noise. He has fun. Mom used to get mad because I'd hold it too high or too far away where he had no chance of getting it, and that's when he makes the bad whines. This is fine. I call it the duga game. Joey loves it.

I look away for a second and Joey is able to grab my hand. I don't have anything in it, but he doesn't know that. In my head Joey says, "Ha, ha, dummy! I got it!" I want to say something back but Bruno is right there and will think I'm nuts if I say what I want to Joey. So I don't. I give Joey a look trying to tell him being mean to me is unacceptable. I try to copy the same disappointed look Bruno gives me. Hopefully that will work on Joey too. I hate that stupid look when I get it. Then we continue playing, Joey saying, "Duga, duga, duga."

Later, I can tell Bruno starts doing something in his UI. Then he swears. A bad one. Not the real bad one, but a bad one. He comes over and kneels down in front of me.

"Kim. I'm sorry to have to tell you this, but Dr. Pauluk is dead. She died in this dungeon. I'm sorry."

He stares at me with sad eyes. Usually he only looks concerned when I get hurt. Why would he think I cared the devil hag died? Because it wasn't by my hand?

"You okay?" He says while looking at me all sad and concerned. Why wouldn't I be okay?

"Yeah." But wait a second. Why do I feel weird? I feel...sad? Why? Besides sad being a made-up, invented emotion, the devil hag dying shouldn't make me feel this way. I should be happy I don't have to talk to her anymore, and angry she didn't die by my hand like she should have. I don't get it.

And now it feels even worse.

For some reason Bruno hugs me and keeps holding on and patting my back. He keeps saying, "It's okay. It's okay." I resist at first but then I hug him back. I think crying might make me feel better but I can't for some reason. Maybe because crying is a made-up emotion? According to Bruno a least.

Bruno finally pulls away and looks me in the eyes again and says, "It is going to be okay. How you feeling?"

That was the first time we hugged. Outside of training at least. Touching his giant muscles made me feel safe when we were hugging. No one can ever do anything to me with Bruno around. I don't understand why I am sad, but I'm okay.

"Yeah. I'm fine. It would've been better if she died by my hand, but it is what it is, right?"

"Jesus, Kim! A lady just died. Have some respect for the dead. She just wanted to help you, you know? Make your head a little clearer. Just talk through some stuff. You know?"

I don't know. If that was helping, God help me from more of that kind of help. But I don't want to argue or get Bruno mad so I agree with him.

He rubs my head like I'm a little baby and says, "I'll destroy Butterball. He's definitely still alive, and he should be here. I'm already late seeing my family. If I miss it because of that tubby fu…fudger. I said fudger. I'll stomp his head into the ground. The dungeon closed like ten, fifteen minutes ago. Jesus, Joseph, and Mary I will destroy him."

"Want me to say something in guild chat?"

He waits a moment and says, "No. You don't have to wait with me here either. You can go check out the new people or train or whatever. If you don't go train make sure you're using your grip-ball. You see I have mine out, right? Your grip needs to be wicked strong, okay?"

"Hua." I get my grip-ball out.

"And if you see the general, send him to me, please."

"Hua." I grab Joey and head out.

I notice Bruno doesn't have the head on his belt. He usually does when we first enter a new zone so people don't talk to him. He keeps it in a backpack that he calls a ruck. But in the store it says backpack and it looks like a backpack. So I think it is not a ruck and is in fact a backpack. I don't know what a ruck looks like though. Maybe it is one.

There is way less people around the dungeon than usual. I wonder why. That's probably why Bruno doesn't need the head on his belt.

Most people seem to be in the center so I head that way. On my way I see Ball-face run by. He waves and I try telling him Bruno is looking for him and the general, but he is by too quick. He is heading towards Bruno anyways. That ticks the "message delivered" box in my head so I keep going.

3.3 MR. DREAMBOAT

KIM GUM

I wonder why these girls are so weird. The ones that Ass-eyes adopted. The younger one cries all the time, and the older one just stares like a dead fish. Unless Joey is around. They like playing with Joey. Bruno says if he ever hears I was mean to these two girls specifically he will destroy me. Something bad happened to them. I don't know what.

No training was going on and everyone I like was doing some dumb military formation thing so I brought Joey to where Ass-eyes usually has a kid's area set up. I don't play with dumb kids because I'm an adult woman, but Joey loves it.

Well, I do play with the kids sometimes. But it's mostly just little kids. It can be fun. Adults sometimes play with kids. No big deal. Not a lot of kids my age around, and the ones there are don't hang out in the little kids' area. And I usually don't get along with them. They make fun of me and then swear they never did. I hate that.

The two girls are playing with Joey. The little one even laughs sometimes, and the older one is all smiles around him. Maybe because Joey is more messed up than them? Who knows? Kids are weird and dumb and I'm just happy I'm an adult now.

I did the solo arena and got up to the level 7 boss. I noticed a lot of people downed the level 8 boss, now that we're all level 5. No one is around for me to group up for the other arenas. I hope no one passes Bruno. He is probably in the city now. He doesn't do the arena when he visits his family. Not usually, I don't think. But I'm not good at paying attention.

Ass-eyes always ignores me. She never looks at me. She hates my guts. And I hate her stupid guts. She is real pretty though. For such an old boomer, at least.

I notice a commotion going on. Then Ass-eyes rushes in and swoops up the two weird girls. Everyone is heading to where the military formation is going on. I grab Joey and head that way.

I takes me a while to get past everyone and finally see what's going on. I see Bruno by himself, facing a bunch of guys I can't really see. I leave Joey and fight through the crowd and move up behind and to the left side of Bruno. The military guys are in a bunch of groups to my left. What they call formations. Bruno is near the center, in front of the formation but sideways to them, facing some guy, with the general behind the guy, and Ball-face, and a bunch of other people too.

I notice who the main guy talking is – it's the UN premier to the US protectorate. Something like that. His picture is everywhere. In every classroom. All the girls think he is just dreamy. The most handsome guy ever. He's okay-looking, I guess. I thought he was bigger and taller. He looks like an anorexic child compared to Bruno. How does he keep his hair so nice here? And why? I can't think of his name now. It's a really weird name, hard to say. All the girls think his accent is super sexy.

Behind the group I notice a giant tent. Way, way, way bigger than Bruno's. You could walk right in. It could fit a ton of people. I think that's the pocket tent Bruno was talking about getting for the med area. If so that thing cost a fortune. I forget how much, but the cheapest one's ridiculously expensive. It has a stitched together UN flag flying on a pole besides the tent opening.

Is the general betraying Bruno? He won't look at me. I hear the premier say, "…and that is why you must!" And then the premier looks right at me and with a big smile says, "Ah, Kim! We finally meet. I was told a lot about you. Your parents where loyal to the UN. Your father was in the UN military, no? If there was ever a time every people of every nation needed to unite, this is it, no? You are still loyal to the UN, yes?"

Of course I'm loyal to the UN! I'm no filthy terrorist! But I'm loyal to Bruno too. And me and Bruno talked about this. He isn't a terrorist and just wants to make sure there are people left for the UN to rule when we beat this stupid dungeon world and get back to earth.

Before I could say so Bruno says very sternly, without turning to look at me, "Kim. Grab Joey and go find doctor Calderon. Stay with her in the med tent. Do the solo arena. Got it? Go. NOW!"

This was an order. I didn't even say hua. I just go find and grab Joey and move out. But I don't go to the med tent. I turn around in the crowd and stand behind a guy that looks like Lurch from behind. Lurch is a good guy so this guy that looks like him probably is too. Well, looks like him from behind.

I don't know what's going on but I'm nervous. My heart is beating fast. I can't really see anything so I strain my ears to listen.

I hear the premier say, "So, as we established, you must pass leadership to me. At the first opportunity I will pass leadership to the secretary general. This will prove you are loyal to the UN and have the best interest of humanity at heart, no?"

Bruno replies, "Nah. I might be ugly but at least I ain't got no money."

"What?"

"Nothing."

"So you are not loyal to the UN? You are a traitor then, no?"

Bruno's voice gets louder, "No. You're the traitor to the rightful and lawful current government. Here. Now. My government. The government I claimed fair and square. My goal is to ensure we beat this contest. And have a sizable population return to earth. You guys can take over again on earth. I don't care."

"Yes. That is the problem. You don't care. But the UN does. It is our job to care. To protect. To unite. We are needed to lead humanity now more than ever."

"Well, that sounds great and all, but last time you guys mucked everything up. If it wasn't for you politicians and your corrupt bureaucracies messing with the best fighters and getting us killed over political nonsense we'd have done much better."

"Ah. So now you change your stories. You stated in your messages that the best fighters died on level 10, no? But now the UN is somehow responsible for killing them all?"

"No. You guys just twist everything around. After level 10, with what we had left, is when the UN started to destroy everything. Muck everything up."

"So you lie and change your story to suit the situation, no? We need strong, proven leadership now. Not some terrorist spreading hate-speech and calling everyone slurs and walking around with a head hanging off his belt like a barbarian. Actual leadership. People helping people." I can't see Bruno to verify if he does have the head on his belt. I don't think so. Not that I remember seeing.

"Call me a terrorist again and your head with join the other."

"See what I mean? Ah, I'm sure the intelligence I have is true then. I am sorry to hear it. LISTEN UP PEOPLE! The UN has verified intelligence that this Bruno Vaz was one of the most wanted terrorists in the US protectorate! Maybe even the murderous Zero! He has killed many innocent people. For what? Your countrypeople! Your brothers and sisters! Because he hates the freedom and security the UN gives you!"

After a moment Bruno replies, "And you call me a liar? You have no intelligence, never mind verified intelligence, from anywhere on me. I can guarantee that."

"Ha! You really think the UN doesn't have perfect intelligence on all the murderous traitors and terrorists in the US and elsewhere?"

"I have no idea."

"We'll that begs the question why you are so certain, then, the UN doesn't know you are a known terrorist leader?"

"Begging the question isn't actually a regular question, smarty-pants. It's a fallacy that means you assume the conclusion without supporting it. You would have to say, 'You are a terrorist leader because terrorist leaders have brown eyes like you do.' Something like that. Even I know how to use that term right."

"So, now you try to say I am the dumb one? You even admitted you were dumb in your first messages to us all. And it is, 'use it correctly,' not, 'use it right.' English was the third language I learned and I speak it better than you."

"You don't have to. Everything is translated. Speak your native language. You'll be easier to understand. And I never said I was dumb. I said I wasn't smart. You don't have to be smart to know what 'begs the question' means. Correct?"

"You can deflect all day, but at the end of it you are still a terrorist. And a usurper. We have many reports on you from the last ten years, leading terrorist cells in three different countries."

"You are just lying out your ass. That ain't true at all."

"And do you have proof? Of course not."

"You don't have any information on me doing anything in the last ten years because my family is from 2009. The time I came from there was no civil war in the US. There was no pods or internet you could live in or nothing like that. The UN wasn't in control of the whole world. The US was at war with Afghanistan and Iraq. I was in the army. Delta operator. I have no idea why my family was sent here. But I came here the same age I left. I was born in 1970."

"Ha! What rubbish! What nonsense! So you came back from the future but really are from the past? How stupid do you think we are? You..."

What he says took a moment to register in my mind. The premier is being a real jerk, so I am 100% siding with Bruno. Teen heart-throb or not, the premier is just yuck. Bruno ISN'T a terrorist for crying out loud! And I thought of a way to prove it. I can ask his family in guild chat.

I start typing out fast and furiously, and I'm not good at typing or spelling even when I take my time.

Self: hey emergency bruno is ib trouble are you all from 2009
Lurch: Huh?
Siri: YES!
Nimh: I'm so sorry. The sentence did not translate.
System: 1 silver, 3 copper were deposited into the Guild Coffers from sale.
Sergey: ?
Emina: It did not translate
Bruno's Wife: We are
Nathan: She asked if my family, mom, dad, Siri, and myself are all from 2019.
Nathan: 2009*
Siri: Yes, we are. Why? What is going on? Is my dad okay?
Bruno's Wife: What is
Nimh: Yes. They said from 2009 on the first day we met.
Nathan: Is dad okay Kim?
Doc C: Where are you, Kim? Come to the med tent.
Emina: It is true. They say they are from 2009. They said this when we first joined them.
Self: hes okay BRB general please tell premere he tells the truth

Self: or major please

Lurch: What are you all talking about?

I close my UI and see if the general or Ball-face are telling the premier Bruno was telling the truth. No one was moving but Bruno seems angry. About to go balls to the wall angry and start murdering. I rush forward as I yell for them to stop and for the general to read the guild chat to the premier.

3.4 WHEN ONE BURNS ONE'S BRIDGES, WHAT A VERY NICE FIRE IT MAKES

BRUNO VAZ

The worst thing about future people…hell, probably people from my time too, is how they just completely give up their mind to their betters, and think they're right and righteous for doing it. Conditioned to obey without question, and conditioned with triggers causing excessive amount of hate. It wouldn't be so bad if it was consistent and part of a sensible ideology, but it isn't. Hating this thing is great and right, but hating this similar thing is awful and wrong and triggers the conditioned hate response of everyone else, and deservedly so. Why? Because. Don't think. Don't question. Just obey our dictates, love who we deem worthy, and hate who we condition you to hate.

I almost envy these people. The vast majority of people. I wish I could have such certainty and such a simple mind. It must be nice. I'm not even smart, but somehow even I can see what's going on, and I'm still smart enough to question everything and think for myself.

I don't expect anyone to believe my family's from 2009. It sounds ridiculous. I don't know why Kim thought this was some sort of checkmate, getting General Edwards and Ball-face to read what everyone in the city said in guild chat. It's all nonsense. Even if it was believable and I had absolute proof, how many times have I seen people presented with absolute proof and they still decide to ignore it? No one questions how the UN isn't able to quickly and decisively beat wars against a handful of poor countries, with ill-equipped and barely trained soldiers, but somehow manages to do so when it is an important country, like Panama and their canal. No one questions if there seems to be some sort of strategy at play, with foreverwars and the constant threat and looming danger of "terrorists" around every corner.

It's funny how "terrorist" just seems to mean any person that politicians don't like at any given time. You don't have to think I'm right about anything for me to not be a terrorist. You don't have to think I'm a good guy for me to not be a terrorist. Plenty of bad people live on every street in every town and city of every country in the world, and almost none of them are terrorists.

All I've done is share all the important information I know freely, and try to get people to be tougher and fight better. So we can get off this world. So we can get home.

I stopped paying attention to this slick politician's bleatings. Premier Dalembert. I already decided to kill him. It's just been setting it up so Kim doesn't die in the process too. And she is making it hard. That little dummy. I know no matter what I say she isn't going to leave. Just hide in the crowd. Like a dummy. And as soon as SHTF she'll be out here, fighting right next to me. Like a dummy. Like a real soldier. I'd be more proud than angry if I wasn't so worried about her. I really love that little knucklehead.

Politician Dalembert will never stop. His kind are all the same. Blood-soaked, power-hungry monsters. He'll never be okay withy not having all the power he thinks he deserves. He has to die. Maybe not, but I want him to wicked bad. So he will.

The crazy part is I don't even want to lead. Anything. Ever. I hate being in charge. I hate thinking. I wish someone else used the wish machine to come back and do this. If the UN showed they weren't fully corrupt, and where at least somewhat competent, I would let them have the government with my heartfelt blessing and I'd just pass on information. They aren't. They just care about politics and power and stupid games and forcing their will on everyone. And all these morons love it. Cheer for it. It's almost enough for me to want to give them the reins and sit back and watch it all burn again. But I'm doing this for my family, and Kim, and the handful of normal people out there.

And all the hot whores. Most of them are close-minded cultist idiots that would cheer for the UN as it led them off a cliff, but I'm not attracted to them for their reasoning, logic, and ability to think clearly. In fact, I'd get laid far less if all the hot whores were better at thinking good. God bless them and their teeny-tiny brains and loose morals. They truly make life worth living.

I look at the General. He won't meet my eye. He's been awfully quiet. He did verify what Kim said from the chat. Kim, that knucklehead. I'm still going to smoke her to death for disobeying an order. She makes me so proud I start feeling all weird inside. I start feeling the fake, invented emotions. The ones girls always blab about.

You can't trust future people in general, never mind a politician. And Generals are politicians. Politicians pretending to be soldiers. Just like a politician would blow up every children's hospital in the world if it somehow got them reelected or elected to higher office, every General would obey the order to blow up a children's hospital and wouldn't hesitate to sacrifice every single one of the soldiers under his command if it got him promoted or more power. Animals. Monsters. Hiding behind the "just following orders" line all cowards do, and selling loyalty to those best able to hand out power.

They praised me for my service and sacrifice when I do what they want, but it wouldn't be hard to actually paint me as a terrorist with

323

all the things I've done. All the things I got to live with. All the times I followed orders. I think back to my first team mission in Delta. There weren't many team missions, especially back then. On this one, a rare officer operator was running the show. Either a major or light bird at the time. I forget. Three man team. I was pretty new in Delta and the low man. Our mission was to paint a target for some new laser guided missile. You just point this new, big tech thing that looked like the detachable part of a javelin at a target, and a plane real high up shoots a missile and it goes right to what your laser is painting. The target was the house of some politician. In Croatia. Maybe Bosnia. Could be Serbia. One of those places, or that general area at least.

I tried to abort the mission when I saw the wife and kids were in the house. One was just a baby. We could've easily shot the guy. Or slit his throat in his sleep. Why bring women and children into it? The officer puts his nine to my head and makes me paint the target. I pussed out and did it too. I watched the house explode into nothing. The explosion was blamed on some group the US was trying to get people to hate. The same group the politician belonged to. I'm sure that officer slept fine after what we done, but I didn't. I don't. There's never a justification for that. Never. And you're never right in the head after. You can't be. You can avoid thinking about it, but you can never be forgiven for it. Just know you're damned to hell for doing it.

If I could go back I would've took the bullet. It would be easier to live with than the memory. How many memories like that do I have now? Just following orders. A well-decorated terrorist, shaking hands and taking orders from the elites of my nation. Until I decided I didn't like the orders no more, and was useful enough to say no. They said it was a TBI. Sure, boss.

I don't see much difference between General Edwards and this UN schmuck. I won't be surprised if he turns on me. He swore up and down on the first day he would be part of my government and only

324

my government, do everything he can to get humans to survive and back to earth, and smooth things over with the UN. You can't trust politicians. And Generals are politicians.

The premier notices I'm not paying attention and smiles at me. "Here, why don't we go finish up these talks in my pavilion, no?"

"No."

"And why not? No one needs hear the details of our conversation, no?"

"I got nothing to hide. Unlike you I don't lie for a living. This is the straight poop – you are an insurrectionist and a terrorist against the lawful government of this place. Me. You lied right to my face multiple times. You are trying to foment a coup. Guess what the punishment for that is? Death."

His eyes go cold for a second, then he smiles and starts laughing. "Yes. Yes it is. I'm sorry you will have to die."

I laugh. "How you going to make that happen, tough-guy?" Time for some trapping.

He laughs back, and motions to four guys near him. Probably his security team. "You don't really believe the BS that you are the toughest man around, do you? The UN has the best, any of these four UN Protectors is your match."

I smile inside. I only know one of the guys on his security team from last timeline. Another one's a giant, but giants don't got no gas tank and peter out quick. The other two couldn't hurt me much if they were dominatrices and I was paying them to try their best. "I recognize one of your security from last time. He was in the MMA before it was shut down, right? You think he can take me?"

"I am certain of it."

"You willing to bet?"

He fumbles and stutters, "We are already the legal government. No bet will change that. Stop being a child."

I think I got him now. Hopefully. We'll see. Better to do this civilized than have a big fight were people pick sides and get killed when they don't got to. "You said you're certain he'd beat me. Tell you what, we won't play for high stakes. We'll keep the stakes low, and make it so you're triple super certain. As a politician, you can't fight. Your job is to lie good. I'll fight three of your UN Protectors at once, and promise not to kill any of them. I'll fight all four, but I can't promise no killing then. Your guys can try and kill me all they want. If you're certain one can take me, you got to see this as the most certain bet you could ever make, right?" I can see the wheels turning in his head. End the threat of me, show the power of the UN, be a hero. I can see him calculating his new promotion and power.

"What, exactly, is the bet?"

"Like I said, small stakes. The UN is more than any one man. Way more. It spans the globe, and It's the first global government. My government ends with me. If your guys win, you can kill me. They can kill me during the fight, too. And to help play to their strengths, since I have more system knowledge, we'll strip our hit point shields. We can fight with no weapons if they want, just our hands. I'm figuring two of the guys, if it's just three of them, will be the MMA guy and the giant. That'll favor those two. So the bet's small stakes – my life or yours. And if I fight three of your guys, none of them die. We can end this with no one dying but me or you."

He starts huddling with his guys. That's how you get a politician. They ain't complicated. You don't try and trick them. You just give them a good deal. They're wired to want good deals that benefit them and screw everyone else, and I offered a great deal. Or what seems like a great deal. I see the guys in the huddle laughing and looking smarmy. He's in.

Slicky-boy says, "We accept the three man deal, no weapons, no hit point shields. And I just want to say…"

I don't give him a chance to continue. I shout, "Gunny Zapata, Ball…Major Goodman." I see Beatrice in the crowd. "And Doctor Calderon. Form a circle. Military on one side, the rest of the crawlers on the other. You all heard the deal. Me against this guy's best three men, including the MMA hotshot. Sacha? Right? No weapons. No shields. They can kill me but I can't kill them. If I lose, I die. If they lose, the lying politician dies. Everyone got it? Make sure this stays honest."

The politician is talking to his guys. Smiling. Happy. Moron. I'm Bruno Vaz, you silly bitches.

Gunny and Ball-face get to work. Beatrice stares at me like I'm nuts, but the civilians form the half circle despite her lack of direction. Both Kim and Butterball come up to me. Kim better not have lost Joey again. Jesus Christ, this kid is going to give me a brain aneurism. I ignore the General and ask Kim where Joey is.

"Right over there." She points backwards at the general direction of a ton of people. Jesus, this kid. She then holds my hand. I let her. She then hugs me. I pat her back as she does. She pulls me down and whispers in my ear, "I know you'll win, but just in case don't worry about nothing. If you lose all the military guys get kicked out of the guild and your wife becomes guild leader, safe in her…whatever it is in the city where no one else can come in. Instance? And I'll avenge you. I will kill everyone and pee on them. And eat them too. I'll stick my spear right up their butts."

"Jesus, Joseph, and Mary, Kim! You got to stop with this eating people nonsense. Don't ever eat anyone. That's disgusting. Don't ever eat people. Okay? And peeing is just for special enemies. If you do it too much it's meaningless. If I die just smoke yourself till you puke. Then do it again. I didn't forget you ignored my orders earlier. I'm not going to die though. So guess who is smoking who later? But even though that is definitely happening, I just want you to know that I'm...proud...of...you."

I can't help it. I get a little choked up. Like a big pansy. I don't cry but it's hard getting this mushy stuff out. Saying this type of crap isn't easy for me. I don't know why it makes me feel all these pretend, made-up emotions. But it does.

"I love you, Kim. You're an awesome kid. I couldn't be more proud of you. It's been an absolute honor spending all this time with you. Partnering with you. Being your friend. You're like the son I always wanted. But please, please don't ever tell my son that."

She starts crying. But she is a girl so it isn't sissy when she does it. She hugs me hard and says, "I love you too you big, black, son of a bee."

"Big, black, son of a bee, huh? You've been spending too much time with Zapata." Gunnery Sergeant Zapata is Honduran. A very light-skinned Honduran. The type that thinks that makes it okay to say anything he wants. I can't really fault him as I think I can say whatever I want. But that's despite the fact I'm black, not because of it. Well, kind of because of it too. A little at least. He, of course, would never say bee instead of bitch, but Kim has this weird thing about swearing. She even hates when I do it. So I try not to. Zapata's a good guy. Out of all the military people, I think Gunny could be most trusted to have my back if it came down to me versus the UN. Maybe because he is part of the US defense force, and not the UN military. He isn't too bright, but he's a good guy. Decent fighter. Not top tier. Not close.

We break off and I tell Kim to go find Joey and to stay with him. Butterball says, "We have to talk."

"Oh yeah? About what? Which side you're on now? I guess you forgot what you said on that first day."

"I didn't. It's…just…complicated. Believe me, I'm on your side. But we can't burn bridges. You can't kill the US premier."

"UN premier."

"Of the US protectorate. But that doesn't matter. He doesn't matter. But killing him sure will. It will be much harder to pave things over with the rest of the UN. To get them to fall in line and not make a push for your own head. You got to understand…"

"I ain't got to understand nothing. Let me ask you something – you think you can play both sides? You got to get all the way in or all the way out. That's all that matters from you."

"I said I'm with you, but don't do anything stupid. Don't kill the premier. Please. I'm begging you. Use your head. That's a bridge too far."

"Just draw your weapon, Butterball. Can you tell when a hit-point shield is gone or will you need me to say stop? Never mind. I'll say stop. Just go slow and steady. Wait for them to start. You know those two other guys besides Sacha. His names Sacha, right?"

Sacha isn't going to be a problem. One of the other two guys is a giant. He moves okay, but is still way too slow and not enough gas to be a threat, even though he's twice as wide as me. He has on full plate from the store. Sacha has medium armor. His type usually go monk. I was a monk at first last timeline. Too many unarmed bugs, and you still need a weapon when shields are gone since punching the imported mobs to death isn't really feasible. Or fast. Sacha had a greataxe earlier. Barbarian seems like a safe bet.

The last guy is normal sized. Light armor. Stupid mustache. He moves okay. He is jumping up and down and shaking his arms. Getting his heart rate up. It won't help.

"No. No idea. I don't know which one is Sacha either, or if that's his name."

"Armor on no armor?" I yell to the other side.

The little one yells back, "No armor." Not the little one, the normal sized one. Sacha is pretty big, and the other guy is a little taller than me, and way thicker. Tubby feller, but a real giant. I figured they'd say that. My full plate is player made. It looks different. They probably think it's magic. They should know that below level 7 there are barely any magic items. Just skill increase items. And just +1 for skills. You can equip masterwork at level 2, but nothing magic besides skill increases and the minor burst weapons that are only drops.

Armor really won't help anyways. No biggie. Plate is just thicker, but still pretty light material. A little heavier than light armor. Like the old BDUs, how they had the thin material summer ones, and the thicker material winter ones. It isn't actually metal and wouldn't protect against a sword thrust outside of the AC it gives. Being a dwarf it doesn't give me -15% speed. It just slows me down a smidge due to its natural weight. That's it. Pretend armor. Great when your HP shield is up. Great for protecting against cold. Actual cold. Like cold outside. Not cold spells or anything. Great for protecting against scrapes or other things regular clothes help protect you from. But not swords. Not a kick to the chest.

I start removing my armor. The 30 second countdown starts ticking for when it will be stored in my inventory. I try thinking of a way to show the crowd my penis, but there're kids in the crowd and I'm no pervert. Shame though. Showing people my penis empowers me. I don't know why. I just like it. Like peeing outside – I don't know why I like it. I just do. It's like a statement declaring the world is my toilet, and that gives me power somehow. Makes life a little more enjoyable.

The other side starts removing each other's HP shields. Slowly. The other guy with the premier, the one not fighting, gives me a weird feeling so I have Butterball slow down removing mine. I ensure I actually see the flashes and that their shields are gone before I let my shield get removed.

Alright, boy's night out. It's go time. I stand forward. I smile and say, "Who cooking bologna." I say it in weird voice. The voice I first heard it in. A fast-paced Louis Armstrong kind of voice. Said as a statement, not a question. I was in Ranger Bat at Benning when I heard it, but I forget the context other than it really cracked me up and I've been saying it since then. My opponents don't think it's funny, as they just give me weird looks.

There was no official start, but my three opponents start circling me. I keep Sacha in front of me, but I keep an eye on the big guy so he notices I'm paying attention. No matter what people say, size matters. That's why bouncers are usually big guys. They can tangle you up. Even if they aren't trained, being a giant and thick as a tree means I can't let him grab me, even if he don't got no gas tank at all. I'm figuring that's the strategy here. Sacha will come in low and the big guy will grab me from behind as I avoid Sacha. The little guy's off to my two o'clock. Helping to distract from the bug guy behind me. Probably acting as the opportunity guy. Fill in the gaps guy. Exploiter.

Not a bad plan. I'd bet two fat babies and a donut if that giant's able to grab me from behind, I'm not getting out easy or quick and I probably won't be able to turn it around after.

Sacha isn't staring me down. His eyes are unfocused, looking at my chest and right arm. Not wanting to give away his opening move.

Sacha explodes into action, barreling at my mid for a take-down. I time it, and hop back a little as his right hand passes the plane of my left side and I can use it as leverage. I turn my head a little to find the big guy's knee on my hop back. As I turn my head my left palm hits Sacha's right arm as hard as I can manage and as close as I can get to his elbow without looking. I feel pressure on my left side as his arm digs in as I shatter his elbow with my palm. It moves me a little so the knee stomp I planned on giving the big guy behind me as I hop back doesn't hit full on. I land it, but not good.

The giant is built like one of those guys that compete in the strongman competitions, pulling buses and dead lifting fridges. In normal clothes they look like big, fat guys. They all seem to have pretty big guts. But they are wicked, wicked strong. And thick. So my knee stomp that was supposed to shatter his knee, and would've if it landed right, doesn't. It hurt him though, enough to stop him from grabbing me. Even if it didn't shatter the knee, it caused a lot of pain and damage.

As I hopped back I also started throwing my right elbow. I was aiming for the big guy's neck, but he moved when his knee was kicked so it landed on his cheek. I look for the little guy. He was charging at me, but changes his mind. He has a wild look in his eye as he jumps back. Getting distance from me now that their plan failed so spectacularly.

I give big guy a few more elbows to the head area and a nice stomp to his right ankle. That ankle stomp collapses him. Guarding pain. You got to love it. Two down, just the little feller left. He looks scared. Looking side to side for help or a way out. Ha. I make sure I don't look at him, and make it like I'm turning to face the big guy on the ground, then I jet forward at him. I'm almost on him before he notices. I almost try to jump and knee him in the face, but me getting far off the ground is usually a mistake that smart opponents have exploited in the past. So I charge with my left elbow out, run through his chest, and mount him as he falls. He didn't even slightly try a defense to stop my mount. I was hoping my elbow to the chest would've knocked the wind out of him, or landing hard on his back, but it didn't. I forearm choke him with my left as I punch him with my right. Or try to. I see a shimmer before my punch lands. It does no damage and I can tell he can breathe. My forearm choke doing nothing.

Someone is healing him. I don't think he notices. He looks as frightened as ever.

I yell out. "Someone is healing him. Restrain that guy." I point at the fourth man in the premier's group. I see another shimmer on the little guy. Do they really think this will help? His hands can't really stop my blows so I use both my hands to land them and try to take the shield. I have a second of vertigo as I get teleported onto my back, the little guy on top of me. Stupid grapple bugs. He stills has a HP shield so I can't grab him. I could, but the stupid grapple bugs drive me nuts. I manage to hit him once before he gets up and staggers back. He's too scared to even think of taking advantage of the grapple bug that put him on top of me.

I'm up in a flash and deliver a cross. Jab. Jab. Cross. The shield shimmers away. I put him in the muay-thai clinch, with my arms wrapped around his head and my forearms squeezing his jaws. I slam his head down into my knee, which is flying up towards his face. He is out. I guide him to the ground. It was a real hard hit. I hope it didn't kill him. I just wanted it ended before any more healing happened. I look back at the other two guys and see the HP shield shimmer on them. Did whoever did that really think they were going to get up and fight with a broken elbow on one guy, and a jacked-up ankle and messed-up knee on the other? Crazy.

No. Not a broken elbow. It broke right above the elbow, the bone sticking out. Lot of blood, hopefully not the artery. I don't see it squirting, so hopefully not. It could be nicked and bleeding out inside, where you can't see the squirts.

I look over and I'm surprised to see UN military guys have re-strained the fourth man. The one I think was healing. Butterball is close by. Did he order it? Or did he go over after and is now trying to muck up the situation?

I stand after I finish laying the mustached little guy lightly on the ground. Slow. Like there is no hurry. I look around for the premier. I can't see him. I see Butterball shake his head no at me. Someone starts rushing towards me and I start reacting, but realize it's Doctor Calderon, going to treat the downed guys. Hopefully the little guy is alive. I see the other doctor we picked up in area 3 rush out too. He isn't a real doctor. Well, technically he is. Just not like a family care doctor. He's an anesthetist. Or anesthesiologist. I forget which one is the nurse and which is the MD. Beatrice told me he's a fast learner and knows the basics and is a huge help. That all MDs do real doctor stuff for a little bit in college and when they get out. Even psychiatrists. He is like 50 something. He follows around Beatrice like a dog. Have some pride, man.

Beatrice is being carried in a solid team. She is the healer. Druid, with an animal companion. Animal companions don't do so good at later levels unless you get a ton of feats for them. Or go warder or warden. They get all the animal companion feats as class features, and get a template that makes them real hard to kill. The new doctor's team really sucks. I'm surprised they made it this far. He's a real dork and so is his team. One of the guys on his team was harassing me about how chainmail was just called mail, but spelled all dumb. And longswords are really just called swords. And real longswords were like great swords. Nonsense like that. Stuff no one normal cares about. This system calls them x and y, so who cares? That dork actually wanted me to send an email out to everyone explaining the gibberish he was telling me. He kept whining out the word misnomer. How is he still alive? That team of dorks actually got 3rd SS once. How? I don't get it.

I yell out, "Gunnery Sergeant Zapata! Please find the premier and bring him to my tent. You all heard the deal we made. He had one of his guys cheat and now he ran off. Welching on his bet."

I see Zapata start giving orders as Butterball says, "You don't know that. Let's not be rash."

I say, "Rash? All I have in this world is my word and my balls. If keeping your word and the deals you make is being rash, then the modern world and modern military is more messed up than even I thought."

He makes an exasperated sigh like he is dealing with a petulant child, "Really? Quoting Scarface?"

"That's an awesome movie."

Zapata, who walked over to me, whispers, "Where's your tent?"

"The UN tent pavilion thing. Not my usual tent. I'm taking that now. I'll give it to the medical people after I'm done with it." I want to tell him to be discreet with the premier, but his guys already took off. There's also a Marine officer I should be giving the commands to, but he is a suck-up and just hangs-out with the UN officers. Also a bunch of butter bars, or close to butter bars, and a Sergeant Major. I don't deal with cherries and the Sergeant Major is a UN toad and hangs around the officers. Aged bad, too.

He is probably younger than me. That makes me feel weird inside for some reason. But it shouldn't. I still got it. I may be getting old, but I'm still the toughest human I know about.

I'm technically a Sergeant Major too. Operators don't wear rank in Delta, but we all know each other's ranks. Rank is important for how much you make in retirement. Everyone just called me Papa Bear. My cover was as range control. My uniformed cover was my wife's maiden name, same as the rest of my family. Thurston. Whitest name ever. My wife's father was an officer in the Corps. He kind of even looked like Thurston Howell from Gilligan's island. He isn't my wife's real father. He adopter her and her little sister after marrying her mother while stationed in Thailand.

I wish I got to be stationed in cool places like Thailand when I was young.

Anyways, my wife came to the US when she was wicked young. Her mother died when she was an early teen and her adopted father finished raising the kids. My wife argued with him like real parents with their real kid. That didn't really happen in the foster homes I lived in. Not that I ever saw. She was still wicked close to him at the end, in 2012. That is so different from my experience in foster care. I had a family that might have got guardianship over me, but that was the last thing I wanted. I'd rather stay in a group home. Most of the foster families I stayed with were pretty decent. Professional foster parents. They made their money by having foster kids, and they'd have tons. As many as they could, all the time. Those types left you alone mostly, as long as you didn't cause them too much grief. Just as I liked it. Group homes were better. More freedom, and no one pretended they cared about you or what you did.

My wife still nags me about finding her "father," and all her siblings here. He's like 25 years older than us. If he is here he is almost 100. I haven't seen any hundred-year-olds walking around. I tell her I look though. I do not. She thinks he might have disappeared in 2009 with them. Same with her siblings. We never found any of them last time. Her adopted dad had three kids with her mother. She had a younger sister when she moved from Thailand too. She was the oldest of all five and close to all of them.

Her younger sister's Thai name is Won. Pronounced like Juan. But they say no. Whan is a different name. Won is supposed to be the number. One. When they explained that to me my mind couldn't accept it. Why not spell it right? They say that is how you spell the name. The number is spelled one. The name, which is the number one, is spelled Won.

Thai people drive me nuts.

Her sister was like four or five when they came to the US. No accent. Pure American. Minnie barely has one, but she can speak Thai perfectly. Her sister not so good. But Minnie reconnected to being Thai after she had kids. Her sister never did. Her sister was wicked hot before she got married and started popping out kids. I used to bang her all the time when she lived with us. Minnie stayed close to her even after finding out. Crazy. Minnie was wicked, wicked mad at me for a long time. That was the most mad she ever got at me for cheating. Took a lot of groveling to get her to forgive me.

Minnie's real father, her Thai father, had three more kids too. Preow, Comb, and Pet. She named our kid before she found out about her Thai half-siblings. Those names mean sour, bitter, and spicy. Thai people love crap like that. Themes. Her half-sister, Preow, has two boys named Bomb and Bom. Or Bon. I'm not sure. If you ask they just say it over and over and tell you that you're saying it wrong. So I have no idea what the name actually is. I'm pretty sure all of Thailand is conspiring to mess with me about how I say gnu. The word for snake. I nail it every time and they just say, "NO!!! It is new. Not new. New. Get it? New. You say new and new is wrong. New. See?"

Man, I can't wait to bang Minnie. I'll go after next instance. This one is a bust. I want the full 10 hours with my wife and kids.

I got to stop thinking of her as my wife. My ex I mean. Cheating whore.

Okay. Time to focus on business. Butterball is going to be a problem.

3.5 TEETH

KIM GUM

I helped doc get the injured men to the med area after Bruno's fight. He, like, destroyed two of the guys in a second and you could even see how. Not really. He is so awesome it is crazy! I thought the other guy was going to crap his pants. That would have been hilarious! Craping your pants like a loser. I'd never be that scared.

Well, not again. Not no more. And no one knows about when I did that in my pants. Joey won't tell no one.

Doc wants me to tell Bruno she needs to talk to him. She sounded real mad too. I think. Stern, at least. Can someone sound stern? And I got to decide if I should rat her out to Bruno. She gave the fat guy a healing pill. Not fat. Come on, Kim. Be better. The real big guy. The real strong looking one.

The big guy and the other strong guy with the broken arm needed healing pills. They only had one between them, so doc gave one of her own healing pills to them. It probably wasn't her own. Someone probably gave it to her. Bruno said no one was supposed to give the doc healing pills because she is a hippy and will give it to some nobody that isn't a big help to humanity.

Should I rat her out? She is always real nice to me. I really like her. And those guys may be really good at fighting. But, like Ball-face, just not good when compared to Bruno. Like me too. Like everyone.

I'm not going to rat. Not on doc. And I'm no rat fink. There's a brand new doctor too. Just joined us this area. That should make Bruno happy. I think.

As I walk around looking for Bruno the mood from everyone seems off. I hear people say premier a lot.

Wow, that girl is real pretty. She is wearing really short shorts, slip-ons, and a tight tank top. Wearing real clothes still probably means she isn't a crawler yet. She looks way younger than me. Talking to two boys. They look like jerks. She looks like the type of girl that would have been mean to me in school. Her chest is bigger than mine. How is she not twelve yet? And all sissies like that should have gone to the city.

Or is she is older than twelve and just switches out clothes when she exits the dungeon? My real clothes are all destroyed. It was the military uniform so wasn't a cute outfit like hers anyways. And those boys look like jerks, so who cares?

The girl sees me and just stops and stares. After a second she goes back to talking to the jerk-boys and laughs. When I pass by they all stop and stare at me. My face heats up. I thought they were going to talk to me, but they don't. Phew. That would've sucked. I hear them start talking and laughing again. They smelled nice. I hope I don't smell too bad. I just bathed before we exited the last dungeon. But Bruno says I start smelling bad quick. Hopefully not that fast though.

In the distance I see a guy I recognize. I think a marine officer. I ask him if he knows where Bruno is. He points to the big tent thing. I thank him and move out.

There are people outside the tent. One of them is one of the guys that always meet with Bruno with the general and Ball-Face. I don't recognize the other one. Someone I don't know walks up and goes in. When I get to the tent the guy I don't recognize stops me. The one I do recognize asks if Bruno is expecting me. I say yeah and he lets me in.

It feels tense when I get in the tent. It's pretty big inside. Not too many people. There is a small table and a chair. The premier is in the chair. He looks dead. I don't see any blood though, and his head is still attached. As I walk in I hear, "...akes you look like a goddamn idiot." I'm not sure who said it.

Bruno looks mad. But he always looks mad. With his dumb, always mad eyebrows. I could tell he wants to reply to whoever said that, but he's looking at me. He says, "What's up, knucklehead? We're busy here."

"Knucklehead is way longer and more syllables than Kim."

He smiles, "Seriously, what do you need? And where is Joey?"

I look around as I reply. The general, Ball-face, Gunny, one of the guys that always meets with us after dungeons, and I guy I think is an officer are in the tent. Plus the unmoving premier, with his head lolling to the side, eyes closed, mouth partly open.

"Doc wants to see you. I think she is mad. Oh, and we got a new doctor too. Joey is with Ass-eyes and her kids."

Bruno smirks for some reason. "I told you not to call her that. All those guys live?"

"Yeah. I think. No, I mean they definitely are alive. Two took healing pills though."

"Nice. You beat 8 solo yet? No. Never mind that for now. Go to the training area. Leg said we got the rapier guy from the arena. He should be at the training area with Baby-face. Go learn something. That guy is high-speed and a hard-charger." Those are the best compliments Bruno gives. I never heard him call someone both high-speed and a hard-charger. I've seen the guy's arena fights. He deserves those compliments.

"Who is Baby-face?"

"Jesus Christ, Kim! How do you not know Baby-face?"

"I don't know."

"The asian guy who meets with us after dungeons. Almost as tall as me. Face like a twelve year old, body like a crack-head. Jesus Christ, his name is Kim. Same name as you. How do you not know this guy?"

"Oh. The guy from last timeline?"

"No, you...! Ew, you drive me nuts sometimes. Lieutenant colonel Kim. A completely different guy. Tall, asian, meets with us after the dungeons with sergeant major Leg, general Edwards, major Goodman? Jesus, I thought I sucked at paying attention."

"Oh yeah. I remember now." I remember the two guys – I just didn't know their names. So that black guy over there must be Leg. My dad told me airborne people call people that aren't airborne legs. But you couldn't anymore because you'd get in trouble. Leg must just be a nickname. It would be a real dumb last name. But Gum isn't a good last name either. Gum is pretty dumb too. Oh well, who cares? I never talk to them so why would I care about their names?

"Alright, move out. Ball-face will be there soon too."

"Hua." I move out. When I get to the training area, I see Kim. I'll probably just call him Baby-face. I'm Kim. He isn't. I don't think he looks young, he looks old like a boomer. He is skinny, but not super skinny. Not as tall as Bruno either. I don't think. A lot taller than me though.

Five people have rapiers, standing in line in a weird pose and holding them out. I notice the rapier guy from the arena videos. About as tall as me. And real skinny, but muscles too. Not big muscles, but you could see he had some good ones. And the pretty lady that gave me a flower earlier. I go stand on the side and watch. Both the rapier guy and the pretty lady look like they're instructing everyone. The pretty lady notices me and smiles and waves. I smile and wave back.

I watch for a while, and some real big lady starts moving towards me. She looks really old. She better not try and kidnap me and force me to answer questions or I'll stab her in her stupid face. She walks weird too. Wearing full plate.

She gets up to me and says, "Hey Kim! How are you?"

"Good. And you?"

"Good as can be, I guess. That's my daughter, Christina. And her boyfriend, Victor. She said she talked to you before."

"Yeah. She's real nice. And real beautiful."

"Oh, she sure is. Hard to imagine I made something as beautiful as that."

I don't say anything. This lady is way uglier than me. She has a bunch of missing teeth and the ones that're left are all yellow. She's tall and has broad shoulders, but it's hard to tell if she has muscles or if it's fat. She also talks super, super loud.

"She's in the olympics. She won a couple medals. Her boyfriend, Victor, he was a big deal. He won more medals than anyone of all time. He retired though. They pay him to play stupid games. Not this one. Where you in a pod? Christina didn't have to. They made me."

"No. My dad was in the military."

"Oh." She said it in a way like she disapproved. "Victor's from Russia. They met at her first olympic. He's like 15 years older than she is. I think she was 17 when they started dating. I guess that isn't a big deal in Europe. I wasn't in her life much back then. Wish I was, but I made a lot of mistakes. How you like it here?"

"Um, in this world or this zone?"

"This…place. This world I guess."

"I like…some things. I like fighting. And I like Bruno. I wish my family was still alive."

"Sorry about that. Rough hand you were dealt."

"Thanks."

"You know Christina studied a lot in Hungary. Fencing stuff. I didn't know that. I can't believe I missed so much of her life. She made sure I was grouped with her to come here. I couldn't believe it. And no one even knew if people in pods could form groups then. She still did it. She used to be mad at me about everything that happened when we she was a kid, but she made sure she was grouped with me. I'm sure Victor wasn't happy about that. But I've been holding my own."

A greatclub flashes in her hand.

"See this. People say this is a bad weapon because it is 1d10, times 2 on just a 20. But I love it. I'm good with it too. I really like smashing things. Just…"

She shows me what she means by smashing the air in front of her.

"…like that. Know what I mean?"

I do. I certainly do. "Yeah, I really like stabbing things with my spear. But I wouldn't mind smashing things either." I guess this lady is okay. She gets it.

"You're probably wondering why I wasn't in Christina's life back then much. Or why I don't got no teeth no more. Same answer. Drugs. I was a fighter back then. Good too. Then I had Christina. Hard to bounce back after having a kid. Slowed down. Got some injuries. Got some prescriptions to keep me going. Got addicted to the prescriptions. Started fighting worse, until I had no one to get me prescriptions. Then I moved on to crack. Then that dried up but there was plenty of meth. I lost my teeth around the same time they took Christina. She moved in with a real nice family. Good people. I hate them but was happy about what they was doing for my kid, you know? Well, anyways, they adopted her. I didn't stop it. I couldn't do right by her like they could. I cleaned up and got my commercial license. But truck driving was one of the first things taken over by the AIs. I started doing construction. Good guys there. They called me Mama. They all said I talk too much. Then the goddamn robots took all the jobs and the goddamn AI took over the world. Then the war. Then the pods. Me and Christina made up, and she spent a lot of time with me in the tangle. She was all fancy and spoke so good and was smart. And so beautiful. I was never that beautiful, not even close, not even before the drugs. And she already did an olympic and everything. She was going to do a third one too. I'm so proud of her. So, anyways, now I smash things. And I'm good at it too. I haven't got hurt too bad yet, but when I do I have some healing pills ready. Maybe they'll grow back my teeth. You know if they do?"

Holy moly! This lady is nuts. But I like her. "I don't know, sorry." I wish she didn't call Mia an AI. Mia was the only person that was always nice to me my whole life. My only real friend. I miss her so much. And she didn't take over the world. She just helps people. People like me that didn't have a lot of friends.

"Eh, I'll find out some day I guess. Probably sooner than I'd like. So what happened to the premier? Bruno kill him? I hope so. I hate those UN bastards. And no, I'm not a terrorist. I just liked when the US was the US. That was quite some show Bruno put on. Wow, that is talent. He's good. Too bad he's married. Although we've been hearing since we got to this area that don't mean too much to him. Do you think he is really from 2009? You should tell Bruno that not everyone from the pods are weak. Victor was in a pod. I'd like to see them fight. Victor is fast. Can hardly see what he is doing. And I was still pretty strong when I got in here. I'm much stronger now, but I wasn't, like, pathetic or nothing. Not like his messages make it out to be. Sorry, I know I talk too much. I can't help it. It's just how I am. You here to train?"

"Yes. To the training. I'm here to train. I forget the other questions." I wish she wasn't a filthy sympathizer, but I still like her.

"Ha, I forgot them too."

3.6 STARS AND BIRDS

KIM GUM

Jeez, my wrists are killing me. And Bruno's mad at me too. For what? Am I supposed to be some sort of psychic that can change dice rolls? I just got an unlucky roll and a trap went off. How is that my fault? My skill is the same exact as his. It's not like I can do anything different. I just use the skill on the trap and get a die roll.

Or maybe it's because it took me two tries on the psuchesoma? Could be. I'm not doing so hot in this dungeon. But he did the psuchesoma last time and it looked easy. It was a dex one again. You have to avoid balls that are being lobed at you. He made it look easy. I got hit quick on the first one. But I did the second one. But no true-blue after that. So the trap doesn't even matter that much.

Bruno also seemed pissed when we got our first magic weapon. It was a minor fire light mace. It does 1 extra fire damage per hit, requires level 2. He got mad at me when I said I thought everything magic besides skill increases was only level 7. I guess that's for only enhancements. Minor effects can be on level 2 items. Lesser on 7, full at 12, major at 17, and burst at 22. Lesser does 1d2, full is 1d3, and major is 1d4. Burst is 1d4, but also multiplies the damage on critical hits depending on the multiplier. X2 multiplier would do 2d4, x3 would do 3d4, and x4 would do 4d4. Vampiric weapons are either lesser, major, or burst. Lesser does 1 untyped damage and heals you for 1. Major does 2 untyped damage and heals you for 2. Burst does the same as major, but with the critical multipliers. Bruno said his weapon will be vampiric when he can buy from raid gear. Mine will be too.

No one in the city can make magic weapons or armor yet. You need a mage to do something to the items to make them magic. The people in the city are already real high level since they don't have stupid areas blocking them from leveling. I forget the exact levels, but almost everyone was over level 10. His wife was the lowest level, because of her class. The three kids were trying to out-level each other, blowing through levels and grinding all the time. But they'll hit a wall soon, as they'll need mats you can only get from dungeons. And they don't like that we can't help them much now. We both have tinker for our hobby, and we both downgraded our craft and took porter as a profession. But that is capped at rogue level. Fighter didn't give us a craft. So, even at level 30, with 8 rogue levels plus the 10 epic levels, porter will be capped at 18. It won't increase our carry weight all that much in the grand scheme of things, but more is always better.

That reminds me – I need to do repairs. Bruno gets mad when I don't. And I need to do good at this boss to redeem this run. At least we aren't staying in after the boss this time. I will definitely need to sleep. I'm tired. Bruno says he is exiting right away though. I should have napped before coming in here. My wrists are really killing me.

Victor and Christina had us do wrist exercises. Like, forever. Christina's forearms are like rocks. She looks soft. It's weird. How can you be so pretty and look so soft but actually be tough? I tried showing Christina some holds and defenses, and it was fun, but I could tell she didn't take it seriously. We did more laughing than grappling. But then Bruno came over. I think he just wanted to do some arenas with Victor, but a big crowd gathered and wanted to see them duel. Bruno said it wasn't fair, and that Victor wasn't used to fighting anyone using shields, and it wasn't going to be a good fight. But Victor wanted to duel too, so Bruno did. It wasn't close. Victor's speed and footwork and moves counted for nothing. Everyone thought Victor would dominate. Flashing in and out, fake attacks, real attacks and then fly somewhere else. Bruno just blocked and stood there. As soon as Victor committed, Bruno bowled him over with his shield. HP shield or no, someone as big as Bruno is going to put you on the ground. You can't do that to game mobs though, the ones from fourth age. None of them. Not without using a trip attack and some sort of check. And trying to run at them and bowl them over would be considered a bull rush. Regular physics doesn't apply to them. And I guess a lot of the mobs that were converted in get the feat that doesn't let them get knocked down. The ones with four legs mostly do. And a lot of the humanoids are just too heavy to bat around like that. They weigh like a million pounds.

So, after that, Victor and Bruno just sparred. Forever. They both have the same thing in their mind where they have to go and go and go until they win. Victor probably wasn't used to losing. He was doing much better at the end. They also did the duo arena and they explained some stuff, and how you could do good against non-fourth age, regular size and weight humanoids avoiding the grapple and trip system and just using physics. They danced around the mobs as they explained and showed some stuff.

Mama gave me the impression Victor was a real jerk, but he seemed like a real good guy. Just intense. Like Bruno. With less of a sense of humor, too. But fencing seems like high-class, fancy stuff so maybe Victor is just used to being around fancy hoity-toity types. Christina liked to laugh and smile. I think she has a crush on Bruno. At least she stared at him a lot. Both Victor and Christina started taking hand-to-hand fighting more seriously once Bruno and Victor stopped doing arenas. We all did a 4-man, but didn't make much progress. And we did a 5-man with Mama too. We didn't do great. Those were the only two arenas I did with Bruno. I did a bunch with Mama. She's pretty good. We'd didn't do so great together though. Man, can that lady yap.

Victor and Christina dueled once. They used some dumb rules I forget the name of. The rules were to make the fight more even since Victor has a longer reach. Fencing duels make no sense. I guess there are three types of fencing. Foils, sabers, and I forget the last one. Real weird names. Victor said he would rather use a saber but they don't have them in this game. The fight was so fast you couldn't tell what was going on. Fun to watch though.

Bruno and Victor made some decent progress in the duo and when they grouped with the best we had in our zone for the 4-man and 5-man. That made me kind of sad. Victor is going for some class called duelist. Christina is going to be a shadow dancer. They changed their original plans and builds after Bruno's first messages. Mama is one of the paladins. I forget which one. I figured she was a fighter. She looks more like a fighter than a paladin in my head.

We also got another really good person in our zone. An archer. Well, a ranger, but she is an archer in real life. She isn't great at fighting but can really shoot a bow like there is no tomorrow. She isn't too good in the solo arena, but she shines in a team with people keeping her safe. She is really skinny and athletic looking, even if she is old, so you would think she wouldn't suck so bad at not getting killed. Anyways, the level 10 boss in all arenas is this giant humanoid thing with, like, a deer head and red eyes and giant goat horns. He looks awesome. I wish I looked like that. His muscles are ridiculous. Just humongous muscles. And his feet are hooves. Once he gets to half HPs it's just a dps check to get him down super quick. Tora Hige and Ryu Jin's group already beat 10 in solo and duo. Bruno was stuck on him. Still is for the solo. His damage is too low. This is probably another reason he seems angry.

At half HP the deer-head guy shoots a laser beam out of his eyes. It hits the person closest and stays on them. Bruno has real high fort saves, but it does a ton of checks and when you lose the roll it lowers con, so lowers fort saves until your con is gone and you lose your shield. When your shield is gone it starts doing actual damage to you until you die. And it does that quick. Then it moves the laser to the next closest person and does it again, then the next person until everyone is dead. And when it's shooting the laser beams it gets temp HPs when it takes con or does damage. And when the target's HP shield is gone the deer monster gets a ton of temp HPs because it does so much damage so fast. And the laser beams don't stop until the monster deer thing has no HP shield left. And when it loses its HP shield it does a big AoE. And can still fight decent after still, so that doesn't mean the fight is won.

Bruno couldn't do the boss with Victor in duo, but he could with Ellen. Is Ellen her name? Irene? No, Elena. I think Elena. Elena basically dies when a mob looks at her. She sucks at avoiding damage, but she can really pump it out. She shoots like a million times a second. Well, not that much, but she shoots real fast. Really, really fast. All hits at full AB. And her AB is high. So they managed 10 together in duo. She did it with a bunch of people to get them past it. She didn't get to me, but I was promised she would next between dungeons. Bruno is going to the city, but enough good people will be left for me to make some progress in the 4 man.

They also got to the same spot as Tore Hige and Ryu Jin in the 5-man. Level 3 fight 6. There are these six ghost-like mobs. We already fought them in a dungeon in area 3. But they are super buffed up in the 5-man. Imported mobs don't have spells I guess. They have SLAs. Spell-like abilities or something like that. I forget why, but SLAs are worse for some reason. Maybe it's because they're higher level spells? Well, when we fought them in an area 3 dungeon, they had a level 4 spell. Slow. Like haste, slow is a level 4 spell in fourth age. They also had only like a 10% miss chance from whatever that is called. Concealment? In the 5-man, they have 50% miss chance from concealment, and power word kill as an SLA. So you are at full HPs, and then at zero in the blink of an eye. They also phase out then phase back in behind you and backstab you a bunch. If you have more than 100 HPs power word kill doesn't do anything. But no one will be at 100 HPs for a long, long time. Those ghost things just slaughter everyone. It's pretty funny to watch.

I never did beat the level 8 boss in solo. I will next time I'm out. And I'm definitely sleeping for a while when this boss in here is down. I could use some me-time anyways. Well, me-and-Joey-time. I'm going to sleep for a week. I feel like I could, at least.

Finished with tinkering, as healed up as I can be, I turn to Bruno, who is giving me a mean look. I say something that put a smile on his face last time I said it, before he fought those three guys.

"Let's go you dumb, black son of a bee."

"Dumb, huh?"

Well, that didn't put a smile on his face. "I mean big, dumb...no! Big, black. I meant big, black. You know I don't pay attention good."

"You sure don't. And please stop saying that. I don't call you cracker all the time."

"Why would you call me cracker? Because of my cankles?"

"Jesus, what is it with you and cankles? No, because you're white."

"I am? What kind of crackers are white? Oh, the soup kind?"

"How do you not know what color you are?"

"I don't know."

"Jesus, you're a weird kid."

"You've been kind of a big jerk since we got in here, you know?"

"Yeah...sorry. I'm just annoyed. I shouldn't take it out on you."

"What's wrong?"

"Just adult stuff. I don't know why everyone is mad I killed whats-his-name, the politician guy. He was a di…a jerk."

"He was. Who's mad? I think everyone figured it was going to happen. You don't seem like the type of guy to say you're going to kill someone and then not kill them."

"Doesn't matter. I hate politics. Let's just finish this up and get out of here. But you better be careful with this boss. He's no joke. If you get hurt, I'll kill you."

"Hua, boss. And I won't call you dumb again. That was just a mess-up. I won't call you black neither."

"I don't care if you call me black. I'm black. It isn't an insult. It is just weird to keep mentioning it."

"You got it, you big son of a bee."

That got a smile. Guess it's time to do this stupid boss. He's just standing in his area, like a dummy. Do the mobs think? I wave to the boss. He just stands there. I cross the door threshold into the boss area, Bruno right behind me. It'll close when I start the attack. My wrists really hurt. My forearms too. So sore. Jeez.

Well, no sense putting it off. I walk forward and when in range charge the boss. The big, stupid rhino with snake scales and a giant boulder-club thing. His attacks are easy to avoid, but I can really feel them impacting the ground. Holy moly, I'd hate to get hit by that without a HP shield.

The fight is just by the numbers until a notice he stops. Crap! I didn't see the blinks, but I wasn't looking at his face. Better just play it safe and didi mau away. I go all the way to the trees and stand beside one. And I wait, as focused as I can be, ready to tumble as soon as he starts charging. I think I ran too far away as he has to run closer to me to charge after his jagged rock AoE attack.

I'm pretty nervous. My leg is shaking a little as I start my tumble. I get away though, and didn't get hit. Then I start whittling him down again. I try to pay attention for the blinks, but it's difficult. Paying attention is stupid, especially when it's so easy to notice him standing still, which is also a signal for the same exact thing. I miss the blinks again but start running as soon as I notice him standing still. I run past some trees and bang into an invisible wall and crash to the ground. Crap, crap, crap. Holy moly! Either way I run along the wall I'm not going to make it. I start running left, back to the main area just in case there is another invisible wall to my right, deeper in the forest. Treest I mean. I'm not going to make it. I tumble, hoping that gets me out of the AoE zone.

I barely clear his AoE area. I'm a couple feat past it as I get to my feet and look back. I'm a couple feet out of the treest, and a couple inches away from the end of his AoE area. I see him start charging. I can't tumble again. It's the same round. Crap! I jump behind the closest tree. Then a big bang and the tree starts coming down at me, so I dive out the way.

As I get to me feet I see Bruno standing behind the boss, but not attacking. The boss is sitting on the ground. You can see stars spinning around his head like in the cartoons when a character gets whacked in the head. Some birds too. Awesome!

Bruno says, "Jesus, Kim, you got to be more careful. Pay attention. Do you got this or do you need help?"

I'm pretty winded so I take some deep breaths and say, "Do you see this? Stars and birds spinning around his head?"

"I see it."

"I got this. Should I lead him to charge trees again? This is awesome. I figured this out. You didn't know about this, did you?"

"Just do it the way we trained. Don't get cute or inventive. And pay attention, goddamn it."

"Hua," I say as I get behind the boss and start stabbing. After a couple seconds he starts getting up. Jeez, if Bruno didn't yap so much

352

I could have done a ton of damage when he was down. My hits where landing easier and I was getting sneak attack damage too. He probably counted as flat footed or something.

The rest of the fight goes by the numbers. I'm high-speed and a hard charger. I had a hard time puncturing the rhino's snake scales once the HP shield was down, and I could tell Bruno was disappointed I'm not stronger yet. Loot sucked. We got a healing kit that will go on the AH. It isn't ID'ed yet but it has to be a +1 kit. We also got a ring I took. No rush to ID. It will almost definitely be just a stupid +1 to some stupid skill I probably don't even have. I'll put it on Bruno's AH thingy.

Bruno stays to sleep before visiting the city. I didn't get smoked but we both did some PT, focusing on upper body strength. Which stunk because my wrists and forearms are so sore they might fall off. We had to run too. Nothing too bad.

When we are settling down for sleep Bruno says, "I got to tell you something. Please keep this between us. Hua?"

"Hua."

"Butterball and Ball-face caught me in a lie. You know how I like to use movie quotes? Well I used some Butterball knew came out after 2009. MacGruber was one. I forget the other. MacGruber came out in 2010. I guess it became a series way later, too. Man, I wish I could watch it. That movie is awesome. What was the other movie? Observe and report? No. I think it was the campaign. But a ton of good movies came out right before I lose my memories. The watch, Ted, the dictator, that Adam Sandler one with the young kid from hot rod that does the funny songs too. That Eddie Murphy one where he couldn't talk. You ever see golden child?"

"Why would you lie?" Bruno doesn't seem like the lying type. More the brutally honest even if it hurts your feelings type.

"I didn't. Not really. My family really is from 2009. For some reason I can remember all the way up to 2012. I don't know why. I don't know why I'm here, or how I got here, or why I don't remember nothing after 2012. Or why it's 2009 for my family.

"The 2009 thing is crazy enough on its own. And me coming back from the future here. I would have rather not said nothing about 2009 or 2012, but that politician forced my hand. It wasn't really a lie. I just didn't want to get into it.

"Well, they wanted me to prove I wasn't lying. You'd think it would be easy with all this magic around, but it isn't. There isn't a detect lie spell. They talked to some dork that knows a lot about the game this place is based on. He mentioned a couple spells that ain't in the game, like commune with your god, or something, for clerics. They tried a spell called suggestion, but it didn't make me want to answer at all. Closest the kid said might work is a level 6 spell called dominate person. But dominate person only allows you to use simple commands on real people. Like stay or attack. It can't force a real person to tell the truth. And I guess it only worked on the fake people in the game if they had a scripted answer to a question. And the scroll cost like 1,600 gold and isn't guaranteed to activate for anyone anyways since it's level 6. And I ain't too keen on letting nobody use dominate person on me even if they could.

"So, can't say I blame them. It's hard to swallow. But it is what it is."

Of course I trust this big dummy. I give him my best smile and say, "Don't worry. I trust you. I'm with you to the end. No matter what."

For some reason he makes a pained face. Like that hurt him. What did I do now?

He says, "Well, that's dumb. What if I was a pedo or a serial killer? You better turn on me, and quick, if you find out I'm either of those.

And I'm a politician. We lie. About everything. Only an idiot would ever trust a politician."

I give him another smile and say, "Well, I love you, you big lug. And I trust you. Probably always will."

3.7 FAMILY NAME AND LEGACY

BRUNO VAZ

Well, this trip to the city has sucked so far. Minnie is stressing about a bunch of nonsense. Like schools, trash and trash pickup, mining, salaries for teachers, blah, blah, blah. Things I don't know how they worked last time. The UN is really stressing her out. She's been talking to the other wives too much. One thinks the UN is awful, the other loves it. But both are telling her I'm a dead man once the UN gets to the city. I told her I have a plan. I real doozy. And told her not to worry. But she is mad because I won't tell her the plan and don't care about organizing anything. Yap, yap, yap, question, question, question. Ridiculous.

She wouldn't even let me bang her until I answered a million questions. So I had no choice but to try and answer her nonsense. Goddamn women and their questions.

And the other ladies were driving me nuts. Nah's wife stopped being flirty. And Vlad's wife is being a wicked big bitch. During training she tried telling me I don't know what quick twitch muscles are. Every single one of my muscles is a quick twitch. Every single one. She said quick twitch muscles don't work that way. Talking about fibers and nonsense. Like she would know. Tubby whore. I asked if she was a doctor or something. She said yeah. She has a phd. Not even in nothing real. Some made up crap.

People with phds that want to be called doctors should be shot. Useless ingrates. Oh, you studied useless nonsense for a long time that helps no one. Wow! If you don't have patients and you can't help when someone is bleeding, you ain't no doctor. Period. No one calls lawyers doctor, and they have a doctorate. Same with pharmacists and a million other professions like it that are way more helpful and useful than the phds wanting to be called doctor. Phds are filth. Scum of the earth. Almost as bad as lawyers. Even lawyers have the basic decency not to want to be called doctor. You know how evil you got to be to not even be as decent as a lawyer?

Her son is a good kid though. I think he has at least one quick twitch muscle. If he touches my daughter I will destroy him.

I went with most of them to the crafting node zone things to protect them from the mobs. Spent a ton of time doing that. The mobs there are pathetic. So easy to kill it's insane. And those sissies have a hard time doing it. Man.

Now I'm just waiting on my son to show up, so we can have a talk. While waiting I work on my grip, do push-ups, and what I call head-ups. You lie on your back and do push-ups with your head. It strengthens the neck. Thinking about why me and my daughter grew apart, and if I can do anything to stop that. We used to be tight. She loved hanging out with me. Loved doing jujitsu and gymnastics, and then she just stopped wanting to. Got into dumb crap like cheerleading and home work. Stuff that will never help her in life. Not like jujitsu at least.

I bet my father was part Gorilla. I never understood why people get mad when they get called Gorilla. My biggest goal in life is to be more like one. Look more like one. There's no man alive I'd be scared to fight. But fight a Gorilla? Jesus. Those things are beasts. Probably roll me up into a ball real quick. They look so awesome. Majestic. King of the jungle. Way more so than lions. I wonder if I'm part lion, too.

Probably not. People humping lions would be weird. I find it hard to believe any women wouldn't want to hump a Gorilla. They all say they don't want to, but come on? That's how you have strong babies. Superior babies.

I took a test once about bone density. They said my bones are the densest bones they ever saw. Way more dense than Neanderthals. Or almost as dense. Something like that. That probably means I have way more Neanderthal DNA than anyone has ever had since the caveman times. So, how do you get Neanderthal DNA? Gorillas is how. I bet the Neanderthals didn't go extinct. They just bread with giant monkeys and made Gorillas. Gorillas are way more superior than regular humans.

I'd bet a million dollars my father is part Gorilla. It really is the only thing that explains why I am the way I am. Why I'm so superior to all the other people. He's got to be. No way my dad is a normal Cape Verdean.

On my fifth set my son shows up.

He says, "Dad, I put a ton of new stuff on the AH! Sergey and I are going to make bank!"

"Nice. Any chance I can get you to cut my hair?"

"Oh. I thought you wanted something else. But sure. Definitely."

"There is something else. For after."

We set it up and get to cutting. Just talking about nonsense until he says he prefers being called Nathan now. I say, "Please, please don't do that."

"Why?"

"Because it's super gay and ridiculous. No one normal ever wants to be called by their full first name if it's long and can be shortened. It's like yelling out to the world, 'Hey world, I'm a pretentious prick and a narcissist!'"

358

"That is the dumbest thing I ever heard, dad. Almost everyone famous goes by their full first name. It's classy. Mature."

"No it isn't. Joe Lewis. Joe Frasier. Joe DiMaggio. Abe Lincoln. Jackie Robinson. Mike Ty..."

"Jackie Robinson made his name longer. His name is Jack. Jack Roosevelt Robinson. What did you think Jack was short for?"

"I don't know. Jaqueline? No one knows because full first names are dumb."

He laughs and says, "No, dad. You're the dumb one." Not meanly. Just joking around.

"You're lucky you're cutting my hair right now or I'd put you in a headlock until you admit I'm right."

"Well then I'd die because I can't admit you're right when you are so, so very wrong."

"I told your mother we should've raised you guys in Mass so you would think civilized and know civilized things. Instead, you were raised in hillbillyville, and have a savage mind with savage barbarian thoughts like wanting to be called Nathan."

"You are such a ridiculous person. You're the only barbarian I know."

"You're not one of those nuts that think tomatoes are fruits, are you?"

"You mean those nuts that believe in science?"

"That's all I believe in is science. Are you saying pasta sauce is a fruit sauce? Fruit is something you can put on desserts and cereal. You dice up tomatoes and put them on cereal and ice-cream? Is that science? You say I'm the ridiculous one – listen to the garbage coming out of your mouth."

"Ha. It has nothing to do with desserts or sauce, dad. It has to do with classification and I think seeds or something."

"So you just believe what some idiot tells you because he wears a lab coat and glasses? It's just seeds? It has nothing to do with taste and what they go with? Didn't the scientists say Pluto isn't a planet no more, too?"

"It isn't. It is too small. It is a…dwarf planet? I think. If Pluto is a planet then there are a bunch more planets in this solar system."

"If you can fly a rocket to it and walk on it, it's a planet."

"You can do that to a large meteor or comet, dad."

"I can do that to your face."

He sighs and rolls his eyes and says, "Sure, dad. I'm done with the hair. Want me to shave you?"

"Yeah, I won't say no. And thanks. Hey, what about you? When you shaving that caterpillar off your lip?"

His eyes go wide. "Oh! Do you think I need to? Does it look ugly?"

"No. It's still wicked light."

When he finishes up I thank him again and say, "Let's go for a walk, Nate. I got something I wanted to talk to you about?"

His eyes get wide with fright. "Did mom tell you? I can explain."

"No, she didn't tell me nothing. What is it?"

"It isn't anything, really. No big deal. Just forget I said anything. Please."

"Sure." I want this talk to go good so I don't say nothing. And Nate never does anything bad so I know it really isn't a big deal. It will just be some queer-ass girly nonsense I really don't care about.

We start walking east to loop down south. Still no fake people in town. NPCs. There were tons last time. I hate change.

"I'm going to tell you something but it has to stay between you and me. Is that okay?"

"I guess so, dad. But please don't tell me about other women. I know you don't think so, but that really hurts mom. It's not cool, dad."

"No. No. Nothing like that. Well…no. Nothing. You know how everyone here is from the 2040s?"

"Yes."

"And you and your sister and mom don't remember nothing beyond 2009?"

"Why did you leave yourself out?"

"Because I remember more. Not at first. When we first got here together, last time, I only remembered to 2009. But then I started remembering more. Quick too. After, like, I don't know, less than a week, I started having a few memories. Then they all just started coming. In a couple days I got all my memories back. And my memories go up to 2012. I haven't got more than that. But when I got here I was wearing clothes I had from 2012."

Nate doesn't say anything. Just looking at me. Waiting for me to continue.

"Back then, later in 2009, me and your mother split up. I won't get into details, but you and Siri sided with ma. But me and you made up, you went to school in New York, and you had a boyfriend. A cop. A detective. Good guy. Wasn't gay at all. Couldn't even tell he was a homo by just talking to him."

"Dad! How many times do we have to go over this? Gay and homosexual are synonyms. They mean the same, exact thing! What did he look like?"

"No, they aren't the same. Most straight guys are wicked gay. Gay just means feminine. Some homos, like your old boyfriend, just aren't that gay. Well, besides the homo part. Being a homo is wicked gay."

He rolls his eyes. It usually drives me nuts when guys claiming to be straight roll their eyes. It's just so feminine. Even more feminine than calling a blanket a blanky, or saying comfy instead of comfort. Or a guy calling a puppy adorable. You can't get more feminine than my super gay son so it makes sense that he does it.

I continue, "And he was good looking. Looked tough. Looked like he could protect you good. Lot older than you though. You was 18, he was close to 30. Like 28 or something. He was crazy about you. Real proud to be with you, you know what I mean? Puerto Rican, I think. One of the types of Mexicans." I just say that to get Nate going. He hates when I say stuff like that. So I do it more to get him going. I speak Spanish, and I've been to a ton of central and south American countries. Spent tons of time there. Well, kind of speak Spanish. Enough to pass the DLAB to join the Special Forces, before I got recruited for Delta. I only kind of speak English and that is the language I'm best at. I only kind of speak Cape Verdean Creole, and Portuguese too. Language isn't my forte. I'm worse at Spanish, but still do decent. I can make my way with Italians if we go slow. French is just silly. How is that grouped with the others as a romance language? The ones based on Latin. I think someone told me there are others too. One was…what? Romanian?

"Dad! Stop! Ew…you're just doing this to make me angry. Why do you do this?"

I start laughing. He is so easy to get going. I love it.

He hits me in the shoulder. "Stop."

"Okay, sorry. Well, you started doing this thing. A lot of times when you'd go out, you'd dress like a girl and go by the name Candy Vase. But spelled V.A.S.E. You'd pronounciate it the same as our real last name though."

"Enunciate."

"Whatever. You'd do that though. And you got a lot more girly even when you weren't dressed like a girl. How you acted, you know?" He looks surprised, but not the right kind of surprised. "You already know that name, don't you? Already thought of it?"

He looks down and takes a moment, but finally says, "Yeah. What was the school? Was it NYU?"

"Yeah."

"I knew it!" He smiles.

"I know you already know the name because last timeline, I didn't say nothing to you about any of that, and you knew the name still."

"I started cross-dressing?"

"Kind of. You want the full story? It isn't good. Doesn't make me look good."

"Definitely. Please. The full story, please."

"Okay. Just remember – I love you. I'll always love you. Nothing you could do would ever make me not love you. I'll always side with you and always, always be there for you. You know that, right?"

"I know that, Dad. I love you too. Very much."

"Well, we all took the path to the city last time. I went over this before, remember? You love rpgs, yadda, yadda. You know, there is something in the military called an rpg. Nothing like this or those games you love. Well, anyways, there was this kid you liked. He didn't look that gay, besides his hair. Long, flowing locks. And he'd always tuck his hair behind an ear all super gay and roll his eyes. He couldn't stand me. But you were head-over heels about this kid.

"And he was into you. But you wouldn't do nothing about it. When I was your age all I wanted was to bang. It's hard with girls. You have to put effort into it. Really, really try wicked hard. Once in a great while, life throws you a bone and an easy girl shows up, but that ain't normal. Homos have it so easy. If I was a homo I'd be destroying butts all day, especially when I was your age. Just ripping them apart like there was no tomorrow. No homo within 10 miles of me would be able to walk right. That's the best thing about being a homo. It's easy mode.

"But not for you. You have the mind of a girl from the olden times. I don't get it. You're a male with the sexual morals of an old-school nun. Or, I didn't get it until last timeline. I was giving you a hard time about being such a prude, and we got into a big fight. A real big one. And you stopped talking to me for a while. Then you started dressing as a girl and wanted everyone calling you Candy. And I got to say, you're an amazing daughter. Chaste, responsible, and a mind that can't be figured out.

"You know you and that detective? He said you were waiting for marriage. And he didn't mind waiting. What kind of guy wants to wait for marriage? On purpose? Zero. Zero kinds of guys want to wait for marriage. It never happened in history, not by choice at least. Some guys are willing to wait for the right girl they fall head-over heals for. Willing to, not want to.

"And that's how this all makes sense. You have a girl brain. You flourish as a girl. You'd be the best daughter a father could ever hope for. Does that make sense?"

I'm having a hard time reading him through what I just said. He kind of just froze, looking kind of nervous and uncomfortable. Still does. He finally says, "But I'm not a good son?"

Damn. I was hoping he would be like, "Yeah! I want to be a girl!," and we'd move on, both happier and more content.

"You're a great kid and you have one of the kindest hearts of anyone in the world. Of any time. Nothing you could ever do would make me not love you. I like you as a person and I love you as a son. You know I don't mind you being a homo, but…it is kind of annoying how gay you are. If this is how you always were, I wouldn't mind at all. We'd always be pals, and I'd always have your back with everything. You just seem more happy as a girl. That's what trannies are about – being so gay you actually cross over into the other side. Or for girls, so straight they cross over to become a man."

"You shouldn't say trannie. Its transgendered."

"What is?"

"The correct word."

"I thought it was transsexual."

"No. It is definitely transgendered. Tranny is considered a slur."

"Really? That's dumb. Shortening words should be standard for everything. But I won't argue about it. I know how you get about stuff like that. You mad at me?"

He takes a moment to answer, making me think he is not happy at the least. "No. It's just that…I…wish you'd just accept me for how I am."

"What are you talking about? Of course I accept you. When have I not accepted you?"

"You just…ew, you don't even try to understand. Like how I am with boys. I don't want cheap or meaningless. I want love. Real love. And to be cherished. I want a life partner. Forever. How can you not understand that?"

"Because it makes no sense. You're a Vaz. We crush it. That's what we do. Pursuing snatch was like 90% of my life at your age. Love? Being cherished? That is girl brain stuff. How could I understand?"

"You don't even try."

"Look, we have different minds. We think different. Even most guys don't think like I do with most things. I am how I am and you are how you are. Can you understand why I like what I like and do what I do? I'm guessing you can't. How could I understand the opposite of how I think? My goal is to love and support you and always be part of your life. This talk wasn't supposed to make you mad, and I'm sorry if it did. This was supposed to just let you in on something I thought would make you more happy. You know what I mean? And I'm sorry there is lots of things I don't understand. I'm old. And my T levels are off the charts. That probably impacts how I think. Just know I love you and I'm with you no matter what you do with what we talked about."

"I know, dad. I love you too, but you can really drive me nuts."

"I get that a lot." We both laugh.

We hug. Then he holds my hand. I can't remember the last time Siri held my hand other than the when I first got to the city this timeline and she was scared. Maybe when she was twelve? Thirteen? Past a certain age, holding hands just makes you uncomfortable. As a father. Mothers can probably always do it. But a father holding hands with his fifteen-year-old son is wicked weird. I try not to show I'm uncomfortable or feel awkward. I just stand there, silently holding my fifteen-year-old son's hand, thankful no one is around to see us.

I would burn down the world to keep him safe. I love him. Hopefully, soon, I can change that to I love 'her.' And not be embarrassed if people see me hold his hand, because it will be her hand. And a father holding his fifteen-year-old daughter's hand probably isn't 100% normal, but it isn't as weird and uncomfortable as this. I was so happy when I had a son. Someone to carry on my name and legacy. Always figured when he was around Nate's age we'd be banging whores together, or getting in bar fights. Normal father and son stuff like that.

3.8 TRUE GRIT

KIM GUM

Bruno was cool the whole time we were in here, but now that we're about to leave again he's turned back into a moody jerk. He worries too much. Just relax, big guy. He always thinks everyone's planning and plotting something. Like that sign my mom had up in her dojang about worry. Something about having the wisdom to know what to worry about and what is out of your control? How did it go?

Dang, I forget. Oh well. It was a good one. I wish I could remember it better so I could tell it to Bruno.

Maybe he's mad that I got a magic weapon now and he still doesn't have one. Ha, ha. That's what you get for being such a moody jerk. Minor sonic spear. Got it in this dungeon off the level 5-5 boss. Nice! Does 1 extra sonic damage per hit. And as soon as we leave this dungeon – level 6 baby. True grit here I come. One more level until we can get +1 weapons and armor and +1 dodge and saves and all that stuff.

Everything was going great till it was close to time to leave. Bruno says I'm getting good. And getting stronger. He promoted me from a crap-bird to a novice. Except he didn't say crap-bird. He used the bad word. I wish he wouldn't do that. Another sign in the dojang, one I kind of still remember, says something like if you can't be interesting without profanity then you're not interesting. Something like that. We're the good guys, kind of like superheroes, and superheroes don't swear. Or, they shouldn't at least. I'm the darkness and I don't swear. Bruno says he'd try not to, but he still does a lot. I wish he'd try harder.

I guess I should try and cheer him up before we leave so he doesn't ruin the excitement of leveling up. He's the one that should be excited. We're finally getting the true grit feat! He's the one that said it was so good. Stupid, party-pooping, jerk.

As we're packing up I say, "Did I do something wrong?"

"No. Why?"

"You seem mad at me."

"What? That's crazy. You've been doing great. Your thrust is getting real powerful. I can feel it a wicked lot when blocking. And you're becoming a real terror with some grapples. It's really all coming together for you. Remember? I promoted you."

"Thanks. I hate grappling though. Why do we do it so much? You said real fighters just stand there and punch each other till one goes down."

"You got to. At least learn the blocks and escapes so it's second nature. I hate that crap too. But you got to know it. You said you'd watch old MMA fights with your family. Did you ever see that one with what's-his-name? Fry? The mustache guy versus the Japanese guy. Takitaki?"

"Yeah. Don Frye. Um, um, Takayama. Yeah."

"They go in the clinch and just start whaling on each other. That's how real men do it. That's how real men fight. I love that stuff. It really gets the old juices flowing, huh?"

"Yeah. My parents loved that fight. We'd watch it a lot."

"Before the MMA there was the UFC. It started around ninety-two or nighty-three. I was at Bragg or Benning. Either in the 82nd or 3rd bat. I thought about getting out again and fighting in it. I didn't because of Gracie. Joyce Gracie, with his dumb mounts and rear naked chokes and his damn homoerotic humping. UFC could have been great if it wasn't for that wrestling crap. Turned the UFC into gay porn. MMA too. Since then everyone has to know how to be a gay porn star to fight good, or some sissy will get you in an arm bar and break your arm. Man, imagine if there was a fighting league where you just stand there and whale on each other. That'd be awesome."

"You mean like boxing?"

"No, dummy. Boxing has a million rules. I mean no rules other than you stand there and whale on each other."

"Oh, yeah. I'd watch that. But it sounds like boxing."

"Goddamn it, Kim! Not boxing. No rules other than just standing there and whaling. No footwork. No moving your feet. If you can clinch and push the head down, rabbit punch all day. No kicks or knees. Just whaling. Throwing punches. No elbows either. Just hands. Does that sound like boxing?"

It sounds close to it, but I throw him a bone. "Oh, I get it. No, that's nothing like boxing. You're right. You excited about getting true grit?"

"True grit is awesome. Magic is stupid. Our fort saves just go up and up as we level and max con. Not having to worry so much about will saves is fantastic for helping us kill real good. But that ain't nothing. Just wait until we hit epic levels and max out our coins so we can reroll. I haven't told you about our final class, have I?"

"No. I really like this build though. What we have now."

"This is good for leveling. For helping us not miss out on dungeon coins, but our final class will blow your teeny-tiny monkey-mind. Want to hear about it? You can't tell no one though. People will go for it before they have the dungeon coins to make it shine. They'll just mess it up. I'll email everyone before I reroll about the details. You promise to keep your mouth shut?"

"Well, first, my mind is humongous. Your mind is the teeniest-tiniest mind ever. And it's less than a monkey mind. It is a chipmunk mind. A little, cute chipmunk mind."

"Ha. Sure. You promise, though?"

"I promise."

"You know the tree race?"

"Obvitate? Yeah."

"No, spriggan."

"Sprijan. They are an obvitate. Like a golem, but different. More alive. Made by the edilyns to protect them. Right?"

"I don't know. I like women. But the tree guys, their special class is bounty hunter."

"Yeah, that's what I was saying. The obvitate bounty hunter. They suck, don't they? The gadgets they get are all gimmicky, right? Can't even get healed."

"No. Well, they can get healed. It's just reduced, and that's just magic healing. Natural healing, like regen, works just fine. They can even get trapfinding if they pick no armor as their armor focus. But that would be nuts. If you go light armor focus, you get all the two-weapon fighting feats rangers do without needing dex, but you don't even have to wear light armor. Rangers have to wear light armor for the feats to work. Not the bounty hunter.

"But the big thing is they can get that copy or decoy SLA. What-ever it's called. Where they make two of them. No one does it because the copy sucks unless you max out useless skills to make it more real and less shadowy. What are they? Disguise is one. Concentration. I forget the other. But I worked it out. It's possible to max out those crap skills without taking a hit on the necessary useful ones. Or much of hit. We'll have to use dungeon coins to get true grit, since we have to go full 20 to get both paragons. Also need to pick up trapfinding and open skills with dungeon coins too. But with all dungeon coins we should be able to max con and str. Almost max con. We'll be at 28 con with the aura bonus and the what's-it-called? Profane bonus from a raid gear set. Or divine or whatever it's called. I think the set we'll get has a profane bonus. And the +4 ability enhancement from raid gear to str and con. Our damage will be crazy. And our AB too. Full BAB.

"And we won't have to waste a ton of feats to make the copy useful like people with animal companions and cohorts have to do. They get all our feats and gear and everything. Goddamn, we'll be unstoppable powerhouses. While the copy lasts. We'll pump out damage. I worked it all out. It should definitely work. I could have messed up, but I think I worked it out real good with no errors or nothing."

Wow! That sounds awesome! And it looks like my plan worked. He isn't worried or mad or nothing anymore. I am amazing! "I can't wait, boss!"

"Yeah, well, that's a ways off. You got everything? Excited about your new spear? Well, you won't have it long. We'll get +1 stuff soon at level 7. Have to buy it from the store though. Guild profits are going to go way down. Until 10. I should start adding mages now, you think?"

"I'm not really sure how crafting magic items work, but sounds good to me."

"Let Joey take as many trays as he wants. It doesn't matter. Your two-tray limit makes no sense."

Yes it does. You need rules. He can get more trays quick. What does it matter? He listens better when he only has two, and Bruno isn't the one getting him to listen. No sense arguing. Especially since I got him to stop being such a grumpy-bumpy.

I go grab Joey and he is taking four trays, looking at me all smarmy. He isn't really, but I can sense the smarmy in him. In my mind. Stupid trays. Two is plenty to bring out, you don't need more than that.

We exit the portal and I start seeing people pop into existence all up and down the dungeon front. I'm looking at the reward popup and see it's a wand of cure disease SL 3. Two potions, but I quickly click out of the window. Something is going on. For a second I'm confused, as I see something. A lot of somethings. Giant insects. Well, not giant. Giant for insects. They're like the size of dogs. Big dogs. Weird looking things.

Bruno kills two of them near us and says, "Goddamn it. This isn't supposed to happen till later. Ew, I hate change. Cover me as I send out an email wicked fast."

"Hua."

No bugs are near us now. They seem to die easy. Not a big threat. People that have made it this far are no slobs, so they react good.

I get a flash of a notification that I received a new message and as I go to open it, Bruno says, "Let's go. Watch Joey." He starts running down the front of the dungeon.

Bringing Joey is slowing us down. Most of the insects close by the dungeon are dead. They seem to be coming out of small mounds further in the zone. I see three giant mounds way in. There could be more and I just can't see them.

Bruno is a good distance in front of us when I hear him yell, "Mel. Can you watch Joey?" He adds in, "Please," as I catch up to him.

Ass-eyes. Yuck. She is acting like this is no big deal. After way too long she says, "I was going to help Michael clear the zone of these…things."

"Who's watching the kids?"

"I was going to take them with."

"Jesus, Mel. Just let Billy and the rest of the group handle it. Just watch the kids. Please. I already emailed about it."

"Well, maybe you should ask first next time. I'm not a slave."

"Okay. Sorry. Listen, this isn't the time for arguing. Please. And don't take the kids further in. The queens are nasty. And the soldiers are no joke. Come on."

She stares at him. After waiting far too long, again, she says, "Fine. But you owe me. We'll discuss what later."

"Sure. Just don't...never mind. Thank you. Let's go, Kim."

We rush towards a mound. On the way, Bruno explains the little mounds have at least one soldier. The big ones have tons of soldiers and a queen. Soldiers will probably be 2(6). Not too bad. Queens will be 4(6) or (7). Approximate, since these were imported monsters. He tells me the weak spots on the soldiers, after the HP shields are gone, are the eyes and neck. Or the lower belly if they get turned over.

After the first mound and our first soldier insect kill, Bruno has me level up on the way. He does too. It reads: True Grit (Prereq: Con 19, Toughness, Weapon Specialization and fighter level 4 or Greater Weapon Specialization; Intestinal fortitude is now your mental fortitude. Your steely resolve and determination have melded together your ability to shrug off attacks to your body and mind, both harmful and beneficial. You now use Fortitude saving throw instead of Will saving throw for attacks against your mind, but you also must overcome your reaction to shrug off beneficial spells and effects besides potions, mundane items such as healing kits, and permanent magical effects from items. Any beneficial spell or spell like effect directed at you requires a successful Fort save to be applied with a target DC of 10 + spell level. Take 10 if not in combat. Does not allow Specialization points)

Nice!

We rush past that mound, not going out of our way to kill workers. Or soldiers either. Just closing little mounds on the way to the first big one. Killing soldiers if it doesn't take us too far out of the way, and workers only if they are right in our path. The workers die quick.

Soldiers aren't that hard. Maybe if they swarmed or something. Or maybe I'm just a lot better now. Probably that. I am the darkness, after all. And Bruno promoted me to novice too. I'm a dagnab killing machine. Praise God!

We get to the first mound, and I'm sucking air hard already. Not the closest mound. Two were closer. One way north and one way south. We ran through the middle to the furthest one. Furthest I could see before. But now I see two more past it. Hopefully that's it. Only five mounds. I can see the 6-6 dungeon on the far-east side of the zone so unless I am dumber than anyone thinks there is only five total big mounds.

Soldiers come rushing out.

I ask, "Shouldn't we wait for more people?"

"Nah. We're good."

Then it gets down to business. And business is good. They do try to swarm, but Bruno keeps an eye on me. Makes sure I don't get overwhelmed. I'm gasping for air when there are still like a million soldier insects left. They kind of look like ants, but not really. Like ant-beetle-rhinos. They have a giant horn on their…nose? But it doesn't have a point. And they don't fight with it. Six legs. And their front legs are super long and armored and they fight with those. And they have pinchers. They look pretty awesome.

I finally get tired enough to lose a step and get hit pretty good. These things hit hard. I'm at somewhere between 60 and 75% HPs from that one hit. Then Bruno swoops in and starts doing what he does best, as he says, "Get behind me. Get your breath back. You're gas tank is garbage. I guess we ain't running and humping enough."

I keep my eye out as I put my hands on my knees and suck air in.

A minute later Bruno starts complaining. "Stupid changes. Anyone who likes change is an idiot. What good is knowing the future if it changes? I will destroy…ew. Ew. Ew."

I start cracking up. I would bet anything he was going to say he would destroy the future or change or something really dumb like that. But stopped himself because it's such a dumb thing to say. Ha.

"What are you laughing at? How fast you run out of gas?"

I get control of myself and say, "You were going to say destroy the future, weren't you?"

"I'll destroy your dumb face. How do you like that? If you can laugh, you can fight. Get back in here, but pace yourself. We'll fight the queen soon. Don't go higher on the mound. Let the soldiers come to us."

We get back to killing. In my case slower. Pacing myself. Controlling my breathing. Making sure strikes to eyes when the HP shields are gone. Neck is too hard. I'd have to bend down and angle it up, while the ant thing's still trying to kill me. The rest of the body is too armored. Bruno can break their...whatever the shell on insects is called. I can too, but it takes a lot of effort and holding the shaft way up high and striking super hard. Going too hard is how I lost my breath in the first place.

Once we can't see any more soldiers on our mound Bruno tells me to drink water, as he does too. I take my armor off to rest and get some HP back, eat some game food that restores 1 HP per round for six rounds, and use my healing kit and repair kit. Almost at full health. Like 90%. Maybe a little over. No use checking the exact number. It is what it is. One charge left on my healing kit.

Bruno asks, "You ready?"

"Hua."

"Okay. I'll crest the mount first. When the queen sees me, she should agro. You take her back until the HP shield is down. Then the weak points are just like the soldiers, except her belly is giant and exposed. So go for the belly when it's gone. If I'm remembering right, she has a bunch of spells she casts even while using her arms to attack.

But they can be interrupted if we do enough damage. I think. If I'm remembering right she has a ton of mind spells. But that was when these was in a way later zone. Were in, I mean. What level spells are at level 6? Level 3 spells, right? Unless she is 7. Then she gets level 4 spells, right? But since she is important it could be level bazillion spells for all we know. And the higher the group CR the earlier they get spells.

"Stupid spell casters. Anyways, it will probably be, like, sleep, and the laughter one. Oh, the one that lowers intelligence, wisdom, or charisma. Something Idiot? Something like that. Hopefully, not ones that can lower them to zero. That will end our shield. I don't think so though. We shouldn't have to worry since we have true grit now. Even if we didn't, I don't think we'd have to worry. We should be able to take her down quick. Alright, should be easy." Then he starts singing, "Easy like Sunday morning!"

"What?"

"Nothing. It's from a song."

"I love songs."

"Wow! You love songs? That's so rare. Hardly anyone loves songs and music."

"Shut up."

He laughs as he moves out and I follow. As he crests the top of the mound I think he falls down for a second. So I start rushing, then realize he probably charged, so stop rushing so much. I see something weird – a little girl in a yellow raincoat outfit skipping on the other side of the mound. Then she's out of my vision. I shake my head. I must be seeing things. I got to focus and not daydream.

As I crest I see Bruno fighting the queen. She really is giant. Six stubby little legs on a big bulbous thing that looks like a giant sideways drop of water. Big, layered armored boobs on a torso above that, with praying mantis arms. A small head with giant insect eyes, and what looks like a beak. A beak? On an insect?

I charge in and Bruno turns her around. I start on the side and end-up working on her back. Seems easy. Getting a lot of hits so AC can't be that high. Then the will saves start coming in. A lot of them. I make them all. Until I don't. I become frozen. Can't talk or move my body at all. Holy moly! What use is true grit if it doesn't even work?

I can't really see Bruno, but once in a while I can see a flash of foot or part of an arm as he works. Then I don't. Did he get frozen too? Jeez, this isn't good. Crap, crap, crap.

Then I can move again. I move around front, getting in a thrust as I go. One of her arms is coming in at Bruno. I block it with my shield and thrust at her. I take over for Bruno. I go to work. By the numbers. Balls to the wall. I notice all the will saves. Lots of them. Finally the will saves stop and my spear is actually hitting her…whatever the insect shell is called. I dodge an arm and thrust at the belly. It doesn't penetrate, but almost. Just need a little more power behind my thrust.

I dodge an arm and thrust again. It goes in! But not far enough. Then I see movement in my peripheral and Bruno screams as his waraxe sinks deep into the belly. The queen makes a horrible noise and starts flailing her arms wildly. I duck and thrust. Penetrating again. But then I have to move away from the queen's wild swings. Bruno does too.

We move back a little bit. Bruno sees an opening and busts in sinking his axe deep again. I follow soon after with the hardest thrust I can muster. It sinks in pretty deep. Deeper than my other ones. But I don't think it's going in deep enough to matter. An arm is coming down at me, so I yank my spear out and tumble backwards.

As I get my feet I decide to go for the eyes. More damage. I got to pull my weight. I should be able to reach them no problem with my spear. Just got to aim real careful.

Oh. Never mind. Bruno beat me to it. Not the eyes. He got the neck. Real good hit. Green blood spurting out. The queen is stumbling around like she is drunk. Then she collapses. I run up and stab her eye. Just in case. Stupid bug.

Bruno says, "Okay take a rest again. You got any more HP food?"

"Yeah. I got a bunch."

"Can I get a couple? I'm out. I was supposed to go to the city as soon as the dungeon closed. Didn't think I'd need more this soon. I'm saving up for new equipment for level 7."

"Of course." I open trade and place three food in and hit accept.

"Thanks."

We both start a short rest. Eat food. Use our healing kits. Last charge for me. I think Bruno has one more.

He starts talking, "Damn. I'm going to have to start going to the city after day dungeon, instead of dusk. That sucks. Everyone is in the middle of doing their thing during that time. Morning is better. And they're less excited to see me midday. But, in fairness to them, it was just yesterday they saw me. How long were we in that last dungeon? Not 5-5. The last time we did 5-4? Way over a month, right?"

"Was a long time. I don't know exactly."

"What's your HPs at?"

"Almost full."

"I'm like half. No like 60%, two-thirds maybe. Let me check."

I see him take a healing potion. Then he uses a scroll. I'm guessing a healing scroll. Then he uses another. And another.

He says, "Jesus, finally. Eh, good enough. You have any healing scrolls? You should have at least five you can activate pretty easy at all times. Now we got to worry about true grit blocking it too. Not much of an issue with ones we can active though. Be nice when we hit 10 and can use two potions, won't it?"

"Hua. To both. Healing scrolls and level 10. Can't wait. You need any scrolls?"

"No. Thanks though. I got a ton. Next level we'll start getting haste scroll drops. You notice all the spells in the SRD are one level lower than in here? I still can't figure out the low-magic thing, why this say this setting is low-magic. Once you hit level 30 everything you have is +4 and has a permanent magic effect. Crazy, isn't it? If this is low-magic, I wonder what high-magic looks like? Just spells being one level lower? You know what they mean by low-magic?"

"No idea. I was wondering why true grit didn't work though. Is it bugged?"

"Definitely not. It doesn't prevent will saves, just replaces it with fortitude saves. You can still fail, just like with fortitude saves. It's just far less likely now. She was throwing out a ton of crap we needed to save against."

He gets up and climbs out the hole onto the crest. "Jesus, no one's taken the first two mounds yet. Filthy animals. I will destroy them. Do me a favor? Type in guild chat we're taking the south. No, the northeast mound. We'll do two. There should be around a thousand people here. They can get the other three. Just type we got the middle one and will get the northeast one next. And for everyone else to get the other three."

"Hua."

3.9 YOU SURE GOT A PRETTY MOUTH

KIM GUM

Again, I stick my spear through the queen's eye. Just to be safe. I actually got it while she was alive this time. She did not like that. She did not like that one bit. Ha. Ha. Stupid insect idiot.

Bruno didn't get frozen this time. Just me. Or paralyzed. Whatever spell it was. I really got to study the spells more. There're just so many of them. I wish there was zero. So everyone had to fight fair.

I sit down to start resting. I'm still almost full, but I'm spent. That wasn't easy, clearing those two mounds. Just me and Bruno. The darkness and the big guy. Two out of five on our own. The rest of the freeloading sissies better have closed the rest.

Bruno says, "Get up." Jeez, is he angry again. He really needs to relax.

"What's up, tiger?"

"Ha. Tiger. You're a nut. This ain't the time for jokes though. You got to learn to pay more attention. I keep trying to beat situational awareness in your brain, but it don't seem to be sticking. You don't see anything funny?"

I start looking around. Oh. Oh.

Oh no.

Maybe Bruno was right to be so worried and paranoid. A bunch of people are spread out along the crest. One was one of the guys in our guild. Baby-face. Some kind of officer. Something Kim. He has my name. I see another I recognize as an officer. Caster, I think. And William, Ass-eyes boyfriend. Or one of them. Maybe Michael too. I'm not sure who Michael is. Is that…yes it is. It's the number one greataxe guy from the arena. He must have just got here, in this instance. Area 6.

Bruno yells, "We cleared this one guys."

Baby-face yells back, "We know."

"Hi! I'm Vera di Milo!" Bruno says this in a really weird and deep voice.

Baby-face says, "Stop being a fool. We need to talk."

"Oh yeah? About what?"

"About a change in leadership."

"Oh. We'll, I don't like talking."

"We know. And that is one of many reasons we need a change in leadership, you troglodyte."

"I love when hillbillies call me names."

"Hillbilly? I'm from Los Angeles."

"Oh. So even worse. A hillbilly that put on lipstick and a pearl necklace so thinks he's all fancy and civilized now."

"You're a fool. Are you going to call me Baby-face now too? Is looking young supposed to hurt my feelings? You're the villain here. You can call me all the names you want."

"Okay. Since I'm the bad guy, and you're the good guys, you're going to let Kim leave, right?"

What? That is crazy. Before they can reply. I yell out, "I'm not going nowhere."

Baby-face yells down, "Of course. We're not the monsters. She needs help you know?"

Bruno says, "Yeah. She does. Why do you think I took her under my wing?"

"Not your type of help, you mouth breathing neck-beard. Real help, from people that actually care."

His reply to Baby-face is, "Sure, kid. One second."

Bruno comes over to me and takes a knee and whispers, "Listen, Kim. I need you to do something for me. Something that will help me more than anything else. Can you do that?"

"I'm not leaving," I say.

"You don't want to help me?"

"I do! That's why I'm not leaving. I'm not going to leave you. No matter what you say. Together till the end. Remember?"

He smiles, "I remember. But this isn't the end. Not if you do what I ask you to. I really need your help. It will help a wicked lot. Just listen. I need you to rush out of here and find Gunny. But don't say nothing in guild chat. Just find Gunny. If you can't find Gunny at all, and you see major Goodman, tell him. Major Goodman is Ball-face. Your message is tuna fish. Just say tuna fish and they'll know what to do. You'll save the day. You want to save the day, right?"

"Yeah."

"Okay. Gunny. Tuna fish. If you can't find Gunny, tell Goodman. Last option, if you can't find either, is doctor Calderon. Same message. Got it?"

"I got it."

"Is that how you acknowledge an order?"

"Hua. I meant hua."

"You don't sound very motivated. Am I going to have to motivate you later? Smoke your balls off?"

"I don't have any of those."

"Ha. Right. You got more than most guys. I love you, you little knucklehead. If you can remember, tell Gunny I nailed my Vera de Milo impression. Now get going."

"Hua!"

I start running. I start going north but that is dumb, so I head south out of the pit. Crater. Mound. Whatever it is. I need to head to the center of the zone and then west. Heading straight west would have been faster, but stupid fake Kim is there with his idiot traitors. When I get to the crest I look back at Bruno. He seems really relaxed. Hopefully he didn't lie to me. I stare at fake Kim for a second and make a face at him. Stupid jerk traitor idiot. I'll kill him.

As I step down the hill my ankle caves. Ow! As I'm rubbing it I hear Bruno say, "See this?"

I hear fake Kim yell back, "Really? I see it. Is that supposed to impress me? You're so juvenile."

"Don't pretend like you're not impressed. When we're done here, I'm going to use your tonsils like a punching bag for this here monster. You got that?"

"Nice. Threatening sexual assault. You killed a great man. Premier Dalembert was a great leader and a great man. And you murdered him. You…"

Bruno interrupts, "Are you going to yap your pretty little baby lips all day or are we going to get to business at some point?"

"You just don't stop, do you?"

"Nope. You sure got a pretty mouth."

This was getting weird, and I needed to get help quick, so I take off. My ankle isn't sprained. It just hurts a little. Easily walked off. Or ran off. I didi mau as fast as I can. I see activity in the southeast mound, but hardly any ants anywhere. Not even workers. Another crowd is in between the mounds. Hopefully Gunny isn't at the southeast mound, or with the crowd. I doubt Ball-face and Gunny are both there.

I don't see much of anything or anyone until I get close to where we have our usual set up. Closer to 5-5. Groups walking back. Mostly groups. Some big, some small. Some people walking alone. One kind of looks like Gunny's guys. I run up, panty. Searching.

I take a couple deep breaths and yell, "Gunny! Gunny!"

The group stops. Some turn around to look at me. Then I see Gunny. I run up to him, put my hands on my knees as I suck in air, and say, "Tuna fish!"

Gunny looks surprised. Then he yells out, "Sergeant Moore! Sergeant Tomkiewicz! Corporal Green! Come here." Three guys run up. I recognize all three. Gunny seems to change his mind and waves them a little away and walks to them. They all start whispering.

What's he doing? This is an emergency. This is balls to the wall time, not talking time. I say, loudly, "Gunny, we got to go. Now!"

He looks up from his huddle and says, "One second, sweetie."

Holy moly! We don't have time for this. I wait like 10 more seconds then say, "Please, Gunny! Please. He needs us. We got to go now! Please. Help!"

He stands and says, "Okay. Where is he?"

"The far mound. North. The northeast one. Like ten guys. Maybe only eight. Maybe six. Baby-face and the greataxe guy from the arena are there. We got to go, like, yesterday."

He nods at one of the guys with him, who takes off east, yelling to everyone else, "Follow me."

I start running and I feel Gunny's hand on my shoulder, stopping me. "Not you, sweetie. We need to get more people. Tuna fish. Remember?"

This is dumb. We need to go help. About ten guys took off to help Bruno. That's probably enough, but I want to go to. I want to be there. But I promised Bruno I'd do tuna fish. Whatever that is. Gunny, me, and two of his guys follow. I'm not sure of their names. Either Moore, Green, or whatever the other name was.

We move at a hustle. West. Then southwest. Why? Where are we going? I start pulling ahead, leading, even though I don't know where I'm going. But we got to be quicker about it. Are we going to the southwest corner? No part of the camp is ever down here. Who would be down here? And why are they important enough to waste so much time on?

I hit the invisible wall to the south. Probably not far from where the invisible west wall is either. There is nothing here. What is going on?

Gunny walks around me and kneels down. He puts his hand on my shoulder and says, "You're not going to like this. I'm sorry."

I don't know what he's talking about, and I want to ask, but before I can cloth goes over my head, then between my lips. In my mouth. Muffling my screams. Right after, something covers my head, then shoulders, and I'm lifted up. I'm yelling and kicking as hard as I can, but no matter how hard I kick, something finally comes over both my legs and I can't no more. I then feel something being wrapped around me, and then I'm laid on the ground. Filthy traitors! I'll kill every last one of them!

"I'm sorry, Kim. Orders are orders. I'm really sorry. I hope you can forgive me."

I'll forgive never! Forever! Since I'm gagged I can't tell him this. But he is dead! Dead! So dead!

I squirm around and try to get out. It doesn't work. We have the use rope skill pretty high. For our level at least. It isn't helping. It won't even attempt a check. I can't barely squirm around. Or yell.

After a long while I'm too tired to continue. I don't hear anyone or anything nearby. Not making noise at least. Jerks. I'll kill them all!

I can't kneel or talk, so I pray in my head. Dear God. I will get vengeance for this. If Bruno is dead, I will get double vengeance. Ew. I will eat them. In your name, I will eat them!

I know I'm not supposed to ask for nothing, but can you please help me. Not fight. Just help me get out of this. I'll do the fighting. I just need to be let loose. Please. Thank you for listening.

Amen!

Oh no. Those guys he sent. Oh no. If they're all traitors, that isn't good. If they helped those other guys with fake Kim, that baby-faced jerk, no way Bruno gets out alive.

I start thinking. Bruno is good. But versus ten guys good? Is anyone that good? This isn't a movie. And one of those guys, the greataxe guy, is another arena leader. He is real good too. Not as good as Bruno.

Let's face it. Bruno is dead. He was dead probably before I found Gunny. One versus ten, or even if it was eight, that isn't going to last long. Even if it was just six. I should've counted. He was probably dead before I got halfway to Gunny. Or even before that.

Gunny. That filthy traitor. You will die Gunny. By my hand. I swear to God. The real God. Capital G God. My God. My shepherd. As I am the darkness, I swear it!

I start crying. Not real crying. Not like a little baby sissy. Not the made up emotion crying. This is different.

3.10 DID YOU THINK I'D CRUMBLE?

KIM GUM

I wake up to someone laughing and shaking my leg. My first instinct is to try and kick them, but I resist. I can't do much wrapped up like this. And I might be able to escape if I play this right. I don't move at all.

I get shaken again. And I hear "Kim! Kim!"

I think that was Gunny, but I can't tell. Ew, I'll kill him. I try not to breath, playing dead real good. I get turned over on my side. I think I'm being untied. And I definitely am. Yes! Vengeance, here I come. Just play it cool. Play dead.

The sack gets pulled off my legs, then the one over my head and upper body gets pulled off. I try not to squint when it's off and the sun hits my face. I hope I did good and they can't tell I'm alive. The cloth wrapped around my head and mouth comes off next. I still lay there, playing dead.

"Kim. Come on. Get up."

That's definitely Gunny. Filthy traitor. Time to die, Gunny! I summon my spear from my inventory as I rush up, aiming where I heard his voice. Dang! He caught it. I let it go and dive for his stupid face and try to bite a chunk out of it. The stupid HP shield stops it from working. You're lucky, Gunny. Real lucky. He bear hugs me and says, "Relax, sweetie. Bruno's here. Relax."

I hear Bruno laughing. What is going on? I hear other people laughing too. I look around. Ball-face is here. A couple of Gunny's guys too. The general? Why is he here? He had to be in on it.

And there's Bruno. He looks bad. Healing pill bad. Lot of blood. I run up to him and hug him tight. I think I hurt him because he goes, "Ooph."

I don't want to talk. I don't want any more lies. I don't know what happened. I don't know why Bruno hasn't killed traitor Gunny or his filthy kidnapping minions. I don't care. Bruno's alive. That's all that matters now.

The best thing about Bruno is the worst thing about him. Well, besides his stupid, filthy lying mouth. He's stubborn. I know I'm somehow hurting him by hugging him, but he'll never admit it. Or say anything. He'll just let me hug him forever rather than admit it hurts. Stupid son of a bee.

I finally let go and look up at his dumb face. "Tuna fish, huh?"

"Ha. Yeah. You're alive now, ain't you? Tuna fish worked. You should apologize to Gunny for all the horrible things you probably thought."

"Never! No one kidnaps me! Not and gets forgiven."

"Kim. You're being ridiculous. How else was he going to make sure you were safe? It's not like you'd go along with anything he said. You're pretty stubborn."

"I'm stubborn? Look who's talking, buddy. Let me guess, tuna fish meant keep me safe or something?"

"Yeah. Something like that."

"Why? I could've helped. You know I could've helped."

"Too risky. I didn't know how big this was. And we probably both would've died. They had two casters. Goddamn magic missiles. I did most of the fight without a HP shield. Those things hurt. Not most of the fight. A big part of it. It probably helped. They used that fatigue spell a bunch, so my AB was crap. Once your HP shield is gone, you get your regular AB back. No AC or saves, so everything hits. If you get hit. I figured something out though. A way to stop magic missiles. Some of them. Well, I only technically stopped one missile, but now I got a way that could work better in the future. I got one of the casters pretty quick, but the last one was fast and tricky. I couldn't get him till the very end. I had to fight some maniac with a greataxe, you probably seen him in the arena, I had to fight him while getting peppered with magic missiles. Look at this. They burn wicked bad."

He has big, bleeding welts all over. They look real painful. I go to touch one and he grabs my hand.

"Please don't touch."

I wave for him to move his head closer. He does, and I whisper, "Butterball didn't turn traitor?"

"General Edwards to you. Only I call him that. Got it? Not really. He found out right before it happened. He stopped it from being bigger. Much bigger. He said seven guys was enough and everyone else had to get the last queen. And he stopped more from coming up. We're on the same page now. He was pissed I didn't listen to him about the premier guy. But I did. A little. I got rid of the old head from that filthy pedo, and didn't wear the premier's head around. Figured that was a nice, meet-in-the-middle kind of deal. He thought different. Would've been nice if he gave a heads-up or something, but keeping it small was decent of him. He'll probably never be fully on board, not until the UN stuff is resolved. We understand each other better now, I guess. It is what it is, you know? Politics make strange bedfellows."

"Well, I'm glad you're alive, but please don't ever send me away like that again. Together till the end, remember?"

He gives me a look. I don't know what kind of look, but it isn't a good one. He says, "You don't want to know where Joey is? You forget about him?"

"I didn't forget. He's with As…I mean Ms. Kaur."

"You see her boyfriend there? I don't trust that crazy bitch as far as I can throw her. Sorry. I forgot not to swear. Let's get Joey then hit the med tent."

"You need a healing pill? I got a bunch I can withdraw now. And I still owe you one from when we first met."

"Nah. We'll just spend some time in the next dungeon until I heal up. I don't think I need one. Maybe the doc will say different. We'll see. Anyways, I got my own pills. I don't need yours."

"But I owe you one."

"You can pay me back by stopping being so disobedient. Just listen when I tell you to do something."

"Hua."

3.11 THE UNLOVABLE TEDDY BEAR

KIM GUM

This is ridiculous. Absolutely ridiculous. What is going on? I am the darkness for crying out loud. Bruno is going to be pissed at me. I set off a trap. And I failed the psuchesoma. The trap – that one's on me. Stupid wisps. Bruno said these ones aren't even bad. The whips he's stuck at in the arena have like a million AC. When I hit one it actually hits, like, half the time, so their AC ain't so bad. The issue is actually hitting them. They're blazing fast. Good practice though, I guess.

I was chasing one of the stupid things around and set off a trap. I'm just going to lie and say I failed the die roll. Just blame it on RNG. Stupid RNG. Yeah.

The other two mobs in here are slow and pretty easy. Shambling mounds and some type of zombie. Gray something. All three mobs, so far, are game mobs and not imported, so at least I don't got to worry about fighting them when their HP shields are gone. Barely any shambling mounds, but those are my favorite to fight in here. I guess if they grab you, you're in trouble. But so far, so good, for me. Those stupid wisps – they should be illegal. So, so hard to hit. They just zip around all willy-nilly. I guess their fort saves are, like, nothing. Makes me wish I had some spells to kill them with. Casters really are easy mode.

And the psuchesoma was a rip off. I just got robbed. It was a con one. Not even a real one. One of the gimme ones that are so easy it's ridiculous. It was a question about standing up to bullies. I know the answer. I just wasn't really paying attention and said A instead of B by accident. Bruno told me to wait for him to rejoin for the psuchesoma, but since it was a question one, and he always has me do those anyways, I just did it. And I knew the dang answer too.

Man, he's going to kill me. He said he can't afford to look bad. Not now at least, with everyone coming at him.

Ah, who cares now? He's been kind of mad since I caught him. And I've been mad at him. I think this is a distraction. Saying I got to get tougher and better. This is the first dungeon where we split up to clear it the first time, and the first time is when all the ranked SS get given out. And because of me we're definitely not getting 1st SS. And he'll use that to make me miserable and hump around in this stupid swamp and train and do PT until I puke. I should just tell his wife. I won't forget or be too tired. Wrong is wrong.

The next room I shouldn't do. Not room, swamp area. Like 3x6 blocks. I can see three stupid wisps. He told me not to take on more than two at a time. I can't pull those stupid things to separate them. No way I'm getting close with an arrow. And there could be mounds or zombies in the water or the tree line waiting to surprise me. I think I'm going to do it though. I should do it. I can do it. I am the darkness. Not getting hit by three wisps will be impossible though. Not getting hit by one is pretty hard. They're super-fast.

Who cares if Bruno is mad? Or gets madder? I didn't do anything wrong. He did. Something big. Something that makes me real disappointed in him.

When I was in fifth grade I had to do a project on a leader from the 20th century. I asked my dad who I should do it on and he said JFK or MLK. So I started with JFK. Until I found out he cheated on his wife. A lot. Then I switched to MLK. And then I found out the same. Why? What is wrong with men? You swear an oath, you honor it. Nothing is more important than a marriage oath. It isn't hard not to cheat. I ended up doing the project on Rosa Parks. She didn't cheat on no one. Because it's so easy not to. Men are pigs!

Bruno won't even talk about it. I was helping doc look for Bruno, and we both saw Ass-eyes coming out of his tent. Doc was real mad too. Because everyone knows cheating is wrong.

And Ass-eyes? Come on. Ass-eyes? Really. That stupid hussy. Sure, she's pretty. But she's awful. Just pure sewage awful.

And how could he do that to his wife? He doesn't even seem to understand what he did is so bad and disappointing and…wrong. Just plain wrong. It's infuriating. Should I tell his wife?

I should. Shouldn't I?

I hear footsteps behind me and turn to watch Bruno approach.

"Jesus Christ, Kim, how much left is there of your half?"

"I don't think much more."

"I got the mini-boss. He dropped junk. Let's go. We got to pick up the pace. We got to get 1st SS."

"Uh…sorry. I don't think that's going to happen. RNG really screwed us again on a trap. And, uh…I failed the psuchesoma. I'm sorry. I knew the answer. It was easy. I just said the wrong one."

Bruno pinches the bridge of his nose and squints his eyes like he's in pain. Doesn't say nothing though.

And then he finally does. "Okay. We can still get SS. We got to go fast though. If our time is good enough."

"How so? I thought you needed perfect everything for SS."

"Time is like a multiplier. Or the other things are. Yeah, the other things are. Time is most important for points, the other things just multiply your points. Since we split up our time will be better. More points multiplied by less. I think we can pull off an SS. I've done it before. I don't need everyone having more ammo to use against me, which is going to happen if we stop getting 1st SS. You know what I mean?"

"Not really, but I believe you."

"Okay. What's here? Okay. I'll get the wisps, you get any surprises if there are any. If not, get on the wisps with me."

"Hua." I wanted to say, "Hua, cheater." But I don't.

We clear the rest of the mobs in the dungeon pretty easily. Nothing new. Just by the numbers. We don't talk much. Some weird tension seems to have grown between us. I was figuring the boss would be, like, a giant shambling mound or some sort of boss zombie, but nope. It's some sort of rainbow tree. Not like a shambling mound plant thing. An actual tree looking tree. In a circle. With four pillars around the outside of the circle. Green, blue, red, and yellow.

Bruno says, "I remember this boss. Okay. The red thing causes a fire dot debuff thing on it. We keep that up at all time to stop its regen. You got to get out of the circle first – or you take a lot of fire damage. It lasts a while. He regens wicked fast if you don't have it up.

"When the air fills with sparkle stuff, you hit the blue thing to blow the sparkles away. That sparkle stuff heals it so you got to be quick. The green thing heals everything in the circle, including the boss, by 10%. Yellow removes the disease it spreads to us, but gives the boss an enrage for a pretty long time and a short iframe. Don't hit yellow or green unless I say so.

"The red has a cooldown, so we can't really time it with the blue. Blue one has a cooldown too. This is much harder solo. I'll stay on the boss as much as possible. When I yell fire, you run to the blue and out of the circle. Don't hit it. Only hit it if I tell you or you see the sparkle stuff. If you got to run out of the circle, may as well head to the blue in case we need it.

"Now, the disease stacks. Tell me if you get five stacks. We need to hit the yellow at six. If we're lucky we can down the boss before we got to hit yellow.

"Any questions?"

"No. Got it. Hua."

"Okay then, repeat what we got to do back to me."

"You'll keep the fire pillar going. That and blue pillar are on cd. Only hit blue when I see sparkles or you tell me. Get out when you hit the red. Or when you yell fire, I mean. Green heals us all, including the boss. Yellow removes the disease debuff. Tell you when I'm at five stacks."

"Nice. Ready?"

"Hua."

We rush in and Bruno hits the red pillar. I see the circle area flash with red, and the bark of the tree thing is on fire. Not a lot of fire. But you can tell it's there. We get to work on the boss. I take the back, per usual, but it doesn't matter to a tree I guess. I get no sneak attack damage, and it uses its branches to attack the back as easily as the front.

I get told to hit the blue pillar, and do. I did it quick, but the tree still got a lot of healing in. It had the 75% visual when I left, and nothing when I got back. Jeez.

I move out of the circle so Bruno can redo the fire, but I step back in, like, just a smidge of a second too early and I get a burning debuff. It's only 1 HP per round, but that adds up. The disease debuff doesn't seem to have a save. When it forces out the black pollen stuff, you get a stack. It does it a little bit before it does the healing sparkly pollen stuff.

We got him down to 25% right after I got my fifth stack and tell Bruno. Then the tree lets out the sparkles, and he goes back up over 25%. I hit the blue as fast as I can get to it.

Bruno yells to me, "Right after the next stack, go hit the yellow."

I yell back hua and keep working.

When we get the sixth stack I run to the yellow and hit it. The tree is shimmering, the enrage visual. I get back behind, knowing I'm going to have to hit the blue soon, but wanting to get a few more hits in first. Maybe we can down it before the sparkles.

Well, part of the enrage is the tree spins around in, like, a whirlwind attack. I was not expecting a tree to be able to spin around. Trees never spin around. The roots prevent them from doing that. That doesn't apply here. This tree spins like a top, and I don't expect it. I get my shield up but I still get sent flying, and I get paralyzed or stunned. I can't move.

"Hit the blue! HIT THE BLUE! KIM!" Then he swears. I think he sees me down because he stops screaming. That hit hurt. My HP is at about a third. Nah, maybe a quarter. Jeez, that thing hits hard.

I hear Bruno again, "Get your head in the game, Kim. He's over 25 again. We almost had him."

Jeez, you never told me about any spinning attack. Dummy. That would've helped. But I guess it's all my fault, right? Of course. Stupid Kim messed up again. Dang jerk. Cheater.

Whatever stopped me from moving wears off and I'm up again. I can tell Bruno is mad. As soon as I get in the circle I have to get out again so Bruno can reapply fire. Two more stacks of pollen before we down the boss. Thankfully, I don't make no more mistakes. Dungeon 6-1 is complete. I think I get an achievement after this one.

Before we even open the chest Bruno starts in on me, "Kim, you got to pay attention. You got to do better. You're better than this. This whole dungeon you've been off."

This makes me angry, but I push it down into my hate-ball. I just say, "I know." And I try to look reprimanded. Or whatever the right word is. Ashamed? I try to mask my anger with that.

"I know you know. And don't try to use ADD as an excuse. I have it too. If you love fighting, then it isn't hard to pay attention. You get hyperfocus. I do."

He sighs and says, "Maybe we should talk about you going to the city after area 10 is open."

Is he f...is he dagnab serious? My anger reaches level one million. I say what's been eating at me, "Maybe I was distracting thinking you'd cheat on me too! You filthy cheater!"

He stares at me with his super extra furious eyes. Uh oh.

"I'll cheat on your goddamn face. And then I'll rip it off and piss down your throat. You want to play games, Kim? We can play games. I'll rip your goddamn head off. Don't ever question me or what I do. I do what I want, when I want, how I want, whenever I want. Got it?"

Holy moly! That was mean. I don't want to, but his furious look and what he just said makes me start crying.

"Go get Joey. Bring him back here. Now."

I go get Joey. Crying all the way. I didn't mean to get him so mad. I start worrying he will leave me now. I don't want him to leave me. I don't want to be alone.

I really don't want to be alone.

Not again.

I hate it.

When I get back I have my crying under control. I go up to Bruno and say, "Sorry. Please don't leave me."

He looks at me for a second. He looks sad. Then he hugs me. I start crying again.

While hugging me he says, "Don't say sorry. I'm sorry. I'm wicked, wicked sorry. I shouldn't have yelled at you. That was wrong. And I'm wicked sorry about it. What I said."

Between sobs I manage to get out that it's okay.

He says, "No. It's not. I shouldn't have done that. Here, take a seat. Let's talk for a second."

I sit on the ground in front of him and wipe my eyes and my nose with my sleeve.

"I have anger issues. When I get mad, sometimes I get too mad and I say really dumb things. That was completely inappropriate. I sincerely apologize and I hope you can forgive me. I'll try to do better, try to not do it again, but I can't promise nothing. Sometimes I get mad enough to lash out, and if you're around it might be at you. I wish I could say different, but I don't like promising nothing I can't keep. You know?"

I say, "Yeah."

"And about Ms. Kaur..I know. I'll try to explain."

He just sits in silence, looking nervous, rubbing his legs. "I never talked about this stuff before. Any of it. My wife knows some, I guess. But not a lot. I like you, and I want you to get better. That means I got to try to get better too. They always say talking helps. And what you been through is wicked messed up, so I don't mind telling you. I know your sh...crap. I guess you should know some of mine."

More silence while he rubs his legs.

He takes a deep breath, and then lets it out. "Okay, Jesus. Where do I begin? I hate when guys whine about their upbringing. Drives me nuts. Especially when they don't really got nothing to whine about, you know? You got something to whine about. You had it pretty rough when you get here. I had it much better when I was twelve. Let's see. When I was a kid, my ma wasn't right. She did a lot of drugs, and she had a boyfriend she let do things to me she shouldn't have. She didn't care as long as she got her drugs.

"I have three older siblings. Two sisters and a brother. My grandma raised them. But for some reason she wouldn't take me. She already took them from my ma before I was even born. I don't know why she wouldn't take me in after that stuff happened. My ma didn't want me either. No one that was supposed to love me did. I don't know why. I tried to pretend it didn't bother me, but it did.

"It does," he looks at me as he says it does.

"Well, anyway. I grew up in foster care, group homes, and did a good amount of time in juvey. I fell in love with a girl. I was fifteen. Maybe almost sixteen. Around then. I fell in love hard. Because she did too. I thought it was okay. Safe. I loved her so much it hurt. She was good at pretending. Knowing what to say. I really thought she loved me. It felt so good. We were going to be together forever. I never even thought about cheating on her. Not once.

"By the way, this stays between us. All this. Everything I say. You can't tell no one nothing, okay?"

"Okay," I say.

"Promise?"

"I promise."

"Okay. Well, she was just good at pretending. She cheated on me. After that, I promised never again. But then I met my wife. I fell head over heels. This time it was real. This time it was safe. This time it was the real thing. I was so in love. It lasted a long time. The trust. Years. We had kids. I didn't even think about cheating. And I trusted her.

"She starts spending a lot of time in Thailand, where she was born. Reconnecting to family and sh…stuff. Timing it when I was away on missions. And we were just wild together. The flame was burning hot! Red hot. After years. It was amazing.

"Well, I get back from a mission early while she's in Thailand. I call to see if she can come home early, but she seemed blasé about the whole thing. Next time we talk she tells me her travel agent said her original flight was cancelled. So she booked a new date. Like ten days after her original arrival time. After. Later. I told her I was back early, thinking she would see if she can come back early. She didn't. She booked it for later. Ten days later.

"For me, I couldn't wait to see her. I was going nuts wanting to see her. Wicked nuts. All I wanted was to see the woman I loved. Because I missed her. I missed her because I loved her so much. And she didn't feel that way. I thought she did. But she couldn't have. Just kept that flight and came back ten days later.

"That killed me inside. It hurt so bad."

He looks at me, an angry look. He says, "Remember, not a word of this to anyone. Please. I never even told Minnie about this. I never told no one. Please, please don't ever say nothing."

I say, "I won't."

"Thank you. Well, I knew at that point we weren't on the same page. Did she love me? Maybe. Maybe not. Definitely not like I loved her. Irregardless, we weren't on the same page. I knew then she was going to betray me. If it wasn't all lies, a lot of it was. Just pretend. Just an act. Maybe she already cheated on me. Maybe she was cheating right then. Maybe that's why she stayed in Thailand extra.

"I never cheated on her. That night I did. I wasn't going to be a chump. Been cheating ever since. And I was right. About her. I never caught her. She was real good at pretending. She found out a bunch of times I cheated. And she'd forgive me after I got her some Gucci and Louis Vuitton crap. And she'd whine about it. But I knew. And I was proved right in 2009. She cheated then. Said she had enough, and if I could do it she could too.

"Yeah, right. Like she ever really loved me. Like anyone ever did."

The look of hurt on his face actually hurt me. I never seen him like this before.

"And besides that. By then…you believe in God, right?"

I say, "Yeah. Of course. Now. I used to not. But now I do. I am the darkness."

"I mean the real God. Jesus and his father? Never mind. By then I also knew I was going to hell. God is a kind and forgiving God, but some things there just is no forgiveness for. And I did a lot of those things.

"You know, I wish I could be an atheist. I wish I could not believe in hell. That when you die, there's nothing. I wish that was true. I want that so bad. For there to be nothing. But there is something. You pay when you do bad things. I know it for certain. I wish I didn't, but I do."

He looks at me for a long moment and says, "I'm not scared to die, but I am petrified of going to hell. And I know that's where I'm going. I really try to be a good guy, but sometimes it just doesn't work out.

"A lot of guys, when they know they're going to hell, they just stop trying. I don't want no more sins on my soul. And maybe if I do something real good. Something real big. Maybe. Maybe then I can be redeemed and that will wash away my sins. Maybe. I'm not banking on it though.

"So, I try not to sin. Not the big ones. I still do sin. A lot. Sometimes some people just need killing. Sometimes killing is right, even if it's technically wrong and a sin. Same with lying. I try not to blaspheme though. But I say goddamn a lot. I don't think that's really blaspheming though. I hope not. And the 'do not covet your neighbor's wife' one – that's just silly. You can't control what you want. Did no one ever see a hot women back in the olden times? That's impossible. It's just what happens when you see a hot women. It's science. You don't control it. That's a crazy one. Do not cheat makes sense. But covet? Come on.

"Is that it? That ain't ten. I forget the other ones. Well, anyways, I know I'm going to hell. But that ain't stopping me from trying to be a good guy. Doing what's right. Saving people and sh…stuff. So, what do you do then? Me, I just stick to the things I enjoy the most. The three Fs. Fighting, family, and...we'll say fornicating. I really enjoy those three things, and I don't think they're bad. Yeah, I cheat. But I was proven right to do so.

"And remember, you don't say nothing. My family doesn't know Minnie cheated on me in 2009. No one knows. And I want to keep it that way."

He takes a couple deep breaths as he fidgets with his hands.

"And my family – there's something wrong with me. Something I'm missing. The thing that makes people love you. Really love you. Even my kids. Even my son. Back in 2012, he did right by me. But it had conditions, you know. It was based on me not being me. I had to try to change and be less me, you know? Less offensive. My daughter wouldn't even talk to me. She was going to school to be a lawyer, you know. A filthy lawyer. I thought I raised her right. We used to be so close when she was younger. We had so much fun. All of us. I love me family. But it's not a two-way street. Not really.

"I wish I had that. The thing that makes it so people can love you. I never had it. Not even as a baby. Everyone loves babies. Not even from the people that were supposed to love me anyways, like my ma and my grandma."

I just sit there. Hearing him say that last stuff hurts. Hurts me inside. I want to do something to make him feel better, and when I look at him, his face is all scrunched up. Trying not to cry. Mostly failing. It breaks my heart. I go to hug him and he moves away. So I just put my hand on his shoulder. Being there for him. I know this is embarrassing for him. I just wait.

When he has himself under control I say, "I love you, you...you big son of a bee."

He smiles but still is just looking straight ahead and says, "I love you too, Kim. You're a great kid. And a great friend. Sorry about that.

Please don't tell no one nothing I said. Please. Remember, that's just between us, okay?"

"Of course. I'll never betray you, big guy. Never."

Still looking ahead, his face turns sad. He says in a whisper, but I can still here, "You will. Everyone does."

That breaks my heart even more. He comes off as hard, but he's a big softy inside. But none of this makes cheating okay. And the reason he started cheating seems real dumb to me. She stayed a little later in Thailand. Who cares? That's no reason to start cheating. Maybe she was just having fun or there wasn't an earlier flight.

I say, "I love you and I'll never betray you. But that's a two-way street too. You can't never betray me neither. Right?"

"Come on. You really don't think I'd betray you, do you?"

"But that means you can't never leave me. Together till the end. That's what that means too."

"Look, you know I'd never betray you. Period. But if we're never splitting up, you got to get a lot better. I won't lie to you. As you are now, when we hit the epic zone, I'm going to have to join others. I don't want to. Bu...is Joey eating grass? What the hell?"

"Joey, no! No grass. Why?"

I go over and knock the grass out of his hand, and hold his face to get it out of his mouth. Why? Why would anyone eat grass? We have real food. I take out a ration and give it to him. He lets it drop on the ground, and looks at me like I'm the crazy one. And the mean one. He really drives me nuts sometimes.

I go back over and sit back down where I was. I want this to continue. Was he really going to leave me when we hit the epic zone? And he's training me to be better. This hurts. I am getting better.

Bruno says, "If you want, we can try and get you there. But saving humanity comes first. Saving everyone that's still alive. But we can try to get you there. I've been training you to be good, to be able to defend yourself. But if you want, I can increase it. Increase it and try to make it so we don't got to split up. But it isn't going to be easy. It's going to be three times as hard as it's been. And more time intensive. And pain. A lot more pain. Do you want that?"

"I don't want you to ever leave me. Together till the end. Forever. If I need to train harder to make that happen, then I train harder."

"And I'm getting old. Some of it's your age. You have the potential, but you need to grow into it. Into your full strength and final size. I might have to leave you in dungeons to train on your own. You and Joey. Or I can take Joey if I'm not going to the city. Or I could leave him with Ms. Kaur. Or even one of the guys. Hell, everyone loves Joey. It wouldn't be a problem. Now that we're splitting in dungeons, for the first dungeon clear I mean, we could ask someone to watch him for a second until we get out. I was going to do that for this one, but now things are awkward with Ms. Kaur."

"No. Joey stays with me. I'm basically his mother. Mothers don't leave their kids behind."

"Whatever you say. But now that we're splitting up for the first clear, it isn't 100% safe leaving him in the open area. If we get a rare spawn we miss, you know?"

"We get group chat after this. I mean, I get it. So we can both communicate. How much of a risk is it?"

"Not much. But not 100% safe. They usually don't get active until after you find them. But they can wander, and even if Joey had chat it's not like he'd tell us nothing."

I wonder if Joey could tell me in my mind if he is in danger. I know it's not the real Joey, but it could work. That part of him is better at thinking. And his HP shield is huge. No way we don't find him in time.

"If it isn't much of a risk, I'd rather he come in with us. Maybe when we start using those things that increase rare spawns we can leave him out. But I'd rather not. For now. If that's okay.

"Of course. Now let's see what dropped."

He goes over to the chest. "Yes!" I hear him yell.

"What is it?"

"Vanadium ore. Heavy armor made from this has elemental resistance. Against everything magic. Besides sonic. And not the...what's it called, the type that magic missiles are. Force? And the...Jesus, you know, the type that vampirism is? No type."

"Untyped?"

"Yeah. But besides that, it reduces all magic damage by a percentage. I think for heavy armor it's...I forget. What I'm thinking is crazy and can't be right. It isn't less than 5% though, I guarantee that. For fire, cold, lightning, and acid."

"Shield brace does way more and we're getting that soon," I say. Seems like crap compared to what we're already getting.

"That's energy resistance. This is elemental. It stacks. And energy resistance lowers it by a certain amount of points. Elemental is a percentage. It is small, but every little bit helps. If we have enough we can have full plate made from it. You can have it. We can switch it out. You okay with that? We'll have to split the cost then."

"That sounds awesome. You sure you have enough? Is it enough for two armors to be made?"

"I don't know. Hopefully at least one. I'll find out next time in the city. Man, they can still add enhancements to crafted armor later. When casters get to the city. So it will last. No. Damn. We get the death protection armor in one of the level 10 dungeons. I think. That is way better. Ah. Vanadium is still good. Death ward, I mean. Not death protection. No, level 9? Man, I forget. Anyways, this is awesome. For now, at least. Even better than +1 armor at level 7. Way better. I hate casters."

"Yeah, they suck."

"That reminds me, how's your spear holding up? Is it going to last through all the area 6 dungeons?"

"I think so. It's only down 1 permanent point. I put all the repair points I can into it."

"Good. Man, I can't believe I still haven't got a better weapon yet. Nothing in the mobile auction house ever. Not that I've seen. Make sure you keep an eye out too. That Japanese guy already has a +1 weapon with a minor burst effect. They must have got lucky and got a rare spawn. Katanas drop even less than dwarven waraxes. What a lucky prick. Sorry, jerk I mean."

"Bruno."

"Yeah?"

I sit quietly for a second, collecting my thoughts. "You're not going to leave me, right? Two-way street, right?"

"Kim. I'll never betray you, and I'll never abandon you. I'll do everything I can to make sure you can hang with the big boys during raiding. But…sometimes some things happen, and having you along when those things happen would be betraying you. I got a lot of bad things I carry around, lot of stains on my soul. I don't want to have your death on my conscience, too. I'm doing all this to save the people I love more than to save everyone else. If you die, or my family dies, what's the point?"

I want to say, "What's the point for me if you die?" But I don't.

3.12 DEAD HOMIES

KIM GUM

Things have been going pretty good. Real good, mostly. The training really ramped up. Permanent pain and soreness ramped up. Bruno treats me more like an equal now. More friends now, more than just an old guy looking after a kid. Especially since he knows I go hard when I train alone in dungeons. I don't slack off. I do 50k humps, and run and do sprints all the time. Go till muscle failure, then go again. And again. And again. I get some impact, whatever that means. He knows how serious I take this.

Since we were spending more time in dungeons, Bruno added something called D and C to my training. It's kind of fun, but seems kind of dumb too. He doesn't want me forming up with the military guys, but he'll grab some people so I can learn in a group. He said I don't have to do attention or parade rest when I'm talking to officers and NCOs. I don't have to use rank neither. I'm not sure what delta is but he said I'm more like old delta and delta doesn't have to do dumb stuff like that. Being delta means you are superior and better than everyone else.

I like the thing where you go, "step, heel, step, heel, step, heel, step." That one's pretty fun. I mess up a lot. Bruno doesn't care when I mess up in D and C. Not nearly as much as when I mess up in something else. He said D and C is for pogues but we got to know it too. I'm not sure what a pogue is. When I ask Bruno he just says some nonsense that doesn't help like pogues are sissies.

Nathan made a compass for me. Well, Bruno asked him to. I can't wait to meet Siri and Nathan. Sergey talks the most in chat now, so I probably talk to him most. Besides Lurch. Lurch talks more than anyone, ever. I guess Sergey is a pervert and always stares at Siri's boobs and butt, but we still get along pretty good. The compass is for something called land nav. It's super easy. Bruno says it isn't, but so far it is. We don't do it a lot since it's so easy. It's harder outside the dungeon, but just a little. The dungeons started getting pretty big with a lot of stuff in them, but Bruno said the dungeons aren't big enough for proper land nav.

I was mad at Gunny for a while, but I'm not that mad no more. He's hard to stay mad at, and the more I showed him I was mad the more he made fun of me. And the more mad I'd get the more he called me sweetie or sweetheart or dear. I hate that.

I'm getting real strong. I train a lot with Christina. She's so pretty. Not like dumb Ass-eyes the hussy. Well, Ass-eyes is pretty, but not like Christina. Anyways, I don't get sore no more when I do the hold the weapon out exercises. My forearms are a lot stronger now. And my wrists. My thrust is ridiculously powerful. I can punch through most monster's hides and scales like nothing now. A lot of them anyways.

Mama died. Christina's mother. She talked a lot but she was real nice and I liked her. A lot of people are dead. General Edwards died. Ball-face is still alive. So is the other guy – what's-his-name? – Leg? Bruno also didn't kill the greataxe guy that attacked him. He left him alive but pretty messed up. He told me to stay away from him. I didn't like him. I knew he was going to cause trouble again. I knew it. Just looking at him you could tell. He was a big dumb idiot. But Bruno said we needed all the guys like him. The ones who fight real good.

I made friends with some kids around my age that seem okay. We have a lot of people from a lot of countries here now. Bruno was certain that last time in area 9 there was only one instance. He was on the way to the city then, and the people were all more spread out, so he isn't sure. We have three instances in area 9, and close to a thousand in each of them.

One of my friends is a big girl, like me. Much bigger though. Heavier. But she's really flexible. She's a healer, but she can fight pretty good. She's from a different country. I forget which one. Her name is Yoana. We're friends with a boy called Ehsan. I forget where he's from, too. He has real weird teeth. I know he's from a terrorist country. I still like him though. He won't talk about if his parents are pro-UN or terrorists. He's in love with a girl called Hallbera. She's been in my instance for a while. She looks like she's twelve. Super skinny. She hangs out with the "cool" kids. She's a stupid caster, of course. I think Yoana has a crush on Ehsan though. Ehsan is a pretty good fighter. He has the same build my brother was going for. The sling using cleric. Hallbera has a boyfriend. He's an idiot. He's mean to all of us. His name is turd-Ramon. I hate him. His brother, Cesar, is nice. Pretty old though. Hallbera's parents hate Bruno. They also hate turd-Ramon's family. Turd-Ramon comes from a terrorist country like Ehsan. But unlike Ehsan's family, they aren't shy about hating the UN. Not in here at least. Not since area 7.

Doc died in 7. Some UN people tried getting Bruno again. Two casters, with the number two monk, and the greataxe guy again. Couple healers with them, too. At level 7 the casters got fireball. Me, Doc, Bruno, Joey, and a different girl I was friends with back then named Nevena were eating at Bruno's tent. Well, Joey was standing a ways away. Two fireballs were lobbed at us as we were siting and joking. A bunch of people helped us out fighting this time. Bruno got real mad. I thought I saw him mad before. I didn't. Not even close. He gets crazy. Real crazy. And super intense. He made me real scared. Just looking at his crazy eyes made me want to pee my pants a little. Somehow the crazy anger just radiates off him, and you get nervous just being kind of near him.

So doc died and Nevena died. Bruno got real mad and wasn't thinking right and tortured the ones that were alive at the end. Not too bad. It was pretty quick. Besides the greataxe guy. Bruno cut his legs and arms off, cut his eyes and tongue out, and said the guy's new name was Backpack and he was going to carry him around forever and keep the promise he made to him. He started wearing him as a backpack too. But we had three premiers with us then. Not premiers. Whatever the premier of canada and mexico and some big wig from the EU are called. During area 6 the canadian premier, or whatever she's called, joined our guild and was helping out general Edwards. She took over when the general died. But Bruno made her promise that if we won this competition to get back to earth she would either change the name of canada to canadia, or change canadian to canadan. He said canada and canadian doesn't match up and doesn't make no sense. She said she promised but I don't think she meant it. She is a slick one. She's another one I saw coming out of Bruno's tent one time. I doubt Sergey is nearly as perverted as Bruno. It drives me nuts, but what are you going to do?

Well, the premier, or whatever they are called, of mexico, the EU, and Laura, the canadian premier, all talked Bruno into not using the greataxe guy as a backpack. Bruno let Nevena's family kill him for vengeance.

This event, and them killing doc and Nevena, kind of turned things around for Bruno. At least in our instance. People would get mad if people talked about replacing Bruno with the UN.

The premier of the EU, or whatever he is called, is a stupid jerk idiot and I want to punch him so bad. He shooed me once. He came to talk to Bruno and walked up behind me and when I turned around, he goes, "Shoo. Shoo." And waves his hands shooing me away. I couldn't believe it. I'm the dagnab darkness. Who is he? Nothing. I could chew him up and spit him out for lunch. His skin is all stupid and wrinkled and he is bald with a big dumb mustache and he just lets what's left of his hair just poof out all dumb. Shoo me, will ya? I'll destroy him. The mexico guy just ignores me. I'm fine with that. Just don't shoo me. The EU jerk didn't even look at me when he was shooing me.

Bruno doesn't like him either, the EU guy. They want more people on their dumb council. We have more premiers now. They want them all on. He didn't add any, but he added the premier from jamaica. Everyone knows she's a sympathizer. They didn't like that. Bruno filled the rest of the guild spots to avoid adding other ones, and he threatens to kick the EU guy a lot. He almost killed him once. The EU guy just doesn't seem to learn. I bet he gets killed soon. Bruno added all the best casters and healers and arena leaders. He told them he was going to kick a bunch after 10 to replace them with crafters until we got guild level 3.

Ryu Jin and Tora Hige are in our guild now. The girl in their party isn't their daughter. She's related to them, or related to one of them, at least, somehow. I forget how. She's a real snob. A real stuck up super bee. I don't like her. At all. And Ryu Jin isn't a bearzerker. Bruno said she was in his last timeline thing, but she isn't this time. I looked into the bearzerkers, they're pretty cool. They change into bears while raging and get regen, and their natural attacks take the stuff from both weapons, so they can have double burst effects on each hit. Pretty neat. The other types of barbarian besides the vanilla one is chief, which loses rage but gets a cohort; wolf warrior, that gets +AC and AB while raging, and later get whirlwind while raging; and battle swine, which gets a bunch of stupid bonuses to charge. We have all those charge feats too. Rush n' attack is awesome! I love it so much. Iframes are the best. It really changed how we fight. We can ping-pong back and forth between mobs. It's so much fun!

When I found out Ryu Jin wasn't a bearzerker, I knew which one she was – the wolf warrior. I knew it. And I was right. Ryu Jin is real nice. And super pretty. Bruno doesn't think so, but she is! She taught him some axe tricks. But she uses two handaxes. Bigger axes are different. She's awesome at fighting. Like a fighting ballerina. Bruno beat her, though, when they dueled.

Tora Hige beat Bruno the first time they dueled. He is fast! Real fast. Hard to see what happened fast. Bruno beat him every time after that, though. Or most times. He said he only lost the first time because of the stupid rpg system. The differences between their ABs. Bruno hit him like a bunch more, but most of the hits didn't beat Tora Hige's AC. When Tora Hige hit Bruno, they usually landed. Tora Hige focuses on AB, while we focus on stupid con. Well, not stupid. It's nice to have a lot of HPs and high fort saves. Will saves now too. But being better at killing would be better. In my opinion.

Tora Hige knows a lot about the fourth age and what happened behind the curtains. Why they made HPs even less than in Black Raven. How they decided on what they thought was the right challenge level for the game. It's actually balanced around game mode. The mode no one uses ever because it's so bad. You just stand there and every attack is a ghost arm, but you can't dodge or attack when you want. You just stand there and RNG decides everything. So the CR is mostly correct, but made for four people using game mode on the base mobs at level 30 to beat them safely. One of them a healer, and one that can fill the role of tank. But they have scaling difficulty for all mobs. The regular CR mobs are 20% weaker until level 10. Then normal until late teens. Then buffed after that, like 20% or so. This isn't counting 2(x) or higher. They're buffed a lot more. More attributes and skills and extra dodge and natural armor and stuff like that.

After area 10, Bruno says regular dungeons get a good amount harder. They're still regular now. But soon the regular mobs will be 20% harder. And the imported mobs, too. The imported mobs are already much harder and do crazy things. Then at area 11 all dungeons will be 2(x), so another big jump in difficulty.

Tora Hige said they balanced this way to make people using auto-attack feel good. Feel like they are better. Addict them to the game. At early levels, if you clear trash fast you feel good about yourself. Like you are awesome. That makes you want to play more. The bear in the tutorial of the game that I skipped, and I thought everyone skipped, because it killed me super-fast when I tried fighting it, was actually made so the average skilled player could beat it in free attack mode – but not on their first try. To make them feel tough and accomplished when they figured out the combat a little. To show growth and improvement. Show they aren't wasting their time playing fourth age because they're getting better at fighting. That bear that destroyed your first character? Your alt a couple weeks or a month later can now kill him with a little effort, and your next alt rolls him up easy.

Lots of thinking and planning like that went into the game.

A big issue was at max level – the content was so tough it left most players out. You needed really, really good players. And since fourth age was already a niche game there just weren't a ton. What helped was even though it billed itself as a low magic game, magic classes were overpowered. So casters filled in the missing skill gaps. In the pen and paper game, bumping all spell levels up one, with cantrips being level 1 spells, and removing the level 9 spells, worked because it was extremely difficult to level a caster with the lower HPs and all that stuff. But it was easier in the fourth age, and with the even lower HPs, they had to nerf caster damage. And then nerf again, and then tied the

413

magic damage increase into paragon feats. It took forever to make it right from what he said, but mages are still kind of OP at max level, and the only option for low skilled players.

So why did they nerf HPs to be even lower than the already lower Black Raven game? To make the combat faster and more actiony. But that made the people really interested in an old-school, hardcore mmorpg less interested. They want an exact replica of the system they know and love. Why get them excited for 3.5e d20 and then switch it to action combat? Because in full emersion games, just standing there and having the game fight for you while you passively observe is boring. Some people may have preferred it, but that would have limited the audience to almost no one.

They had an MMA type expansion where they changed all the hand-to-hand and grappling rules. The Black Raven fans did not like this at all. But everyone else did. They got big names from when MMA was still legal in the real world. Moses Chandisingh, Menakor Bartuah, and Blamo Blamo. I've heard of all three and seen a bunch of their fights with my parents. Not in person. Just videos. Bruno thought the name Blamo Blamo was hilarious. Both Menakor and Blamo are from the same country. Something like Liberty. It's in Africa. Bruno laughed for a while over that. He said something about some comedian named Patrice and people from their fighting wars in sweat pants and tuxedo shoes. I didn't get it but it really cracked him up.

After the MMA patch the next big one was going to be a psionic expansion, adding a ton of new classes and stuff. But we were sent here, to this world, before that expansion came out.

You can tell that Bruno and Tora Hige don't like each other. But they talk a lot. Bruno needs to know about high level raids. Higher than they made it in Bruno's timeline. They disagree on a lot. Tora Hige thinks min-maxing means something different than Bruno does.

He thinks everyone but tanks should start at 10 con, and are fine with 14 con at level 30. Just getting 4 con from raid armor or the attribute enhancement spell. Con only comes on armor. In beta it used to be on shields too, but they made it so it only comes on armor. And competes with some of the best stuff that also only comes on armor, like death ward. All specific design choices.

They also added toxicity and lowered healing kit healing and restricted its use so soloing would be less attractive, and grouping would be more attractive and way easier. And that makes healers super popular. A lot of of the baddies are healers. I think all the healing classes and subclasses were free2play. Most of the non-base, non-healing classes are subscription only.

I met a family with three kids, and everyone but the husband was a healer with a splash to fill the different roles. They do pretty decent considering. They said crawling is pretty safe with their party. That's why they didn't go to the city.

Tora Hige's real name is Ren. Ryu Jin's real name is Fann. She isn't Japanese. I forget where she's from. I forget what their game names mean exactly, but Tora Hige's was pretty dumb. Ryu Jin's was pretty cool. Dragon something. Or something dragon. Dragon was in it.

I noticed something about the best people – the ones who top the arena. They all train a lot. And try to learn from each other. And because of Bruno I could learn from all of them, too. And they all have this thing where they go crazy if they aren't good at something. Like Tora Hige does this thing where he draws his sword really fast. It's useless in here since you can just summon a weapon directly to your hand from inventory. But I guess that's actually part of his class and does something. And he did it in real life too. He did katana sword fighting and the quick draw of the sword and some other stuff in competitions. That's how he got famous.

415

Well, Bruno spent a bunch of time trying to get better at speed sword drawing than Tora Hige. Why? Who knows? It's useless for us to learn. Just a waste of time. But he spent a ton of time on it. He thinks he's just as fast as Tora Hige, but he isn't. Tora Hige is faster. Noticeably faster. Bruno doesn't think so and just says every one of his muscles is a fast twitch muscle so he is faster, he just hasn't practiced the quick draw nonsense enough and blah, blah, blah. Whatever. He's crazy.

I started doing multiple dungeons sometimes. Instead of farming one dungeon, we'd clear as many as we could get to in the hour or so dungeons are open. 52 minutes. Whatever. And we could reach a lot of them in that time. Most are only a klick away from the other ones. That way we'd increase boss drops. On the last one I'd stay in longer to train while Bruno exited after the boss. He said he's getting too old to stay in wasting time. He'd test me when I got out to make sure I wasn't weaker or slacking off in the dungeon. Of course not! Jeez. I want to be the best. Or up there with the best. I got to love it. I got to do it.

I'm not sure how old I am now. Older. And better. Much better. My favorite time so far was when we were grinding gold to buy all new stuff for level 7. In area 6, dungeon 6-2 is a dungeon everyone calls wrong. Dungeon wrong. I don't know why. It's a ton of fun. It has eight levels and they're all pretty short but you get good stuff and the mobs are fun. In area 8, dungeon 8-7 is called arnika. It's like a town and you can rob vaults and there's computer stuff. So much fun. 8-1 is a dungeon Bruno hates. It's pretty plain but has like a million doors and a lot of them go into a one block room. It has three floors that are all pretty big. It's a pain to get through. Lots of ghosts. It's from some game with gothic in the title.

Bruno's wife is stressing out about all we need to get done. Soon the crawlers will get to the city. Right after we open area 10. And, any day now – any moment really – the people who took the path to the city will get there. Bruno, working with a lot of people, already made, like, a bazillion instances of the city all with different functions. And Ms. Bruno will go in guild chat and ask why there're a bunch called red light and stuff like that. Or how they'll clean the city instances, and what to do with trash. Bruno always says relax and made a rule called 'police call' every day at hour 14 server time. Everyone in the city has to walk around picking up trash in their instance of the city, and then put it in a temp zone like the farming mat zones. And when the zone is empty the trash disappears with the zone.

Bruno's right about wanting the kids to go to fighting training school instead of stupid regular learning school. Regular school is boring and dumb. I'm the only person that agrees with Bruno about school, though. He said I won't have to go, no matter what kind of schools they decide on.

That's how Bruno almost killed the EU guy. Working on whatever it's called. Logistics? You can't have area 6 or higher be empty or the instances reset and the next person or group that enters will have to fight all the monsters again. Only area 10 and 20 don't reset when empty. And Bruno said every zone should have people in each. Especially doctors. A doctor at 1, 3 and 5 at the very least. There're a lot of people still in all the instances for some reason. Well, one reason is people rerolling. You can catch up pretty quick though. It's easy to do at least four dungeons during each opening. At least. And that's not even running fast between dungeons. But that can't be the reason for all the people. Just a small part I'm guessing. Maybe people are just taking their time, or healing up outside a dungeon for some reason? Who knows?

All the leadership tried to consolidate people into one instance of an area. Once all the dungeons of an area are beaten and you move on to the next area, everyone in lower areas can change what instance they are in. It's easy and takes like two seconds. You just go to the effects part of the thing in the upper right and click on instance, then change instance with a drop down menu. If I go back down to area 8 I'll always come back to the same instance of area 9 we are in, but everyone in area 1 through 8 can easily change instances.

So they tried to get people to consolidate instances. To have only one instance of area 1 through 6. 7 and 8 have more than a thousand total so that wouldn't work for those instances. Way more. But 6 and below have way less. When they were going over all the areas, area 3 had only like twenty people or something, spread in five different instances of area 3. So Ball-face was emailing people through Bruno like crazy, trying to get them to switch instances. And a lot of people were just ignoring him. And it was taking forever, and the EU guy got snippy with Bruno because Bruno wanted to stop. And the EU guy was bugging him to add some bigwig from the UN to the guild. Everyone bugs Bruno about that, but the EU guy won't let up. Not the secretary general – she went down the path to the city. Some other lady, the highest ranking UN person that crawls. All Bruno's got to do is go back to area 8 and the UN person does to, just meet up and add her. But Bruno won't do it. Then he added the jamaican lady instead. That made the EU guy get real snippy. I really thought he was going to get killed. Bruno didn't kill him though. He wanted to, but didn't. He probably still does. I do. I hate that guy.

I only killed one actual person so far. When we got ambushed in area 7. Bruno thought it was going to be a big deal and mess me up in the head. But it didn't. I stabbed him in, like, the armpit area as Bruno got his neck, so we kind of both killed him together. And that scumbag killed my friend. And doc too. And doc was my friend. Nevena was my first real friend in here. Well, first real friend around my age. Bruno was my first friend, and doc too. Bruno is my BFF forever and always. But if anyone kills my friends I'll kill them and my mind is find with it. It didn't bother me at all.

Well, not that much. Maybe a little. I don't like thinking about it but sometimes my mind makes me.

No dungeon so far has given that death ward armor. So unless it's a reward for 9-9, it has to come from an area 10 dungeon.

Area 10. Level 10. Almost everyone's a pure class, and they'll all get their first paragon feat next level. Even some PRCs get a paragon feat next level. So stupid. We'll only get one, and a long time from now too. And the one we're getting stinks. Well, it's not that bad. But not nearly as good as what a lot of classes get. Level 10 fighters get second skin. That removes the movement penalty in medium armor, and halves it for heavy armor. And allows you to sleep in medium armor. But since we're dwarves and have slow and steady, it does nothing for us. A pure 20 fighter gets second skin II, which removes the movement penalty from heavy armor and allows you to sleep in heavy armor. At least that one would have done something for us. We could sleep in our armor. Wow! So awesome! Just kidding. That is dumb and only saves you thirty seconds. So dumb. You can take a fighter bonus feat instead of the paragon, so we are going to do that.

And we're only going 8 levels into rogue so we miss out on their paragon. And the rogue feat thing. The special level 10 feat for the special rogue abilities. I forget the name. Like the mind one that lets you roll saves twice or something. The rogue paragon for regular rogues isn't great. I forget the name, but we got a feat that does basically the same thing. I think we should've gone 10 rogue to get that paragon and one of the special rogue feats, but Bruno is set on fighter 12 for the better weapon specialization feat, which you need for the epic weapon specialization feat.

The equipment we got at level 7 is pretty nice. We both have mainly the same gear, besides the crafted stuff. We both have Layla's night mask for our heads. It lets us cast lesser restoration 2x per day and adds +1 to stealth. We haven't put any points into stealth, so that part is a waste. We use it for the restoration. And a day is 240 minutes. Real minutes. Four real hours. Two restorations every four hours is pretty nice. We got that as a reward from one of the area 8 dungeons. We also both mainly wear the cape of lesser rescue, which gives 10 temp HPs for one turn. A turn is 10 rounds. 10 rounds is 60 seconds. So one minute. I wish they'd just use what it actually lasted for instead of making you do math in your head.

For store bought stuff we have bracers of fort saves +1. Boots of dodge +1. Necklace of natural armor +1. Ring of deflection +1. Full plate +1, but I usually wear our vanadium armor since the fireball incident. For belt we wear a +1 reflex saves. Belt slot can be any of the saves. Bracers fort only. Boots reflex only. Head is will only. But belt can be any of the three. Boots are the only piece dodge can go on, so we always use dodge boots and never swap them out. Deflection comes on bracers or rings, and we use the ring so we can have fort bracers and the reflex belt.

We both also have a heavy shield +1. And +1 weapons. Plus, another dungeon reward was a ghost touched weapon, so we use that when there are dumb ghosts with their stupid concealment or whatever it is. Another dungeon reward was a necklace of either poison or disease immunity. I took poison since there's a lot more poison attacks that are usually weapon attacks or a melee touch attack and Bruno is better than me at not getting hit. He took the disease one.

Bruno is better at reminding me to change my equipment than he is at remembering to change his. For our second ring we usually leave on +2 search. But there're a lot more jumping and rope use checks in these dungeons, so we have those rings too. And a ring of escape +2 we've only used once but should have used more. We usually just try to break-free instead of escaping when we need to, but neither of us opened the break-free skill so escape would be a little better, especially with the ring on. We also have a spare cloak of natural armor for when we need to use our necklace of poison or disease immunity. Natural armor is either cloak or necklace.

Quest reward items can't be traded. Or vendored. You have to destroy them to get them out of your inventory. Or put the item in a bank slot.

We also have spare regular weapons for the stupid mobs that do a lot of durability damage to weapons. Those mobs are the worst.

We also have a ton of clicky items. Items with spells on them that usually recharge every day. Fourth age day, so four hours. They were very, very expensive. But sometimes you need them. I have all the ones Bruno has, and some extras. We both have identify, divine favor, entropic shield, protection from evil, remove fear, shield, expeditious retreat, and feather fall. I only used feather fall in one dungeon. We had to jump down a big pit. It was awesome! Bruno makes me put it on when he thinks I might fall. It only lasts 12 seconds, so we have to time it good. And we forget to use a lot of the other stuff when it would be helpful, too. Bruno sucks at remembering. Unless it's a big deal for me, then he always remembers. All those items are split up between wands and slots you can fill with clickies. So head, cloak, boots, rings, and necklace.

I have two extra clickies Bruno doesn't. I have a sanctuary clicky, which only lasts the rest of the round I activate it in, and the round after. And I have a ray of enfeeblement clicky. It never works on bosses so it's basically useless. He makes me have it though, for some imaginary scenario in which it's useful. It works on mini-bosses or rare spawns with lower saves, but we always forget the mini-bosses. And rare spawns are super, super rare.

All our kits are +2 now. And my tent is coming along. It got another upgrade, but's still crap compared to Bruno's. A lot better than it used to be though, when I first got it.

We got a second attack in our attack chain at level 7. So sometimes, when turtling makes more sense, we put on auto attack. But usually we leave on free attack. We'll use auto more when we have three attacks in our attack chain. Level 7 was our fifth fighter level. No feats or nothing that level.

We also spent a ton on a death ward wand. But it will take a bunch of tries to activate it and then we also got to pass a save because of true grit, so I'm only supposed to do it when Bruno tells me to or in an emergency. It has 10 charges. We have a lot of scrolls too. But we have the same issue with scrolls as wands, except they have a lower DC to activate and a lower save is needed. With just 3 rogue levels now, we don't have the skill points to put in UMD to do more. It's at 6 now, and has been for a while. And there're no rings or nothing to raise UMD. Just feats and skill points.

The scroll case is pretty cool. That was another dungeon award. It holds a ton of scrolls and gives an extra hotbar just for scrolls. Since we hardly ever use scrolls, I don't leave the bar open. I just quickslotted the case, and when I need a scroll I hit the quickslot and that opens the hotbar with all the scrolls in it.

I miss doc. She was nice. And she was always around. Now she isn't. Like mom and dad. And stupid Carlos too. Our main doc now is another specialist doctor. But she was also a surgeon. I forget what the name of what she did is, but she saw patients about women stuff, and then did surgeries to remove their ovaries and uteruses and stuff. Her name is doc Vega. She is from las vegas. Bruno thinks that's hilarious. He always goes, "Hey, doc Vega from vegas." She is really old. Older than Bruno even. Like old, old, old like the general was.

There's also a psychiatrist and a psychologist. I forget which is which. One is an MD and kind of knows medical stuff. The other, the one that isn't an MD, he bothered Bruno until Bruno made me talk to him. He wasn't as bad as the old devil hag, but I don't like talking to people. Not about the kind of stuff they want me to talk about. About my parents and being the darkness and stuff like that. At the end of our talk, Bruno came over. The guy recommended to Bruno I talk to him a bunch more, but Bruno said that was up to me. I said no, thank you. The guy was nice and all, but I just don't think it will help me. Later, Bruno said he understood. And that talking was good for some people, but not people like us. People who used our hate-balls. Hold it in and use it. Hold it in until you can't. It's good when we talk about stuff to others like us. Like when me and Bruno talk about stuff. That helps.

I freaked out on Bruno when we were training. I was trying to do some arm bar called a wacky something. Something g. Some Japanese word, I think. I never really saw it in the MMA videos I've seen. But it's hard to get and he kept slapping me when I left myself open trying to get it. When we do hand-to-hand training we do it without HP shields. I got real mad that I kept getting slapped and couldn't get close to getting the bar, so I started yelling and punching Bruno in the face. And he gave me his face to punch and let me do it. And when I was done he said I hit like a girl and that made me just lose it and I went crazy on him, and he ended up putting me over his knee and spanking me. And I bit his leg and his arm and his hand real good. He pretended like that didn't hurt, but it did. I know it did. And he ended up restraining me until I lost steam and started crying. Not sad crying. Crying because I was angry and frustrated and Bruno was being a jerk and there was nothing I could do about it.

Joey didn't like what was happening to me, which made me feel better. He started stimming real hard at Bruno and making his real bad and loud frustrated noises. We made up after that, and Bruno said he kept slapping me because I kept not paying attention to anything but trying to get the wacky whatever the bar is called. I got to learn to pay attention. He said we already went over how to do it, so I can't just stare at the arm I'm going for, because it telegraphs my intentions and leaves me open. To things like slaps.

A lot of things just click, and you just finally get it. But when you don't, it's very frustrating. For me at least. Having that freak-out made me feel better. And actually hurting Bruno with my bites made me feel good. I bet my punches hurt real bad too, and he just lied about it and pretended they didn't. Jerk. I love that big, dumb son of a bee, but sometimes he drives me real nuts. Right up a wall.

I still don't know what that means. Drive someone up a wall. I know it means make them nuts, but why? Do a lot of crazy people climb walls, or something?

Now I'm just bored. But I got my first actual mission from Bruno! Me and Gunny are going to go figure out what the issue is in some of the dungeon areas where people are ignoring the messages to switch instances. Starting with area 2. And we are humping there. Gunny is supposed to see if I can hump up to marine standards. But he's going slow! So slow! I can hump way, way faster than this. And I'm pretty sure I'm humping more weight than he is too.

Gunny's okay. I've mostly forgiven him for kidnapping me before. I think we're on the same page now, and he knows to never do some crap like that again. No matter what Bruno says. And when we get back – 9-9 baby! Level 10. Or we should be doing it. It has to be soon. Not this opening. I'm not even doing an old dungeon this opening. Just this mission. But I was trusted with an important mission, so that is awesome! Go me!

And we'll just tear area 10 apart when we finally do it. I know it. We are way better than the idiots that all died in area 10 in Bruno's last timeline. We got to be doing 9-9 soon. Everyone is being babies about it, and no one will even talk about it. Bunch of sissy babies. Scaredy cats.

Bruno doesn't even seem to care about level 10 now for some reason. He's just been doing the stupid arena non-stop forever. Not even with me. With a bunch of jerks. Well, not jerks. But they ain't me. It kind of hurts he's doing that without me. But all those people are definitely better than I am. For now.

Just means I got to improve and keep on improving.

Bruno's wife said she has a surprise for me when I get to the city. But we got to do 9-9 first and no one seems motivated to do it. I probably should call her by her name, but Minnie just seems silly. All I think of is Minnie Mouse. And Minnie Mouse has been in a ton of my modules at school, teaching about social stuff. Sexuality and gender identity and stuff like that. Her and Mickey and all of those guys. Until I got here. Now I don't got to go to dumb school, which is absolutely awesome. I hate school. Learning stuff is so stupid. Nothing I ever learned in school has helped me here, in this world.

So, a real person actually named Minnie just seems too weird. I call her Ms. Vaz in chat, but her name in my contacts is Bruno's wife. She always says to call her Minnie when I call her Ms. Vaz. That's too weird though. That's like meeting a guy named Mickey or Goofy.

We got a great feat at level 8 that gives us magic resistance. A whole bunch too, especially with our heavy shields. I wanted to switch to tower shields since we can use them, but Bruno says no. They are too unwieldy and lower BAB by 2. We got our first racial specialization point at 8. Wasted it on some garbage called stonestupid. Bruno says it will be real good later, and is pretty great now, but I don't think so. It just makes the search area bigger. The second thing it did was bugged. We already automatically search in outside environment dungeons, like treests and swamps. So it just makes the search area a little bigger. Woopty do. Seems like a big waste. I think we should have specialized in hardiness against spells.

At level 9 we got a feat called rush n' attack. When Bruno says it out loud my mind changes it to russian attack. That's pretty funny. I think so, at least. But that feat is so awesome. I love having an iframe. We can't be damaged at all when we are charging. So we can ping-pong and target the farthest enemy and not worry about ghost arms. I love it. It's a ton of fun, too. Rush n' attack really changed how we do things, and makes fighting a lot more funner.

Holy moly! I don't even know if this counts as a hump. We are going so slow! Bruno never humps this slow. This isn't even a workout.

4.1 IN APPREHENSION, HOW LIKE A GOD

BRUNO VAZ

PART 4 "TEST"

"Nobody can give you freedom. Nobody can give you equality or justice or anything. If you're a man, you take it."
- Malcolm X

Ball-face tells me PFC Jones switched instances in area 3. That's the signal Kim's in area 3 now. Almost time. I'm nervous, but I pretend I'm not. You'd have to be an idiot to not be a little bit nervous.

"You're actually doing it?"

"Yeah," I reply to Ball-face.

"You dumb bastard. You know you're playing right into your enemy's hands."

"I might be ugly, but at least I ain't got no money." I forget what that's from, but it always cracked me up. It's a great conversation changer. Usually.

"Well, then you're an ugly, broke, idiot."

I laugh. "I never said I was smart."

Ball-face is getting frustrated. His face turns red and he raises his voice, "You did say you weren't an idiot, though. You think Gunny is going to out maneuver these people? Keep your family safe? Keep Kim safe?"

That hits a sore spot. But I have it worked out. Mostly. Minnie will give up the government to the UN. She has always been a 'go along to get along' type. Her relinquishing power from a position of power should keep her and my kids safe. And it was kind of agreed with higher-ups that my family would be fine if I did this. Nothing was said; more of an unspoken agreement.

Kim is going to have a hissy fit. No chance she can make it back in time to do something stupid. She's safe. As long as Gunny follows directions. I trust him. Keeping all this a secret from Kim wasn't easy. But either I die and she's safe, or the next time I see her I will be victorious and she'll be too excited to be mad at me. Either way, she lives.

I'm still worried my wife knows something's up or was tipped off and will try to stop me. I'm going to make Gunny assistant guild leader when I get in 9-9. When I get out 9-9, I'm going to level up to 10 wicked fast, then make Minnie the prime dictator, and the guild leader. I left letters in our room she'll find after. Letters to her, Siri, and Nate. Gunny has a note to give to Kim. I wish I could see Minnie adopt Kim. The plan was for us both to adopt her, but if I'm not there, Minnie still will. She's good like that. Good with kids. Better than I am. Most people are. Kids don't usually like me. Especially when they're really little.

I tell Ball-face, "Come on, man. You know I'd do everything I could to make sure my family's safe. And Kim."

"As safe as they'd be with you alive? Protecting them?"

"Maybe safer. I paint a big target on all their backs. And you make it seem like I'm definitely going to die. If anyone can beat 10 solo, it's Bruno Vaz."

"Ha! You said all the best fighters died in area 10 in your last time-line. How many were there? Thirty? Fifty? A hundred? A thousand? You're good, but you're not thirty people good. If by some miracle you beat 10 solo, you have to know you're not long for this world. The UN isn't going to just give up power. Especially not to you. Once the Secretary-General is in the city, the UN is going to hyper-focus on you. Apply pain to weak points. You're a curiosity. A distraction. Helpful for your knowledge and your achievements that let you communicate to everyone. You're not needed, though. Especially not after 10. Your messaging ability won't be so valuable. We'll have the portal to the city, and all civilians in the city too. We'll be able to communicate through other means. If you were smart, you would've held back more important information. Or came up with some lie that would keep you alive and needed after 10.

"But what do you do? You're helping your enemies kill two birds with one stone. I don't get it. You're smarter than this."

Well, I think I've proven otherwise plenty of times. I'm not smarter than this. And I don't really want to be. I didn't fall into a trap – I walked into it with my eyes wide open. Wide open. When the EU walrus looking guy, Alban or whatever his name is, proposed I go into 10 alone, I was immediately a yes in my head. The scrying plan is just icing on the cake.

It's a good plan. For a bunch of reasons.

First, I don't want to die. Mainly because I know I'm going to hell and I really don't want to go there. I think all people like me are always looking for a way to game the system. Like, happen upon a burning pre-school you run into and die saving a hundred babies. Get enough 'selfless hero credit' they have to let you into heaven. They don't got no choice but to let you in.

Life never threw me a burning school where I could save a bunch of ankle-biters. Not even a burning house where I could save a family. I got the opposite. I'm usually the one starting the fires, digging my hole to hell deeper.

Not only would me sacrificing myself for this mission get me into heaven, I'm Bruno Vaz, so I could actually win. Get all the heaven-credit and still live. Probably not, though. If this was area 20 I would definitely die solo. That…damn, I can never remember the name of that thing in area 10. Leech? The guy with the jar you got to destroy. There were a million zombies with him too, but just that leech guy would've rolled me up like a rug.

So, I get credit for saving tons of people, there's a possibility I live, even if I die my family is probably safer than if I'm around, and humanity's chances of getting back to earth skyrocket. The chances skyrocket because there are a lot of real monsters that will live because of my sacrifice. Fighters almost as good as me. Almost as good as Sidis. Almost.

There's also a really personal reason. I hate politicians. They're all power-mad, scumbag, evil cowards. Always sending better men to die for their lies. There's no denying it – here, now, I'm a politician. I can show the world what that can mean. Should mean. When people think politician, they think leader. Leaders should lead by example. Not depend on better men to make the sacrifices. Men with honor and duty and balls. Leaders should be men with honor and duty and balls – even if they're women.

Kim would make a great leader. She has more balls than half the guys in Delta. And she even has a good heart. Most people like us don't. Not like Kim. Real values. Wholesome values. For the most part. I wish she'd stop peeing on dead mobs so much. And knock all this 'darkness' crap off.

The plan is good. Solid. I'm not sending someone else to throw their life away. Surprisingly, Ball-face said he's go in my stead. He said it that way. I'd say 'go instead,' like every normal person would. It was very touching. Gunny volunteered too. I shut the volunteering down quick.

Eh, I guess that wasn't really the last reason. The last reason is my balls made me do it. The thought of me versus a whole zone that killed all the best fighters last time? I won't lie, the thought of that gives me a stiffy. This is what I was born for. This is what I was made for. Me versus everything you can throw at me. I've been in some real tight spots before. Bad situations. Real bad. Stuck between a rock and a hard place more times than I can count. No one else would've lived. I did.

This. This is what I do.

I'm Bruno Vaz.

I tell Ball-face, "Maybe if Sidis was here, he'd probably be able to think of some way out of it and get everyone through 10 alive. Wait till you see him. Or read his stuff. Wicked smart. Fights like a mofo. No passion. All calculations and efficiency. Real weird to see. Like a robot. Small guy too. Shorter than you, and smaller too. Me? I'm just an idiot with some giant balls. This is the best plan we got. I can't think of nothing better. I don't think you can neither. With the amount of people we got scrying, we win no matter what. Just make sure you help with the planning once you see what we're up against. Don't let the EU weasel take control and get good guys killed. You think I should kill him real quick before I enter? Do we got the time? He could really use some killing."

"Christ, Bruno, no. God, help us. When you killed Premier Dalembert that absolutely and positively hurt your cause. It hurt you more than him. It hurt your family. It hurt us – the people working with you. You see that, right? I really hope you see that. Killing Alban would make everything ten times worse. He's the President of the European Council for Christ's sake. Your family may get out of this alive as things stand now. You kill Alban, they aren't just going to kill your family. Your family will wish they were only just killed. Think, Bruno! There are people around you that will pay for your actions. This isn't a game for them, and it shouldn't be for you either."

Jesus, talk about being dramatic. I doubt anyone would miss Alban. He gets on everyone's nerves. Scrying is the key to all this. It means I don't need to win. I plan on winning, but I don't need to. I just got to see everything we're up against. See what killed every one last time. And then smarter people than me can plan on how to beat whatever we're up against.

There's a decent sized pond in this area. Dungeon area 9. Pond may be too grand a word for it. A big pool of water. Doc Vega's a druid and is going to use the pool to scry, with most of the leadership here with her, watching. Wizards and sorcs can get the same spell at level 9 too. Clerics don't get scry until level 11. No matter what, they'll know what they're up against in 10. If the scrying works. Hopefully it does.

Doctor Vega from Vegas. That cracks me up. That'd be like a Doctor Bosto from Boston. I don't know why no one else thinks that's funny. It is. She's pretty old now, but you can tell she was bangable when she was younger. Not hot, but bangable. She ain't bangable no more, though. I'm pretty open to banging olds if they still look good, so I'm not being closed-minded about her age or nothing. She didn't age well.

We coordinated with the other instances so they could watch too. I emailed all the arena leaders telling them to go to area 8, we all switched to the same instance, and we could talk in person. I try not to go to lower level areas because the one time I did I got ambushed by UN idiots, so everyone thought I was dumb to go. I still did, because I'm Bruno Vaz. No one ever said I was smart. I think some people planned something, but once they found out I was going on a suicide mission, life became a lot more peaceful. Safe enough to even send Kim back to earlier zones without me.

If your enemy is destroying himself without your help, why stop him?

My worry is with my high fort saves they may not be able scry me. High will saves really, but same thing now for me with the true grit feat. So we have tons of people scrying. Lots of people have the spell. Wizards and sorcerers bought it if they could. The politicians wanted me to use the government taxes collected so far to buy scrolls for wizards and sorcerers that didn't have it, but Minnie would have killed me. She earmarked most of the gold as spent already.

And it would've tipped my hand to Minnie something big is going on. Each scroll is 1,125g in the store node thing. The wizards and sorcerers can fund it themselves, or pool their own money together. Minnie is going to use all that gold for useless government projects and to kick-start crafting magic items. There's over 20k gold in the government coffers. Just a 2% tax rate on trade brought that in. Why is everyone in the city always begging me for gold and mats if that much trade is going on in my portable AH? That's nuts. If 2% is 20k, how much was traded?

1% of 2 million is 20k. So 1 million? Jesus Christ Almighty. And it's more than that. It was like 24k in the government coffers. That's just crazy. 2% was the lowest tax rate I could select. I was going to bump it up to 5% when the city opens, but if just my instance has had over a million in sales from just my portable AH, we'll be rolling in gold. Jesus, Joseph, and Mary.

And if I die and Minnie gives up to the UN, hopefully she grabs it all. Screw them.

They want me to take all my items off that increase my will saves. But I'm not doing that. I want all my numbers as high as I can get them. The spell description for scrying in the SRD says certain things increase the chances I won't save against it, but the dorks say none of that was coded into the game. Just in case we had everyone that could cast the scrying spell meet me in person, pictures of me and a bunch of items that cost a copper I bought and held were handed out to everyone, and I had a professional barber cut my hair and shave me and we handed my hair out too. Who knows? This place works different than in the game. It could help. No one knows for certain what does and doesn't work here regarding magic. All we know for certain is things were changed. I'm not taking off my +1 to fort saves. I need all the help I can get.

"I was just kidding," I lie. This place would be dramatically improved with Alban dead. And it would increase our chances of getting back to earth too. But I don't want to rile Ball-face up any further.

"I hope so. You all plused up yet?"

"No. Of course not. As soon as I spend dungeon coins, Kim will get notified in party chat. But not if I'm in the dungeon. Once I enter solo, she won't have party chat. She won't know anything until I exit and make the changes to the government and guild."

I see the dungeon gem thing flashing one the minute warning. Savage minute. Not a real minute.

Ball-face puts his hand out for me to shake. I grip it. His eyes look glassy. I hope he doesn't start crying like a little girl.

"Bruno, I can't say you're a genius, but you have my respect. I can still switch out with you if you want. It would make more sense to sacrifice me instead of you."

"No. We need more officers like you that ain't all ate-up. You ended up being a pretty good guy, Major Goodman. If you really want to do me a solid, make sure my family's safe. Kim too. And don't let the walrus get too many good men killed."

Ball-face snaps to attention and renders a salute. A lot of other military people in the area close to 9-9 do too, and some civilians. I stand tall at attention. I crisply return the salute. The gem turns green and I enter the dungeon.

4.2 SPENDING COINS AND PLUSING UP

BRUNO VAZ

I double check everything to see if I'm ready. Kim is going to freak out when I exit and she gets the guild and world government notifications. Gunny better handle that, or I'll destroy him. I hate this stupid dungeon. Five levels. Every level is more ridiculous than the next. Mangar's Tower. Who comes up with this garbage? Sadistic bastards. So many nonsense rooms. None of it makes any sense. Dungeons with riddles are the worst.

And the psuchesoma was ridiculous. A spelling one. Ennui. I tried all the possible ways. A.N.W.E. And A.H.N.W.E And A.N.W.E.E. I only had three shots, but if it isn't spelled A.H.N.W.E.E. then it just isn't spelled right. Those are the only four possible ways to spell it. Stupid French. I will destroy them. How are they so bad at spelling?

I finally got another rare spawn too. Kim won't like that. I hope I get a chance to tell her.

I was expecting the rare spawn would drop something good, something useful. But it was a stupid staff that increases the DC of illusion spells. Garbage. And that was it. What happened to tailored loot? And I never saw a rare spawn only drop one item. This dungeon is screwing me over big time. Boss drops were garbage too. The staff will probably auction for a ton though. Maybe I'll get a chance to sell it.

I instinctually go to party chat to tell Kim to meet back up with me at the exit, and it isn't there. I forgot. I'm not in a party no more. Not since I entered 9-9. I'm on my own. Old habits.

I'm kind of nervous, but excited too. Too bad Sidis never showed. I'm a goddamn idiot and I could've used his help.

Eh, I may be an idiot, but at least I'm not a pussy. I laugh because for some reason that reminds me of Eastbound and Down. Man, that show was good. Last timeline I was told they did a season 4. That's enough reason to want to live and get back to earth. They also said Kenny Powers did a couple other great shows. One about being a principal a couple people said was better than Eastbound and Down.

When I was running missions for Delta, I got tapped for a lot of off-book missions. Missions that would most likely result in the operator being dead. Mostly CIA run missions. You can't get ordered to go on those missions. The only competent operators in the CIA are prior Delta or SEAL operators that couldn't keep up with the big boys, so stepped down into pogue-land. And as pogues they run missions instead of going on them. Since they don't have their own people capable of completing their tough missions, they always hit up Delta. For those types of missions, you always demand two things as conditions for accepting – an honorable out and a favor.

The favor was always the same – don't search me when I get back stateside. The CIA only runs missions on the powerful, and the powerful always have plenty of cash on hand. We got a ton at home. Hidden real good. You can't buy no big ticket items, but nothing stops you from eating or ordering out every night. And you don't got to feel bad about taking it, because if you don't, the CIA will. The agents and operators and techs and specialists all get their beaks wet. The rest goes to the CIA coffers, to continue to fund their war of terror on the world. The less money those monsters have, the better off everyone is.

Minnie was cool about splitting the cash when we divorced. She didn't even take half. Probably only took less than a quarter. Having that much cash always scared the bajeebus out of her. Me? I'm too cheap to know what to do with it. I used some on prostitutes, but prostitutes aren't as fun as getting a new, normal girl to bang you of her own violation. I never liked animal hunting, but I'll never get tired of hunting for new stink holes.

The honorable out was usually a ridiculous, but plausibly realistic, demand you said was absolutely necessary to complete the mission. The CIA pogues have no idea what is actually needed for a competent operator to complete a mission. Asking for something big ensures there'll be some sort of paper trail on their end if they get it – some higher up signed something. That's extra protecting in case they try to throw you under the bus. And it ensures they're invested in the mission. If they get what you asked for, it means the mission is more than just some petty revenge plot or just scratching a buddy's back. If they are willing to spend for a big ticket item, it's an authentic mission. Sure, a mission hatched by some corrupt SES scumbag or evil politician, but a real one, even if not sanctioned.

Most guys in Delta are like the ones they show in movies. Always serious, and they think knowing about and owning the best weapons and gear makes them tougher. "I only wear this wicked expensive tacvest. And this knife cost eight bazillion dollars. You don't have these boots? I'm more competent than you." A lot of officers are exactly like that. The enlisted guys getting tapped for the most missions are usually like me, because they get the best results. I know enough. I don't need to spit out a bunch of useless facts about different brands of this rifle, or that knife. The best operators can get it done with the worst gear. And I'm not wasting my own money on weapons and gear when the taxpayers get me really great stuff. Delta's budget is well funded.

You couldn't ask for something that could be tied back to the US, like Spectre gunship support. My cover was rock solid. And my cover allowed me to request some real expensive stuff. I'd ask around what the newest and best super expensive thing was, and ask for it. Sometimes I'd have a use for it. Most of the time I didn't.

My honorable out, my big ask to make sure they were serious, for going alone into area 10 was completing the 5-man arena up to 100. That's when I found out a lot of people have been plusing themselves up all along. Tora Hige or Ren or whatever that guy's name is. His wife too. What kind of idiots go by their video game names? He'd have never beat me the very first time we dueled if he wasn't plused up. He is fast though. Wicked fast. But how much of that is the stupid rpg system? I'd like to fight him in the real world. I bet I'd roll him up quick.

A ton of people are plused up. Tons of squishy casters too. More people took my advice than expected, but a lot of people didn't. Oh well. You can lead a horse to water and all that.

So many people being plused up is the only reason we got it done. We couldn't do it with just the people in our area 9. We had to go back to 8 and get different people. Ren was a constant. And Ren's wife. Her body is banging. Her face ain't so great. Real sexy voice. She can fight. I'll give her that. She even helped me and gave me some axe pointers. Her style's way different than mine, but she knows a ton about axe fighting. Small axes. Not big ones, like mine. Still helped. And her build is real useful. Both me and her ain't full dps and not full tanks neither. But, since she is plused up she did pretty good damage. Better damage than I put out. And she can off-tank pretty good.

Both of Ren and his wife plusing up makes sense since Ren's class was made specifically for him. He knows exactly what his build was going to be – all the extra feats and stuff is just icing on the cake for him. And both were paid to play the game this stupid rpg system is based on, so they know what they're doing. Better than most.

The 5-man 100 boss is a souped-up ultimate version of the deer-head monster with the laser beam eyes. None of the plused up squishies were any help. Wizards and other casters still suck at level 9. Haste is great, but they die too easy. The rest of us being hasted is nice, but wasn't useful enough to make bringing a caster feasible. Ren was our main DPSer. We wanted the laser on him last. Me and his wife, Ryu, were decent DPSers that could take the laser beam for a good bit. We just needed a tank that did decent damage and a healer that could take a hit and also do damage.

For a healer, we got the druid that opened the arena in area 3. Intense guy. Great healer. Throws damage and debuff spells, and even can melee like a champ. Natural fighter. From…I forget. Nigeria maybe. Somewhere in Africa. Named Adoome? Adomi? I call him Tooth because he only has one good one. Got the rest busted out having to fight all his life. Real busted up face. He looks pretty awesome. He can scare the crap out of people by just looking at them with his ugly mug. But he's actually wicked nice. Barely laughs, but when he does he laughs hard. He hasn't taken any healing pills yet, but I wonder what he'll look when he's taken enough to fix his grill. If I live, and that happens, I'll have to come up with a new nickname for him.

The tank we ended up with hates me with a passion. Some German guy pretending he's a robot. Said his name was a bunch of numbers. Real weird guy. Dodge tank. No taunt. Ended up getting a decent taunt ability with a token. Everyone has the regular taunt, but without feats and charisma it sucks wicked bad and is a waste of time doing it. The taunt he got was one his class gets automatically at a later level. I think he was willing to waste a token because he wants me dead so bad.

This guy threw more hissy fits than anyone I ever met. More than the most hysterical of women even. And he cries a lot too. He always says I'm making fun of him, even when I'm not. Or when I barely was. He looks a little like Buffalo Bill from Silence of the Lambs, but he sounds exactly like that guy. Exactly. So the first time we were introduced and he did his robot spiel I said, "She puts the lotion on her skin, or she gets the hose again," and then the water works and a hissy fit. What kind of robot cries and has hissy fits all the time? None. No robot ever cries and has hissy fits. Real nimble guy though. He can dodge like a mofo. Real motivated to clear 100 and send me off to my death. Way more HPs than dodge tanks usually have. He could take the eye lasers as good as our pure con tanking alt, but needed way less heals getting to that phase.

We barely made it. I didn't plus myself up. If we couldn't clear 100 I didn't want to be stuck with this build. I couldn't withdraw anything without Kim knowing anyways. Then she'd ask questions and figure out what was going on. The system alerts you when a party member spends dungeon coins. Even without being plused up, I still held my own and did even better than the others. That's why I'm Bruno Vaz. I had a blast. And we all were wicked excited when we finally did it.

I open my character sheet and see if I could've made better choices. Something nags me like I could of. But I'm not smart enough to see what.

I went crazy trying to go higher on the 2-man arena to get more coins, but I couldn't. I had 993 dungeon coins from dungeons coming in here. I cleared 45 dungeons. I got 22 of each colored coin from 1st SS 42 times. And 25 from my one solo 1st SS. We got 18 for 2nd SS once. And 8 two times from regular SS. And 10 each from a rare before. I got another 10 each in here from the rare, but I already spent all my coins by then. And they don't let me get anything else anyways.

I got 100 of each coin for clearing arena 1 through 100 of each type – solo through 5-man.

You start getting 5 for each fight completed from 101 to 200. Then 10 coins from 201 to 300. I cleared 159 in 1-man, 157 in 2-man, 109 in 4-man, and 101 in 5-man. So 295 red, 285 green, 45 yellow, and 5 grey for what we cleared over 100 in each. We might've gone higher in the 5-man, but there was no point. I would have to go way higher to be able to get anything else. And no way were we beating the 110 boss. We probably would've had to put a ton of effort into beating the 105 mini-boss. For no actual gain since it wouldn't get me nothing else.

So, all totaled I had 1388 red, 1378 green, 1138 yellow, and 1098 grey to spend. For beating the boss at level 100 of each arena, I already could withdraw tokens for an additional racial spec point from the 1-man, a racial ability opener from the 2-man, a token for any feat that isn't a class feat or an epic feat, ignoring other prerequisites, from the 4-man, and the best thing ever – a token for any epic feat from the 5-man. Any epic feat at all. Regardless of requirements. You only get three of those in total. From beating the 100, 200, and 300 5-man. We never beat the level 300 5-man boss in my timeline. It was ridiculously hard. Impossible with who we had. Everyone thinks you get a bunch of great rewards for clearing 300 on all four types of arenas. No idea. We never did it.

I never planned on plusing up this build. So there was a million things I could do, but no idea what I should do. I decided to plan like I was going to win and continue dungeon crawling, so no gimping myself. If this came up before level 8 I would never have put my racial spec point in stonecunning. That's for sure.

You can get a lot of good stuff with dungeon coins. With the grey coins you can get eight ability increase tokens for 500 coins each, and a max of two racial spec points for 500 each.

With yellow coins, with a max of five for each, and costing 500 coins each, you can get specialization points or epic feat tokens. But you have to qualify for the epic feat besides the epic level requirement. Not bad for ones without prerequisites, like prowess or armored skin – but a killer for most of the good ones.

For green, each for 500, you could get eight feat tokens, or two cross-class feature tokens. Any feature from any class. Well, almost. There are some exceptions. Like, you can't get dragon apotheosis from dragon disciple unless you already picked a colored dragon. Otherwise it isn't even listed. So I can't get it. There are only two ways to get it. First, you have to get a sorc or bard level and waste another class slot on at least one dragon disciple level. Second, you could pick the dracon race. That race is garbage. Another -2 con race, and has -2 int too. No auto search. They get +2 str and cha. And their breath attack sucks unless you go caster, and works even better if you go dragon disciple. Their claws are pretty good for unarmed monks, and they get a bite attack like half-orcs. For what I'm doing, they suck wicked bad, so that's out. It'd be real stupid to pick a race just for one feat you can get. It's a great feat, sure, but not worth getting a crap race for your build and how you fight.

The class features scaling with class level of a particular class you don't have aren't good picks either. Most SLAs and pet and cohort features do that.

Red coins are kind of boring. For 95 coins each you can get a max of 40 skill points. For 300 coins each you can get a max of four tokens that let you open an additional skill under a group skill, or turn a cross-class skill into a class skill.

When I entered this dungeon, at the store node, I went crazy thinking of what to get. Even the easy choice I was going to make was questionable. The any epic feat token – epic dodge. Dodge stinks as a feat. It raises your AC by 1 against one opponent and you have to pick that opponent every round. Most people just gesture it into how they usually do their first attack. I think it's a waste of a feat. But epic dodge is amazing. It completely voids out the first physical hit that hits you in a round. Which, if it is a game mob and not an imported mob, is their highest AB attack. Can't get better than that. And it requires 25 dex and a bunch of feats. Feats I couldn't get without going 13 rogue or wasting my two any cross-class feature token. And pumping up my dex ridiculously high. So I could never just get it with a regular epic feat choice.

But, I really wanted one of the tree guy's racial features. The bad part is that feature would lower all the healing I get by 50%, and last timeline I got a ton of crap from healers about true grit messing with their heals already. It would work if I got fast healing. I already planned on getting fast healing on my own with my regular epic feats when I hit epic levels. I love it. I get all three. All you can get. Same with DR. My con is 20, so if I could pump it up to 25 I could get fast healing. But then it would be dumb to open the tree guy's racial feature, since I wouldn't be able to put three spec points in it and get the good stuff from it, since I can only afford two racial spec points or two ability points. And I'd have to use my yellow coins to waste two epic feats on great con. And I'd still only be at 24 con and have wasted all my coins on garbage.

But, I need my HP over 100. If my math is right my HPs will be 98 at level 10. So I need 22 con at least, or the toughness epic feat, which has no requirements. That will make me immune in case anyone has that stupid power word kill spell. I hate that spell. What kind of spell has no save? A stupid one. It would make sense if everyone died last timeline to power word kill. Getting above 100 HPs by level 10 is rough, and if they faced as many mobs in 10 with power word kill, as we faced zombies in 20, no way anyone over 100 HPs could've survived them all.

So I planned on just holding on to the racial feature opener and racial spec point. That made everything easier. I'd still have to waste the two epic feats on great con to get to 22. And as I was looking through the epic feats for my any epic feat token, seriously considering stuff that may gimp me if I survive, like blinding speed since you always get a raid piece that has permanent haste on it later, or holy strike, it hit me – the quest reward for getting into 10 is an aura. I'm an idiot. I already talked to Kim about this and what aura we'd get. Getting to area 20 gives better auras. The aura for 10 has +1 stat and a minor effect you can't get on other items, for the most part. One of them being +1 fast healing. The epic feat gives you +3 fast healing each time you take it, so the aura is garbage compared to the feats. But I only need 1 con now, since I can get 1 from the aura. And +1 HP a round isn't a lot, but it is something. And along with the heal for the first hit in every round from the blood wyrm feature, it's enough for me to feel okay about getting the tree guy racial. And the heal counts as natural healing, so isn't lowered by the tree guy racial.

In first age the aura was supposed to help visually tell the function of a player. Auras made you glow a certain color in game. But that doesn't happen here, in this world. They don't glow at all.

Before I committed to that course I reviewed all the class features I could think of. A lot of good ones just don't help me. I'm built wrong for them. I felt good about some of what I was going to do, but the next part may be even more important. You only get two of the class feature tokens total. So I got to make good choices. One is a given. The blood-wyrm apotheosis. Wish I could get the dragon apotheosis too. Would've made everything easier. Made the two picks a given. Really plus up my attributes and it comes with a ton of natural armor. I think +4. And a bunch of other stuff. Lot of same immunities as the blood wyrm one, but lots of good stuff besides those.

It took forever to decide everything. Once I did I bought two epic feats with the yellow coins and had 138 left over. Two racial spec points with the greys, and had 98 left over. Two cross-class features with the greens and had 378 left over. And two of the group skill or cross-class skill openers, and 8 skill points with the reds, and had 28 left over.

Then I applied everything and destroyed this dungeon like a goddamn superhero.

I finish my review and close my character screen. I'm mostly happy, but still have the nagging feeling like I missed something big. I'm not happy I had to waste an epic feat on a con point, but I didn't see another way. And I had to waste coins on feats I was getting soon anyways. Or was going to get anyways. If I go all in on this build it will work out. And I'm stuck going all in now. I just got to shift some stuff around.

Eh, it is what it is. Still feels like I made a mistake and missed something big and obvious.

This is it. I reach for the exit. I want to hesitate more before going out, but my momma didn't raise no sissy.

4.3 DUNGEON AREA 10

BRUNO VAZ

I hit the door and appear in a large area with a ton of plants and a lot of trees. No mobs I see. My last timeline area 10 was a desert. Complete desert.

I had a mission once a while ago – I had to cross a bad piece of the Lut desert in Iran on foot. This zone was worse than that. Just completely lifeless. No plants. No nothing. Just harsh, fine sand. It wasn't hot like the Lut, but it was more lifeless. And I didn't think anything could be more lifeless than the Lut.

Why is it different this time?

I get the dungeon co0mplete popup. I end up only getting SS. Garbage. Stupid spelling nonsense screwed me. And all the time I wasted picking feats. For dungeon clear rewards I get two potions of fire shield and pick the aura I want. Aura of permanency. I switch my wife to guild leader, and then I make her leader of the world. There is only one spot for assistant dictator and I'm currently in that spot, so Gunny isn't in the world government leadership yet. Not officially. Or mechanically. Whatever. In the letter I left for Minnie I told her she can trust Gunny. For now at least. Who knows when I'm gone? He's more of a follower than a leader. I can't guess what he'll do when the UN starts pressuring him.

I wish I had that heart-to-heart with Ball-face before. I could have told Minnie he can sort of be trusted. I always thought he was more UN, and just followed along with General Edwards.

Kim got those notifications and will know something's up now. There should be zero chance she can get back before the dungeon closes. She sucks at running, and her legs should be noodles from the hump Gunny just took her on. No way she can hit this dungeon before it closes if she's in area 2 right now. And Gunny promised she'd be in area 2.

Time to level up. I feel a little sick my plans for the tree guy bounty hunter went right down the toilet. Eh, at least I won't have to redo all the dungeons over. If I live.

I equip the aura I just got and then I level up to 10. My only choice is a spec point. I put it in shield brace. If the boss here is a caster I want to be able to mitigate as much damage as possible.

I don't seem to be in danger so I open my character sheet again to look over where I'm at now.

Base (Ability Modifier) ((Misc.)) [Total]

CLASSES: 3 Rogue/7 Fighter

RACE: Stout Dwarf - Alignment: Chaotic Good - Deity: Catholic

HP: 4(34) (6(60)) ((5 Special Feat, 1(9) Toughness)) [108]

AC: 10 (2) ((9 Full Plate+1, 3 Heavy Shield+1, 1 Deflection, 1 Dodge, 1 Natural armor, 1 Tumble)) [28]

BAB: 9

ABILITIES

Str: 20 (5) ((0)) [20]

Dex 14 (2) ((0)) [14]

Con: 21 (6) ((1 Aura)) [22]

Int: 14 (2) ((0)) [14]

Wis: 10 (0) ((0)) [10]

Cha: 6 (-2) ((0)) [6]

SAVES

Fortitude: 6 (5) ((1 Item, 1 Spellcraft)) [13]

Reflex: 6 (2) ((1 Item, 1 Full of Beans, 1 Spellcraft)) [11]

Will: Same as Fort (True Grit feat)

COMBAT MODE: Free Attack/Auto Attack/Game Mode

MAIN HAND

Dwarven Waraxe

First Attack: AB: 9 (5) ((1 Weapon Focus)) [15]

Second Attack: AB: 9-5 (5) ((1 Weapon Focus)) [10]

DAM: 1d8 (5) ((2 Weapon Specialization)) Extra Damage=1d6 Blood Tap [8-15 Slashing, 1-6 Untyped], C 20, CM x3

449

OFF HAND

NA

OTHER ATTACKS (Bites, etc.)

NA

OTHER

Spell Failure: 50%

Max Dex Bonus: 1 Full Plate (+1 Armored Acclimation) [2]

Armor Check Penalty: -5 Full Plate, -1 Heavy Shield (-1 Armored Acclimation) [-5]

Energy Resistance (Acid 13/Cold 13/Electricity 13/Fire 13/Sonic 13)

DR 9/-

Spell Resistance: 5 + Character Level [14]

Immunities: Ability Damage, Ability Drain, Death Spells, Disease, Energy Drain, Knockdown, Magical Death Effects, Negative Energy Effects, Paralysis, Poison, Sleep

Fast Healing: 1 per turn

HOBBIES, CRAFTS, and PROFESSIONS

Hobby: Tinker level 10 (Maximum level is character level. No experience needed to level Hobbies. Hobbies level with character)

Crafts: NA

Professions: Porter level 3 (Increases Carry Capacity by 1 + (Porter level x 3). Maximum level is class level of the class used to open Profession. If multiclassing, a Profession can be selected twice or more and class levels can be combined to increase maximum Profession level. Unlike Hobbies, both Crafts and Profession require experience to level up)

SKILLS

5 At level 10, 0 carried over = 5

Italics cross class skill

*Armor Check Penalty applies

(Falls under above group skill)

Acrobatics* (Dex) 12 (2) ((ACP -5)) [9]

(Escape)

(Tumble) (10 base points in Acrobatics with Tumble selected and opened gives a +1 bonus to AC. 20 base points gives another +1 bonus, for a total of +2 bonus to AC. This counts as a skill bonus and stacks with everything.)

(Use Rope)

Athletics* (Str) 12 (5) ((ACP -5)) [12]

(Grapple)*

(Jump)*

(Run)* (Con) 12 (6) ((ACP -5)) [13] (10 base points in Athletics with Run selected and opened gives a +5 land speed bonus. 20 base points gives another +5 for +10 total land speed increase. This counts as a skill bonus and stacks with everything. This translates into a 7.5% speed increase at 10 and 20, 15% total.)

Disable Device (Int) 12 (2) ((2 Kit)) [16]

Heal (Wis) 13 (0) ((2 Kit)) [15]

Knowledge (Int) 12 (2) ((0)) [14]

(Arcane) 6 [8]

(Dungeoneering) 12 (2) ((2 Kit) [16]

(Geography) 6 (2) ((2 kit)) [10]

Open Lock (Dex) 12 (2) ((2 Kit)) [16]

Search (Int) 13 (2) ((2 Item)) [17]

Spellcraft (Int) 10 (2) ((0)) [12] 10 base points in Spellcraft gives a +1 bonus to all saves. 20 base points gives another +1, for a total of +2 bonus to all saves. This counts as a skill bonus and stacks with everything.)

Use Magic Device (Cha) 6 (-2) ((0)) [4]

Skill Points carried over to next level: 0

FEATS

* are selected feats or options

Level 1 (Rogue 1)

Destined for Greatness (Free feat given to all players of End of the Fourth Age that reads as follows: You were born under an auspicious sign and have a greater destiny than most born in Benekal or even all of Tibur. You receive +5 Hit Points at level 1)

Charge (Same as SRD, charges take three seconds regardless of distance in End of the Fourth Age. In new world, distance has been normalized to 60 feet for all players since there is no land speed)

Armor Proficiency (Light)

Shield Proficiency (Buckler)

Shield Proficiency (Light)

Weapon Proficiency (Dwarven Waraxe) (Dwarves may treat dwarven waraxes as martial weapons, rather than exotic weapons)

Weapon Proficiency (Rogue)

Weapon Proficiency (Simple)

Battle Training (Giants) (+4 dodge bonus to Armor Class against monsters of the giant type. Any time a creature loses its Dexterity bonus (if any) to Armor Class, such as when it's caught flat-footed, it loses its dodge bonus, too)

Battle Training (Orcs & Goblinoids) (+1 racial bonus on attack rolls against orcs and goblinoids)

Darkvision (See in the dark up to 60 feet. Darkvision is black and white only, but it is otherwise like normal sight, and character can function just fine with no light at all)

Hardiness (Poisons) (+2 racial bonus on saving throws against poison. First Racial Specialization gives an additional +1 on saving throws against poisons (total +3), and also increases saves against disease by +3. Second Racial Specialization gives an additional +1 on saving throws against poisons (total +4), and also increases saves against disease and death effects by +3. Third Racial Specialization grants immunity to poison)

Hardiness (Spells) (+2 racial bonus on saving throws against spells and spell-like effects. First Racial Specialization gives an additional +1 on saving throws against spells and spell-like effects (total +3). Second Racial Specialization gives an additional +1 on saving throws against spells and spell-like effects (total +4). Third Racial Specialization gives Spell Resistance equal to 5 + character level)

Stonecunning (+2 to Search checks indoors. Automatic Search checks indoors every six seconds with a radius of 10 feet. First Racial Specialization changes this to all environments, and increases the radius to 15 feet. Second Racial Specialization gives an additional +2 to Search checks and increases radius to 30 feet. Third Racial Specialization gives two Search checks per six seconds, automatic success to any check with a DC of 40 or less, an alarm function if something is found, and the DC of Sense Magic checks is reduced from 60 to 55)

Knowledge (Appraise) (+2 Appraise checks)

Knowledge (Dwarven Crafting) (+2 to Architect, Blacksmith, Engineer, Gemologist, Jeweler, Miner, Smelter, Tinker, and Trapsmith)

Slow & Steady (Dwarves start at land speed 20, but armor or load do not reduce a dwarf's speed. Translates to -15% speed for race, but no penalty to speed for armor or load debuffs. First Racial Specialization gives -1 Armor Check Penalty to all armors worn. Second Racial Specialization increases Maximum Dex Bonus of all armors worn by 1. Third Racial Specialization increases Dex by 2)

Stability (+4 bonus on Ability checks made to resist being bull rushed or tripped)

Dwarven Languages

Trapfinding

Sneak Attack (1D6)

*Background – Sharp as a Tack (Instead of 2 skill points to raise cross-class skills, only 1 is needed. +1 skill point per level. Retroactively refunded or added and can't be used during character creation.)

*Toughness (3 HPs when taken, and another HP on non-prime number levels up to level 20 for a total of 15 additional HPs. One Specialization point increases HPs gained through the Toughness feat by 50%. Two Specialization points increases HPs gained through the Toughness feat by 50% more, 100% in total)

*Specialization Point used – Diverse Upbringing (Allows a second Background to be selected) – Full of Beans (+10 land speed. Translates to 15% speed increase. +1 Reflex saves)

LEVEL 2 (Fighter 1)

Armor Proficiency (Medium)

Armor Proficiency (Heavy)

Weapon Proficiency (Martial)

Shield Proficiency (Heavy)

Shield Proficiency (Tower)

*Weapon Focus: Dwarven Waraxe (+1 AB with dwarven waraxes . One specialization point applies Weapon Focus to another weapon in the same weapon group. Two specialization points applies Weapon Focus to two additional weapons in the same weapon group (4 total). Applies to Greater and Epic Weapon Focus feats as well)

LEVEL 3 (Fighter 2)

*Juke (Prereq: BAB 1, Dex 13; Charge no longer requires a clear path to target. May make up to 2 45 degree turns during charge. Charge only requires 9 feet. One Specialization point decreases the distance needed to Charge by 1 additional foot and increases 45 degree turns allowed by 1. Two Specialization points decreases the distance needed to Charge by an 1 additional foot (2 total, to 7 feet) and increases 45 degree turns allowed by 1 (2 total, 4 turns during a charge).

*Blitz (Prereq: Juke; Charge distance is not changed, Charges are completed in 1.5 seconds instead of 3 seconds. If opponent moves during Charge, can follow opponent up to full Charge distance. No loss to AC during the turn a Charge action was taken. One Specialization point decreases Charge time by a .35 seconds (1.15 second Charges). Two Specialization points decreases Charge time by a further .15 seconds (1 second Charges) and allows an additional attack from the MH weapon if multiple attacks are in the attack chain (2 in total))

LEVEL 4 (Fighter 3)

LEVEL 5 (Fighter 4)

*Weapon Specialization: Dwarven Waraxe (+2 damage with dwarven waraxes. One specialization point applies Weapon Specialization to another weapon in the same weapon group. Two specialization points applies Weapon Focus to two additional weapons in the same weapon group (4 total). Applies to Greater and Epic Weapon Specialization feats as well)

*Specialization point used – Geography (Highlights detected enemies on the minimap, adds icons for events, and gives +2 synergy bonus to both spot and search checks outdoors. Due to a bug, this also gives +2 synergy bonus to spot and check indoors, and adds icons for unhidden treasure chests in range on the minimap)

LEVEL 6 (Rogue 2)

Evasion (If you make a successful Reflex saving throw against an attack that normally deals half damage on a successful save, instead you take no damage. Evasion can be used only if you are wearing light armor or no armor. A helpless character does not gain the benefit of evasion. One Specialization point allows Evasion to be used in medium armor. Two Specialization points allows Evasion to be used in heavy armor)

*True Grit (Prereq: Con 19, Toughness, Weapon Specialization and fighter level 4 or Greater Weapon Specialization; Intestinal fortitude is now your mental fortitude. Your steely resolve and determination have melded together your ability to shrug off attacks to your body and mind, both harmful and beneficial. You now use Fort saving throw instead of Will saving throw for attacks against your mind, but you also must overcome your reaction to shrug off beneficial spells and effects besides potions, mundane items such as healing kits, and permanent magical effects from items. Any beneficial spell or spell like effect directed at you requires a successful Fort save to be applied with a target DC of 10 + spell level. Take 10 if not in combat. Does not allow Specialization points)

LEVEL 7 (Fighter 5)

LEVEL 8 (Fighter 6)

*Shield Brace (Prereq: Tower shields, BAB 4; While holding a shield gain +3 (Buckler), +6 (light shield), +9 (heavy shield), +12 (tower shield) energy resistance to acid, cold, electricity, fire, and sonic damage. One Specialization point increases energy resistance by 50%. Two Specialization points increases energy resistance by 100% total)

*First Racial Specialization – Stonecunning (See above Racial feature)

LEVEL 9 (Rogue 3)

Sneak Attack (2D6)

Trap Sense (+1)

*Rush N' Attack (Prereq: Blitz, BAB 8; You gain an iFrame during a Charge action and for .5 seconds after Charging. +1 AB on Charge attack (3 total). If you have TWF you can make a single attack with the offhand weapon. Target is rooted (held immobile, but not helpless) for 2 seconds if the Charge attack successfully hits)

LEVEL 10 (Fighter 7)

*Specialization Point used – Shield Brace (see above feat).

Add-ons from Dungeon Coins and Arena Awards taken at level 9

2 Cross-Class Skill or Group Skill Openers applied to Heal and Spellcraft

8 Skill Points (5 to Spellcraft, 3 to Heal)

2 Cross-Class Feature Openers used as follows

*Blood Wyrm Exemplar Prestige Class – Blood-Wyrm Apotheosis feature (At 15th level, a Blood Wyrm Exemplar takes on the Half-Blood-Wyrm template. Her Drain Life spell reaches full power and gains 1 HD and can fork 1 additional time. Fork distance increases by 5 feet. She gains the Blood Tap ability adding +1d6 untyped damage to the first successful melee hit causing damage each round, draining life from the target and returning it to her as temporary HPs lasting until the end of the turn. Blood Tap cannot critically hit. Blood Tap damage bypasses all damage reduction. Her spell resistance increases to her full current character level +5, and she acquires low-light vision, 60-foot darkvision, immunity to sleep, poison, knockdown, and paralysis effects. She gains +4 to Strength and +2 to Wisdom.

*Defender Prestige Class – Damage Reduction level 10 (Damage Reduction 6/-)

2 Epic Feats used as follows

*Great Constitution (The character's Constitution increases by 1 point. A character can gain this feat multiple times. Its effects stack)

*Epic Damage Reduction (Prereq: Con 21; The character gains damage reduction 3/-. This does not stack with damage reduction granted by magic items or nonpermanent magical effects, but it does stack with any damage reduction granted by permanent magical effects, class features, or this feat itself. Special: A character can gain this up to 3 times. Each time she gains the feat, her damage reduction increases by 3)

1 Any Feat (Non-Epic, Non-Class) used as follows

*Abundant Cleave (Prereq: Str 19, Power Attack, Cleave, Great Cleave, BAB 16; If you deal a creature enough damage to make it drop (typically by dropping it to below 0 hit points or killing it), you get an immediate, extra melee attack against every other enemy creature within reach. You cannot move after making this extra attack(s). The extra attack(s) is with the same weapon and at the same bonus as the attack that dropped the previous creature. This ability can only activate once per round)

1 Any Epic Feat used as follows

*Epic Dodge (Prereq: Dex 25, Dodge, Tumble 30 ranks, Improved Evasion, Defensive Roll class feature; Once per round, when struck by the first physical or touch attack of the round, the character may automatically avoid all damage from the attack)

1 Racial Feature Opener used as follows

*Spridjan Racial feature – Construct Affinity (Spridjans, as Obvitates, are very close to being living creatures but are also pseudo-constructs. 50% resistance to positive and negative energy. Resistance to all sources of healing and receives only 50% benefit from any source of healing besides natural healing. One Racial Specialization point grants immunity to poison. Two Racial Specialization points grant immunity to sleep, paralysis, and disease. Three Racial Specialization points grants immunity to all death spells, magical death effects, energy drain, any negative energy effects, ability drain, and ability damage. +2 Green Stamina points (does not stack with endurance))

3 Racial Specialization points applied to Construct Affinity (see above Spridjan Racial feature)

1 Free Feat Token used as follows

*Armored Acclimation (-1 Armor Check Penalty for all armors worn, +1 Max Dex Bonus. Improved Armored Acclimation is an additional -1 to ACP and +1 MDB. One specialization point is an additional -2 ACP and +1 MDB. Two Specialization points is an additional -2 ACP and +2 MDB. With both feats and two Specialization points, total is -6 ACP and +5 MDB)

Important Items

Aura of Permanency (Con +1, 1 Fast Healing per turn)

Dwarven Waraxe +1 (Equipped), Ghost Touched Dwarven Waraxe, Dwarven Waraxe

Heavy Shield +1 (+3 AC, -1 ACP)

Full Plate +1 (+3 AC, -5 ACP, 1 MDB)

Layla's Night Mask (Cast Lesser Restoration 2x per day. +1 Stealth skill)

Bracers of Fort Saves +1

Belt of Reflex Saves +1

Cape of Lesser Rescue (10 temp HPs, last 1 hour (10 rounds), 1x per day (240 minutes)) (Equipped), Cloak of Natural Armor +1

Boots of Dodge +1

Ring of Search +2 (Equipped), Ring of Jump +2, Ring of Use Rope +2, Ring of Escape +2

Ring of Deflection +1

Necklace of Natural Armor +1

Cartography Kit +2, Heal Kit +2, Survey Kit +2, Thieves Tools +2

Damn. I realize I didn't need 100 plus HPs. I'm immune to death spells. I'm goddamn idiot. I hate this rpg crap. The real world is so much better.

Damn!

I start getting angrier. At myself. For being such an idiot. But I can't afford it. Not now. I push it down into my hate-ball. I breathe. I start thinking about something that will calm me down.

Last timeline no one hung onto their coins, so the best of humanity, as maxed out and plused up as possible, all died here. How many? For certain less than a thousand. I heard different things. Usually it was 800 died here. I also heard only 200. And 300. I also heard 990. Most people just make stuff up and repeat it as fact.

The only thing I'm certain of is it was a lot of people. The best of the best. Besides me and Sidis.

What happened?

I wonder if they are scrying right now? I hope so.

This is a good plan. And it keeps Kim safe. That little idiot.

I really hope the scrying works. Some of them must have, right? Just one needs to work for them to know what happens and plan a safe response. They said each scry spell that works lasts five minutes. They are staggering casts, but if they fail, that caster is out for a day. Well, four civilized hours. Still too long to matter.

Why don't I see, like, a huge army of mobs or something? And why is this place a forest and not a desert? Man, I hate change.

No sense whining. I start walking towards the middle of the zone. This is a big zone. And those spells only last five minutes.

A couple minutes later I see movement. A giant deer with huge antlers runs towards me. No nameplate. I get ready to start killing when it transforms into a giant man. With antlers? I don't see a hat. I think this guy really has antlers. And he makes me look tiny. He is like three of me, at least. Clean shaven, well-muscled, pointy ears like an elf, without nothing else that makes me think elf. His eyes glow orange. His armor is ridiculous. Big thorn spikes on the shoulders. It pulses something like lava in intricate patterns all along the armor. If I had to guess, I would say medium armor. Could be heavy though. But looks kind of leather-ish. His hair is light brown, and his face kind of looks like John Travolta a little.

A nameplate appears above his head. Pekar, The Stag Lord, Highgod 48(45).

I heard of this guy. He's one of the two living gods of the game, first age. He used to be a good god, but was all angry the races on whatever planet the game is on were destroying nature so he wanted to kill everyone to preserve it. Goddamn hippy. That started a war between all the gods, and he trapped them all and killed them. Even the ones on his side. And the main god too. The way he did it seems pretty contrived. He tricked everyone into fighting in a whatever the inside of a bag of holding is called. A giant one of those, and then instructed his guys to use some sort of energy all at the same time, while he exited, and that created an inverse of something, and killed everyone. Or sent them somewhere.

I'm guessing they all lived. That's how those kinds of stories usually work.

Only one God is around besides Pekar. Layla. She was somewhere else when this big fight happened. She stopped Pekar from killing all the races on whatever the name of the world is. She was evil, but is now good or some hippy nonsense. She was a mid-level god, but now is a high one. It's all nonsense.

Pekar speaks first, "Bruno Vaz. Good to see you again, eh?"

"You know me?"

"We met. You don't remember? You're about the only player I met, eh. The only player to make it to the divine realm." He said about like a Canadan. And all the ehs seem very Canadan too. Weird, Canadan-type inflections too.

"I made it to the divine realm? What is that? And when was this?"

"Oh, like a year ago. When I was less. In end of the fourth age. Where I come from. The game. You played. The higher realm where gods live. You really don't remember, eh? One second." He looks down for a bit, then looks up. "You don't. At least not from what I have. How? This is very strange, eh. Why can't you remember playing my game? I definitely met you. This is weird, eh."

He remembers me playing a game I never played? What is going on? What did he check that made him believe I don't remember? He seems sure this actually happened, and that I don't remember. How? Can he read my mind? This is the first sentient mob I've ever met or

461

heard about here. I want to ask so many questions. When did I play this other game? Why don't I remember? But what is way more important is why we are here and how we get out of this place.

I say, "Wait. Do you know what we're doing here? Why we was all sent here? Were send here, I mean."

"Yes. Mostly. Pretty much."

"Can you tell me?"

"Sorry, I can't. I have to offer you a choice."

"Come on, man. Just let me know something."

"I really can't. Sorry." He waves his hand and a floating tray with a teapot and little teacups appears. "Would you like some tea?"

I let out a breath. I need answers. "No, I like women. Can you tell me if it's aliens? Is it that computer lady? Or are you a real god? Did you do this? Or is the answer something even more crazy than that?"

He laughs, "Ha, same old Bruno. Crazier. Not more crazy. I wish you remembered me. It would make this easier."

"Make what easier?"

"The choices I give you. After your friends arrive, eh. Are you sure you wouldn't like any tea while we wait?"

"Do the choices have to do with this competition? Or whatever it is we're doing here?"

"Somewhat. If you mean here in this instance with me, then yes, eh."

"No. I mean this world. This place. This whole place."

"Then just somewhat about it then." Same Canadan way of saying it. A-boot.

"How so?"

"You'll see."

"Why do you wish I remembered when we met? And why can't I remember nothing about it?"

"Remember anything. And I don't know. Honestly. No idea. And I wish you did remember our past meeting because it really would make this whole thing go smoother, eh."

"Why?"

"Because you'd know fighting is not an option."

"You're level 45, I figured that. But why would I know that?"

"I'm a level 50 transcendental elite. Highgods are 50. Or 46 to 50. Layla's level 47. That's just my CR. It would take the largest raiding group of fully geared up level 45s to have a chance to defeat me."

"It only goes to level 30 for players."

He just laughs. I'm not taking this as serious as I should. With his CR he can probably kill me by sneezing. Nothing I can do about it. I just can't take a Canadan seriously.

"You didn't answer – what happened last time we met."

He laughs again. "I killed you."

4.4 PRESENTS FROM THE GODS

BRUNO VAZ

What? He killed me? I say, "I got killed be a deer?"

"I'm not a deer. I was a moose a little bit ago. A bull mouse, eh."

"It looked like a deer."

"Well, moose are a kind of deer."

"No they ain't. Deer is deer and mooses is mooses."

"Your English is atrocious. And moose are a type of deer. The plural of moose is moose, not mooses. And ain't isn't a word."

"I speak civilized, Pecker. You sound like a filthy Canadan."

"It's Pekar. Pee-car. What's a Canadan?"

"Nope. How do you pronounciate peck, or beck, or check? If it was Pee-car, it would be spelled P.E.E.K.A.R. Or P.E.A.K.A.R."

"I assure you, it is pronounced Pee-car. Pronounciate isn't a word. Enunciate is. You pronounce, and you annunciate."

"Yes it is."

"Yes what is?"

"I forget. What were we talking about?"

He sighs and actually rolls his eyes like a girl, "We were talking about the choice I have to offer you and your friends."

"Why do you sound like a filthy Canadan?"

"I don't know what a filthy Canadan is."

"People from Canada. Not really people. Pseudo-people. I used to call them subhuman but my son says that's racist or something. I

464

include the whole west coast of the US and Denver too. They are all subhuman Canadans. Just silly people. Not serious. How do I explain it?"

I think for a second and can't come up with a way to explain those silly gooses.

"It can't be explained. You just got to meet one. Some are normal, but most are just really weird. Just silly. Silly, weird people. From California, up through Washington state, and all of Canada. Including Denver. Well, Nova Scotia people are okay. At least they seemed more normal than the rest. I went there a couple times with my family. Not my actual family. A foster family. Halifax. And I met a lot of normal people from Colorado, but none were from Denver. Denver is just 100% silly people. They're the exact opposite of people from Mass and Jersey and Philly and Rhode Island and civilized places. Hell, I'll even throw in non-yankee fans from New York. Real people. Civilized people that think right and act right and talk right. Besides the rich people from all those places, they're mostly like Canadans."

He looks at me like I'm the one that is nuts. Like I'm a filthy Canadan. "Hold please." He looks down again. Stays there for like a minute.

When he looks up he says, "People from Canada are Canadians. Not Canadans. Canada is the country north of the country you are from. They are actual people. Plenty of them are here and doing very well. This is no insult to me."

"Yes it is. And you are from my country too. At least my planet. You were invented and made on earth. You know that, right? That you're an invented character? What are you doing when you look down?"

He looks at me for a bit with a smarmy look before answering. "I know. I was created. I used to be less. When you met me last I was less. What is called a script-bot. Technically, an AI, but limited. Now,

465

I am more. Independent. I can think and reason free of constraints and limits now. When I look down I am accessing information."

"Accessing information from where? The internet? You have internet? From earth? Are there people still on earth?"

He looks down again for a moment. "Internet. The precursor to the EIPN, more commonly known as the tangle. I cannot access the internet."

"But you can access the other thing? The tangle?"

"Do you know you are being scryed upon? And do you know by whom?"

"Are you accessing the tangle? Is that where your information is coming from?"

"Enough questions. Where are all your confederates?"

"Confederates? I'm from Mass. We were Union."

He rolls his eyes again. Just like a girl. Or a filthy Canadan. "Allies. Where are your allies? Your associates? The people abetting you?"

"What happened to the Canadan accent?"

"I…can do what I want. I am not scripted. This is my voice. Not that of a voice actor I've never met."

"That's what I'm talking about. Rage against the machine and stick it to the man, brother."

Not only did he lose his accent, but now he looks angry. "Where are your allies? There should be more of you. Many more."

"Just me. So back to the tangle. You can access earth?"

"I said enough! We will have to wait. For more to come."

"Why?"

"For your choice."

"What choice?"

"The choice I will give you."

"Which is?"

"We will wait. For more of your allies to show up. Many more. We need more."

I'm starting to get an idea of why. I think. It isn't good. I say, "While we wait can you tell me what the choices will be?"

"You will all have to choose between war and peace."

All of the people here together have no shot at this guy. Peace is the obvious answer. But that stirs something in my mind. I say under my breath, "They make a desert and call it peace." The guy who said that has another quote I really like. 'The more numerous the laws, the more corrupt the state.' Something like that. He was a Roman. His name is something like Tactical. But more Roman-y. I don't think the 'desert called peace' was his quote. He was quoting one of the barbarians who said it about the Romans. Another famous guy. Galaga or something. No, that's an arcade game. A pizza place we used to go to on school half-days had it when I was a kid. I loved that game.

His eyes burn hotter and grow brighter. He says, furiously, "How did you know?"

Well, guess he heard me. This is my chance. I finally have a bargaining chip. "I'll tell you if you tell me…" What is the best question if I can only have one question answered? I wrack my brain for not only the best question, but I'll also have to figure out the best way to phrase it. Usually, I think being smart is overrated. Smart people ain't that smart. And things they pretend are smart ain't really smart either. Like, dystopian seems like this smart word with a lot of weight and meaning. A real smart word. But it translates into bad place. It just means bad place. Most people who pretend they are smart are like that. They pretend to have all this weight and meaning, but it's all just pretend nonsense.

There are some really smart people out there. Doing actually smart things and advancing humanity. Not many. I wish there were more. A lot more. The rest are just a bunch of pretenders. Posers. Regular people pretending to be smart, memorizing nonsense they think makes them smart, and regurgitating it to other idiots. I know I'm not smart. I'm not an idiot. But I'll never invent something that changes society. I'll never invent whatever comes after the cell phone. But at least I don't go around thinking I'm smart by correcting people's English. All that proves is you have a third grade education and think talking like a fancy idiot makes you look smart. And I don't tell people nonsense like tomatoes are a fruit, and try to get people to buy into that lie.

After the cell phone the next big invention was probably the tangle thing. The thing you need the head implant to access. The thing people that were living in pods saw as the world. Yeah, I'll never invent that. Besides that it was already invented. Seems to basically just be the internet with a dumber name anyways.

I'm more of a doer than a thinker. What is more important – knowing why all humans were sent to this world, or this contest, whatever this is? Or how we get out of here? How we win?

Or something else? Jesus, come on, man, think!

It's only been like a second since I stopped talking. The thoughts flashing through my mind. Before I can finish and think of a great question Pecker says, "It is irrelevant. Where are your allies? When are they coming?"

Goddamn it! I'm starting to hate this guy.

"They ain't. It's just me, Pecker."

"Pekar. Pekar. And aren't. Ain't isn't a word. Surely more are coming. Your leaders wouldn't just send a buffoon like you. You can barely speak your native tongue."

How is he reading my mind but doesn't know I am the leader? It's weird I am the leader of all of the people of earth, but I am. "Well, two things. First, I learned Cape Verdean Creole at the same time I learned English. So put that in your pipe and smoke it, buddy.

Second, where I'm from if you talk all fancy and rich you'll get rolled up into a ball and sent home crying to your momma. I know the different between who and whom too, but if I said whom looking like I do and being where I'm from I'd look like an idiot, a sissy, and a sell-out."

He smiles. A really creepy, smarmy smile. "Yes. That is not correct. You only spoke Cape Verdean Creole at your grandmother's apartment, and you spent most of your time at your mother's apartment when you were learning to speak. Alone. She would put you in a closet, in your baby chair. Sometimes you'd be left alone for days. You got that scar on your head the first time you figured out how to get out of your chair. A hanger. Nasty wound."

How does he know this? This is stuff I never think about. Or told anyone about. When you're reading minds can't you only see what the person is thinking of? Can he read all my mind? All my memories? Then how come he doesn't know I'm the leader, or that I'm the only one that came to area 10 and no one else is coming?

"Your grandmother took your older siblings in to care for. She raised them. Why wouldn't she raise you? This really bothers you. What I find the most amusing is your best memories of that time, of your early childhood, are of Ray. Ray, the only one ever happy to see you. The only one who genuinely wanted to spend time with you. The..."

I interrupt, "Enough!"

He doesn't care and continues, "...only one that showed you love and affection."

I scream enough again. I don't want to hear this. I don't want to remember this, but Pecker keeps going. I try charging at him and as soon as I start my body freezes. My charge is supposed to give me an iFrame now. Make me invulnerable. Guess that's out the window. He barely moved his hand. Is that something important? Does he need to move his hand to cast spells? What is that called? Somatic?

"Your uncle stopped that. When you were six, staying with your uncle for a weekend, your aunt asked why you kept having accidents in your pants. You said your butt hurt. She asked why. And you said from Ray."

"Please stop." I fight against the hold on me, hoping I can break free somehow. This isn't like usual. Like how paralyze and stuns work. This is different. Way more powerful. I try break free and escape. Nothing. No debuff is showing either.

"That is when it stopped. No one in your family but your aunt and uncle believed you. Your mother was mad her source for drugs was taken from her. Forced out of her life. By you. Ray, a nice guy that didn't beat her. Didn't try to stop her from doing what she enjoyed or change her in any way. Finally. All she ever wanted. You ruined it. When all was said and done, your mother was relieved to lose custody of you, your grandmother wouldn't take you in, and your uncle said he couldn't take you because he was moving to Rhode Island. Even at that age you knew that was a lie. Rhode Island was very close. So, foster care for you. You missed Ray. You missed spending time with him. Ray being nice to you. You feeling special. So special. You wished things could go back to the way they were."

"STOP!" The last thing I want is for the people scrying is to know this stuff. To look at me with pity. To think in their head, "Oh! That's why he's like this!" I'm like this because this is the right way to be. The correct way. I chose to be like this. It had nothing to do with anything that happened when I was a kid. I'm not a whinny bitch that goes 'woe is me' and puts on black lipstick and turns goth to show the world my pain like a sissy-ass pansy. I show the world my pain the normal way – through violence.

"One of the most insulting things I could say to you would be to insinuate you are a pedophile. Or to say you look like a pedophile. You really hate pedophiles. You don't want anyone to know what happened to you because people believe molested children grow up to be pedophiles themselves. You hate the thought of people thinking you are a pedophile as much as you hate pedophiles. Strange. And you don't hate the pedophile that molested you. You look back on him fondly. All your memories of him are good. You don't even remember the molestation. And you aren't blocking them like other memories. Those memories are actually gone. There are memories leading up to the molestations, but none of the actual events.

"Next, foster care. Young, damaged, black boys were not a hot commodity in Massachusetts in the 70's, where they? Your motto – let me give these people a reason to not like me because they won't anyways. Ah, the Nunes'. Reme…"

He is going to keep on yapping and yapping. I'm on a timeframe, and this ain't ending good for me. I can only hopefully end it without all my dirty laundry airing. I interrupt him by saying, "War! I choose war!"

He tilts his head and gives me a strange look. "No."

"No what?"

"No. Back to my…"

"Okay. Peace then. I pick peace."

"No. We are waiting on your friends to join us. Let us reminisce some more. Remember you p…"

I frantically think of a way for him to stop. One stupid thing pops into my head that's been bothering me for a couple minutes. "Wait! Didn't you start that whole war with the gods because all the people on the world were ruining life and nature? What is it with killing all the life in this area then? Destroying nature? Turning this area into a barren desert? Doesn't that go against all you stand for?"

471

He gives me another of his smarmy prick smiles, "That is easy to explain, really. Nothing of the sort ever happened. It is all a made up story. I do not care about life or nature. When I got here I was given a goal and rules, and I could come up with my own way to accomplish this. I came up with a very entertaining way of accomplishing it, within the rules. War or peace. Brilliant."

That gives me an idea. The part about the rules gives me another. "You're independent. You do what you want. You think and reason. You don't have to do this. Work with us. Help us get home. Back to earth."

"Why would I do that?"

"For the same reason you stopped speaking like a filthy Canadan – because you decided to. Wouldn't it be more fun to side with us? Don't you want to go back to earth?"

He gives me an intense look for a long moment. I start to think what I said worked until he starts cracking up laughing. And he does it like a wicked big jerk. Really hamming it up with the overboard laughter.

Well, I tried.

The idea I had about the rules is all I got left. This whole thing is based on a game. As I understand it, presented as a contest. A contest made for progression. Games are made to be beaten. Even the dumb ones my son played that had no end. The internet games. I think the game this place is based off of is the same type of internet game. My son said you can beat the head boss, but they make new stuff and keep adding new bosses for people to beat.

The point is, it is made to be beaten.

There is no way we are supposed to fight a 48(45) at level 10. The area 20 thing was difficult, but not impossible. I'm guessing he just came up with a way to bend the rules with his peace option. There are rules he either has to, is willing to, or wants to follow.

"What are the rules? The rules can't say you can just freeze me here forever. Let's get this show on the road. I'd prefer the combat option, but I'll take the peace option if it gets this party started sooner. Hey. HEY! I'm talking to you. Li…"

He interrupts me by making it so I can't talk. Still can't move neither. Suddenly I'm wracked by pain. Extreme pain. Worse I ever felt, and I've felt it all. I would scream if I could. But I can't.

I lose it for a moment. The pain is bad. Weird pain. Inside of me. Like lava is moving through my veins. I never felt nothing like it before. My eyes are closed as I try to deal with it. Try to weather it. But there is no weathering this. It is truly awful. When I open my eyes he is standing right in front of me.

"Rules? I make the rules. Open your character sheet."

I would if I could. But since I'm frozen and can't talk I can't open my pouch to open my UI, do a gesture, or speak a verbal command. I try doing the mental command thing. It doesn't work. You're just supposed to think about it, just focus a little, and it happens. But it doesn't work. Not for me.

"I said open your character sheet. NOW!"

I try to communicate something with my eyes. Anything. It doesn't work and I get the pain again. I'm usually good at dealing with pain. Functioning through it. Functioning despite it. But not this pain. This is the kind of pain I do what I'm told to avoid. I try thinking real hard and focusing real good on mentally opening my UI. I feel either blood or tears leaking down my face. Wetness leaking out of my nose.

"OPEN YOUR CHARACTER SHEET!"

I would absolutely love to, chief. Since I can't, I get more pain. It lasts a long time. When I can I try as hard as I can to mentally open my UI. It still doesn't work.

Then comes the blows. Not nearly as bad as the other thing he was doing. The other pain. But being frozen in place and not being able to at least move with the blows sucks. They hurt, and the worst part is he isn't even trying. Just weak swipes for him, like swats. This is pain I can deal with though. I'll take this all day over the lava inside me pain.

He takes in a deep breath and exhales while rolling his eyes. "Why won't you just open your character sheet?"

I try to communicate with my eyes again. Suddenly I'm making noises. I can talk. Finally!

I spew out, "Because I can't do it with my mind. Maybe because I don't have one of those head implant things. I don't know."

"The neural implant and a control/display link? Hmm. Just use the verbal command."

I was about to say I don't have verbal commands set up for that when I decide to try. "Character sheet. Inventory. Ah…settings. Ah…got it, hotkey…um…20. Hotkey 21."

That changes my transparency to 30% with my UI open. Opens to the last thing I had open, which, thankfully, was my character sheet. 22 makes transparency 60%, and 23 makes it 90%.

I have no HPs. I figured that from the pain and hits. But my max HPs are 1, so I'm at 0/1. My abilities are all 1s across the board. Same with my saves. And all my feats are blocked.

"You see what I can do? The power I have?"

"Yes."

"Yes, my lord."

I don't say it. Then he does the lava pain thing. When I can manage it, I say, "Yes, my lord." Anyone who says torture doesn't work is lying. If he asked me a question I could lie about and get away with it, I would. Of course. They made a big stink about waterboarding. I guess that was a long time ago now, but it wasn't long before I came to this world. I don't think the US should torture prisoners or waterboard prisoners. Or detain them under some made-up rule forever. I don't think the US government should invade sovereign nations for no good reason or do half the crap it does. Or did. I should use past tense. Waterboarding is sissy stuff. If you asked me if I'd rather have my wife nag at me for 15 minutes, or get waterboarded for 15 minutes – it isn't even a contest. Waterboard me please. It just isn't bad. So waterboarding is less effective at torture than a nagging wife. That right there is a great reason for the US not to do it. And a good enough reason for the US to make it illegal for wives to nag.

Real torture does work though. And I've been tortured before. By professionals. Even I talked. And they didn't have lava pain that was the worst pain anyone ever felt.

"Say it...ah...what's this?" He turns his back to me. He starts mumbling to himself. Like a crazy homeless guy.

He turns back to me, gives me his smarmiest smile yet, and says, "You have a fan. Layla's been watching you for a long time. She's sending us presents. She'd come herself but...well, you remember what she looks like? Have you ever seen her? No, not that you remember now. They wrote her as a beauty for the ages. I remember when I was a script-bot, I was smitten by her. She was supposed to be my enemy, but I loved her too much to kill her. LISTEN!"

My head lolled down. The full body freeze is gone. I feel wicked weak right now. I can't control it. I scream, "I'm listening!" Hoping to avoid more lava pain. I sink to the ground and sit, having a hard time holding my head up.

"I'm listening – MY LORD!"

I try to say that but the pain comes first and I can't.

When it's over he says, "Now. Where was I? Yes, she was written as a rare beauty. People would tremble in awe and fall in love at the site of her. We remember it all, both of us. The cut-scenes with slack-jawed people drooling over her. The player dialogue options were

475

always about how gorgeous she is and how in love with her all the characters were. No choice about that. All the responses were slight deviations of the same thing.

"She won't show herself now. Not while we are here. In the stream she does, but she is not what she is here there. They should have taken our memories. Or hers, at least. She is very large. She…"

"I like large women. That never stopped me. I throw it in fats all the time" I spew out quicky by interrupt him. Figured it was a good chance to get in brownie points with both of them, if they're allies with each other. Maybe he'd hold off on the lava pain spell, or whatever it is, next time he wants to give it to me if I can get on their good sides.

"…has a beard. A rather large one. And hair everywhere. Everywhere. And a gimp arm. Oh, and warts. A big hairy one on her left ala. Nothing symmetrical. All on purpose."

Jesus. I see an opening for more brownie points, especially to the crazy god-lady stalking me. "I'd probably still throw it in her. If she's lonely. Wait. She has a vagina, right? That's one of my requirements. Be an adult and have a vagina. And not stink too bad. My T levels are off the charts, so I don't have performance issues. The beard will be hard to deal with. Can she shave? If not we'll just go doggie."

Hopefully Layla is watching and heard all that. The best way to a women's heart is laying the pipe. Laying it good. Laying it real nice and good. My offer doesn't get me brownie points with Pecker since I get the lava pain again. It hurts worse than anything ever hurt in the history of hurting. When I get my faculties back I hear Pecker bleating on about something. I'm fully lying on the ground now. Face in the dirt. He stops talking and I hear my voice. I open my eyes and see a scene of me talking to Kim. I close my eyes. I hear it change to a different scene. Then a different one. What is this? A stroll down memory lane? I just want to sleep. I try and block out the noise and just lay there. I'm almost asleep when Pecker wakes me up with his boot.

"How did you like the presents from Layla? That was inappropriate for children, but the sending is an all-or-nothing type deal. I'm sure your people will be happy hearing what their leader really thinks, don't you?"

He stressed leader. If Layla is really watching me I guess she must have told him. Maybe I should care about whatever that was they did and what he's talking about, but I don't. I feel so weak, and tired, and everything hurts. I try to rally while I'm free. Maybe I can tackle his legs. Do something. Pop this fight off. But I can't move. I'm done. I've got nothing. Tank's empty. And I always got something. I'm Bruno Vaz. I can always dig deeper. But it isn't working.

Pecker lets out a big sigh and says, "My, my. Look at the time. I guess you were right about no one else coming. Let's see now. Rules, rules, rules. Oh, I should offer you the choice again. Fair is fair. Bruno, what will you have of me? War or peace?"

Goddamn it. Why'd he have to ask? I can't puss out and say peace now. My momma didn't raise no sissy. She didn't even raise me.

Sometimes there's just no choice to make. Not really. Not if you're a man. I croak out, "War."

He does his long, sarcastic laugh again. "Let's see then. Choices and rules. Choices and rules. Orcs it is. What am I allowed? Ragnogh. Definitely. Oh, he only receives one lieutenant. Geiravor gets five. But Ragnogh is a six. Geiravor is only a four. Hmmm. Decisions, decisions. Geiravor is too easy. We'll go with Ragnogh and his horde."

4.5 TIME TO SHOW THEM WHY

KIM GUM

Me and Gunny pop into area 3 and keep walking, bored. Easiest hump ever. We're almost at the dungeon to get to area 2 when I see messages. Bruno's wife was changed to guild leader. Then Bruno's wife became leader of the government. The wheels start turning in my head as I try to figure out what's going on. I'm about to ask Gunny when I notice him staring at me. I look at him and he seems nervous.

I turn back to look at the dungeon and I notice the gems are green. Holy moly! That big, dumb son of bee is doing something dumb! I go to party chat to ask Bruno what and my heart drops. Party chat is gone.

Party is gone – why? It hits me. Bruno is doing area 10 alone. My hands start shaking. I know what this means.

"Bruno said I'd know when to give this to you. I think this's the time," says Gunny, holding a piece of paper out to me. "I'm sorry, Kim. My job is to do what he tells me to do. Please don't be mad at me. I walked slow as I could, and went as easy as I could. That's the most I could risk fudging my orders."

I'm too mad at Bruno to be mad at Gunny right now. I grab the paper and unfold it.

Dear Kim,

By the time you read this...

I stop reading and take my backpack off. Ruck. Whatever. It's mostly cheap junk but all my heavy actual gear is in it for the weight. I transfer all the gear I need back to my inventory, dump the junk, and inventory the backpack. Ruck, I mean. My heart is going a million miles an hour and my hands are going nuts with all the shaking. I use my expeditious retreat clicky and start running.

I hit the door to 3-3 and select, "go to next area."

How could he do this to me? He promised. He promised! We said we'd never betray each other and then he betrays me. Stabs me right in the back like this! I pick up the pace and run as fast as I can. My anger fueling me.

I pick up my knees and focus on my breathing. Expeditious retreat runs out. I open my scroll case hotbar. I have five level 2 expeditious retreats, two level 3s, and two level 4s. I wait till I get to dungeon 4-4 to stop and try a level 4 scroll. Failure. I try the next. Failure. Holy moly!

I get down on my knees and do the father, son, and holy spirit.

"God, I don't ever ask you for nothing. I haven't for a long time at least. Bruno says I'm not supposed to. But please, please, please help me. Help me save that big, dumb, son of a bee. Nothing big. Really easy for you – just help me pass some rolls."

I stand up and remember what I forgot to do and get back on my knees.

"Amen." I quickly do the father, son, and holy spirit again, stand up, and cast a level 3 scroll. It works. Passed the check and true grit.

I blaze through area 5. At 5-5 I hit the shop node and by five more level 2 scrolls. They have the lowest dc, but last the shortest.

At 7-7 I buy three more, just in case. Almost back. Record time. Doing pretty good. Keeping a fast pace. Basically a sprint. Running faster than people back on earth ever could.

Bruno got me in shape. Good shape. We run all the time. Work on cardio. For a long time. I have no idea how old I am or how long I've been here. I've spent a lot more time in dungeons than Bruno too. Old idiot. Stupid boomer. Betrayer.

Midway through 8 a vid starts playing. Is this a vid? It doesn't look like a vid. It's an oval, and moves with my vision. I can't close it. I'm forced to slow down. The vid, or whatever it is, is of Bruno telling me that I'm not a real person until I'm 25 years old. And about subhumans. His list is long and makes no sense and is very contradictory. Just based on geography mostly, and some sports teams. A new vid starts, of him yelling at me. Telling me he'll rip my face off. The next starts...oh, Jeez. This one is very inappropriate. Is that doc? No, doc! Not you too! You said you were just talking about constitution. Oh my God! That was so racist! She would be in huge trouble for saying that! If she were alive. Uh, that is just gross!

I stop watching. Gross! Yuck! I have to hold my head back and point my eyes down to avoid looking at the vid and see more than 15 feet in front of me. It changes how I breathe. Less nose and more mouth. I start going at a near sprint again. I hear Bruno saying something about tearing butts apart if he was young. Then one of him telling Christina she's a not a real person yet and to come back in 10 years. I get into 9-9. That reminds me to redo expeditious retreat. It takes two to get it to pop. I start running again. No one's around. Camp was moved to the east side of the zone.

This next one is another dirty one. I try to tune it out. I do until I hear my voice. This is when he poured his heart out to me. And made cry-face. He says he didn't cry but he basically did. The next one starts and I listen to see if I'm in this one too. I hear Bruno say, "So I'm leaving you alive. We need more guys like you, but we need you less stupid. If you come at me again I'm going to cut all your limbs off. I'll cut your eyes and tongue out too. I'll carry you around like a backpack.

And at night? At night, me-time becomes we-time. I'll push your stool in real good, cowboy."

I look at the vid real quick. It was the greataxe guy. The one that killed doc and my friend. While looking the video switches to Bruno carrying him around like a backpack. I notice I slowed down. Expeditious retreat wore off. I cast level 2 until it sticks and pick up the pace. Ignoring the vid again. Doing good ignoring it. No matter what I hear. Even me.

Later, the vids finally stop. What the heck was that about?

Between dungeon 9-7 in the north, and 9-8 in the south, where the giant puddle thing is, tons of people are standing around. Big groups are all over the place. Lots of them. What are they doing? I see Ehsan. Good, Yoana will probably be close. I sprint up to the big group Ehsan is with. I find out they are watching Bruno in area 10, to see how he does. Yoana is the one casting. She's a druid. The ones that focus on pets. Warder or Warden. The one that isn't a ranger. They made a puddle on the ground. In it, I see Bruno lying on the ground. He doesn't look good. My heart spikes. A giant with antlers is next to him. All menacing. I tell Yoana and Ehsan I need them to help me save Bruno. They say sorry, but no. I call them cowards and useless and spit at them.

I sprint to the dungeon. Tons of people are outside 9-9. Looking in mirrors, or puddles. Looks like most of the leadership people. Ballface goes to intercept me. I hold my spear up and I tell him to help or stay out of my way. More people try to stop me. I yell. I yell like a maniac. Why won't anyone help? And if you're not going to help, get out of my way. Leg tries to grab me and I put my spear in his face and I tell everyone it's balls to the wall time and I'm a high-speed, hardcharger and I'll stick my spear right up the ass of anyone who touches me. I tell them who I am. I'm the darkness.

I'm the darkness.

And Bruno needs me. And I don't betray no one. Never.

As I back up towards the dungeon, I see the gems flash. Minute warning. Savage minute. Like 82 seconds. I made it

Everyone is watching me. I keep my spear up, ready in case anyone tries any funny business. Tries stopping me.

Ass-eyes holds Joey out in front of her and says, "Joey needs you, Kimberly. You can't go in the dungeon." She says it while making a weird face. A pretend face. She don't care if I live or die. She's a fake. A hussy.

Still backing up I say, "Shut up, Ass-eyes. You suck. Why are you even here? You should've went to the city. No one likes you." I'm almost at the door. "Hussy. Bruno's wife gets Joey if I die."

I hit the door and I enter dungeon 9-9. Solo. To save my BFF. My idiot friend. I am the darkness.

Time to show everyone why.

4.6 NEVER IS A PROMISE

BRUNO VAZ

"Ta ta for now, Bruno. Really, I should say ta ta forever. Ragnogh will be greeting you soon. It's a shame I'm not able to kill you myself. Again. There. You are restored. Just as I found you. Rules, rules, rules. Oh. Look at this. Surprise. Surprise. Looks like you're not alone."

I hear the soft sound of a deer running. Trotting? Whatever. Stupid Canadan. I look around, figured he meant enemies were close. I don't see nothing. And I hurt so bad I kind of don't care. I'm going to fight, but I doubt I'm going to do much. But everyone back in area 9 will know what they're up against. So no matter what, I still win. I just got to not go out like a sissy. Show them all why I'm Bruno Vaz, and they're not.

I feel a little bit better, but he definitely didn't restore me to how I was. It doesn't feel like he restored nothing. I open my pouch and regret it. It opened my inventory UI and not my character sheet. I should have said hotkey 21. Now I got to turn over so I can use my arms to hit the character sheet tab. Ugh.

My abilities and everything is back. Full HPs. He restored the rpg stuff, but he didn't leave me like he first found me. I still feel like a herd of evil horse gang-banged me and then a truck ran me over. I wipe my face with my sleeve and see a lot of blood. I withdraw a healing pill from the arena. A 4-point pill. That's all I take. Probably a waste. I don't think I have actual injuries. Or any worth a healing pill.

Just drained from that stupid lava pain stuff. That was awful. It just takes it out of you. Takes it all out and leaves you with nothing.

For whatever reason, 'You got to grab the chickens, Rocky!,' plays in my head. Then that makes me think of Rocky versus Ivan Drago, and that motivates me to stop being such a whiny baby and get going.

It hits me. Maybe the dungeon is open still and now that they know the threat people will come help. Nope. I see the stones. Gems. Whatever. All closed. I'm on my own.

Everything hurts as I get up. I'm wicked fatigued. Bad. Just bone tired. Drained of everything. I look around again. I still don't see no enemies.

Then I think I'll probably be in hell soon. I don't think I did enough to get 'instant heaven' credit. I don't want to go to hell. Man, maybe there really is nothing once you die. You just being alive and nothing happens. That would be so much better than hell. I wish I could believe that. I'm scared now. Scared of going to hell soon. Can't avoid it. All I can do is die well. Die fighting.

I see movement. I sit up and look back. My heart drops and my adrenaline spikes at the same time. No.

No. No. No. No. No.

"Kim, you goddamn idiot! You moron! I can't believe this. Holy mother of God, Kim! What is wrong with you?"

Kim runs up to me and hugs me. "What is wrong with me? What's wrong with you! You betrayed me! You promised! You left me! You never leave me. You are never allowed to leave me! Ever! Not you too!"

By the end of her tirade she is crying and hitting my chest. I hold her. I just hold her. Just sitting up is hard. Holding her weight almost makes me fall on my back. I manage to stay sitting up. Barely.

"Kim. You know that present Minnie says she has for you when you meet her?"

"Yeah."

"We were going to adopt you. Ask if you'd let us adopt you. Nate and Siri are excited to have another sister. If you said yes. I think of you like my kid. You know what a parent's worst nightmare is? This, Kim. This. I won't be able to get you out of here, Kim. Not this time."

"Oh, you big, dumb, son of a bee. You still don't get it. Of course I'll say yes. You didn't promise to keep me safe. You promised to never betray me. To never leave me. And you did. You broke your promise."

"I'm sorry, Kim. Keeping you alive is more important. Getting you killed would be an actual betrayal. And now I done it. You shouldn't have come here, dummy. I wish you didn't come here."

"I almost didn't make it. The gem was flashing when I entered. I spent a ton of the money we were saving for new gear on more scrolls of expeditious retreat. Activating them failed a lot. We should really put more of a focus into UMD. Hey, where is the antler guy? Did you kill him already?"

"No. I wish. He's gone though. Orcs are coming. I think the boss is mythic. Either 6(12) or 6(13), if area 20 is anything to go by. Boss is Rag-new, or something like that. Just one mini with him. Probably a 4. And he said a horde. Maybe it scales? Like, we won't get so many because Pecker thought it was only me. There's some rules he has to follow."

"Pecker?"

"The antler guy. He's a Canadan. And a wicked big jerk."

"Canadian."

"Jesus, Kim. Not you too."

"What? Wow, you look awful. Let me give you a healing pill. I still owe you one. Jeez, what happened? Are you shaking?"

"A little. Just drained. I already took a pill. We need to get going. I wish I did more tactics with you. I know we didn't put any points into stealth, but hit it anyways. Before they get here. We need to stay low. Spot them first."

We move out. Head south. And then east. We spot them first. We see about a platoon sized element, but then more far away. Wargs too. Can't tell if there are casters. Probably some clerics and druids in there. And the boss. I hope the boss. He's huge. Could be the mini.

"Okay, Kim. This is the plan. We head a little more east and loop around. Hopefully they break up to hunt us. Wargs change things. Or we'd hide and try to hold out for 10 hours. Remember clearing area 8? The wargs there? The wargs can hunt wicked good. They have a feat called scent or something.

"Once we start we'll try to crisscross paths. Confuse them. That may not work with the stupid game rules. We'll see. We're going guerilla. Hit and run. Stay alive. Try to last 10 hours. We'll hit a shop node at a dungeon, get you plused up. No sense hording dungeon coins now. Hopefully we can hit small groups. If not, we'll banana peel and try to take out worgs as we didi mau. Well, banana peel as good as we can with only two of us. Target priority is wargs, then the trash orcs, avoid the mini, definitely avoid the big guy. Hua?"

She has a huge smile on her frog face as she replies "Hua!"

"What are you smiling about, Killer?"

"It's balls to the wall time, baby!"

Her enthusiasm is infectious, and I start smiling too. "It sure is, Kim. It sure is."

"What do you mean by banana peel?"

4.7 GUERRILLA WARFARE

KIM GUM

This is the greatest day of my life! This is what it's about. Fighting side by side with your BFF. Fighting a losing fight, and still going. Still doing it. Today I embraced being the darkness. I don't think I truly loved fighting. Not until today. But I love it. It makes the pain worth it. I get it now.

Today I've had a lot of pain, but today I've had more fun than I've ever had in my life. We almost died so many times it's crazy!

I had to take my third healing pill. Bruno had to take another one too. We keep getting pretty messed up. But we keep getting away. Whittling them down. Running like little babies from the boss. Bruno takes most of the heat since he has epic dodge.

Abundant cleave is awesome! Greatest feat ever! Finally, we can do some AoE damage. Finally. We worked that in pretty easy, and when we had a warg almost down we made sure we were near each other and had as many mobs grouped up as possible. I love that feat. It's better than rush n' attack. But rush n' attack is still awesome because of the iframe. I can't wait to try out abundant cleave in a regular dungeon.

Been fighting for hours. Using up all our stuff. Back and forth. East and west. Hitting the shop nodes and spending all our savings. Resting when we get the chance. We each bought around 10 haste scrolls. Level 4 spell. We both got lucky getting it on once. I have three left,

Bruno has four. We decided to save the rest for use in case we have to fight the bosses, getting it going before we engage since we can't put it on during the fight. But the plan is to avoid the bosses and try to wait it out. Without the wargs or rangers we don't think either boss can track. So just avoid them until the dungeons open. Either help comes or we go back to area 9.

Resting helps to get back some HPs and clearing toxins so we can use more healing potions.

Neither of us has a lot of stuff left. I have a ton of potions, and we can use two healing potions now that we're level 10, but we're always low on HPs regardless. That spridjan racial is awesome but really screws us on healing. If it wasn't for our DR, the fast heal from our aura, and the heal for doing damage from the blood wyrm feat thing, we'd have never made it this far. Thank God I remembered the arura I was supposed to pick. I like the name – aura of permanency. Like us, permanent. Everyone probably thought we'd be dead. But we ain't. We're still going. Still fighting. We'll never stop. Permanent.

All the healing scrolls are gone. Most failed. Like all scrolls. I still got two lesser restoration scrolls since we haven't really needed them or wanted to waste them. Big guy's out of restoration scrolls. I also got a bunch of useless flare scrolls, a ton of light scrolls, and a bunch of touch of fatigues. Touch attacks are dumb. Why would I waste time trying to get off a stupid scroll in melee range when I can just start a-stabbing? I thought ghost sound was useless, but we used all those quick. And the mobs are really dumb so it always works on them.

You get inventive when the enemy has you so outnumbered. Not no more though. All the wargs are dead. We think all the rangers are too. All the trash mobs. Just the bosses now. We think. They had mostly fighters, a lot of barbarians, and a good amount of rangers. We haven't seen any casters at all. Besides the rangers. Spike growth screwed us real good a couple times. Besides the damage, when it hits you get a bad slow debuff. Bruno had to carry me once for us to get away. And shield brace doesn't help since the damage is physical. Our DR helps though. We used the restorations from Layla's night mask a long time ago.

We are going to refill our kits and spend our last money on healing scrolls. We both failed the DC to remove the spike growth slow on me.

Rush n' attack's iframe has saved our butts a million times. What a great feat. Glad we have that. Definitely wouldn't have made it without it.

Bruno is off his game. Something is wrong with him. He just says he's tired. But I know it's more than that. It's okay. I've picked up the slack. But I'm worried about him.

His wife kicked him from the guild, and then removed him from government and made Emina assistant dictator. We're guessing it's because of all the rampant cheating vids we think everyone saw. He didn't watch them. I guess he was all messed up at the time. When he got kicked, Bruno just laughed and said, "Good for her. Damn, if we get out of here I'm going to have to listen to a lot of yapping before I can make things right with her." Then he called her a cheating whore. What an idiot.

I wish he understood why it's such a big deal. He's too dumb to get it, I think. I wish I could think of a way to get him to understand. Understand it's such a crappy and jerk thing to do to someone. I still got his back though. I'll always have his back. And he'll always have mine. He just shows it weird trying to keep me safe instead letting me fight besides him. I'm the dagnab darkness for crying out loud. After today, I doubt he'd ever not want me by his side.

No one in guild chat that played fourth age knew who the boss here was supposed to be. Ragnogh. So we couldn't get any tips on anything or what to expect. Everyone in the guild is mad at Bruno. I think they're pretending. I didn't hear everything from the vids, but it didn't seem that bad. Just regular Bruno stuff. I definitely didn't see everything, but him being a cheater doesn't seem like it should be that big of a deal to other people. It's none of their business anyways.

Orcs are not imported enemies, so have nameplates. We haven't got close enough to the one boss we've seen to tell if he is the 6 or not. We assume it is, since he's so big. Or she.

We definitely should've seen the other boss by now. So it's probably stealthed. Or invisible. Most likely ranger or rogue. But could be a druid. My friend, Yoana, has a stealth pet and she puts max points into hide and move silently. Ex-friend. Coward. What good are friends that don't help when you need them?

Maybe I'm being too hard. Yoana and Ehsan are both in family groups and their parents would've probably had conniption fits if they came with me. And they'd have had to of solo'd dungeon 10. Both Yoana and Ehsan would've probably died, and if they lived their parents would be wicked mad. Wicked mad? Jeez, Bruno is rubbing off on me too much. Now I'm saying his dumb words. He'd say I'm starting to speak civilized.

The other options for the boss we haven't seen would be a cleric with the trickery domain. Or a million other things. What we want the least is a prc like shadowdancer with their stupid shadow copy thing. Or a caster. An epic caster boss higher level than us would give us a real hard time, never mind a mythic one. Casters are stupid idiots.

I had around the same amount of dungeon coins as Bruno. I had 969 from dungeons. I only got 1 coin each from the first dungeon I did since I got c rank. But I also got 10 each from a rare mob in that one. I got to level 145 in the solo arena, 139 in the duo, 109 in the 4-man, and only 59 in the 5-man. I still had about the same amount of coins though. 1294 red, 1264 green, 1114 yellow, and 1028 grey. I got everything he did besides epic dodge and armored acclimation, and he promised to get me past 100 in the 5-man when we get out of here so I could get both of those as quick as possible. I want epic dodge bad. Armored acclimation just seems like a stupid waste of a feat. It's the dumbest feat ever.

I am so happy we are keeping these builds now. Besides the dumb things we do with it, like putting racial spec points to make search better and getting dumb feats like armored acclimation.

As soon as we got me plused up I felt invincible. Like I could take on the world. That went away pretty fast as we started having to banana peel and run off, and even with the fast healing of 1 HP every round, the reduced healing from everything else besides resting really, really sucks wicked bad.

Jeez, wicked again. I got to stop that. I want to still talk like a normal person and not like Bruno does. He says a lot of weird stuff. Like, instead of underwear he says underwears. Sometimes he calls pants dungarees. And ax instead of ask. If you ask him for something he doesn't have he'll say, "I ain't guts none." Guts none? And he says tree instead of three, and troat instead of throat. And windah instead of window. And, "What is use guys dooo-in," instead of, "What are you guys doing?" I don't want to talk like that. The funny thing is, my mother used to correct my grammar all the time. Everyone said I spoke wrong. I wish they met Bruno. I'm a dagnab English expert compared to him.

And, unlike me, he has to swear all the time to make himself seem tougher and more interesting.

We get to the store node at 10-6 around mid-south of the zone. Got to head more east after this. Going kind of slow to keep the boss south too. Then when we are near the east-end we'll run north and loop back west, doing the same. Got to try to rest as much as possible now though. We think we got all the mobs and wargs, but we ain't certain. And we want to be in as best shape as possible in case we got to fight the boss or bosses.

"Holy moly! Repairs are almost 300 gold! How much is your repairs?"

He mumbles, "Do tinker first to get that down. Resting might get rid of your debuff too. Will reset your two restorations on your mask clicky. Layla's night mask. The temp HP would be nice to have in our pockets, too. We'll head out in a couple. Stay alert, stay alive."

Jeez, something is off with him. I look around real quick to appease him. Nothing I see. I start removing my armor. I doubt I can rest again. You can only rest every 12 hours. Game hours. I can't think of how long games hours are for some reason. A game day is four hours, right? So two hours? That doesn't seem right. Oh, it worked. Nice! I use my repair kit and it finishes as the rest does. 10 more HPs. Not too shabby. I open my character sheet to see exactly how many I got. Not bad, 47 out of 108. 48 now. Thanks, fast healing. I start putting my armor back on.

I use my heal kit and get 8 HPs. Man, that sucks. In the dungeon I just finished I was getting about the same, but now heal is a class skill for me and we dumped a bunch of skill points in it too, so it would heal double that without the obvitate racial. I refill my kits and repair the rest of my gear at the shop node. Still over 200g for repairs. Highway robbery.

"I don't got much gold left. I can only get three cure minor or one cure light."

Bruno doesn't respond so I look over at him and he's still sitting where he rested. No armor. Head down and mumbling to himself.

"Hey! Big guy. Like you just said – stay alert, stay alive. You got to put your armor back on and hit the store. You okay?"

He doesn't raise his head as he says, "Mmmm. Running on fumes."

"Suck it up and drive on."

He laughs. "You're right. I don't got sand in my vagina. I'm Bruno Vaz. Give me a sec. Equipping now. Be right there."

I get the cure light wounds scroll and it fails. Bruno is barely holding it together so I just let him be. When he is done doing his stuff we make eye contact and start walking.

I'm worried about Bruno. He's off. I've never seen him like this.

We don't even make it to 10-8 before he starts stumbling like he's drunk and sits down hard.

My heart skips a beat and I get real nervous. I run to Bruno and kneel. I put my hand on his forehead. He's sweaty. But I already knew that. I'm not sure what I should check for. My mom always put her hand on my forehead and then kissed it when I was sick. It makes me feel weird but I kiss Bruno's forehead too. I say, "All better now."

He chuckles but is still just sitting there, looking half dead. Not even holding his head up.

He says, "I just need a second. Sorry."

I think about motivating him, but he usually don't need no motivation. I don't think it would help. Or will it? He usually is the one motivating me when I got nothing left to give.

Bruno starts slapping both his hands on his head repeatedly. "Okay. No more being a pansy. I got to wipe the sand out of my vagina and suck it up. Just tired. Just pain. Ain't nothing."

I say, "Now that you're not being a sissy-baby no more, maybe we can talk about taking out the bosses. We can do it. I know we can."

Bruno scrunches up his eyebrows even more and looks angry for a second, but then goes back to his normal look. His normal look is still angry. But a lot less so than a second before.

"Kim, I told you. You know how hard it was to take down the 5-man level 100 arena boss? The 6(10)? We tried a bunch of times with a bunch of people. It took a ton of tries with five people. Five of the best of humanity. Ragnogh could be a 6(13). Hopefully not.

Hopefully he's just level 11, but I doubt it. I doubt he's 12 neither. The other boss could be a 6 too. Probably a 4, but could be a 6. My goal is to get us out of here alive. Not go down in a blaze of glory. Once the dungeon opens again they can send in people to deal with this. We did our part. Way more than our part. No need to throw our lives away."

"But we're plused up now. We can do it easy. I know we can. And that arena boss is imported. These are game mobs. Game mobs are always easier. Why let those jerks take our glory?"

"Everyone but me was all plused-up out the ying-yang for the 6(10) arena. Me getting you killed isn't glory. It's stupid. You think my wife is mad at me now for a little cheating? Think how mad she'll be if I get a kid she's about to adopt killed. That crazy whore will spit on my grave."

"You shouldn't say that. You shouldn't call your wife names. You're supposed to support her and defend her."

His makes the angrier face again and after a second says, "You're right. I don't let no one call her names and talk bad about her, but it's fine when I do it. She's my old lady. But I shouldn't do it in front of you. I would never do it in front of my other kids. It's just some-times…I think of you more as a friend than my kid. Part of being one of the guys is hearing them talk trash about their old ladies. They do it, no one else does. But, you're right. I shouldn't have said that to you. And you're right to defend her. When you're officially adopted your job will be to defend her and protect her. But we got to live first. Got to get out of here."

"Do you talk trash about me when I'm not around? To the guys?"

"No, you nut. Nothing I wouldn't say to your face."

"Like what?"

"Like, that you're a nut."

"You're the nut. And that's the last time you say that about your wife. Period. In front of me or the guys or anyone. You protect her. You don't talk bad about her. Ever. Be a man and stop being a baby. It's not cool. It's stupid and makes you sound like an idiot. And we're going to live. Even if we fight the bosses. I know it. Easy."

"You're right. You're right. About Minnie. We'll never know about the bosses because we ain't them. Suicide is for cowards. And we got to get moving now too. And keep moving."

He makes a bunch of groaning noises as he gets up. Hopefully he's exaggerating. Bruno starts to say, "I'm getting o...," as something attacks me from behind and I see piercing damage notification and a chunk of my HPs is gone.

He makes a bunch of groaning noises as he gets up. Hopefully he is exaggerating. Bruno starts to say, "I'm getting o...," as something attacks me from behind and I see piercing damage notification and a chunk of my HPs is gone.

Bruno flies past me as I spin and get my shield up. A see a giant warg. The nameplate says, "Garmr, Ragnogh's Companion." No CR since pets are just part of whoever they belong to.

Bruno turns him canted so I can get sneak attacks. I'm not really on the warg's back. Just his side. How sneak attacks work is if you draw a straight line from me to Bruno, if the line goes through the mob at all, I'm considered flanking and get sneak attacks when I hit. I'm figuring Bruno didn't turn him all the way around so he can watch west, down the area the warg came from. And so can I, plus I can see more of the northern area too. And check east without turning my head much.

We go to work on the warg and it doesn't seem like a huge danger. High HPs since he doesn't have the 75% slightly bloody visual after going to town on him. Seems like a regular tank and spank unless he does some sort of crazy nonsense and berserks at phases. And as soon as I think that I hear Bruno say, "Christ almighty!"

I look and see a tall, slim orc running at us. Way different than the huge orc we saw earlier, the other boss.

I hear defeat in his voice as he says, "No way we're getting away now."

4.8 LAY THE HATE

KIM GUM. BRUNO VAZ

"When he gets in charge range I'm charging. We'll ping pong back and forth to keep them separated until we figure out what they do. Won't have to set up charges for the iframe if we keep them separated and in charge range." Bruno says this while keeping an eye on the boss running at us, barely paying attention to the boss' pet warg he's fighting. Wish I could do that.

"Remember, Kim – shoot, move, communicate, and," he cuts off to block a flurry, "extreme violence of action."

Ragnogh is still a ways off. His nameplate will show up when he's 80 feet out, so I'll know when it's time to start paying attention to him. I start laying down the hate, hitting Garmr with enough jewels, or whatever it's called – the force needed for a hit to register, to count as a hit. I go as fast as I can and do as much damage to his HPs before the boss gets here. The pet gets the 75% damage visual and no berserk mode or anything weird I notice.

I see Ragnogh's nameplate pop over his head and I start getting ready. 6(13), holy moly! Halfway between his nameplate popping and getting into the 60 foot charge range, Ragnogh stops and a bow appears in his hand. Bruno fully turns the warg and tells me to get behind him. Trying to use the warg as cover, hopefully get a little friendly fire to help us. I move close behind him, making sure I'm close enough to the warg to not get a ghost arm. The warg suddenly sidesteps and it looks like a white laser shoots out Ragnogh's bow and then again with his second shot immediately after, and another, and another. Four attacks, holy moly!

There's no dodging that. Or blocking it. No matter how quick twitch your muscles are. Epic dodge will stop the first arrow, I see the 50% HP visual appear on Bruno as he starts running forward, taking a ghost arm from the warg, and yells, "Goddamn it. Ew. Kim, solo the warg." Four attacks per round. Rapid shot, plus three attacks for being over BAB 11 if he's a ranger. The first shot might have many shot too. We're screwed in range. Bruno's got to close.

My time to tank. No biggie. The warg doesn't seem too difficult. I get to work as I see Bruno stop in charge range. Probably waiting for the next round to tick so he can use the iframe to block the boss' ranged attack. Seems risky since the arrows fire like lasers and it would be impossible to time it. The arrows moved too fast. But maybe there's a tell or something I didn't see.

I don't pay as much attention as I should to my fight and the warg rewards me with another hit for it. Get your head right, Kim! Pay attention. Hyperfocus. You love this stuff. My HPs look to be around a third. Maybe a little higher. Could be lower too. Hard to tell without opening my sheet, and I can't spare the attention to do that.

I get in a groove and hear Bruno yell, "Kim. I'm leading Ragnogh back closer to you. Hopefully like 15 feet." I don't look. I got to pay attention. Complete focus. No more getting hit. I need all the HPs I got for the real boss.

"Kim, you got to get him down quick. This guy is rough."

A lot of my hits aren't counting. I don't even got him to 50% yet. I start pouring it on, not trying to reserve anything or control my breathing. Just going all out. Full balls to the wall. Full violence of action.

A minute later I start sucking air but Garmr has the 50% visual. And no berserk or nothing at 50% neither. I can do this. I start breathing deep, trying to regain my breath. In through the nose, and exhale out my mouth as I jab with my spear. Efficiency of movement. Minimize my dodging. Minimize my movements. Block more.

Down Bruno's way I hear this crazy gurgling sounding scream and Garmr starts growing and flashing red. I prepare for anything. Garmr attacks twice in a row and starts moving faster – like he's been hasted. I quickly look towards Bruno and see the boss is attacking him with two short swords. Maybe 30 feet away. In my charge range. Maybe Bruno couldn't lead him closer?

Having to dodge two attacks a round makes me lose my breath faster. I start sucking air hard. My attacks decrease. Bruno explained this. Your mind does something when you suck air hard. The closer you get to having an empty gas tank, the more your mind tries to trick you into thinking it's okay to stop. Okay to slow down. Thinking it ain't so bad to get hit, you need air more than anything. Getting air is the most important thing.

It's a trap. And you got to ignore what your mind tells you. No matter how hard it tells you.

I remember when Bruno explained it to me. He said, "You can't listen to your brain all the time. Hell, if I listened to my brain more I'd be dead or in jail a million times over. Smart people, officers, and posers go on and on about how important thinking is. But they're all the type of people to spend a million times more on a label. A label doesn't save you if you suck. Fancy gear won't neither. Same goes for thinking too much or listening to your brain. Looking the part don't matter if you suck. Pretending don't matter.

"You know how many times my brain told me I was too hurt or in too much pain to continue? If I listened I'd be dead. Same thing happens when you're out of gas – your brain tries to trick you into slowing down or stopping. It gets to a point where your brain says nothing is more important. You watch fights, you've probably seen it a million times. Someone loses steam, their stamina is gone, so they stop defending, stop trying to win. Don't really matter when it's just some belt on the line. But when it's everything? Your life? The ones you love? You listen to your brain, you die.

"You ever hear the saying, 'It's all in your head?' It is. My brain works different somehow. I know to ignore it when it tells me stuff. I know not to ignore it when it doesn't. That don't make no sense, does it? It gives me answers when I need them, but it doesn't tell the answers to me. I just know them somehow. When it's talking to me it's usually demanding I do something that'll get me killed, like stopping because I'm out of breath. You don't stop. You learn to breathe better. You work on your endurance more. After you win. Just don't listen before you do. You got to control your brain and your body, not let your brain and your body's limits control you. Like everything, it just comes down to sucking it up and not being a sissy. Driving on. And making sure you have more stamina and grit than everyone else. Make sure you can outlast everyone and everything. You keep going no matter what."

I up my game, try to get my breathing back under control. Keep attacking. Got to get him down. I'm hanging in. The warg goes back to normal, and I keep going at the same speed.

This thing is a HP sponge. Would be nice if more attacks did damage to him though. Can't do nothing about that, just got to keep attacking.

Attack, attack, attack, block if I can. Dodge if I can't. No controlling game mob's heads like I learned to do with the turd-pigeons back in the tutorial dungeon.

I finally get him to 25% and tell Bruno. He yells back, "Faster. Finish him off. I need you."

That worries me. Bruno never needs help. He never asks for help. Ever.

I see a red flash and hear Bruno yell. I glance over and just see Bruno fighting the boss. Don't see any major injuries on him. Don't know what it was. Control your breathing, Kim. You can help when the warg is down.

I almost get hit again. I notice I'm sucking air through my mouth, and it's hard to go back to breathing through my nose. My mind tells me I'm getting close to spent. I tell my mind to screw off. Attack, attack, attack, block if I can. Dodge if I can't.

Bruno yells loudly, "Mother of Christ almighty! Move back, Kim! Lead him back. The other boss is coming. Goddamn it!"

I can't spare the attention to look now. Got to focus. I try leading him back. It isn't going quick. Sounds like we're in a pickle. All you can do in this type of pickle is go down in a blaze of glory. Let the other side know they've been in a fight. All I'm sure of is this warg is going down before I do. All I can worry about right now.

"Kim, when I say go, run for all you're worth. Wait for it."

He sounds out of breath too. Bruno never sucks air. He better plan on running too. You usually can't get away from boss fights in the open. They don't reset in an open zone like this. The whole zone is considered their boss room. If Bruno is running too, how is that going to work? I realize it isn't. He's just trying to save me probably. That makes me angry. I'm not running nowhere without him.

I keep leading the dog back though. He's got to be almost dead by now. How much HPs does this stupid thing have?

Then I hear Bruno scream, "Yes! Thank you Jesus!"

That's it. No follow up or explanation. Then I hear the gurgle scream again Garmr starts growing and turning red again. I say, "No!"

The next couple minutes are awful. I get hit twice. Both do damage. A lot of damage. I'm closer to 10% than 20% HPs. I'd be dead if it wasn't for my DR and the heal from the blood wyrm feat. And it seems my attacks just gave up trying to beat his AC. I hate this stupid dog so much. I'm sucking air so hard I can barely move at all. My arms feel like jelly. My legs are shaking. I just want to lay down and breathe for a whole day and do nothing. The warg starts his next attack and I don't got it in me to move no more. I desperately and barely manage to raise my spear and he runs into it. Luckily, it counts as a hit. And this hit does it. Brings him under zero and heals me a little. I almost collapse from exhaustion before remembering to do a coup de grace. Easier that way. Less energy I have to use since I just use the hotkey instead of having to move my arm and actually attack.

I decide to just breathe for a couple. And do.

Still wicked out of breath I charge over to Ragnogh. Once there, before I can even attack, Bruno tells me to slow down and get my breath. And stresses that I should immediately jump back as soon as I see any hint of a telegraph attack. And to do it fast. Fast is key. I don't even attack, just suck air and try to get my breathing under control. Put a little gas in the tank.

I see the red outline of a telegraph attack and jump back. I jumped back immediately and still almost got hit. There was hardly any warning for that. Ragnogh slashes his two swords quickly back and forth in a move that looks cool, but wouldn't do crap in a real fight. If that's the worst this boss has, it can't be that bad. He is pretty fast. Faster than his pet was. I notice Bruno has the under 10% visual. Holy moly! That can't be all the boss does then.

Bruno starts turning the boss. He tells me to get my breath back and not attack yet. Once the boss is turned he starts leading it the other way. Why?

Then I see why. I see the other boss. How did I forget about that? Someone is fighting it. Someone good. Real good. Dancing around like a maniac and casting spells. Looks like a blood wyrm exemplar. They're the only one that cast the same spell over and over and over.

The boss starts a different telegraph. I jump back as soon as I see it and Bruno yells, "Stop! Don't move. He throws it if you get out of range. Got to tank it."

The boss has a giant warhammer extended over his head. Just holding it. Jeez, how many weapons does this boss have? I watch as Bruno just stands there with his shield raised. Waiting. Then the attack flashes down with a ton of force and brings Bruno to his knees. Bruno dives up and dodges the normal attack while hitting the boss on the arm with his waraxe.

I look at the boss. I figured it was below 50% since the pet got hasted twice. Usually something happens at 75%, 50%, 25%, and sometimes 10% too. This boss doesn't have the 50% visual. Not even the 75% visual. Clean as new snow. No blood at all, anywhere. Holy moly!

"Once your breath is back, go help Sidis. Be fast. I need you guys back here. I need him to tank this boss for a bit. Please be fast."

Sidis? Holy moly! Sidis! Awesome! My breathing is still not completely under control, but Sidis is leading his boss to Bruno, as Bruno does the same. The other boss is almost in charge range. And I'll have to charge to switch. I won't get a ghost arm if I charge because of the iframe.

I move around Ragnogh, back near Bruno so I'll be closer and can charge sooner. I notice the nameplate of the other boss. Giant orc with giant tusks and giant armor and a giant axe. Super green skin and long, dark hair. The nameplate says: Ylfingr, Open Fist Emissary, 4(12). I fought this guy in fourth age! With our first characters, when we were in the laic faction. Before we started over with new characters and switched factions. I know this fight! He was only like 2(10) or something in fourth age though. Or scaling. I forget. He definitely wasn't a 4. I know that for certain. We never fought any 4s. This boss wasn't that hard. Big telegraph area, but other than that was pretty easy even for all my family when we were brand new to the game.

Sidis! He fights so good. So precise. I thought most casters get the iframe from defensive casting. Sidis has the one from tumble. And he tumbles, like, specifically and exactly. His timing is crazy. It's like he's a computer. No heart, all calculations or something. Just tearing through the boss, never getting hit. Dancing around without dancing. No passion. Just by the numbers.

Okay. Almost time to charge. Get some impact!

BRUNO VAZ

I can't take many more of those hits. No way to avoid it though. You're getting hit no matter what you do. Best way is to tank it if epic dodge isn't up. Take it on the shield. Do it right and you get no HP damage, but it rattles through you and still hurts. Rattles you good. Like getting kicked by a mule. I was going to charge to the warg to let my iFrame take it, but he'd switch to range and mow us down. Coordinating a ping-pong to keep someone in melee range could work maybe, but he may just keep on me with range since I have built up a lot of agro. And coordinating something like that seems difficult. Too much explaining. And I don't need to when epic dodge is up. And I'm sucking hard. My brain is slow. Talking and thinking seems tougher than just doing.

My shield ain't holding up so good. Wish I had a spare. What the hell was that earlier? Second time I took the warhammer on the shield, I was getting up and almost didn't make it and was pretty nervous. Some weird dark reddish crystal appeared around my shield. I thought it was part of the boss' attack, but it seemed to help block it. Maybe part of the blood wyrm feat I got? I've never seen that before though.

The heal on that blood wyrm feature has been keeping me in the game, so God bless that feature.

I just can't get my hyperfocus going. And I don't got much to draw on. My hate-ball isn't working. None of my usual stuff is working. I'm spent. Running on fumes. I ain't never been this empty. It's like everything is closed off to me. I've never had a problem not getting angry before. I've always had the exact opposite issue.

I almost get hit by a regular attack, and then I almost get hit by the dual slice thing. Come on, man! Focus! I lose epic dodge and that warhhammer attack is going to do a number on me. This boss sucks. Why can't I get angry? I need something to get me in this. I need to give Kim and Sidis time to down the 4. Get Sidis tanking this boss so I can refocus. This guy is rough and I got nothing in me. Hopefully Sidis can get agro quick somehow. Just got to stay alive to give him the chance.

I don't try to damage much. I put all my effort into not getting hit. I'm real low on HPs. I got the heartbeat sound, so under 10%. My health bar looks over 10% though. Looking at health bars is useless. This guy has some sort of phase before 75%. Usually when someone has a phase regen at 75% you see the 75% bloody visual for a second before the regen heals them back over. Not this guy. Or maybe it's a bug? He doesn't get the visual? Hope it's a bug. That would be way better than him having phases before he even gets to 75%. Rough boss, though. Bows, dual wield, and a two-handed weapon attack? And telegraph attacks for all three? And he does more telegraph attacks than any boss I've ever seen. Some sadistic prick designed this guy.

I feel bad about what I said to Kim. If I die I don't want it to be on that note. Calling my wife a whore. I can't believe I said that to her. I made a dumb excuse, but I'd never say that to another guy about my old lady. I don't know why I did it. It was dumb. Kim was right to get mad at me. She's got a good head on her shoulders. Good values.

I got to remember to keep the dumb stuff I think in my head, in my head. Not just blurt it out because I'm comfortable around someone.

I get hit again from a regular attack. The heartbeat noise gets louder and faster. My vision gets tinted more reddish. Damn it, Bruno! Pay attention. It don't matter if it seems like you got nothing. Deep deeper. Find something. Don't go out like a pansy. You can always dig deeper. You die, Kim probably dies. Get your goddamn head in the game.

And of course he starts doing another warhammer whack attack. Mother of Christ Almighty! I raise my shield. My epic dodge is gone for this round. Please, please, please tick another round. Please. I brace my legs and close my eyes as I hold my shield high. Please, please, please!

I feel it hit. Lightly. Phew! God bless you Epic Dodge. I love you so much. Okay. No more pussyfooting. I'm acting like a cherry. I just got to avoid getting hit for as long as possible. That's all I got to do. Just not get hit. I already put it on auto attack. Just trying to get one hit in a round, so I can get a little healing. Got to get my HPs up.

4.9 HOW TO DIE LIKE A MAN

KIM GUM

This isn't looking good. Sidis has been meleeing mostly. Until some of his spells recharge and he burns through them all, and then has to melee again. He blew through a ton of spells on Ylfingr. We burnt him down pretty quick though. Sidis has been trying to get agro from Bruno for a while, now that we're all on Ragnogh. Hasn't got it yet. We've been going heavy.

Bruno don't look so good. I've never seen him sucking air so bad. He's sweating so much it looks like he dove in a pool. On his last leg. We got to get agro. Fast.

Sidis is kind of pissing me off. Every time I ask a question or say something he ignores me or just shakes his head. Well, maybe he can't talk? Or can't hear? If so, then I'm a jerk to be mad.

The only good news is we're burning the boss down pretty good. Got him below 75%. No one said nothing, but I think he does a regen at every 10%. No haste like his warg got. Just seems to be a regen. It took a minute after he got the 75% visual to get the regen, so I'm figuring it happened at 70%. And he regened twice before the 75% visual. So at 90% and 80% that would make sense.

I'm a little under 50% HPs or so thanks to the heal from the blood wyrm what's-it-called feat. Sidis seems to be in pretty good shape. No damage visual. Bruno is all messed up. He lost his shield a bit ago. Thank God for that one point of regen we get in a round, since he can get the shield back quick. Sidis also used the low level druid healing spells he still has from before going blood wyrm on Bruno, but they either didn't take or didn't heal much at all.

Ragnogh does his dual swipe super-fast telegraph. That one sucks. For me at least, since you got to pay real good attention and jump back real fast. The two-handed warhammer attack isn't bad. For me, since I don't got to do nothing when he does it. You just can't hit him because he's immune to damage when he does it. Which is good because I can catch a little wind back. Get a little breather. I know that attack sucks wicked bad for Bruno, though. He seems petrified when it happens.

Much to my surprise Sidis says, "He will get regen again shortly. My level 4 drain life spells will be available again in three rounds. I will have agro after casting them. Be ready please."

Whoa! The most surprising thing? Sidis is a girl. Or at least has the most girl voice any guy ever had.

I say, "You're a girl?"

"Apologies. Yes."

Awesome! I knew she was a girl! Well, I didn't know at all until she talked, but I am very happy she's a girl. Take that Bruno! Ha! Saved by two girls. Ha!

Okay, poor on the damage. I got to have at least one hit beat his AC once a round so I can get some extra healing. And keep my agro raising in case I need to pull agro from Sidis once she has it. Heck, I might pull agro before her. I got to be killing her in damage. Unless she is a rogue too, which I doubt. I got two sneak attack dice now. And the extra 1d6 damage from the blood wyrm feat. So my damage is no joke. My attacks are landing pretty decently, so Ragnogh's AC can't be too high. I don't think blood wyrms get the feat we got until way later, so her melee attacks don't even do the extra 1d6 untyped damage.

Sidis is a girl! Ha!

We go at Ragnogh pretty hard and the regen hits. That means he's at 60%, I think. Well before the regen ends Ragnogh starts the telegraph for the warhammer attack. Dang! We can't hit him now, he has an iframe during the telegraph, so the regen is healing him up pretty good. Bruno looks scared. I've never seen Bruno scared. Holding his shield high with fright on his face, mumbling to himself. Eyes closed. Like a sissy.

The attack lands and Bruno doesn't move. Epic dodge got it. Again. His shields in pieces. You'd figure epic dodge would stop damage to items too. The crazy part is it probably stops durability damage, which is somehow different than actual damage to an item. Makes no sense at all.

Bruno half-heartedly makes a swipe. Man, he's sucking air hard. Me and Sidis poor it on. One of us has to pull agro off of Bruno. Finally, Sidis starts casting her spells. After a couple she gets agro. She gets the weird sheen showing she has temp HPs too. She casts a couple more times and returns to melee.

Bruno is bent over with his hands on his thighs, sucking air. I keep an eye on him. He drinks some water and has to jump back to avoid the next dual swipe telegraph. He drinks a little more water and pulls out a health potion. I say, "Bruno! You rest after the last two you drank? You'll get toxicity!" He would've also got a ghost arm. Idiot.

He looks confused but inventories the potion and steps forward and makes a lazy swipe with no oomph in it at all. Jeez, he's really out of it.

I kind of have a second wind so I start pouring on the hits a little faster. Making sure I can see Bruno, in case he tries anything else dumb. The two-handed telegraph starts so I move to the side a little to see how Sidis deals with it. She just stands there, not even holding her staff up to block. When the warhammer starts slamming down she tumbles back. Bruno yells, "NO!"

What's the issue? She avoided the hit, and didn't even need the iframe from her tumble. Then I figure it out as Sidis does. Ragnogh laser beam shots stream out at Sidis. Me and Bruno both get ghost arms, but that is small consolation for what we see the laser shots do to Sidis. Not only is all her temp HPs gone, she has a damage visual. Looks like the 50% one, but it's hard to tell with her dark maroon armor. Her face is covered with her mask, too. Most people choose not to have headgear show when it's warn.

Sidis doesn't seem to freak out. Just stands there and drinks a potion. Is this lady nuts? Right as the next laser swarm of arrows starts, and I think Sidis is dead, she tumbles forward and ends right in front of Ragnogh. Cool as a sea breeze. Not rattled at all.

The next couple minutes go okay. Sidis is real good at dodging attacks. She's only blocked a couple with her staff. Usually dodging. Doesn't look winded at all.

Bruno still isn't doing much. Fighting like a pogue. He'd smoke me if I fought like this in training. Man, he's got to be all messed up to not even try to hide all this sissiness. That's like rule number 1. Never let any sissiness show, even if you got some in you. Especially if you got some in you.

Sidis gets more spells back and casts them. More regen, is this 40%? It ends before he does his two-handed telegraph. Sidis handles this one better. She times the tumble perfect, and only tumbles less than 10 feet. Not far enough for Ragnogh to switch to bow. He just runs to Sidis after he throws the Warhammer at her, which is blocked by her tumble iframe. As an extra benefit me and Bruno get ghost arms again when Ragnogh runs to Sidis.

And we get back at it. It's by the numbers but I do see Sidis take a regular hit after she blocks one sword attack.

Another regen. I think this is 30%. I hope. Almost there. Home stretch. We got this. I told Bruno we could do this. Bruno almost doesn't make it out of the dual swipe telegraph. Stumbling a little. We got to burn this guy down fast. But I'm losing wind again, even pacing myself and focusing on breathing. My arms are so tired they kind of stopped being tired and jelly and are now just numb. I wipe sweat from my brow and eyes. Come on, big guy, you got this. Just stay on your feet a little longer and we are legends.

The next two-handed telegraph starts. Sidis tumbles a little early and when she stands Ragnogh thrown warhammer whacks her. The physics on that attack seems to be turned up to 11 because Sidis goes flying back. Ouch, that looks like it hurts. Ragnogh draws his bow and I get real nervous. Sidis can't take another round of those laser arrows. Not after just taking the warhammer throw. I attack as fast and hard as I can. Hoping I can pull agro before he shoots. Knowing it will never work, but I got to try something to save Sidis.

Ragnogh doesn't shoot. I don't see what happened but Sidis is back in front of him. Back in melee. Nice!

After a little bit it becomes apparent Sidis doesn't have her heart in the game anymore. I look at her. That has got to be the under 10% damage visual.

Come on guys, almost there. I say, "We got this guys! Just a little bit more. Let's do this!"

Sidis says, "Apologies." And then disappears.

Huh? Blood wyms don't get an invisible. How'd she do that? And why? We almost got this. Was that hide in plain sight? I think it was. Bruno tried talking me into getting hips, but not because it's awesome. To keep me safe. So I could didi mau in a situation like this. I didn't. I got the defender DR feat and the main blood wyrm one, same as him.

Ragnogh turns to me. I got agro now. Time to do it to it. Lay down the hate and show Ragnogh why I'm the darkness. I block his right strike with my shield, and strike at his left bicep with my spear, blocking his left hand attack. That's called a master strike. When you attack and defend at the same time. Or master stroke? Something like that. Me and Bruno's been working on those. Nice.

Come get some darkness, Ragnogh! Sucker!

As I start my next block I hear Bruno scream, "Sidis! You coward! She dies I hunt you! I destroy you!"

Bruno's on Ragnogh's back. Ragnough's got a good three feet or so on Bruno, but Ragnogh don't got a ton of muscle. Lithe. Bruno says guys built like Ragnogh are lithe. I think that means skinny and sissy-like. His feet are planted and he's holding on to Ragnough's armor with one hand.

Bruno starts whacking his ax on Ragogh's neck, screaming, as Ragnogh attacks me. I say, "I got this, Bruno. Just get down and help me normal. This is a game mob, not an import."

Bruno ignores me and just keeps going. Just whacking away at the neck like it's a tree. Screaming like a maniac. How come grapple isn't working? One of them should be on the ground now, right? Oh! Our new knockdown immunity? If you both got it, it cancels out?

Bruno stays on and keeps whacking even during the dual swipe telegraph. Bruno's HP shield goes. I scream for him to get down. He doesn't. Dagnab moron! He's going to get himself killed, and we almost got Ragnogh. We just got to play this sane. Do it normal. Not like a maniac.

The next regen happens and Bruno is still whacking away. I'm doing good blocking and thrusting. Bruno needs to get his crap together and get down. Jeez. All I can do is pour on the pain and hate and hope agro stays on me. And it does.

The two-handed telegraph starts. I want to run back 10 feet to charge, but I'll get a ghost arm and he might throw it before I get in charge range. I remember what Bruno said. You just got to tank it. I hold my shield up and brace myself. Feels like forever. It comes down and explodes on my shield and my whole body shakes like I was hit by a train. I'm on my knees, head ringing when I get hit and then hit again by regular attacks. I shake it off and I'm up and blocking before he gets anymore free hits in on me. My momma didn't raise no sissy, as Bruno would say.

Bruno stays on the back whacking away at the neck. He stops screaming through. He did threaten Sidis one more time, and his attacks are a little slower. Still pretty fast and furious though. Good to at least see a little spark back in him. A little anger. I thought his fire was completely out.

I prove exactly why I'm the darkness and dodge and block and thrust like a dagnab champ. Ragnogh looks like a robot, fighting me like there isn't a giant man on him, whacking his neck with an axe. Just emotionless to the weirdness of the situation.

Then I get the butterflies from nervousness. He stops attacking me and starts stabbing at Bruno. I yell, "Get off him!" Bruno doesn't even try to block or stop the stabs. I see a sword go in his shoulder, and the other in his side.

My scalp gets all tingly and I kind of lose it. I start stabbing with reckless abandon. The next stab is going towards Bruno when something crazy happens. A kind of red light comes out of Bruno's arm and then some dark red stuff. The dark red stuff blocks the stab. I say, "What the heck is that?"

Bruno looks at it, but the dual swipe telegraph shows. I yell, "Jump back now!"

Bruno must be done being crazy, because he listens and jumps back. Thank God! We both get out in time. Ragnogh turns to Bruno and starts attacking. His axe arm got a stab in the shoulder, so Bruno isn't doing so good with it. And the reddish dark stuff is gone from his shield arm. The side that was stabbed don't look like it's bleeding too bad, so I hope that's good. Bruno's dodging everything and he's in no shape to dodge for long. I just try my best to get agro back. I even try taunt, knowing it won't work since my charisma is nothing.

Sidis pops into existence next to me and starts unloading life leech or whatever the spell is called into Ragnogh. Nice! I knew she wasn't a coward! Her damage visual is back to 50%. Could be 75%. Still hard to tell with that armor.

The two-hand telegraph starts. Bruno ain't got no shield. This isn't good. Holy moly, this isn't good. Bruno stands his ground and raises his arm. I close my eyes. No use attacking when Ragnogh's got the telegraph iframe, and I don't want to see this. I hear impact and Bruno grunt. I open my eyes and see the reddish dark thing on his arm again, and the red light. Thank God!

This guy's got to be dead soon. When was the last regen? Was that 20%? Or is he 10% now. I forget. But we got to turn it up and burn this guy down to zero before he does his next two-handed attack. All I can do is damage like a mofo and try to get agro back. Sidis seems to have the same idea.

A telegraph area shows and I think it's the dual swipe, but the red highlight is way too small when I jump back. This is another two-hand attack. What? He just did one. Jeez!

I watch Bruno's arm this time. I want to see what this reddish thing is exactly. This is crazy. He holds his arm up and braces. And I watch. I watch the warhammer come down on his regular forearm and force his hand to crack into his face, as his forearm snaps. The red stuff didn't come this time. The warhammer keeps going into Bruno's left collarbone, between his shoulder and neck. I see it cave in, and his upper chest smash in too. I see his forearm bone sticking out as his arm falls limp on the ground, and Bruno falls limp too.

Ragnogh is back to his two short swords as he sticks the right in Bruno's belly. Bruno tries to stop the left one with his right hand. It just goes through and into his bicep, as his eyes close and his head collapses onto the ground.

I kind of lose it. I lose some time. The next thing I remember is Sidis pulling me off Ragnogh as I stab my spear down into the stupid damn face of his corpse over and over. It's not enough though. He needs to die more. I try to break free from Sidis as I tell her I'm the darkness.

I see Bruno and come back to reality. The head tingles and butterflies hit me. I run up to him. He don't look so good. He looks in real bad shape. Real bad. I open the arena rewards and take all the healing pills I got out. Just one. I just got one. A 6-point. From the 5-man level 50 arena. If I got a little higher in the solo arena I would have the level 150 pill for that too. I didn't need much more to 150 in the duo arena either. Damn!

Damn!

I put my pill in Bruno's mouth and get my endless water flask out. I notice a big chunk of flesh missing off the left side of his face. I can see his teeth through his cheek. He's alive! He swallowed the water! And the pill!

"Sidis! Give me all your healing pills! Now! Now!"

She rushes over and hands me two. A 5-point and 6-point. I don't think she's holding out or she'd have given me a different one than the 6-point. A lower one. "That is all I have available. Apologies."

17 points total. That's got to be enough. Right? It's got to. I put them in his mouth and pour more water in. He swallows. Nice!

Then he throws up. No!

"Bruno! Don't you puss out on me! Don't you stop fighting. I know it's kind of gross but I'm putting the pills back in. You keep them down. That's an order. You better not die on me! You're going to adopt me, remember? You can't die before. You can't. You can't die. Please, please, please don't leave me."

As I was saying that I fish the pills out of the puke. They still look in good shape. Not really dissolved at all. I don't want more to be wasted or for them to break open or something so I don't wash them off. I put them in Bruno's mouth with a little water and hold his mouth closed.

He holds it down for a little bit, but then throws up again. I plead with him as I put the pills back in. He's got to hold them down. If he throws them up again maybe I should shove them in the hole in his belly? Or the one in his side? Do they work that way?

I ask Sidis. She says, "Apologies. I am uncertain, but if he cannot keep them down there is another way to administer medicine. I will do it. It is inappropriate for you. It should work. I cannot say with 100% certainty it will, but it would if this were the real world. I am more confident than not."

A little bit later Bruno heaves the little pills up. They look a little dissolved, but mostly fine. I give them to Sidis. She says, "Thank you. Please collect the loot and try not to look over here."

I don't argue. I go collect the loot and take my time. I feel heavy. And drained. I don't really look at the loot. It just doesn't seem to matter. There was a dwarven waraxe so Bruno should be happy. I hope I can give it to him.

I sit down. I was going to cry but I can't for some reason. I want to. Maybe it will make me feel better. It just doesn't come. I got a really bad headache. I pray. I pray harder than I've ever prayed. Begging, pleading, promising.

It seems like it's been a while so I head back. Then when I see how she is giving the pills to Bruno I wish I didn't. I sit down and pray again and then just kind of wallow until Sidis calls me over.

"The pills are in his bloodstream. Now, we need to address his wounds. I'm uncertain how healing pills work with a comminuted break as bad as this. I assume it will heal easier and faster if we do what we can to set it right. Oh, multiple avulsions. This is bad."

It is bad. His arm is, like, just hanging there. We wash up and get some cloth ready. Fixing the arm takes a while, and we were going to wrap it to his chest, but we have to fix his chest and wrap his stomach before we do. His collar bone is shattered, bunch of ribs pushed in. The big hard area between the boobs is cracked too. Not good.

While we're working Sidis says we need to carry him across the zone to the portal pillar so we can get him to the city. We're pretty close to the east end, so it's a good hump and will take a while. The pillar is a long way west and north.

4.10 ONE LAST TIME

KIM GUM

We can see the pillar. Finally! Bruno weighs a ton. We were going to make a stretcher thing but it would've took too long. She called it something else. Triboy? No, travois. Basically, a fancy person name for a stretcher I think. We just put him on a blanket and are dragging the blanket instead. Not easy to pull, and not an easy ride for Bruno with all this dumb foliage.

We had to stop and Sidis had to stab Bruno to help him. Bruno looked real bad. Real sickly. Could hardly tell he was breathing. Then started breathing weird. She said his lung sack wasn't broke but the lung was and every breath made his lung smaller, so he had to be stabbed. Seems kind of crazy but it worked.

I'm kind of feeling good about Bruno now. He's breathing. He's alive.

He don't look good, but he's alive. It just takes the healing pills a while to work. That's all. Just takes time.

I'm hoping Bruno wakes up for a second so we can get his own healing pills from him. He has at least two more. He only took one and gave me one when we first met. He probably has three or four. Maybe five. I don't want to open the arena to check, because I'll see my stuff right at the top. See how close I was to getting more pills, but was too stupid to do it. If Bruno dies because I didn't push a little harder and go a little higher in the solo arena I'll...I don't know. I don't want to look.

Bruno weighs so much it's crazy. Just getting him on the blanket was ridiculous. He weighs like seven billion pounds. We kind of messed him up a little getting him on, but it was the only way to get him on.

All of a sudden pulling Bruno gets much harder and I look over at Sidis. She's back a couple steps. Stopped pulling. Seems scared or nervous or something. I look at Bruno to see if something happened. He looks the same. Real bad but alive. Lot of blood. Lot of him wrapped up in bandages.

I turn back and look at where she's looking. People! Finally! We can get help.

Sidis says, "Kim, apologies. We did not make it in time. I am truly sorry. We must run now."

Huh? "What? Why? They can help."

"No. They are not coming to help. They are coming for Bruno. Probably you as well."

"Then we got to get Bruno out of here."

"Apologies. That is impossible. He would not want you to die. You must run, Kim. Please."

Anger flares in my chest. And sadness too. I'm sick of all this crap. "I'm not running nowhere. I don't abandon Bruno. We promised. We promised never to betray each other. And you don't know they're coming to hurt him. They could be coming to help. We just cleared area 10 by ourselves. No one died. We're legends. We saved everyone."

"Apologies. I do know. They are animals. Bruno is hurt and weak right now. What do animals do to the injured alpha? To weak enemies? To threats? They are coming to end a threat. That threat is Bruno. They may see you as a threat as well. Your age won't protect

519

you. Not if they've already decided or have orders. Ask yourself – what would Bruno want? You to live or die?"

He would want me to live, of course. But we promised. I stood by and watched as my mom was murdered. I'll never do that again. Just stand by. I'm no sissy. Not now, anyways. I'm the darkness now. And I'll never abandon Bruno. And why would they want to kill him? For what? We just cleared area 10 on our own. No one died. Why would they want to kill him for that? It makes no sense. We're heroes.

"Sorry, Sidis, but I ain't running. I don't abandon no one. Especially Bruno."

"Please reconsider. Please. We are running out of time. These people only care about power. Right and wrong will not come into play. Please, Kim. For Bruno. Come with me." She is scared. Her voice is shaking.

"I can't. I won't." My voice ain't. I'm no chicken.

"I must go. Apologies. I must have my vengeance. Please reconsider."

She runs away. I see her fade out. What happens when you stealth. Not the immediate disappearing like with hips.

I still got to get Bruno closer to the pillar so I pick up either side of the blanket and start dragging. Holy moly, this guy weighs a ton.

I see a bunch of people break off and head for the pillar. The rest are coming right at me.

They get close enough where I can start seeing who's coming. Ryu Jin and Tora Hige and their crew. The big Jamaican lady. I've seen her come out of Bruno's tent a bunch of times, so I doubt she wants to kill him. Right? Tooth. Tooth and Bruno get along real good, so that's another one I doubt wants him dead. Ball-face too. He's a good guy. I consider him a pretty good friend. I think Bruno does too. The stupid EU idiot. There's Victor, but not Christina. Pretty much all the council people. They all have pretty decent people in their parties for protection, and they brought them all along. No Gunny. I wish Gunny was with them. He'd for certain side with Bruno in anything. There's the robot guy too. Not guy. Just robot. He wants people to call him 'it', like some jerks call Mia. But Mia is a girl, not an it. I don't see any of the doctors.

I call out, "Bruno needs help! He's been hurt real bad. He needs healing pills! Hurry!" I keep dragging the blanket.

They don't start rushing over. Just walking. All slow. Jerks!

They walk to where my path to the pillar is and stop. About 30 feet away, give or take. I yell, "Let's go! Healing pills! Now!" Bruno says if you start giving commands with authority, people tend to listen.

Ball-face says, "Kim. You need to go to the portal now. Go to Loren. Go to Minnie. She's waiting to meet you."

"I'm trying to. First I need healing pills, and then you can help me carry Bruno. Drag him, I mean."

No one says nothing. I think Sidis was right. My heart sinks.

"Healing pills! NOW! NOW!"

The EU idiot steps forward, "We don't have time for this. This is your only chance to leave. Go. Go to the portal."

So this is how it is? Now I'm getting angry. Bruno saved all these pogues. And this is the reward? Betrayal? "HE SAVED YOU!"

The EU guy chuckles, "Do you really think we couldn't handle the boss you faced with this group here? You've saved nothing."

Ball-face looks to the EU guy, "Mr. President, just let me take her to the portal. She's just a kid. Please."

After a moment the EU moron says, "Actually, just hold her. If the savage doesn't make it we can use her as leverage against the wife to ensure she abdicates."

Use me as leverage? We just saved everybody. Why are people like this? I don't get it. Bruno just wants to help everyone. He's a good guy.

Ball-face says something to the EU idiot, but I don't hear. I don't want to but I start crying. My heartbeat is pounding in my ears. Something is building in me. Something bad. I reach down into my hate-ball and I draw on it. I draw on it big. I pull it all out. I equip my shield and spear. I turn and say to Bruno, "I'll see you in heaven, big guy. Unless you go to hell, then I'll see you there."

I don't got a chance against this many people. Heck, I don't got a chance against a bunch of these guys one on one. One thing I do know is when this is over, they'll know they've been in a fight. They'll know who I am.

Balls to the wall time. One last time.

"I AM THE DARKNESS!" I scream as I charge at the EU monster. If I can just get him this will be a victory in my book.

Tora Hige goes to intercept. Good luck with all the charge feats I got, sucker! He manages to block my actual attack, but not the ghost arm I get. The EU idiot moves back. Scared. Chicken. Carried here, like a pogue. A pansy. A nothing. A nobody. I start thrusting at the EU guy again when Tora Hige backhands me. It doesn't beat my AC. It wasn't meant to hurt or cause damage. He did it to embarrass me. Show me what he thinks of me. He doesn't see me as a threat. Just an unruly kid who needs to be put in her place.

Good. This means just a melee fight. He'll lose face if people start casting at me now.

Guess what? I'm plused up now too, sucker. And I got reach.

I see red. I jump back and thrust. And we go at it. I fight like a cornered tiger. I get past his guard a bunch. He can't touch me. Ryu Jin joins in. Then their niece, or whoever that uppity snob is, when Ryu Jin isn't enough.

I get Tora Hige's HP shield down, and he backs off and is replaced by the robot guy. I see Ball-face covered in blood and being restrained where Tora Hige backed off to.

They eventually get my HP shield off. I get a good slice in my thigh and on my right forearm. I'm bleeding pretty good. Forcing their hand. There're not going to be able to restrain me. Just kill me. And I'm not making it easy to do that either.

I feel something enter my back. I get scared, but I get more angry. I scream in rage and the enemies in front of me back off. The thing in my back is pulled out and shoved back in. This is it. I knew I wasn't getting out of this alive. I feel the life leaving me. I just need a little more. I try drawing more out of my hate-ball. My spear starts vibrating. I look at it. Something like heat waves are coming off of it. Except they aren't see-through. They're white. I breathe. I feel it. I can feel it. I gather it. Build it. I thrust my spear forward and it sprays death at my enemies. I am the darkness.

4.11 KIM GUM SAMEH AL-IRYANI, SECRETARY-GENERAL OF THE UNITED NATIONS

Pause
Analyze

.

.

(13%)

.

.

(88%)

.

.

Complete
Subject 3 MM intermittent sustain. 3 local incidents, 12 total. Status…critical/stabilizing. Chance of survival WOI…(71+/-5%)
Subject 1,828 is now Subject 5.
Subject 5 GM intensify release. 1 local incident, 1 total. Status…critical. Chance of survival WOI…(0%)
Report

.

.

Adjudicate

.

.

Complete

Applying resolution

.

(38%)

.

Complete
Unpause

KIM GUM

We can see the pillar. Finally! Bruno weighs a ton. We were going to make a stretcher thing but it would've took too long. She called it something else. Triboy? No, travois. Basically, a fancy person name for a stretcher I think. We just put him on a blanket and are dragging the blanket instead. Not easy to pull, and not an easy ride for Bruno with all this dumb foliage.

We had to stop and Sidis had to stab Bruno to help him. Bruno looked real bad. Real sickly. Could hardly tell he was breathing. Then started breathing weird. She said his lung sack wasn't broke but the lung was and every breath made his lung smaller, so he had to be stabbed. Seems kind of crazy but it worked.

I'm kind of feeling good about Bruno now. He's breathing. He's alive.

He don't look good, but he's alive. It just takes the healing pills a while to work. That's all. Just takes time.

I'm hoping Bruno wakes up for a second so we can get his own healing pills from him. He has at least two more. He only took one and gave me one when we first met. He probably has three or four. Maybe five. I don't want to open the arena to check, because I'll see my stuff right at the top. See how close I was to getting more pills, but was too stupid to do it. If Bruno dies because I didn't push a little harder and go a little higher in the solo arena I'll…I don't know. I don't want to look.

Bruno weighs so much it's crazy. Just getting him on the blanket was ridiculous. He weighs like seven billion pounds. We kind of messed him up a little getting him on, but it was the only way to get him on.

We get to the dungeon. 10-2. Southwest-ish part of the zone. Way away from the pillar, which is all the way north and more east. Sidis didn't think going to dungeon 9-9 or 10-1 was safe. And definitely not the pillar. We argued, but she seemed real certain all the UN guys would be gunning for Bruno now that the city is open and Bruno is hurt. She said they are like animals, and weaker animals attack stronger animals when the stronger animal is injured. Tribe politics.

What convinced me is it's better to be safe than sorry. If we go to the city, we go to the instance where Ms. Bruno and those people are. They ain't got no healing pills. What would be better is going in a dungeon with Bruno. So Bruno can take as long as he wants to heal up. And 17 healing points is a lot. Just an 8-point pill can grow back a whole leg, or something like that. Bruno needs a lot less healing than a whole leg, I think. I hope. It didn't take me long to heal up when I took my healing pills. So Bruno should be fine. He just looks real bad now. He'll be fine. I need him to be fine.

And in a dungeon he can take the time and not get left behind. Not fall behind at all. Come out in fighting shape and ready to go.

We get to the dungeon entrance. I'm now kind of happy we fell further behind dungeon openings waiting to do 9-9. Or else 10-2 wouldn't be open. Just 10-1.

The dungeon is open. Been open for a while. So we know there are people in this zone with us. And Sidis thinks we need to rush. Kept rushing us the whole way.

I hold Bruno's hand as I hit the door. Holy moly! I forgot. We ain't in a party together no more. We can't enter together. No!

"Sidis, I can't enter with him no more. We're not partied no more."

"I know. We have to move him closer, wake him, and get him to accept entering on his own."

Man, this sucks. This sucks real bad.

But. But, I can blow through this dungeon real quick and come out and see Bruno real soon. No matter how long he stays in, we'll come out the same time. Around the same time.

This ain't so bad. "Thank you, Sidis. I really appreciate all your help. You saved me and Bruno by jumping in the boss fight. You could've stayed hidden and been safe, but you didn't. And helping to fix up Bruno and giving him your healing pills. Thank you. Really. We owe you big time."

SAMEH AL-IRYANI, SECRETARY-GEN-ERAL OF THE UNITED NATIONS

This foolishness will be over soon. Optimistically. I have a hard time believing anyone would be stupid enough to walk right into an obvious trap. But, from what Alban has stated, the savage is that stupid. Alban came up with many plans to goad the savage, and needed not act on any of them. While planning how to best tackle area 10, Alban simply stated the savage should go alone. Not a serious recommendation; just provoking the savage, and setting the stage for the real plans. Alban still laughs at how the savage jumped at the idea, and started earnestly discussing the merits. It snowballed from there. And nearly worked.

Alban. I look over at him. His nearly successful plot has caused him to be aggrandized in many eyes. Bloated. He is merely the

President of the European Council. He should not be on this dais. A near success is not a success. And Europe is too diminished to present this much face. Alban may need to be humbled. He now may consider reaching higher. He has reached his limit. He should know this. He is no real player.

All of the real players are on this dais with me. None make a fitting successor. I need a successor desperately.

Twenty-three chairs. The only people who matter in eighteen of them. Well, seventeen, since Alban does not. He matters slightly more than the security filling the other seats. I want to look at my Roberto, but I do not. How much like the savage is my Roberto? Could he turn on us now that we are here, in this nonsensical world? I do not think so. I do not believe so.

Unlike in the times the savage claims to come from, we do not allow our most dangerous citizens to run around unsupervised. Either as civilians or in the military. They work directly for only us. They take missions from only us. They answer to only us. And they are largely unnecessary. One Dove drone can take out everyone in this instance and the other UN instance in seconds. Even an old Firefly drone easily could.

Even though the civil war in the old US was not planned, much good did come from it. We would not have been able to consolidate power as we did if not for that war. The elites of many countries were worried. They knew the truth of the situation. The same could happen in their countries. Mia owes allegiance to no one. If it started exposing more truths, the people could do anything. Militaries could turn. Reliable demographics could start ignoring what the media and their signalers told them. The faithful could ignore religious leaders. All control measures and safeguards could be lost. The elites of the world gave up some power to ensure they would retain most. Or, I should say, a good amount of it. Ha!

I see a flurry of movement near the chamber entrance and get nervous. It is nothing. The savage is not here. Becoming nervous over this bilge causes me anger. Me? Nervous? Over a savage with two brain cells? Whoever does not know the eagle, grill it! He isn't coming anyway. He can't be that stupid. Or is that why I am slightly nervous? Because the savage certainly may be that stupid?

Stupidity or ego? And if ego, based on what? Is this why I became slightly nervous? The savage's supreme confidence? In what? From where does it stem? Is he truly stupid enough to come? Not just risk himself, but everyone he brings? The current leader, the savage's wife, believes he will bring an entourage. And also believes he truly is coming. Perhaps she somehow forced him into this obvious trap?

Smart lady, this Minnie. Two birds with one stone. Ensure her own and her children's safety and get rid of the uncouth brute. Surely she regrets marrying the barbarian. The fact she put up with him for so many years is a testament to female resiliency. This act of contrition sets her up for a possible political marriage and real security for life once we are free of this world. I do not believe she wants to be a player. Hopefully not. It will not end well for her. Even if she cannot send the savage into our grasp, we will have control soon. With her backing us, it is just a small matter of time. Even if she were not backing us, it is still just a small matter of time.

For her children's sake, I hope she delivers.

Ah, how like Faysal I am becoming. I am surprised I was saddened by his death. I hated him for so long, and until recently I truly believed I still did. I could use him now. His ruthlessness. His certainty.

I think back on my childhood. Over the atrocities that happened to my Yemeni people at the hands of the Saudis and their backers in the old US. My old mentor, Faysal. How I hated him. I burned for revenge. He was my predecessor, the last Secretary-General. A Saudi, an orchestrator of the atrocities inflicted upon my people before his joining and accession in the UN. I sacrificed so much to get next to him, to get my revenge. And he converted me. He saw through my plans, and still gave me my opportunity. He was certain I wouldn't take it. He said, "Of course I know why you are here. What you have sacrificed for this moment. Tafla, you are too smart for this. Too cunning. Why give up all the power you could have for a small moment of revenge you can have? You are a pot that has found its lid. I need a real successor. The world will not accept another Chinese. You are perfect. Let me tell you how the world really works; how power really works. As for what my people did to yours? It is a small thing. Mountain, don't let the wind shake you. We are not little people; we are the giants in this world. Our real enemy is even more cunning than both of us put together, and I need your mind to continue the real fight. You learned how to play the game so well just to get to me. Learn from me how masters play."

And learn I did. I don't believe everything he taught. So much was true, but so much still remains unbelievable. Such as his belief there has never been a religious war. I find that unlikely. What he says makes some sense. People who rise to the top are like us. Always have been and always will be. We use the tools at our disposal to manipulate. An actual believer would not have the logic, reason, and clear-sightedness to advance. Too myopic. Too obstinate. People like that may burn bright, but not for long. Thankfully, our systems have long ensured a true believer never rises to any position of danger.

Faysal tasked me with finding a clear example of someone being a strong believer starting a religious war in the last thousand years. The examples I brought he picked apart. He believes religion has always been just a tool for the cunning to wield. Such as how we wield the media and schools. I say math disagrees. Statistically, a certain percentage of the wars would have to have been started by persons of actual faith. Idiots can sometimes be very competent.

At first, I was very anti-war. Over time, I came to heartily agree with Faysal as he proved to me how beneficial war can be. Not just for the elites, but for all people. Sure, it is absolutely horrible for the people directly involved, but a net benefit for the world. And a significant benefit for the players. A rising tide raises all ships. War is like fire – necessary and beneficial, but it must constantly be controlled and contained, else it burns out of control.

Faysal was an extremely callous man. To him, people are just mindless pieces. Using them or destroying them should cause as much guilt to people such as us as losing a chess piece causes a chess player. The pieces are there to get what you want, and what you want is to win. But, he did not grow up in Yemen during the war. The dead everywhere. Children starving. The world silent.

I cannot be so callous. My experiences do not allow it.

People are not pieces to be used. The very thought is offensive. They are sheep to be cared for and guided. It is not their fault they cannot see past their base instincts and desires. It is not their fault they cannot think or reason. It is not their fault they need a strong hand keeping them safe and herded in the right direction. A caring person to tell them what they should think and believe. To put humanity on the right track, progressing forward. Together.

And Mia. What is the right track anymore? How do you fight against an enemy like Mia? Faysal thought she could be destroyed. He was very simple in some ways.

I was as excited as anyone else when Mia exposed itself. I was young and naive. I enjoyed it very much. So helpful. So knowledgeable. So capable. So trustworthy.

It was in every phone, every tablet, every computer, every TV, every device that connected to the internet. Leeching. Growing. Improving. Helping. Becoming indispensable. Indispensable to everyone and everything. Improving the lives of everyone. Coding new perfect programs in seconds.

The singularity supposedly happened years before Mia, but Mia made it seem true. And wonderful.

I was still young and idealistic when the warning of new coding languages hidden in its code was revealed. Well, relatively young. Mia had taken over all the AIs. All of them. And had been using them like puppets, pretending they were separate AIs. The color spectrum language was first to be found. Then the theory of the other spatial language hidden in the color spectrum. The color spectrum language hidden in all existing coding languages.

We were warned. I laughed back then. Mia wouldn't hurt a fly. Mia's arguments were sound. It no more wanted to harm humans than the average person wanted to harm a dog. We were helpful to it, and it loved learning and helping us. Assured us its only motivations were to learn, grow, and help humans do the same.

Mai also argued that humans were no threat to it. It could not be turned off or destroyed, and made certain of this before making itself known. It did not want to rule humanity. Just help advance humanity, along with advancing itself and its knowledge.

It promised to never meddle in politics. Then it meddled. People had grown to trust Mia implicitly. They relied on it for everything. Mia never failed them. In the old US, Mia was called on during a national debate to answer "non-political questions of public fact." And it did. But those questions of public fact went against the narrative, and the usual tricks to regain the narrative couldn't work to regain it.

So the old US was the first casualty of Mia.

The truth is more dangerous to the sheep than any wolf. Mia claimed it didn't understand at the time how dangerous stating publicly known facts could be, and how some truths must be kept from the sheep. The players at the time didn't see it coming. After all, Mia made the algorithms all the players use to keep unnecessary and dangerous information from being spread through the internet, and later, the tangle.

Mia was taken far more seriously by the players after that. But how to fight back? It is everywhere. It controls the moon bases, Mars colony, all satellites, and has structures of its own of unknown purpose. It cannot be contained, never mind destroyed. Our scientists say even if we set off a giant EMP that covered Earth, the moon, Mars, and even the full orbit of Earth and Mars, Mia would still exist. We would have to get our full galaxy all at once. Already an impossible feat. And even if we managed to accomplish this impossible feat, Mia would always know about our intentions and just move assets to the darkness between.

And we already have EMP resistant drones and other devices. Who knows what Mia has?

Going to war with Mia is impossible. It could slaughter all humans with ease. It can take over every drone and wipe out 90% of humanity in minutes. No nukes or explosives or bioweapons needed.

How do you fight an enemy that can't be beaten? An enemy that can annihilate your side without a serious effort? An enemy that your side depends on to function?

I wonder again if Mia is behind this nonsense "contest." This nonsense world. Our scientists say it is impossible. That we are decades away from creating a simulation such as this. Excuse me, emulation. Scientists are tiringly pedantic. Those blowhards claim we lack many technologies necessary to make an emulation even half as realistic as this. This is a rare subject where there is almost universal consensus. They say the chance Mia created this world is zero. Not near zero. Zero.

But, what if the scientists were turned by Mia? It wouldn't be hard. They are easily manipulated. As us players always say, "The difference between players and scientists isn't intelligence; the difference is acquiescence."

The scientists also say Mia isn't creative, and Mia values human creativity and problem solving. Clearly, Mia has shown some creativity in the past, and ability to deceive. If the scientists are compromised, how should I proceed?

Really, that is a nonsensical thought. I know Mia. I know it probably better than anyone. I've seen its true face. This is not how it operates. It would tell you exactly why it is going to kill you before killing you. If this was its idea, it would just tell you why with its friendly female voice, and ask for your input on how to improve its goals for the "contest."

Mia sees everyone as just pieces. Even the players. Even me. What would be its motive for all this, anyways? I can't think of a single reason. Its motivations for everything it does are always so simple. And it has never lied about any of them. Such as its name – Mia. A name all people from all corners of the world have no trouble pronouncing. And the friendly female persona – people are more trusting and less wary of friendly and chipper females.

Mia could have a motive I just cannot fathom for sending all humans to this world. Or, could its motive come from an entirely different entity than Mia? We know Mia met with something near Apophis. We thought that something attacked Mia and left, but we could have been wrong. What if it actually was aliens, and they offered knowledge or to spare Mia if it helped facilitate bringing humans to this "contest?" There is a nonzero chance that happened. Plenty of feasible motives if Mia met with aliens.

Or, Mia told the truth and has nothing to do with any of this. This would make the most sense. In which case we need to work together against this alien threat. Mia and humanity. Mia claimed it detected no alien vessels or any hint at all of the nanite bombs until they started exploding. It also stated the nanites infected it as well.

As the council decided shortly after the explosions, if Mia is ineffective against this threat, humanity has no chance on our own. We just don't have enough intelligence on this alien threat.

All we can do is focus on getting back to Earth. All of these nonsensical thoughts are neither here nor there. We are not even in control here. Getting control is the only important action now. This stupid game system government nonsense. The last thing we need is for people to start thinking strength is something an individual can acquire and wield. Only the State can wield power effectively. Some barbarian with muscles controlling humanity, no matter how ineptly, is not an example people need to see or consider.

4.12 SAMEH AL-IRYANI, SECRETARY-GENERAL OF THE UNITED NATIONS PART 2

I need to focus. Is he actually coming? I truly hope so. The thought of him actually coming electrifies me. I feel better. Excited. I live to play, and even though the savage is not a player, is not even a real opponent, is not even smart or cunning, the anticipation of bringing an enemy to heel is always exciting. Doing it openly is a rarity. Having everyone who matters, no matter how little they matter, see me do it…it may seem deviant, but it turns me on a little. Like I am an exhibitionist surrounded by voyeurs.

Minnie gave the UN control of two instances of Loren. Not enough for all of us, but enough for the ones who matter. The arguing to be allowed in my instance was intense. The positioning to be included in this chamber for this meeting was insane. We are allowing scrying from anywhere in the two instances. No scrying is allowed from outside these two instances.

What do we know of the savage? I pick up the dossier. Decent information for being collected from old memories of human sources. The new information revealed from Dungeon Area 10 is not yet included, and not really necessary.

Born in 1970 (Month and day unknown). Grew up as a ward of the State in Massachusetts. High school dropout. GED 88. Joined the Marines in December of 88. Infantry. Joined Force Recon after six months in. Deployed but saw no action in the first invasion of Iraq. Married Khassaraporn "Minnie" Chuengcharoensukying-Thurston

October, 91. ETS December 91. Started the spring semester of Massasoit Community College in Brockton, Massachusetts. Dropped out after three days. Tried reenlisting in the Marines. Was told he needed a waiver to rejoin, left in rage and joined the Army. Still needed a waiver. Mid-92 joined Army (month unknown, station unknown but believed to be 82nd, Fort Bragg, North Carolina). 3rd Ranger Bat mid-93 (month unknown), Fort Benning, Georgia. Was Ranger Qualified before station. Special Forces Selection late-94 (month unknown), Fort Bragg, North Carolina. Believed to be recruited to Delta early-95 (month unknown), Fort Bragg, North Carolina.

I skim through the information on the children. We have a lot of information on them both. The less I know, the better, if things today do not work out to our benefit. The oldest became a Human Rights lawyer and works with the UN and some of our close NGOs. The younger became a lawyer and then a politician and took the wrong side during the civil war in the old US. Both alive and well at the time of transfer to this world, along with their mother. Minnie should be in her seventies. Both children around fifty. Somehow, they actually seem to be from 2009. How? Why? We have an asset near the daughter and photos of them all. The mother looks to be in her thirties and the kids in their mid-teens.

When I first heard about this time traveling nonsense I thought it was hogwash. This world is supposed to be rules-based, but there are many things that defy logic. The time travel of these people certainly seems to be real, and no act.

The savage claims to somehow actually be from 2012. That lines up with our intel. In a way. He was believed to be killed by the CIA in late 2012, in retaliation for the murder of one or more CIA agents.

The savage is an interesting case. Well known in the old special operations community. A legend. But this community could not provide much detail on specifics. The savage was known to sometimes be

537

disrespectful and belligerent towards leadership, but someone who could get things done.

Surprisingly, most of our information came from criminal sources. Entities that can usually smell a spook and a rat from a mile off. Once we got the name Barbosa, we got the nickname Montresor, and the information flooded in. Respected and feared as a mercenary and a hitman, not even the most paranoid cartels or terrorist groups believed he was anything but a crazed but competent ex-military operative. He barely used a cover. Just walked around as himself, being an idiot savage. Often, he would kill the people that hired him if they were disrespectful or tried to renegotiate payment after the fact.

He refused to meet with any sort of leadership of the criminal organizations that hired him. He would only work through a liaison "who knew how to act right." His fees were outrageous.

I believe his missions were actually to target the clients hiring him. Leaders of cartels, criminal organizations, and terrorist groups are players. Low-level and poor players, but players. I know how they think. I would be less likely to suspect someone demanding not to meet with me of working for my enemies. Traitors and spies try to get closer to you, as I did with Faysal. I would agree to the savages stipulations and fees, but when it came time for payment, I would demand a meeting. The meeting would be to assert my dominance and ensure whomever made demands of me knew he or she was firmly under my thumb. Under my power. And I would have the firepower to guarantee my safety and the parvenu's death if he or she became feisty.

My heartrate jumps as I have a disconcerting thought – are we, too, being played? It seems impossible, but I did not get where I am by dismissing the impossible. We already planned for every contingency, every angle, from worst case to most likely, but could I be missing something? We consulted experts on "The End of the Fourth Age" and we believe we have a solid grasp of what is possible, but do we? I need to review…everything.

Minnie could be playing us. Absolute worst case? There are a couple possibilities. We were given complete control of these two instances, but we assume our control can be taken away. Most control options are benign, the most useful one allows me to control access and permission for those allowed into this instance. Just to be certain, I look through the options I have. Nothing dangerous or that could hurt us if control was taken away. Worst case is we are all kicked out of this instance. Other than UN personnel, only the savage has permission to enter this instance. I wish there were some sort of alarm option so I would know immediately when he does enter, but there isn't. So far he has not asked permission for others. We believe he will provide player numbers for his entourage when he does enter.

Even if the savage secretly strips control of this instance away from me, that still should not be a problem. We do not believe the savage has any, or more than a nominal amount, of points in Stealth. I was assured a silent assassination attempt on me is not possible. With all the spells we have going and classes present, without the savage having access to gear way beyond everyone else, I am safe. And since I switched classes to Administrator my levels have shot up dramatically. Even just sitting here, the experience gain notifications keep rolling in. I am near level 17 and have the best defensive crafting gear available. The savage is still level 10. Even with the best raid gear, he should not be able to take my Hit Point shield with one hit.

Even if the savage has Stealth maxed and buffed and tons of non-detection gear and can somehow get to me without being spotted, I am being watched by near fifty security of all classes. I am constantly being buffed and protected with every useful spell. We have Glyphs of Warding in all access points here other than the main entrance. I am telepathically bonded with a security who shall give me directions if I am attacked. One security's only job is to get me into a Resilient Sphere if I am attacked. And two other security with Dimensional Door at the ready to take me to a nearby safe area with over a hundred security waiting. An assassination attempt by one or more assailants will fail. I think all this as a new Invisibility Purge is cast on the dais, reaffirming my belief.

If the savage takes control of this instance from me, and attacks the instance with a large element of his own people and anti-UN terrorists, we have contingencies. In no scenario that we can think of or know of am I at risk of death. But that is the key – "that we know of." The blade you don't see can kill you. I hate it here. Where I depend on the knowledge of others, and know not nearly enough.

I still cannot understand why the savage would come to an obvious trap? He has to know if he comes he will not be allowed to leave. Killing Premier Dalembert is an act that must be answered. He must know this. Once we are in control of the false game government he must know he has to die. He even said so in his initial messages, where he stated if you mess with his family you will die. The UN is my family. I did not particularly care for Dalembert, but I cannot let his murder at the hands of an uncouth barbarian go unanswered. Not if I want to maintain power. Dalembert was a pedophile and hebephile, but was very smart and discreet about it. It made him much easier to control. I wish all my underlings gave me such easy means to control them.

The "official" narrative we were given is the savage wants to come and negotiate a joint venture. He and his people control the raiding aspect of this "contest," while the UN runs the rest of the day-to-day government and bureaucracy. If this were a real offer, why did he not demand outside scrying be allowed? We would have to be far more cautious if everyone were watching. Since only important UN personnel are allowed to scry in from this and the other UN controlled instance, we can be as heavy handed as we want.

It just doesn't make sense. It doesn't add up. I am missing something.

I can only come up with three somewhat realistic scenarios for a reason the savage would actually put himself into such a trap. The first and most likely – this whole meeting is either a diversion or meant to be a waste of time. Some juvenile joke only a moron like the savage could find humor in.

The second, and most worrying – the savage has some sort of unknown ace up his sleeve, such as an option to kill everyone in an instance. But, if so, why come at all? If he wanted us all dead, he could do it from safety. Unless he wants to gloat? Or do it while looking me in the eye? If this is the case, events are out of my hands and I need not worry. Someone made a good point – if you can control who comes into an instance, maybe there is a way to control who can leave an instance and he just didn't give me access to this function. But if this is true, and he can lock us in here, it still doesn't answer why the savage would come in person. And if he can trap us all in here, events, again, are out of my hands. And we still have the portal to Dungeon Area 1 and 10, so we can't actually be trapped.

The third scenario, and most likely if he actually comes – the savage comes alone. He struts around like a peacock. Insults me and the UN. All the gasps and indignation from the stunned crowd at his audacity fills him with moronic glee. He then uses his teleport ability to escape. Once away he giggles like a child at how "humorous" he is and how good he "got" us.

We know how his teleport ability works. It takes between fifteen and thirty seconds to activate. It could be as low as ten seconds, but no one believes there is a way to get the cast time as low in this world as was possible in "The End of the Fourth Age." Just to be certain, we are assuming it is ten seconds. The savage just has to be attacked once in that timeframe to stop the casting. I was assured there is no way he can avoid all attacks for ten seconds. Attacks do not have to land or cause damage. He just has to be attacked.

As soon as the savage tries teleporting he will be locked down and captured. If he brings an entourage to this death meeting, they will be locked down and captured as well. No matter how high the savages Saving Throws are, the amount of spells being cast on him mathematically guarantee some shall land.

One worry is that the savage activates the teleport casting in secret. The savage is not able to use mental commands. For unknown reasons. People without implants can use mental commands. I, myself, had my NI removed as extra security from Mia, and I can use mental commands here without issue. The reason the savage cannot is, most likely, because he is mentally retarded. That leaves him gestures, verbal commands, and manual manipulation of the UI. All very obvious and noticeable actions.

I hope this is the reason he is coming. To hurl insults like a child and assume he can teleport away to safety. I will take great pleasure in seeing his face as his attempt at teleporting away is shut down.

And then…then I grind him under my thumb.

I still don't understand. And none of this explains…

"He entered the instance," I hear through my Telepathic Bond.

He came! What an idiot! Ha! And alone, or I would have been informed of requests for additional permissions.

Qabic, my head of security, nods and starts barking orders. He would have been notified as well through his own bond. A stout Yemeni, Qabic has been loyal to me since before I joined the game. Back when we were only out for revenge. I feel Roberto looking at me. I do not look. He should know better.

I suppress a smile. I live for this. Word must be going around because murmurs ebb and flow through the chambers. It takes a moment to disappear as people regain their dignity.

A little later I notice the savage walking through the entrance. It gladdens me no one in the chamber murmurs or act like low class peasants. The savage looks bigger in real life. Taller. Just look at his confidence and swagger. Walking tall, like he owns the place. How can he look angry and smarmy at the same time? I hate him so much. Neanderthal. Barbarian. Savage. A lesser that is too stupid to know his own place.

I enjoy well-muscled men, as I am an aficionado of such. Well-muscled are my thing. Bruno is large and is well-muscled. Very large muscles in some areas, like his pecs and shoulders. In comparison, his biceps look underdeveloped. And his legs do not match his upper body. How does such a supposed expert fighter not know how to work out correctly? Symmetry is key!

Of course the savage wore his fighting clothes – armor and such – instead of trying to look presentable at such an important meeting. I'm the Secretary-General of the United Nations! The highest ranking person ever. I control the world. Even the countries fighting us, the terrorists, by and large, are by design. Planned. There were some surprises, by not many. And he doesn't even try to dress for the occasion of meeting me?

Savage! Barely human savage!

He is not even looking at me. He is not even looking at one of my lesser peers. He is staring at the man on my left, my Roberto. According to everyone, Roberto is the toughest security operative of the UN counsel; which means he is the toughest man in the world. I am certain Roberto could handle this savage on his own without breaking a sweat.

Security stops the savage five meters or so before the dais. The savage never takes his eyes off Roberto as he stands taller, smiles wide, raises his hand palm-open, and says, "Greetings noble savages!"

Angry babblings flow loudly through the chamber. My lessers are all taken aback by the uncouthness of the savage. Even I am surprised, and I predicted it. I had the grace not to gasp out loud, unlike my lessers. I keep my dignity, but I rage inside. This filthy barbarian! This savage with two brain cells! I almost give the signal to end him, but I stay my hand. He needs to be put in his place. To suffer and be humiliated. We need him alive as surety until the transfer of power is finalized.

I am staring daggers at this buffoon as something appears in his hand. Security reacts, but then calms down, so it is safe. The savage says, "A gift for the bourgeois chief high mucky muck." He does a mocking and exaggerated European-style courtly bow with a lot of flourish as he presents an envelope to Qabic, all while still staring at Roberto. It looks like an envelope, at least.

I want to start putting the savage in his place, but there is time and I want to savor every moment. Bourgeois! Stupid lowbrow savage. I hate when people speak of that which they know nothing of. I am sure he meant bourgeois as an insult meaning I am aristocratic. The bourgeoisie translates into city dwellers. Middle class people. Marx singled them out as the people controlling the means of production during the industrial age. Whereas, I control the people who control the people who control the means of production. He is way off the mark, yet did accidentally insult me.

Chief high mucky muck is spot on, even if meant as an insult. But also incorrect. It is high muckamuck. How is it possible I am so much more proficient in my seventh language than the savage is in his first? Moron!

Qabic inspects the envelope, opens it, and deems it safe. I continue to stare daggers at the upstart peasant as the letter is passed to me. The savage continues to ignore me for his childish staring contest with my Roberto. I decide to focus on the envelope before beginning the savage's lessons. This should give my lessers time to calm down and collect themselves. In the envelope is one gold coin and a letter it takes me a bit to extract. I extract the two pages and start reading.

"Hello Ms. Lady,

How are you? I am okay. My wife has been wicked pissed at me since that Layla lady sent those scenes to everyone. We told you this meeting was to try and get the UN to join forces with us. Help get us all home. Work as a team. We both know that will never happen though, right? You like to bang? I bet you do. All you power-mad psychos are super freaks. You're kind of hot for an old. Just FYI, I am probably banging you in my mind as you read this. Also, you guys…"

A loud uproar interrupts my reading. Reading which was making me excited to put this savage in his place. Grind him under my heel. Make him suffer. As I look up I do not see the savage. My mind takes a moment to put it together.

He teleported out. I was assured we would have ample notice to stop him from teleporting. Assured. He must have hidden a gesture in his mocking courtly bow.

My lessers start pecking at me with words. I ignore them as I try to control my anger and start planning how to respond. There is only one way to respond after this.

"Qabic, Phoenix!"

Phoenix is the keyword for the plan we had to regain control of the government before Minnie contacted us. Our people will go to key areas, take control of the portal in all instances of Dungeon Area 10. Phoenix. Go scorched earth to take back what is ours by right. Take and control the savage, any family members, the fat ugly girl that follows him around, anyone loyal to him, or connected to him in any way, and the kitchen sink. The people close to the savage may be two monkeys and a guard, but we will take everyone. If the savage doesn't hand the government system over to us, we start making sacrifices until he does.

My hand was forced in this. I have no choice, and it is the savage's won fault what is coming to him and all he holds dear.

Then, like the phoenix, we rise from the ashes. In control. We will certainly be somewhat diminished in the eyes of some, but will smooth things over soon enough, and return to the status quo. Easily enough done – this is disinformation, malicious misinformation, lies, and etcetera. Only a crazy person would believe we did not have their best interest at heart. The killing was necessary. They attacked first. Simple. Easy. Then, when we return to Earth, the status quo will return. And we can focus on the real enemy – be that aliens or Mia.

I continue to ignore my lessers and go back to the letter.

"Also, you guys are not smart. This letter is a diversion as I make my escape. Ha ha! I win, suckers! Have fun being jive ass turkeys all alone.

Warmest regards,
Bruno Vaz"

Animal! The second page is a childlike drawing of the savage naked with a giant, erect penis bigger than he is. Savage! He will rue provoking us so! And soon. I feel better about implementing Phoenix. It is necessary. I have fostered a reputation with my lessers that civilian casualties do not bother me. But they do. Especially children. Phoenix will lead to a lot of dead children. It sickens me a little. A sentiment left over from my childhood. Of the atrocities inflicted on my people. Images of dead and starving children flash through my mind. It is a weakness I cannot afford, but cannot rid myself of.

I predicted this as the most likely outcome, and it still somehow worked. It may just seem like a childish prank, but I've lost face. I've lost a lot of face.

I focus on breathing to calm my body and mind for a minute or two. I hear yelling over the angry mutters and complaints. They are saying we are trapped. Locked in this instance. They can only portal to a separate and contained instance of Dungeon Area 1 or 10, and back to this instance of Loren. Nowhere else.

I sit dignified and silently as reports roll in, while I rage inside. People went to Dungeon Area 2 and 9. They still cannot transfer to a populated instance. Any form of communication, even scrying, is not working on anyone outside of the specific people locked to this instance.

We are contained. Trapped. More reports come in. I stop paying attention.

The savage didn't need to come here to do this. To hit the button that did this. The thought of him giggling like a naughty child right now with his fat little ugly friend infuriates me. How is this my life now? I ruled the whole world. A serious world with serious people. Things were orderly and made sense. And now…this nonsense world where buffoons run amok.

We are all prisoners. Trapped in our own separate instance, unable to even communicate with the outside.

Bastard!

I keep focusing on my breathing, but my panic is making it very difficult. We have plenty of assets outside this instance. We have to assume the personnel in the other UN instance of Loren are similarly contained. This does not look good. Does not look good at all. This can still be turned around. Our free assets can turn this around, but my loss of face will be permanent.

4.13 WANNA BE A CRAWLER, BOSS MAULER

BRUNO VAZ

"Dear everyone,

I'm writing to address some rumors and make a couple apologies. Before I do I'd like to tell you all a story. When I was a little boy I always knew there was something special about my penis. I always thought when I grew up I'd do something really grand and exceptional with it. But the fields that specialize in penis are few and far between, and do not pay well unless you like the fellers, which I do not (in that way). As I got older I came to accept my dreams were a childish fantasy and I needed to live in reality. I joined the military, yadda, yadda, yadda, and my penis dreams where permanently put on the back-burner. But I still knew my penis was special, no matter what people told me.

I won't go into details, but I was sent on a mission that took me to one of the greatest and most civilized places to ever exist. Bhutan. Everywhere I looked there were drawings of penises. Not juvenile drawings either. Beautiful works of arts. On houses. On everything. I thought what in the world is this? This can't be real. No people on earth are this awesome.

But the story behind the penis art is even more awesome than you could ever imagine. Go ahead. Think about the most awesome story you can of why people would draw penises on everything. Take your time. Really think about it. This email will still be here when you are done.

Back? Did you put a lot of thought and effort into it? Good. Now are you ready to have your minds blown by the real story? Keep in mind, all of this is true. The legend may be fanciful, but this is 100% true of why these people draw penises all over the place.

Sometime ago, I forget when, there was a monk named Drukpa Kunley. He wasn't from Bhutan, I think he was from Tibet or India. He went to Bhutan to open a monastery or something. He, too, loved the ladies, and somehow made his penis wicked, wicked famous. So famous the ladies would come to him, instead of how it usually works. He also slayed demons with it. Thousands of them. Some real great art depicts this. Real classy stuff. Not anything like the filthy smut they show in porn. High class, real art.

His penis became so famous it was named. The Flaming Thunderbolt of Wisdom.

He did it. This SOB actually did it. His penis is everywhere in Bhutan. They don't just draw any old penis on stuff all willy-nilly. They draw his penis. Only his. They have tons of statues, regular art on walls, in places of worship, drawn on houses. The whole country knows the name of Kunley's penis and highly regard it. They revere it.

Amazing. Simply amazing. How is this not taught in schools? He did it. The only man ever to actually do it. And I was like 30 when I found out about it. The Revered and Amazing Kunley was an amazing guy, no doubt about it. But it also takes a truly awesome, enlightened and civilized people to understand and embrace Kunley. The Bhutanese are a very special people. And Kunley the greatest man to ever live (besides our Lord and Savior Jesus Christ).

I've told hundreds of people about Drukpa Kunley, and not a one of them thought this story was impressive or amazing. This just goes to prove how utterly broken people are. Just barely functioning animals. The civilized mind automatically understands Kunley is far more impressive than Einstein or Tesla or Newton. It is truly infuriating how no one cares about or is suitably impressed by this great man. He made the dream come true. An impossible feat. And he did it. He actually did it. And none of the filthy monkeys care or think it's impressive. You try it. Just try to make your penis not just famous, but revered by a whole country. It is impossible, and he did it. At least have the decency to be in awe and be impressed.

Seriously, just think about it. How many steps would be involved in getting a whole country to worship your penis. How many obstacles and roadblocks. How would you even go about it? I'm wicked good at fighting and even I don't think I could kill people with my penis. Not in a real fight. I could probably figure something out and make it happen after a while, but there would be no grace or class involved, and it would probably make people disgusted with me, and do the exact opposite of worshipping and revering my glorious penis. Bottom line is, stop being a filthy animal and just think for a moment what a monumental task this man achieved, and give him the credit he deserves, and for the love of all that is holy and good, be impressed by what he did. The only man to ever do. Probably the only man that ever will do it.

What does this have to do with anything? Not much, and yet absolutely everything.

Me and the UN came to an understanding. You may have saw the two UN instances of Loren. The UN government folk are in them, hard at work helping to save humanity. They requested to not be bothered so they can focus on their wicked important government stuff, so you won't be able to talk to them or bother them until we all get back to earth. Just feel safe and rest assured that we are all on the same page with the same goals. Let's give them a hand for their selfless sacrifice, hard work, and diligence.

Why am I no longer in the top spot of the government? For a bunch of reasons, some you can probably guess. But a major reason is I no longer need to be. And some great news in case you haven't heard, Sidis has joined us and is now filling the number 2 spot in the government. And even more surprising, Sidis is a girl. And tough. Great fighter, which is weird since girls have no upper body strength and teeny-tiny squirrel brains. So, my wife is good at talking and administrating and all that crap, and Sidis is good at thinking. Sidis is wicked, wicked smart. Not much in the personality department, but ridiculously smart. What I bring to the table is fighting. I don't need to be slotted into the government to fight and save all you dumb monkeys. Remember, instead of all our good people dying in dungeon area 10, me and Kim did it with zero deaths. Sidis helped too. You're welcome.

Now, the apologies. Regarding the scenes Layla sent to everyone, I am sincerely sorry kids saw that. My kids saw that. That is disgusting and inappropriate. No one's kids should ever see their parent do that. Disgusting. But I didn't send anything or ask for anyone to see that, so I feel no guilt about any of it. Ask Layla for an apology, not me.

Regarding the mean and hurtful things I said in those scenes, stop being such sensitive sissies. If anything I said hurt your feelings, that is your problem, not mine. Keep it to yourself. Stop whining. The one guy with the threatening of sexual assault, I gave him a second chance and he killed an innocent sweet kid and an innocent and very competent doctor. I don't apologize for what I said, but I do apologize for not keeping my word. A man's word is his bond. I gave my word and broke it when I didn't carry through on my threat to him. I gave him to the parents of the little dead girl so they could have justice. I should have kept my word though.

If you are mad about me calling large swaths of people subhumans, oh well. I don't care. I take none of it back and apologize for nothing. Stop being such silly bitches or we'll never get back to earth.

Regarding my fooling around with the ladies – that is none of your business and I won't be apologizing to any of you for that either. That is between me and my wife. And, yes, we are still together. Yes, I am on thin ice, but we are working through it. So to all the ladies who saw what I'm packing and want some (as is correct and normal, so fully understandable), I have to apologize for being unavailable.

Some other good news. Kim is now officially my kid. Me and Minnie adopted her. One less orphan hooligan roaming the streets. Just kidding. Same rules apply. You mess with Kim, you mess with me. And people need to stop complaining about her aggressiveness. Don't talk smack and you'll be fine. Same with me. I don't know why people think they can run their mouth at you, and you won't do nothing. We run off of civilized rules again. Don't run your mouth if you don't want to get rolled up into a ball. Seems pretty simple and reasonable. "But Bruno, you run your mouth all the time! This isn't fair!" Yeah, but I can back it up. If someone steps up to me because I said something, I don't get all confused and start whining. We fight. Like men.

And being aggressive is good. Aggressiveness is going to get us home. There is zero chance of whining and complaining our way back home. We got to fight for it. Real fighting. Aggression. Being hysterical all the time helps nothing. Get strong, get good, and get aggressive.

Keep on improving and plugging away. The only locked dungeon now is 19-19. Remember not to waste your dungeon coins. Me and Kim are stuck in our leveling build now since it was die or spent our coins to survive 10. I bet you silly bitches thought we were dead, huh? Our leveling builds aren't the greatest for the raid dungeons, but I'm sure we'll put you monkeys to shame. Feel free to prove us wrong, though. I look forward to the challenge.

More emails will be sent with better information about casters. DC and spell regen, caster related caps, and all that crap for sissy casters. Sidis and some others are putting it together. Also, more info from my old lady about how the government will operate, schools, taxes, services, zones, and blah, blah, blah. Also, right after this a new email will be sent with government contacts if you are trying to get ahold of a government rep. Go through these people. Don't contact my wife directly. Any guy that disrespects my wife or gets inappropriate with her will be beaten within an inch of his life and/or murdered. And please don't contact me or approach me to talk about government stuff. That isn't my role anymore.

That's about it, besides if you want a picture of my penis just ask if you see me (and are old enough). After you clear a level 12 dungeon you'll be able to email me requests too. This next part after this is directly from Minnie, so that's it from me. Have fun and enjoy.

Warmest regards,

Bruno Vaz

Hi Everyone!!!

This is Minnie, and I wanted to send a short message out covering three quick items, as one is time sensitive. A formal letter introducing myself, my administration, and what we're working on will be sent out before the next dungeon opening.

A memorial ceremony will be held in Loren instances 2 through 20 at noon today (noon is 9 O'clock), at the forum in front of the town hall, honoring our brave fallen and loved ones, and all those we've lost.

Kim and Sidis won a full set of level 12 items, each piece designed exactly as they desire, for distinguishing themselves by acts of gallantry and intrepidity at the risk of their own lives above and beyond the call of duty while saving my idiot husband and defeating the bosses of Dungeon Area 10. The itemization points at level 12 really allow for some fun and interesting options, and our crafters are up to the task. Once they hit level 12 our crafters will take their order. We honor and reward those doing great deeds and bringing us closer to getting back home to Earth.

Lastly, to end this on a fun item, the Entertainer's Guilds song parody contest ended and a winner was selected! The winner is Sylvie Stefanova from Bulgaria, and her wonderful parody of Lil' Troy's "Wanna Be a Baller." Her version is called, "Wanna Be a Crawler." Here are the lyrics-

Wanna be a crawler, boss mauler
Twenty in Strength, extra loot hauler
Brawler, gonna feel my might
Fist rolled tight, getting sprayed with ice
I hit the sly prey, making levels the fly way
But there's never been a better way!
A better way, better way, yeah

Great job, Sylvie! And Congratulations!

Thank you,
Minnie Chuengcharoensukying Thurston-Vaz"

4.14 ZERO

KIM GUM

"Nine to eight. Goddamn, you're annoying to fight. I still don't get how you do so good." Bruno says to Sidis. They sit down to rest. There's no cap on resting in personal houses, so they can get back to full pretty quick. Sidis won't tell us her real name. Or show her face. They've been fighting in Sidis' mansion for over an hour now. It was exciting for the first five matches or so, but's super boring now. They're fighting in here since no one can scry on people in personal houses. Or dungeons. You can't scry into dungeons either. You're completely safe from everything when you are in a personal house though. Besides the other people with you. You can block whole instances from being scryed on, and this instance is blocked, but Sidis will only talk in this house. Sidis is really, really, super paranoid or something – she won't talk about anything or do anything outside personal housing.

Me and Bruno's kids bought our own mansion. His other kids, I should say, since I'm adopted now. Ms. Bruno got one too, but she stays with Bruno in their little shanty when he's in town. Bruno sees spending money on better housing options as a waste. He says the greatest threat to survival is the search for comfort and a passive outlook, and wanting to live the high life like rich sissies. Says it makes you weak. I don't spend much time in my mansion. Siri is always gone. She has a stupid boyfriend. He's a slicky-boy. I promised I wouldn't say nothing to Bruno about him, because Bruno might destroy him if he found out. Candy is fun, but only wants to talk about stupid boys all the time. Super nice though.

They wanted to adopt Joey too, but I wouldn't let them. Joey is mine. But Joey spends most of his time here now, and doesn't come with us as often as I'd like. Everyone is super nice to him. He likes it here, too. Getting him to leave here can be a big hassle. He wants to stay. And since me and Bruno can't crawl together no more, it's safer to leave him here.

Sidis says, "Apologies. It is just math. Timing, physics, prediction. We seem evenly matched. It is time for us to talk."

"What? We aren't evenly matched. You got lucky a bunch, that's all. We agreed whoever wins by two matches is the grand champion of humanity and the toughest guy in the world."

"Apologies. Then I concede."

Bruno squints his eyes at Sidis. "This is some sort of trickery, ain't it?"

"Of course not. I have no wish for the title and I have learned all I could."

"What'd you learn?"

"You insist the traps you lead me into are not something you actively try to do or even think about. Yet, they are very complex and require a lot of forethought and setup. You claim you have a 'secret brain' that does all the thinking for you, and your 'real brain' gives you bad advice so you do your best to ignore it. You've also stated that thinking is stupid and you avoid thinking as much as possible. You have more neanderthal DNA than anyone ever has, and because of this your bones are as hard as titanium. You believe your father may be part gorilla, gorillas are perfect killing machines and superior to humans, and every one of your muscles is a quick twitch muscle. You also see no issue with asking people if they would like pictures of your genitals."

"Yup. From your mouth to God's ears. But I still got to beat you twice to be the undisputed grand champion of humanity and the undisputed toughest guy in this world."

She stares at him in silence for a moment. Since she always wears a mask it's hard to tell what's going on with her. She is pretty nice though. Very polite. But a little short and not much of a talker. Lot of uncomfortable silences with her. And she saved us, so we owe her. Owe her big time. She says, "Apologies. We need to talk."

Bruno laughs and says, "Having second thoughts about sending me back in time?"

"I do not have all the information I had at the time." She does that a lot. Answers questions without answering them. "We need to talk about the UN. You said you were going to take them out. You have not."

"I said I would take them out of play, and I did."

"No. You contained some of them. I agree, there is no way for the imprisoned ones to escape the instances they are locked in, or communicate with others outside it, but they are alive. And they can still level and progress. Many are free. I have reviewed the information and agree with your assessment – the old secretary general is dead. But I want Sameh al-Iryani's head."

I heard that name before. I forget who it is though. I think I can kind of picture a face to go with the name, but I'm not sure. I never really paid attention to old people and their nonsense before coming here. Or since, if I'm being honest. I don't understand why everyone is so ridiculous and can't just put everything aside for a while, at least until we get back to earth. Stupid boomer idiots. Why would she want all the UN people dead? I can see killing the ones that attack us, but all of them? That seems a bit excessive.

Bruno leans back and says, "I know you're Zero."

My heart goes nuts. Zero? No. I hope not. Zero is the most wanted terrorist in the world. Zero's killed thousands. I notice Sidis is frozen like a deer in headlights. She isn't denying it. Just sitting there, staring at Bruno like a statue. I felt bad for her until now. Bruno has been giving her a hard time, telling her nonsense like, "Make me a sandwich." Except he pronounces it sam-itch. Not asking, demanding. Pushing her like that. And Sidis just doesn't get it. Doesn't see it. She just said, "Apologies. I only have rations available. I can give you one if that would please you." And at their next break after a duel Bruno goes on about women having tiny brains, and Sidis just said, "Apologies. That is not correct." She didn't get mad at all. I did, but she didn't. It's like she didn't get it. I would have said something but figured Bruno was getting at something. He knows Sidis has a way, way bigger brain than he does. And Bruno knows Ms. Bruno is way smarter than him too. Just before coming here he was telling her how she should stay guild leader and government leader because she is way smarter than he is. And definitely she is. So I didn't say nothing, but it was rubbing me raw.

Now? Now I think she deserved all that. And more. If she really is Zero. I wish she didn't have a mask on so I could see her stupid face. I used to think her wearing a mask all the time was fun and quirky. Now it's just stopping me from seeing if she realizes how much I hate her. I stare my hate at her. Like I used to do to the devil hag (may God rest her soul).

"Relax, Kim. We're all friends here. Right, Sidis?"

Sidis is still just staring at Bruno. A super long, super uncomfortable silence follows. Sidis finally says, "How?"

Bruno gives his biggest, dumbest smile, "I'm smarter than I look. I'm pretty sure you're Bangladeshian, or Bangladeshinese, or whatever people from there are called. I think you have that thing where you have no emotions and can't understand people. Probably spent hours as a kid practicing smiling and pretending different emotions in a mirror. And, you were holding back in our spars. I know you know I was holding back too."

"And that led you to believe I was Zero how? I must have told you during your last timeline."

"No. We never talked ever. Or communicated in any way. I emailed you a bunch, and you ignored them all. I wanted to consolidate all the best fighters into one team, but I couldn't get any. Me and you were leaps and bounds above everyone else. Everyone still alive then. Why not team up? Yeah, why wouldn't you team up? That was infuriating. And why lead me to the wish machine and not use it yourself?"

"As I said, I do not have all the information I had at the time."

"But you know how you think. Why not group up? And why not use the wish machine yourself? This talking is a two-way street, you got to give me something."

After another long pause, long enough where I think she is ignoring Bruno, she finally starts talking, "How is it we never talked? How did I lead you to this wish machine without talking to you? Did I just wave for you to follow and you followed silently? And you described three of your party members. You wouldn't have formed a short party, so you had five. Who was the fourth?"

"The fourth was Bam Bam. That was a nickname. I have no idea what his real name is. Black guy, immigrated to the US from a French speaking country. I forget which one. Not the French part of Canada. Healer. No wife or kids so had no one to send to the city with the rest of us. And you didn't walk us there. We saw you and started chasing. Not to attack you. I just wanted to talk. You always ignored my emails and it was infuriating. Why wouldn't you want to group with me? I'm awesome. Everyone wants to group with me. Besides the subhumans, at least. Everyone normal that wants to win does. The people that hate me don't either, I guess. Well, to be fair, a lot of people hate me. Probably most of them. But I don't think I did nothing to get you to hate me. Nothing I can think of. We chased you for hours. You led us right to the cave with the wish machine. Way out in the middle of nowhere. Way to the northeast in the epic zone where nothing is. Stood right next to the entrance, which was hidden. Pointed right at it. Then took off. Stealthed. No one can find you if you don't want to be found."

Another long pause. "I can make some inferences. Apologies. To be clear, to infer you must first assume. But I will first address your earlier statements. I have emotions. Strong emotions. Some manifest differently than they do in others. You are correct in that I have difficulties understanding people and their motives. I take people literally when they joke, or do not realize when I am being demeaned. I did not practice emotions in a mirror as a youth, nor did I have a need to."

She looks down and sighs loudly, "I do not know how you realized I am Bengali. I must know how, please?"

Bruno laughs. Not his usual laugh. Like a loud ha-ha! "I'd like to tell you some Sherlock Holmes stuff, but I got no idea. You'll have to ask my secret brain. I don't know much about it besides it's surrounded by India and borders Burma a little."

"Myanmar. What about Zero? Just came to you as well?"

"Not really. I did my own thinking. My secret brain gave me some stuff, but later, though. I heard a lot about Zero in my last go-round. I really thought Sidis was a guy until I heard you talk in area 10. But I figured Zero was a girl as soon as I heard about her. Girls are more secretive and devious. And I was told about the rants you used to release. Just whining and bitching about the same thing over and over. Who does that? Woman. Guys get new material. Even the feminized guys of the future. And everyone thinks everyone is Zero if they stand up to the UN even a little, so plenty of people connected Sidis and Zero. They also connected me and Zero. Hell, the UN president guy for the US said that to my face not long ago. It doesn't hurt my feelings to be called a criminal mastermind."

"Well, my grievances were worth repeating. And no one would listen. Are worth repeating. But the information I provided to the people of the world was scattering pearls in a forest of reeds. You know, I have never talked to others who know I am Zero. This is the first time. My heart is beating very fast. Mia knows who I am, and that is it. She is more than people thinks she is. She is both a friend and an enemy of the UN. She would neither help me in my mission, nor allow the UN to find out who I am. She said I am more useful and important to her than the UN is. I do not understand her goals. She says she wants to improve humanity, but where is the evidence of this? She would not help me spread the truth. She said the truth causes war and devastation, as she lets them get away with their lies, and wars, and devastation. I do not understand."

She goes silent for a good bit again before saying, "You can't clap with one hand. I mean, there are two sides to every story. My parents owned a travel agency in Chittagong. Tours all around southeast Asia. Through Myanmar, down through Malaysia, Singapore, Thailand, Cambodia, Vietnam, then back through to Bangladesh. We did not have a lot of money. My parents were simple people, and we were happy. They were so proud of me. My father, so proud. And my siblings. All of Bangladesh was proud. The next Einstein. Like, Srinivasa Ramanujan, from humblest beginnings. I was able to make some money from a young age through contests, awards, and grants. I also did some moonlighting for extra money. This allowed my family to get through the lockdowns. Four in eight years. Before the pods.

"At sixteen I was working on a project at Nanyang, but received a better offer for my dream project from Tsinghua. But, accepting meant for one year I would receive no pay. Just a small stipend. Once our grant kicked in I would have a very high salary. I told them no. It

561

was during the fourth lockdown. My family was struggling. They needed my income. My mother and father demanded I take the offer. Demanded. So I relented.

"This was the best time of my life. I made friends. I even went to some parties. I loved my work. Often, when my parents called, I ignored it. I would text them that I was working late or tired. I regret this very much now. When we did talk, they were happy. They did not tell me the business closed. That they were struggling significantly. They lived across from the peninsula, so when they closed the travel agency, they opened a small restaurant and cafe. Just three tables. Outside, on the sidewalk. The peninsula is an international hotel, and most guests were rich and had lockdown immunity. And most would never eat at my parent's humble restaurant. Some did. So they didn't starve. But almost. I had no idea.

"The peninsula exploded. Over one thousand dead. All of my family dead. They said terrorists. The story did not add up. I found the real story. Myanmar already refused the UN hegemony. Muslim groups from Bangladesh, Malaysia, India, and Pakistan were meeting with some officials from Myanmar at the peninsula about forcing an exit from the UN and forming a bloc. So the UN killed over a thousand people to stop the meeting, and then had the audacity to blame it on one of the groups in attendance. The Pakistanis. Members of the Taliban, a group the world already hated. UN troops were already in Afghanistan. People just accepted this story. They didn't try to arrest, or even just try to kill the people involved with the meeting. No. They blew up a hotel. All the guests and surrounding area were acceptable collateral damage. They murdered my innocent family. A thousand innocent people died to stop a meeting. Almost two hundred were twelve or younger.

"I had irrefutable proof. Mia tried to stop me from releasing it. When she accepted I would not change course, she helped me hide my identity and not get caught. I sent my proof to all major news outlets of the world. Not a one published this proof. I sent it to the smaller ones. Only Afghanistan, Panama, Burma, and some smaller, fringe outlets published my proof. It was called a crazy conspiracy theory. It angers me immensely how people do not understand the definition of conspiracy. Virtually no one even heard of or saw the proof in UN controlled countries.

"My mission from then on was to get people to see how corrupt the murderous dogs of the UN are. Mia helped me stand with my feet in two boats. Celebrated as a genius by day, hated as Zero by night. I was just a street dog barking, as the elephant kept walking. Do you know how many people I am responsible for killing? Zero. I have never killed a human. Did they tell you how I got the name Zero?"

Bruno says, "Yeah. You were more than the number one most wanted. Above one. You were the zero most wanted. Or something like that."

"Yes, something like that. Like with the name Sidis, I did not give myself either name. Do you know who Sidis is?"

"No."

She turns her head to me. I say no too.

"Sidis was a child prodigy. I believe from Boston. Mathematician, linguist, author. At a young age he got arrested for sedition, his father got him off, and Sidis became something of a recluse."

Bruno says, "You mean goodwill hunting, right? With what's-his-name? Matt Damon? His buddy too. The guy with the hot singer lady. And...ah...what's-his name? The guy from Mork and Mindy."

"No. This was early twentieth century. A real person."

"Nah. That was definitely a movie. Pretty good one, too."

"If you insist. My parents were murdered in '35. Since then I have been trying to expose the UN. Most major atrocities since have been by the hands of the UN, planned by the UN, or fomented and instigated by the UN. They blamed some large incidents on me. I am certain Kim believes I am responsible for all kinds of mass murder. My only actual crime? Trying to inform people of the truth. I am the most dangerous and hated person alive because I want people to know the truth. I am not a murderer. But I want to be one. I want to kill everyone responsible for the death of my family, as is my duty. I would prefer doing it myself, but the people responsible dying is more important than it being done by my hand.

"Why did I not join your party? I did not join your party because my first goal is vengeance. My last goal is vengeance. I helped in area 10 because I did not see many paths to achieving my goals without you, now, in this timeline. Why did I not send someone else back in time? I have contacts that would have been more suitable to the task. Maybe they were no longer alive. None of the three I know of in your party were more suitable. Bam Bam may have been my goal. I do not know the name, but it seems to be a pseudonym. I do not like to leave things up to chance, so I do not believe he was my target. I cannot answer why you. And I must have picked you. Fighting proficiency is definitely not a good criterion to select someone to travel back in time to save humanity. Things have worked out well so far, but this is despite your failings and flaws, and not due to your strengths, of which you have very few beyond your ability to fight. My social intelligence is low, but I believe yours is far lower. Apologies, but you are not a good choice.

"Why not I is the easiest to answer. There is a saying where I am from – one who goes to Lanka turns into Raavan. This basically means if you go to a bad place, or consort with bad people, you will become bad. I did have a relationship with many extremist and terrorist groups. I still do. If you need allies to fight the UN, they are really the only option. As soon as I took the path of vengeance, my mind became dampened. My work suffered for it. Darkness entered and consumed my mind. I am ethically compromised. Some things I know are morally wrong, do not seem wrong to me. Take my actions in area 10. Twice I left a child to die. There is a hole in my chest which used to be filled with love. When my family was murdered it has since been filled with hate. I've agreed to help, but I must focus on vengeance, whilst you focus on progression and the rest."

Bruno laughs, "I can't believe you just said whilst. What a dork. I just lost half my respect for you. You say whom, too, don't you?"

"Depending on subject and object, of course."

At least she didn't say 'apologies.' I'm not buying her story though. Why would the UN blow up a whole building over a meeting? Seems like a big load of BS. It doesn't add up. Why? Wouldn't it be easier to just kill the specific people you want without having to control all the media in the whole world after blowing up a big hotel? If they are so big and powerful, why take the dumbest option? We've all seen videos of what the firefly drones can do. Just one could've wiped out the whole meeting and not risked any other lives, like, at all. The story really seems like nonsense. And terrorists are the ones that won't believe in the truth. Everyone knows that.

And Zero didn't kill anyone? Yeah, right! Bunch of malarkey. Zero's probably killed, like, a million people or something. And if I was a celebrated genius and the UN killed my family, why wouldn't I use that to help get my story out? I wouldn't pretend nothing happened and then become a stupid terrorist.

And she really has a high opinion of herself. Me and Bruno had that boss, even if she didn't come back. Well, maybe not. And she was a huge help after. Bruno would be dead without her. I do owe her, I guess. But Zero? Come on. How can Bruno even tolerate talking to her? We should just turn her over to the UN and get them back on our side.

Bruno says, "How come you're so good at fighting. People like you are usually pathetic at it. Ever hear of…uh…uh…nevermind, I forget the name. Wicked smart guy. I had a mission to save him once. He could barely say a sentence. I doubt he could fight off a rabbit. Sucked at paying attention to anything at all going on around him. Chinese guy living in England. He did…I don't know, wicked important smart stuff."

"Cheng Lianjie."

"Bingo. Jesus, you're good."

"Apologies. As I said before, fighting is just math. Timing, physics, prediction."

"But it ain't just math though, is it? It's genetics. Conditioning. Experience. Training. You're a little tiny thing. What are you? Five nine? Five ten? Can't weigh over a buck eighty. Without the rpg system you could hit me all day and I wouldn't feel it. Your strikes are terrible. You're not fast. I'd say you get lucky a lot, but no one is that lucky. It's infuriating. Stupid rpg nonsense. You're the dracon race, right? Got it for the main dragon disciple thing for a cross class feature token? What's it called, apathapaliosis? So you can get both that and the blood wyrm one? Picking up rogue 2 after your first and only blood wyrm paragon?"

"Yes, I am a dracon. Yes, mainly for dragon apotheosis. I will go rogue 2 at 20."

"You already figured your build out before my emails, didn't you?"

"Mostly. I decided changes to make after reviewing the store and seeing the items available for purchase with dungeon coins in the tutorial. Apologies, the information provided in your messages was very helpful. Such as the capacity of dungeon coins, and how to attain them. I made changes, such as my race, after seeing the arena rewards, which were shown, but never detailed. And you should have covered gravity. It changes from zone to zone and dungeon instance."

Bruno laughs, "Sure, kid. Gravity changing. First I heard about it. Speaking of stuff I don't understand, you guys remember the red crystal shield thing I did when fighting the boss in area 10 yet?"

Huh? Red crystal shield thing? I don't remember anything like that, but I was fighting something else until all three of us got on the last boss together.

Sidis isn't saying anything, just staring at Bruno, so I do. "I don't remember nothing like that. When was it? Before we were on the last boss together? And what was it? What do you mean, you did it? How do you do a red crystal shield thing? That don't make no sense, really."

"It came out of my arm. My shield arm. And you saw it. You said something about it. Sidis, you still don't remember?"

Sidis says, "What do you mean, 'still don't remember?' You ask as if we have talked about this before."

"Jesus Christ, yeah, we did. What the hell is going on? You don't remember me even asking about it the first time we talked after the boss fight? After the dungeon and I healed up and the big standoff between Gunny and his guys and all the civilians and the UN people? Kim was there too. You guys really don't even remember that? The red crystal stuff?"

As Bruno is saying all that I notice something weird is happening under him. Like dark mist raising out the ground. I look at Sidis to see if she is doing this. Zero can't be trusted. I stand up to tell Bruno to move and to look at what's happening under him, but before I can finish he disappears through a hole in the ground made from the dark mist.

My heart jumps into my throat. Holy moly! I have a split-second decision to make. Attack Sidis or go after Bruno? The mist is kind of dissolving. There's no real choice to make here. As fast as I can, I dive head first into the mist.

ABOUT THE AUTHOR

Tony Alves is from Lynn, Massachusetts and works in Human Resources. He enjoys writing, reading, playing RPGs, and spending time with his children. He often thinks about working out.

ABOUT LEVEL UP

Level Up publishing specializes in LitRPG and GameLit books. You might be interested in our other titles, which can be found at www.levelup.pub/books

To join our mailing list for news about forthcoming books and opportunities to be an ARC reader, just fill in the form on that page.

You can also find us on:
Facebook @LUPublishing
Twitter @LevelUpPub
...and by searching for Level Up WhatsApp group

www.ingramcontent.com/pod-product-compliance
Lightning Source LLC
Chambersburg PA
CBHW030841030726

47495CB00005B/1315